A HUNT OF SHADOWS

ELISE KOVA

Silver Wing Press

A HUNT OF SHADOWS

ELISE KOVA

Published by Silver Wing Press

Cover Artwork by Marie Magny
Developmental Editing by Rebecca Faith Editorial
Line Editing and Proofreading by Melissa Frain

ISBN (paperback): 978-1-949694-36-9
ISBN (hardcover): 978-1-949694-37-6
eISBN: 978-1-949694-32-1

Also by Elise Kova

A Trial of Sorcerers
A Trial of Sorcerers
A Hunt of Shadows
A Tournament of Crowns
(More to Come)

Also set in the Air Awakens Universe

AIR AWAKENS SERIES
Air Awakens
Fire Falling
Earth's End
Water's Wrath
Crystal Crowned

GOLDEN GUARD TRILOGY
The Crown's Dog
The Prince's Rogue
The Farmer's War

VORTEX CHRONICLES
Vortex Visions
Chosen Champion
Failed Future
Sovereign Sacrifice
Crystal Caged

Married to Magic

A Deal with the Elf King
A Dance with the Fae Prince
A Duel with the Vampire Lord
(More to Come)

Loom Saga

The Alchemists of Loom
The Dragons of Nova
The Rebels of Gold

See all books and learn more at:
http://www.EliseKova.com

for Danielle

Table of Contents

THE
MAIN CONTINENT
VANGAR
GRAYSTON
SOLARIN
"THE CAPITAL"
RIVEND
MOSANT
THE GREAT IMPERIAL WAY
TIX
OPARIUM
THE
SOUTH
LYNDUM
PACA
LEOUL
CR
SHAN
THE FINSHAR
DELTA
HASTAN
THE
EAST
CYVEN

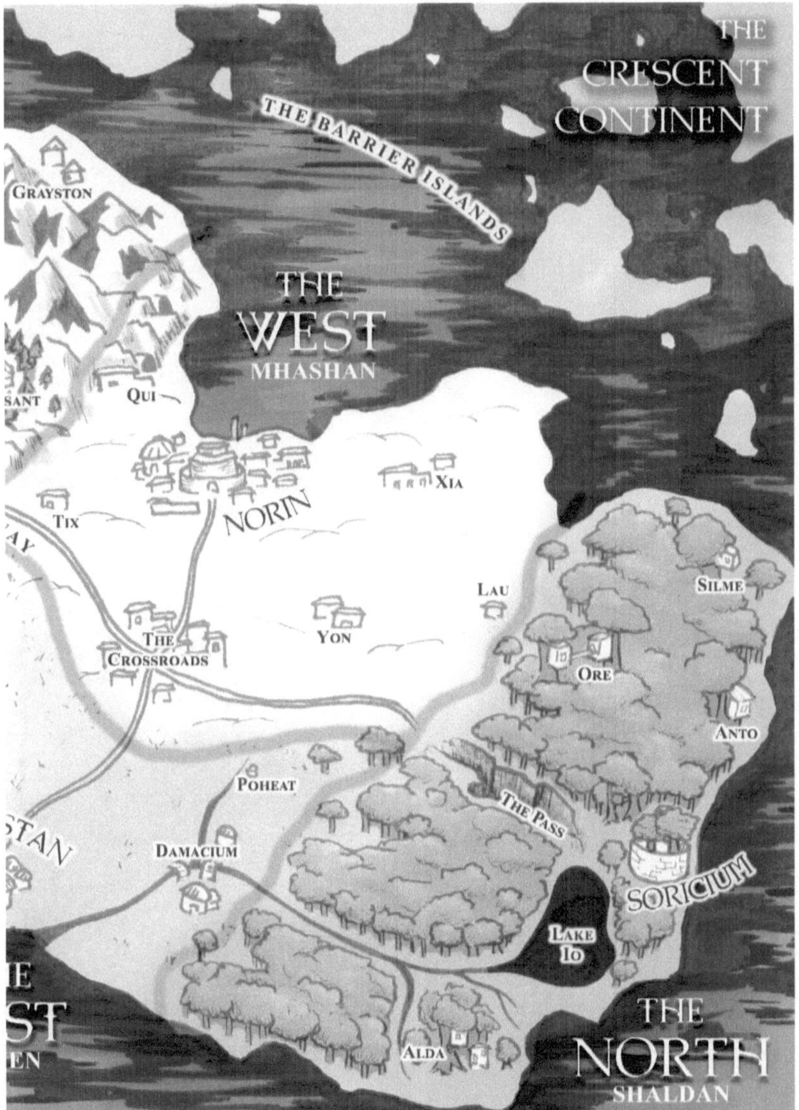

THE
CRESCENT
CONTINENT
THE BARRIER ISLANDS
GRAYSTON
THE
WEST
MHASHAN
SANT
QUI
XIA
NORIN
TIX
AY
LAU
SILME
ORE
THE
CROSSROADS
YON
ANTO
POHEAT
THE PASS
STAN
DAMACIUM
SORICIUM
LAKE
IO
E
ST
THE
NORTH
EN
ALDA
SHALDAN

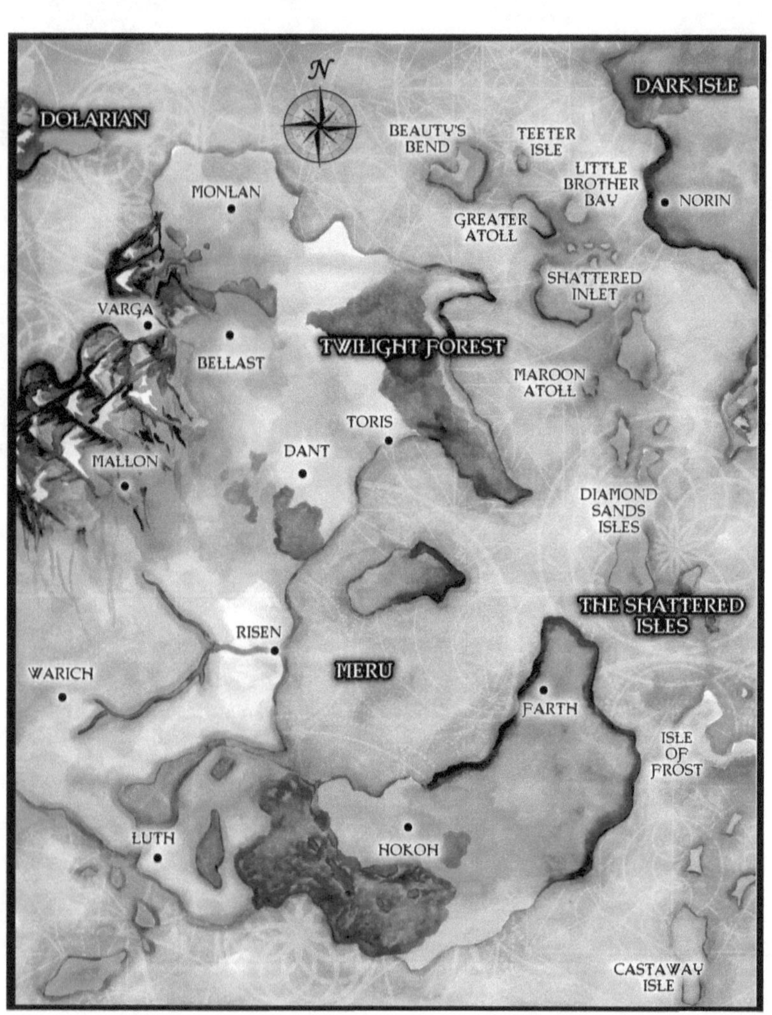

N
DOLARIAN
DARK ISLE
MONLAN
BEAUTY'S BEND
TEETER ISLE
LITTLE BROTHER BAY
NORIN
GREATER ATOLL
VARGA
SHATTERED INLET
BELLAST
TWILIGHT FOREST
MAROON ATOLL
TORIS
DANT
MALLON
DIAMOND SANDS ISLES
THE SHATTERED ISLES
RISEN
MERU
WARICH
FARTH
ISLE OF FROST
LUTH
HOKOH
CASTAWAY ISLE

Need a refresher on what happened in the last book?

Head over to this page of my website...

https://elisekova.com/a-trial-of-sorcerers-summaries/

... to read a full summary of what happened in book one to make sure you're ready to begin book two!

ONE

Dark water surrounded her. Deeper and deeper, invisible hands pulled her under, into the arms of death. Eira didn't fight their chilling grip as the ghostly fingers plunged through her skin, into bone and soul. She didn't try to swim up toward the glyph of light that swirled above her.

Not until her eyes landed on Marcus. Her brother struggled up toward the shining light, mistaking it for sunlight—for a dawn they weren't destined to see. Eira opened her mouth to try to call out to him, but cold water rushed into her lungs, silencing her.

Marcus.

He swam as hard as he could manage. The watery hands clung to him, reaching, ripping into his flesh. They dragged him down, demanding his life. Couldn't he see them? Feel them? If he did, he still strove toward the light anyway.

Don't.

Eira pressed her eyes closed and allowed herself to be pulled farther under. Take me, *she mouthed into the inky tides, to the hands of fate that were hungry for blood.* Take me instead.

Farther and farther, she sank. The light dimmed to nothingness. Marcus swam upward and far beyond her reach as the shadows crushed her. Eira inhaled deeply. She would become one with the dark and the cold. She would be its willing servant if it meant he'd be saved.

Eira awoke not with a jolt but with a frosty exhale. Her breath curled in the air as a white plume, as though her spirit was leaving her body. She stared at the now familiar wooden ceiling, covered in a pale blue frost.

It had been two weeks since her brother died. She was a champion for the Solaris Empire. She was in a cabin on a ship of the Imperial Armada and on her way to Meru to compete in the Tournament of Five Kingdoms.

The facts grounded her back in reality, separating her from the dreams that haunted her. Eira sat. Her cabin was small, her things neatly packed in two bags and a large trunk that were wedged between the wash basin and the door.

She held out her hand. This was not the first time her magic had reacted to the dream and she'd woken covered in frost. She much preferred the ice to waking up soaked. Eira twirled her fingers in the air, beckoning the magic back to her.

Except, it didn't come.

Tilting her head, Eira tried again. But the frost didn't budge. Instead, as if protesting, the coating of ice on the walls around her was getting thicker by the minute.

This wasn't her magic.

Eira threw her blanket from the bed and jumped to her feet. She raced to her bag, sending ice shards scattering as she quickly tugged on a pair of trousers underneath her sleeping shift. Who was making the ice? And why?

This was another dream. It had to be. She'd wake up soon. Yet her hands trembled as she fumbled with the buttons of her trousers.

The frost kept closing in around her. She was living the nightmare of three years ago. This was what the room of the Tower apprentice she killed must have looked like. First that girl, then Marcus. Death and magic followed Eira wherever she went. She wouldn't be able to escape. She would die here, finally punished for her crimes.

"Focus," Eira hissed at herself as she pressed her eyes closed.

She wasn't dreaming and she wasn't in the Tower anymore. She was on a ship, heading to Risen, the capital of Meru. And something was going terribly wrong.

Eira yanked open her door, freeing it from the doorjamb with force. The frost had covered the hall and was encroaching on every room. Eira slapped her face, twice. It stung. Definitely not a dream.

"Wake up!" she shouted. "Everyone, wake up!"

Nothing happened. Her heart was beginning to race. All Eira could think of were her traveling companions—her friends—frozen and dead in their beds.

"Wake up!" Eira tried again and then crossed the hall to Alyss's door. She banged on it several times before she heard movement.

"Eira? Eira! Is that you? What's happening?" Alyss shouted through the door.

"I don't know but—" Eira was interrupted by a sudden burst of flame over her left shoulder. Where a door once stood was now nothing more than a charred frame and wet ashes.

Noelle emerged from the steam and narrowed her eyes immediately at Eira. "Is this your fault?"

"It's not me." Eira ignored the stab in her gut at the suspicion. It was another reminder of three years ago—of two weeks ago, when she was sitting in a jail cell, arrested for her brother's murder. *I'm not a killer*, she wanted to say, but now wasn't the time for objections. "We have to find out what's going on."

"Move aside." Noelle barely gave Eira a chance to step back before incinerating Alyss's door.

Alyss stood, teeth chattering, snow and ice covering half her nightclothes. "What in the Mother's name is happening?"

A thud rattled the door next to Alyss's, shaking ice from its coating. Noelle turned her flames there next, revealing an even less dressed Cullen. He was in nothing but a loose-fitting pair of shorts and halfway to turning blue.

"I could use more of that fire," he grumbled, wrapping his arms around himself. His hazel-gold eyes swung to Eira. "Are you—"

"This isn't me!" Eira snapped. Other doors were beginning to rattle as their occupants woke. "You two put on something warm." She pointed to Alyss and Cullen. "Noelle help anyone else who needs it."

"Commanding me? I thought we hadn't decided on who the team leader would be?" Noelle folded her arms and arched a dark eyebrow.

"Just do it!" Eira started for the stairs at the end of the hallway that led to the main deck. A commotion was rising. "I'm going to see if I can figure out what is going on."

She was gone before any of them could object.

Eira grabbed the railing of the stairs, *hard*. She pressed her magic into the ice coating it that was trying to block her entry upward. Magic battled against her own. Whoever was doing this was strong. But she was stronger.

Glaring, Eira turned the ice into harmless steam, emerging onto the dark main deck of *Daybreak*. Sailors were running about, slipping and fighting against the frozen surfaces. Rigging clattered in a frigid gale, shaking snow from the sails.

It was nearly summer. The weather should be temperate. Eira turned her gaze over the dark water and, in the distance, made out the haze of what looked like a massive ghost ship.

Deneya emerged from another set of stairs that led into a different region of the hold. Her eyes were fraught and panicked; rage twisted her brow. She swept her gaze across the deck and out to sea, ignoring Eira.

"The witch." Deneya cursed loudly and rushed to the deck railing by a dinghy. "Drop this boat," she demanded of a sailor. "We have to go after her."

The sailor shook his head, eyes wide. "We're not going after the pirate que—"

Pirate queen. The words echoed in Eira's ears. *The Pirate Queen Adela*—the woman who might have given birth to Eira. Who might have some idea as to how to control the depths of her powers. She stared out at the massive ship slipping between the shadows and past the edge of her cognition.

"This is an order!" Deneya roared. The sailor nearly wet himself at her ferocity.

"I'll help you!" Eira rushed over. Speaking only to Deneya, she said, "Cut the lines when the water rises."

"All right." Deneya gave her an approving nod as Eira lifted her hands. Seawater heeded Eira's commands, lifting to meet the keel of the small vessel. "*Mysst soto sut*," Deneya murmured and an axe woven from light appeared in her hands. She made quick work of the ropes and stepped into the boat. Eira was close behind. "You—"

"You need me to move this boat, unless you intend on rowing?" Eira cut off the woman.

"Carry on, then." A wild and somewhat approving smile snaked across Deneya's lips. As Eira lowered her hands, easing the dinghy back to the waves rocking the *Daybreak*, Deneya shouted up to the sailors, "Light a beacon for us to find our way back!"

Eira didn't wait for a reply. The ocean had been calling to her from the first moment they'd embarked from Norin in the west of the Solaris Empire. It called to her power with a ferocity Eira had ignored until now. With a pull of her fist, the dinghy was sent speeding forward, racing through the waves as the water itself propelled them. All the might of the sea was at her command.

"Yargen bless." Deneya stumbled with a hard thud and a groan. Luckily, she wasn't thrown over. "You really can make this move."

"We have to catch up to them." Eira squinted ahead. There was only the ghostly outline of the vessel, striking between black waves in a moonless sky.

"I know." Deneya grunted, working her way to her knees. Eira had found she had natural sea legs, something Alyss had been bemoaning for days as she upturned the contents of her stomach. The ocean whispered to Eira, telling her of every swell and dip right before it happened. "*Mysst soto gotha*." Deneya held out her hands and a bow condensed from strands of light. She pulled and released an arrow that sped ahead like a ribbon of sunlight over the dark waves.

Eira blinked several times, not from the sudden brightness, but because of how the magic light shone on the dark water—just like her dreams, just like on Marcus's face when he died. Right before the sight returned her mind to that nightmarish place, the arrow was eaten by the darkness. Deneya fired another as the boat slowed to a stop, drifting in the water.

"You're right," Deneya said. Eira didn't think she'd spoken. "We can't catch up to them, not with them sailing the infernal *Stormfrost*."

"*Stormfrost*?" Eira shook her head, trying to banish the ghosts that haunted her. She had little success. But she did jostle a memory from one of her early meetings with Deneya. "Adela's flagship?"

"Unfortunately." Deneya let out a string of curses that Eira didn't recognize, each angrier than the last. "She hasn't been spotted in these waters for decades. She's not supposed to be here," Deneya growled.

"Was it an attack?" Eira continued to stare at where the ship had left, wondering what secrets it carried with it. Was her birth mother on that vessel? Did she really want to know the answer to that question? Eira still wasn't entirely sure.

"No, it was a targeted strike." Deneya frowned, her expression barely visible in the darkness.

"What did they come for?" Eira finally sat. The air was beginning to warm, already becoming balmy in the absence of the ice-covered *Stormfrost*. The summer heat worked its sticky fingers uncomfortably up Eira's spine, wrapping themselves around the back of her neck with a grip more unwelcome than Death's personification in her dreams.

"Not what, but *who*."

"You don't mean…"

Deneya looked her right in the eyes and said, "Ferro has escaped."

Ferro. The man who murdered her brother. Who'd manipulated and tried to kill Eira. He was supposed to be brought to justice on Meru…

Now he was free.

***

The atmosphere of the *Daybreak* was perpetually thick and uneasy, heavy with a pregnant silence. Everyone knew of Ferro's escape from the hold, but no one spoke about it outright, as if, by saying it aloud, they'd somehow make it more real than it already, horribly, was. Or, perhaps, the superstitions surrounding Adela were what kept people's tongues still.

It made the final days of their journey utterly unbearable.

Eira was up with the dawn on the last day of their voyage. Standing at the bow, she stared at a sight she'd only ever dreamed about: Meru, golden and glittering in morning's first light.

"Is it everything you'd dreamed of?" Cullen interrupted her thoughts.

Eira jerked and grabbed the railing for support.

"Sorry, I didn't mean to startle you."

"I shouldn't be so lost in my head." That would get her killed, if she wasn't careful. Being too wrapped up in her own thoughts and plans, in perceived safety, had led to Marcus's death and nearly her own. It had led to Ferro escaping. She had to be more vigilant. She had to be the one making the moves—not the one paying the price.

"What thoughts are you lost in?" Cullen eased his elbows onto the railing next to her, looking out over the ocean.

"It doesn't matter."

"It does to me." He glanced back at her, speaking volumes she couldn't understand with a look. "You hardly even speak to Alyss these days. You've spent most of the voyage holed up in your room."

"Don't concern yourself with me. You have enough to worry

about." Eira looked back toward the city in the distance. She could make out Queen Lumeria's castle now, perched on a hill. The Archives of Yargen sat opposite—a library so vast and ancient it was said to house all the knowledge in the world.

"I want to worry about you." Cullen swallowed thickly. "He would've—"

"Don't." Eira stopped him with a glare. "Don't bring up my brother."

Cullen sighed heavily and joined her in staring across the sea. "It looks just like the painting at court," he said with a note of wistful longing. Her heart agreed with his tone. Those days had been a simpler time, indeed.

"No," Eira said softly.

"No?"

"It's more beautiful than an artist could ever hope to capture with oil and canvas." Eira inhaled slowly.

"So it *is* everything you dreamed of, then." He smiled slightly.

"The place? Yes. The circumstances? No."

Cullen's smile fell. "Eira, if you ever want to speak, I'm here for you."

"Don't worry about me," Eira repeated. Perhaps if she repeated it enough times, he'd understand. She didn't need him. She didn't need any of them. What she *needed* was Ferro in irons.

Cullen's expression turned wounded. He straightened away from the railing. His hand shifted, fingertips brushing against hers. Eira followed the line of his arm up to his chest, remembering the sight of him in his sleeping shorts and nothing else the night Ferro escaped.

The thought of Ferro being free squelched any soft emotions or tender longing. It was a dagger as cold as the air that night, cutting any warmth from her. It was the dark waves she was lost in dream after dream—the dark waves the *Stormfrost* had escaped into.

Eira curled her fingers, breaking the contact.

"Listen, I—" He didn't get to finish.

"Cullen!" a man called up to them. Senator Yemir, Cullen's father, stood on the main deck below, his narrowed eyes darting between them. "Come, we have preparations to go over for our arrival."

Cullen's attention switched between her and his father, finally landing on the latter. "I'll be there in a minute."

"*Now.*"

"Go," Eira encouraged. "I'm fine, really. Thanks for checking on me."

"Are you sure?" He took a half step closer to her. "We're all worried about you."

"There's nothing to worry about." She was still breathing, wasn't she? That was more than her brother could say.

"Alyss said you'd say that, and not to believe you when you do." Cullen leveled his eyes with hers and Eira cursed Alyss for saying anything to him. She knew Eira too well and had been hounding her for weeks. "Talk to her, Noelle, Levit, if not me then *someone*, please. We're all worried."

"Cullen!" Yemir snapped.

"I'm coming!" Cullen pulled away with one last, long look at Eira. His stare seemed to linger long after he vanished with his father belowdecks.

Eira shook her head and refocused on Risen. Cullen wasn't her concern. He was from a different world than her, destined for different things. He would spend the weeks leading up to the tournament dancing and dining with Risen's nobility.

She was headed for the Court of Shadows.

Belowdecks, Eira ignored Cullen's advice and avoided Alyss and Noelle. She'd learned their habits and used the knowledge to her advantage on board. Other than the few times Alyss had cornered Eira in her cabin, she was mostly spared interaction. She needed the time and solitude to keep reliving that cold, dark night in her mind. To try and find some detail she might have overlooked, something that might give them a clue to where Ferro had been taken.

Because she would find him, Eira vowed both to herself and to the memory of her brother. She wouldn't rest until he was brought back in chains. Ferro would see justice for Marcus's and all the other apprentices' deaths.

Eira dressed in the clothes that had been prepared for their arrival. Fritz had said that the competitors were going to have tailors in Meru attending to their needs as they arose. But the Empire would ensure they disembarked pressed and clean.

Each competitor wore a variant on the same style—close-fitting black trousers and patent leather boots. A tunic made of cotton, dyed in a color that was reminiscent—and a little too on the nose for her taste—of their affinity: Eira had a Solarin cerulean shade, Alyss a deep viridian, Noelle was in a dark crimson, and Cullen a sort of hazy purple that he somehow still managed to make look attractive. It was truly a testament to how handsome he was that he could pull off *that* particular shade.

The four competitors stood together on the main deck as their escorts—Senator Yemir, Senator Henri, Tower Instructor Levit, and Ambassador Cordon—inspected their attire a final time. Eira's attention drifted from the men making their adjustments and humming over fashion, instead admiring the city they were docking in.

The city of Risen was unlike anything Eira had ever laid eyes on. A wide river snaked between tall buildings and the sloping hills the city rose up along. The architecture wasn't entirely unlike Solaris...yet it somehow made the capital of Solarin look like a hovel by comparison. Risen was twice as large, the buildings twice as opulent, and magic was as thick as summer air. This was a city that had been steeped in histories Eira could barely understand and desired for nothing more than to learn. Her eyes dragged up toward the Archives of Yargen, high on the hill.

All the knowledge in the world was there. If that were true, perhaps there was something on Adela that could help them find Ferro. Perhaps there was something that would lead Eira to her own truths.

The thought cast the city in another light. Suddenly, the dawn had become harsh, the glints from the ornate, bronze gutters on the buildings becoming almost violent. Ferro had escaped. He was still out there. He'd killed before and he could kill again.

Deneya walked before them, drawing Eira's attention back on board.

"All right, you four, listen up." She spoke with the authority of a military commander.

Eira had heard Gwen use the same tone many times. She promptly pushed thoughts of her family away. Her parents never sent word following Marcus's death. They hadn't even bothered to come and bid her farewell when she left. Her uncles and aunt had held her fiercely, but by then Eira had been well out of reach of their arms.

"You're not going to have the welcome parade we planned for."

"Excuse me?" Senator Yemir blinked. "You did not—"

"Senator, you are not privy to everything that happens on Meru, especially not discussions with my queen." Deneya looked at him from the corner of her eye. Ambassador Cordon pulled Yemir to the side, speaking in hushed tones as Deneya continued addressing the four competitors. "Since Ferro has escaped, Queen Lumeria has decided to lock the city down."

"Lock down an entire city?" Cullen asked.

"The West did it for a decade while holding out from the Empire's conquests." Noelle tossed a fan of dark hair over her shoulder, not bothering to hide a proud smirk.

"Let's hope it doesn't take a decade to find Ferro," Deneya said severely, drawing the attention back to her. "The queen is using everything at her disposal to locate him. However, his motives aren't entirely known. And it is possible he might be working with accomplices…"

Possible? Eira knew he was. She and Deneya had found out that much with certainty when Eira had still been in captivity and they had investigated Ferro's room together. It was obvious from the fact that Adela had been the one to free him. He had help in powerful places.

"If the city is locked down, then how will the tournament's opening gala take place?" Yemir asked, charging back into the conversation. "Or the dignitaries' dinners in the royal halls? Or the competitors' display of skills? Or—"

"Nothing of that sort will take place until we ensure the streets are safe for competitors and citizens alike." Deneya drew a slow breath and seemed to inflate until she towered over the senator. It was a trick Eira wanted to learn so desperately she found herself inhaling slowly without realizing it. "Until then, all the competitors and dignitaries will be sequestered in safe houses, provided by Her Majesty."

"*All* the competitors?" Eira asked.

"Yes, all. Now, come along. Our escort is here."

Sure enough, a legion of elfin were waiting on the docks at the end of the gangplank for them. Half wore armor plate covered in white with deep purple sashes around their shoulders, pinned with a medal. Each had a short sword on their hip with a bejeweled hilt cast in gold. The other half of the honor guard were in plain silver plate and had capes of red.

"What do the different soldiers mean?" Alyss whispered to Eira.

"I think the ones with the swords are the Swords of Light—the militia of the Faithful of Yargen. Think of them like a religious army. And the red capes I think are the queen's knights?"

Deneya gave a glance over her shoulder that Eira caught. It almost looked approving. Deneya wore a red cape today.

They marched up the docks, surrounded by guards, and into the empty streets of Risen. The hush of the city was prickling. The silence made the buildings and iron window boxes loud with whispers Eira's magic snagged on. She worked to keep the echoes of voices out of her mind, an easy feat when distraction was so readily available. Already, Eira was looking over her shoulder and scanning for the violet eyes of Ferro.

More than once…she could've sworn she heard his whispers among the echoes.

He was one man—a horrible, twisted man, certainly—but only *one*. Risen had to have its share of murderers, as all cities did. So why was every man, woman, and child sequestered? There was so much more to the web Ferro was tangled within than Eira had realized back on Solaris.

Without issue or discussion, they arrived at the safe house. It was a large compound in the heart of the city with a manned gate upfront, archers in roosts overlooking the front courtyard, and a five-story building of curling marble, wooden shutters, iron balconies, and domed roofs around decorative leaded windows.

"This is where you'll be staying," Deneya said as two of the soldiers opened the heavy wooden doors.

Alyss gasped. "It's marvelous."

"It truly is," Noelle agreed.

Eira opened her mouth to speak but was cut off by a rogue whisper. *How I have…* She jerked toward one of the large door knockers as though it had sprung arms and struck her. The voice had come from there.

"Are you all right?" Cullen asked under his breath.

"Fine." The word was a little too sharp, but Eira was more focused on tearing her gaze from the knocker and stepping into the main atrium. She was imagining things. That voice… it couldn't be. She returned her focus to Deneya and the quick overview of the manor she was giving.

"Beneath us on the ground floor are the public common areas," Deneya said. Eira hadn't realized there was a basement on entry. "Then every kingdom has their own space. The first floor is Meru; second is Solaris; third is the Twilight Kingdom; fourth will be Kingdom of the Draconi; and fifth will be the Republic of Qwint. The last two have yet to arrive."

Eira stared at the doors opposite her at the other end of the atrium. Behind them were the competitors from Risen. Her competition. But also people she desperately wanted to meet.

"Senators, you and the ambassador will be staying at another manor. There's only room for one chaperone here per group and that will be Instructor Levit, as a fellow sorcerer."

"We should be—"

"I wouldn't question it, Yemir," Ambassador Cordon discouraged. He plastered on a fake, placating smile. "You'll be with the other dignitaries, nobles, and guests of honor in our own safe house. There are many coming for the tournament. We can't all stay in one building."

"Oh, of course." Yemir bowed his head at Deneya. "Your queen is most generous."

"She really is." Deneya smiled thinly then said to the guards, "Escort them to their lodging." Then, she faced the four competitors and Mister Levit. "You five, come with me."

They wound up a curving stair that reminded Eira somewhat of the Tower of Sorcerers. It spun up the atrium, a landing at every level. Deneya led them through the doors of the second level and into a common area that stretched toward the back of the house.

This...way... Voices continued to follow Eira's steps. The house was noisy, its din threaded together by her paranoia. Ferro could be anywhere. She could almost feel him lingering in her shadow, ready to pounce. She heard him in every shadow.

"You should have everything you need. Your personal effects will be behind shortly." Deneya stepped away from them, oblivious to Eira's plight. "If anything is amiss, tell the guards. Otherwise, you're not to leave this compound without approval and an escort. Understood?"

"Yes, thank you, Deneya," Mister Levit answered for them.

"Take care." With that brief goodbye, Deneya left them all.

"Look at this place." Alyss spun. "It's a dream—just like a storybook!"

"It is magnificent," Cullen agreed.

"Surprised it's good enough for the Prince of the Tower." Noelle grinned. Eira didn't miss the brief flash of pain in Cullen's eyes. She knew he hated that moniker, yet he didn't seem to stop anyone from using it…anyone but her. "How do we pick rooms?" Noelle walked over to one of the six doors lining the common area, yanking it open to reveal a four-poster bed.

"It seems they've already been chosen for us." Mister Levit held up a note.

"What's that?" Eira asked.

"A brief welcome from the queen via Mistress Harrot, the caretaker of the house. She has assigned each of us a room so that there would be no debate." He chuckled.

"As if we would debate." Noelle crossed her arms. Her offense made it clear there certainly would have been debate if given the chance. "Which one is mine?"

"The doors are marked with our colors. Black is mine, apparently," Mister Levit answered.

"Then I'm going to get changed," Noelle declared.

"Into what? You don't have your clothes off the ship yet." Cullen arched his eyebrows.

"I shall wait naked, then. These 'ceremonial' rags they designed for us just aren't my style." Noelle grimaced at her attire and sauntered off to the door marked with a diamond-shaped, red, glass inlay.

"I'm going to go and catch my breath," Eira said, starting for her own door.

"Don't you want to explore the house?" Alyss caught her hand. "See if we can meet the other competitors?"

"Desperately." Eira squeezed her friend's fingers. "But first, I want to see where I'll be sleeping. I'll be right back."

"I'll check out my own room, then. Knock when you're ready."

They parted.

Eira slipped inside her door, looking to the four-poster bed, the nightstands, the dresser, and then the desk that overlooked the back windows. The letter left for Mister Levit had given her the idea that maybe Deneya had left a note for Eira with some kind of instruction as to how to find the Court of Shadows. Now that she was here in Risen, she would meet the court, wouldn't she? That was what they had agreed on, wasn't it?

Eira pressed her eyes closed and tried to remember, but her thoughts were interrupted by Ferro's voice, whispering in her ear.

"I've been waiting for you."

EIRA'S BLOOD TURNED to ice; she went rigid, frozen in place. Her heart stopped beating and her breath hitched. She was back in that dark forest, cold, helpless, fighting a man who was far stronger and vastly more skilled.

Impossible. Not real. It couldn't be. Eira blinked several times and grounded herself in the warm sunlight that coated her face through the sheer curtains.

Magic pooled in her fingertips, dark tides rolling within her, ready to attack if her theory was wrong. Eira turned, facing the suspected source of Ferro's voice: a landscape oil painting hung by the door.

The words had sounded so real. As though he had been standing right there, whispering in her ear. She swallowed thickly. He wasn't there. But the ghost of him was.

He haunted the city, the manor, the room she had to *sleep* in.

Eira gripped her head and took a shaky breath. If she was going to hunt him, she had to come to terms with hearing him. He was her prey.

Gathering her courage, she faced the painting. "Well? Anything else?" she whispered.

Nothing.

Who was Ferro waiting for here? Or, perhaps the painting had changed hands several times? Perhaps Ferro had said those words in a different place altogether, or the painting wasn't the source of the echo. Eira rubbed her eyes and collected her thoughts. She needed to speak to Deneya and let her know that Ferro's presence was in these halls.

Two knocks on her door had her quickly clawing together composure. Alyss was on the other side.

"Ready to explore yet?" Alyss chirped cheerfully.

Eira tried to keep her panic contained. It swelled in her throat, making her force a smile and the words, "I am."

"Can I join you both?" Cullen asked. He'd just emerged from his room across the main living area.

Eira shared a look with Alyss. Her best friend had gathered on the journey that something had changed between Cullen and Eira. But Eira had managed to dodge most of Alyss's questions. Mostly because Eira herself wasn't quite sure what that "something" was beyond a deepening, uncomfortable tension every time Cullen was around.

She met Cullen's amber eyes. "I suppose it'd be fine." Then Eira looked to the door with the red diamond. "Should we ask if Noelle wants to join us?"

"You heard her, she's not emerging from there until she has her clothes. She doesn't want to be seen in *these rags*," Alyss said dramatically.

"Alyss has a point." Cullen shrugged. "And I've no interest in seeing Noelle naked, assuming that wasn't an empty threat."

"I don't think Noelle does anything in half measures," Alyss murmured.

"I can agree with the lack of interest in naked Noelles," Eira said. "So just the three of us then."

"Should we let Mister Levit know we're leaving?" Cullen paused at the first door to the left of the entry, glancing at the black diamond.

"I'm sure it's fine; we're not wandering far." Eira was already pushing the main doors open. She didn't want a handler. She wanted to meet the other competitors without the tension of someone hovering over their shoulders. She had enough distracting her already.

"Eira's right, it's not like we're allowed to leave the manor itself." Alyss brushed past Cullen, following Eira out to the landing, her heels clicking on the marble floor. "How much trouble could we really get up to?"

"Knowing you two? A lot," Cullen said, but followed them anyway. He had an approving smirk despite his words.

"If you're so worried, then *you* can be our chaperone." Alyss peered up and down over the railing. "Where to first? The Twilight Kingdom? Meru? Or the communal areas?"

The waters within Eira were churned by the echoes around her and made murky by the infinite, unseen possibilities the halls held. Were those possibilities unknown delights—knowledge and experiences she'd yearned for her whole life in Solaris? Or was her demise lurking somewhere above, or below, just beyond the curve of the stairs?

What are my orders? Ferro's voice. Her head jerked toward the right of the door to the Solaris area. Even though it sounded like he had been speaking over her shoulder, there was nothing there.

"Are you all right?" Alyss asked, touching her arm lightly.

"I'm fine."

"A voice?" Alyss's voice dropped to a whisper. Cullen took a half step closer. Eira hated how they circled around her protectively, as though she were some broken and pitiable thing.

Eira shifted the topic as quickly as she could. "It's nothing. Let's start in the communal areas. I doubt the other competitors appreciate strangers barging in on their personal space unannounced."

Cullen and Alyss shared a worried glance. But they didn't press the matter of the echo she'd heard.

"Surprisingly restrained." Cullen sounded like he approved.

"Glad I can surprise you." Eira gave him a slight grin and started down the stairs, walking with her shoulders back and relaxed as if she didn't have a care in the world.

As if Ferro's voice wasn't lingering in the air around her.

They wound down the way they came, arriving at the main atrium. The doors to the Meru competitors' quarters were still shut, so they continued down and ended in a single room that spanned the length and width of the entire house. The back wall was stone archways, chiffon curtains wafting effortlessly on the afternoon breezes. They teased glimpses of terraced gardens that tumbled down toward the main river of Risen the house had been built along.

Inside, the room served multiple functions—from the kitchen and its marble counters with copper pots hanging overhead, to the three fireplaces and seating areas, to the billiard and gaming tables off to the right. At the last of which, two men were playing.

They sat around a carcivi table, only a few moves in judging by how many pieces were on the board. The first man, with bright orange hair, had a book balanced on his knee that he was constantly referencing. The other brushed his fingertips lightly over the pieces as he waited.

"We could just ask them about the rules." The man touching the pieces stopped and looked their way. He had deep, gnarled scars over half his face—the half that was originally facing away from them—and both his eyes were a pale, milky color. Alyss took half a step back and Eira grabbed her friend's hand, squeezing it tightly so her startle didn't offend. "You're the ones from the Dark Isle, aren't you?"

"Yes. It's nice to meet you." Eira spoke for the three of them. "I'm Eira, this is Alyss, and this is Cullen. And you two are?"

"I'm Ducot," the man answered, "And my woefully inept opponent is Graff."

"Nice to meet you both." Eira's eyes darted between their faces. Instead of eyebrows, they each had faintly glowing dots along their brow. Their ears were rounded like a human's, unlike the pointed elfin's. "You're from…the Twilight Kingdom?"

He gasped. "Graff, our reputation precedes us."

"Or, they know that it's them, elfin, and us here, and she can manage a process of elimination." Graff rolled his eyes and held up the small, worn book he'd been consulting. "This game— carcivi, you call it?"

Eira nodded.

"Your princess brought it to Meru and it's apparently quite popular in Risen right now, but we cannot, for the life of us, figure out the rules."

"I can help with that." Cullen stepped forward. "My father insisted I learn when I moved to the capital. It's not too hard once you get it, but can be tricky to pick up."

Eira and Alyss followed Cullen over, hovering as he pulled up a chair. He wore an easy smile, confident, even meeting people from across the world. It was a trait Eira admired.

"This piece is your general." He pointed. Then looked to Ducot with a guilty expression. Cullen picked up the piece, holding it to the man's hand. "Here, let me—"

"If I need to touch something I will." Ducot brushed the piece and Cullen's hand away. Graff snickered under his breath. Cullen looked absolutely horrified at the notion he might have offended. "I'm blind, more or less, not mute, lame, or dumb."

"Right…" Cullen lowered the piece back down to the board. "If your general should be defeated, the game is over…" Cullen proceeded to explain the game in as brief of terms as possible. Which ended up not being very brief at all. There was a reason Eira had never bothered to learn carcivi. "…and that's the basics."

"My head hurts." Ducot groaned.

Eira couldn't stop herself from laughing. "I know how you feel. My brother loves—" She stopped herself short. Her throat was suddenly thick with a substance that tasted like tears. "—lov*ed*, carcivi. But I never took the time to learn," she finished softly. How she wished she had taken Marcus up on his offers to teach her. Time she'd let slip through her fingers like a fool.

"I enjoyed playing with Marcus." Cullen caught her eye and Eira promptly turned away. As though she could put her back to the pain and move along as easily as her long strides.

"I'm going to explore the grounds. Please excuse me."

"I'm coming with you." Alyss grabbed her hand.

"It's all right." Eira wanted to be alone these days. Her friend just hadn't caught up to the shift in her preferences.

"If both of you are going, then I'm going, too." Ducot stood. "Cullen lost me after the explanation of the knight that can move both forward and back, and behind walls."

"Well, I'd still like to learn, if you're willing to play a practice round?" Graff said to Cullen. "Not every day we get to learn a Dark Isle game directly from an expert."

"I wouldn't say I'm an expert… But I'd be happy to play a round or two." Cullen moved into Ducot's abandoned seat.

"You enjoy that, Graff. I will be walking by the river with a lady on each arm, so do take your time." Ducot held out his elbows with a lopsided grin; the scarred half of his face didn't seem to move as well as the other. Alyss took one elbow with a giggle. Eira followed suit and they stepped out into a sunlight-drenched back patio. With every step, tiny pulses of magic radiated off Ducot.

"Ducot, may I ask you something?" Eira couldn't contain herself any longer.

"I got the scars saving a princess from a horde of bears. But I was blind from birth. That's why both eyes are the way they are even though just half of my face is shredded so handsomely."

Alyss gaped up, horrified.

Eira blinked at him several times, utterly caught off guard. "That… I… I'm sorry."

"It's all right, everyone asks." He chuckled.

"Well, that actually wasn't what I was going to ask."

"It wasn't?" Ducot stopped, arching his eyebrows—well, glowing dots—at her.

"No."

"You weren't wondering about my scars?" He turned to face her, leaning forward. Eira wondered if he was somehow trying to intimidate her. It wouldn't work.

"I don't see how they're my business to wonder about." Eira freed her hand from his elbow, folding her arms over her chest.

"Then what were you going to ask?"

"I wanted to ask what is the proper way to refer to someone from the Twilight Kingdom. Someone who has the markings on their brow like yours. I've only read about the Twilight Kingdom tangentially in books brought from Meru, so there hasn't been much information. And—" She was interrupted by his laughter.

"I suppose if you've never seen a morphi before, you'd have questions."

"A morphi?" Alyss asked. "Is that what you and Graff are? Is that like elfin?"

"Indeed. But morphi possess the magic of the shift, which is unique to us." Ducot leaned forward and broke a branch off one of the carved topiaries. Magic rippled out through the air from his fingers, as though reality itself had become the surface of a still lake that he was casting stones into. The branch blurred, hazy between each ripple. Then, at once, Ducot flicked his wrist, freeing it from the magic. However, it wasn't a branch any longer. It was a pale blue, faintly glowing, long-stemmed rose that he handed to Alyss.

"What was that?" Alyss whispered in awe, accepting the rose. She turned it over in her hands and looked to Eira. "It's real."

Eira sought clarity. "The shift can…transform things?"

"More or less." Ducot began to meander down the stairs that led toward the river. "The shift is the ability to bridge the gap between what is, and what could be."

"Amazing," Eira breathed and followed after him. "So you can transform anything?"

"To an extent."

"What about this bench, or that plant, or that boat on the river?" Eira's excitement at new magic made the words blend together a little.

"It depends on the strength of the morphi, of course."

"Is there anything you can't—"

"I'm sorry for my friend." Alyss stopped her. "She's a bit over-eager."

"Alyss—" Eira hissed.

"You can't go interrogating the first people you meet," Alyss hissed back.

"I can hear you both perfectly." Ducot pointed to his ears. "These make up for a lot of the sight I don't have, and then some."

Alyss put her hands on her hips and gave Eira a pointed glare.

What? Eira mouthed.

Apologize, Alyss mouthed back.

"Still here. You're not as quiet as you think." Ducot sighed.

"Ducot, I'm sorry if I asked too many questions," Eira forced herself to say. She had about a thousand more, but Alyss was right.

"You've nothing to apologize for."

"Ha." Eira couldn't stop herself from blurting. Alyss rolled her eyes.

"Honestly, it's nice to have someone genuinely interested in the morphi…someone who hasn't been tainted by the Faithful of Yargen."

"Tainted?" Alyss repeated.

"Not literally, just your perception of us. We were worried, you know. Since your princess is marrying the Voice." They arrived at the lowest walkway that ran along the river. Ducot rested his hands lightly on the railing, spreading them out, feeling the metal, before leaning against it. His milky eyes stared out over the water. "The Twilight Kingdom and Meru haven't historically been the closest of friends. Things have been better under our current rulers, and hopefully better still with this treaty. But when you said you'd read about us in books from Meru… I was worried. Every historian's penmanship seems to have a different *slant* when writing about the truth."

"Isn't the Twilight Kingdom on the Crescent Continent as well?" Eira asked. She would presume their histories to be closely intertwined enough that the truth was well known.

"It is. And border disputes have been but one of the sources of our tension."

"*One* of the sources?" Eira pressed. Ducot just shrugged. She was in the middle of figuring out how to rephrase her question to try and get him to talk when Mister Levit interrupted them.

"Eira, Alyss," Levit called down the terraces. "Your trunks have arrived; you should come and get dressed for dinner."

"Coming!" Alyss called for them, then looked to Ducot. "Thank you for taking the time to speak with us."

"It was my pleasure." He scooped up Alyss's hand and kissed it lightly. Alyss let out a giggle.

Yet Eira saw a different man. She was reminded of Ferro, transported back to that firelit room in the dark of night. She looked out over the river, imagining herself diving under the waters, just as she used to when she wanted to feel numb. But the imagery no longer helped. All she could imagine were other dark waters, pressing in around her, around Marcus.

She shivered.

"Eira?" Alyss jolted her from her thoughts. Her friend was already several steps ahead. "Are you coming?"

"Yes, sorry." Eira shook her head and turned to give Ducot her thanks and found him no longer focused on the buildings across the water but staring expectantly at her.

"You won't go to dinner tonight," he said under his breath.

"What?" Even though the sunlight was warming her shoulders, Eira felt colder still.

"You will be too sick to eat dinner with the other champions. Wait in your room."

"For what?" Eira breathed, glancing between him and Alyss. Any second and her friend would turn again and see her lingering.

"Your guide to the Court of Shadows."

CHAPTER THREE

"LET ME LOOK you over," Alyss insisted for the hundredth time. "I'm sure I can do something."

"Alyss, it's just a stomach ache. What will help me most is being left alone to suffer in peace." Eira groaned, rolling onto her side and clutching her stomach. Alyss and Levit were on either side of her bed. Cullen hovered in the room. Noelle leaned against the doorframe, more worried about her cuticles than Eira's condition. "I'm sure I'll be fine soon."

"They warn us about this with sea travel." Levit sighed heavily. "The food never keeps as well as you intend it to, even with Waterrunners packing ice around it." He rested his hand on Eira's shoulder. "Are you sure you don't want to come to dinner?"

Eira weakly lifted her head off the pillow as if it was a great effort. "I… No, just the thought of food." She collapsed back onto the plush mattress with another whine.

"Don't push yourself. Stay here." Levit patted her shoulder.

"I'll gladly save you my table scraps and regale you with tales of the other competitors," Noelle quipped.

"Noelle, you're *so* generous." Alyss rolled her eyes then crouched down so she was almost nose to nose with Eira. "Are you sure you don't want me to take a look? I can unpack my salve and potion supplies quickly—"

"I'll be fine." Eira grabbed her hand. "You go and have fun. Bring me back all the stories."

"There will be more dinners with the competitors and we don't want to be late to this one," Levit declared. "Let's give her the space to rest."

The three of them departed. Alyss stared at Eira with a frown, worrying her lip between her teeth.

"Really, I'll be okay." Eira squeezed Alyss's fingers, feeling guilty for lying to her friend. "Maybe I just need some quality time with the chamber pot."

"Gross." Alyss slapped Eira's shoulder lightly with a laugh. "Fine. Get better soon. You'll hate yourself if you miss too much." With that, Alyss left.

Her friend was right. Eira was already regretting not going to dinner and meeting the other competitors. But she would have time to mingle with the elfin and morphi; they were all stuck in a house together after all. She didn't know how often she'd have the opportunity to meet with the Court of Shadows.

As soon as she heard the outer door shut, Eira was on her feet. She changed out of her sleeping shift and into a pair of dark trousers, a black long-sleeved shirt, and a hooded cloak. If she was meeting with, helping, or possibly joining the Court of Shadows, she needed to look the part.

Once dressed, Eira paced her room as she waited. Her feet and her mind were in competition for which could be more restless. With every step she was being wound tighter and tighter by the echoes of Ferro that singed her ears whenever even the slightest bit of magic wriggled free of the iron-fisted hold she kept on it.

...I was worried...

...ambition will be...demise...

...sure?

...bring it to her...

Halting, she bit her lip, keeping in a groan as she gripped her head. Eira inhaled slowly and exhaled, forcing the tension from her shoulders.

"He's not here," she whispered. Her own voice gave her ears something real to focus on. "He's not here," she repeated just for the calming effect it had. "But...he was. He had to be." This many echoes of him couldn't be mere coincidence or moved relics.

She ran her fingertips along the gilded frame of the first

painting to speak to her. They trembled slightly. She already hated what she knew she had to do. But hunting Ferro had been her choice. And her magic might just be what helped her find him.

Letting her powers unspool like invisible thread, Eira reached out. She brushed against objects, walls, doors, every surface with invisible fingers that probed for traces of Ferro. But the words were weak and fractured, conversations diminishing with time as the traces of magic left on them slowly faded.

There was more. Something stronger. There had to be.

Opening the door, Eira stuck out her head to make sure the others were gone. No one was in sight. The room was still. She padded over to the main entry and rested her hand on the knob, pressing the side of her face to the door that led to the central stair and listening with her ears, rather than her magic.

Silence.

Eira cracked the door, scanned the stairs, and slipped out, her back to the wall. Her magic stretched around her, rushed over the wall, searched…but found nothing.

Pushing away, she glanced back at the unassuming expanse of stone. "I know what I heard," Eira insisted to herself. Ferro's voice was truly an echo. It had to be.

Once we possess…

His words were a siren's call. She slipped back into the Solaris common area, silently shutting the door behind her. To the left of the main entry was a large hearth, ornately carved with painfully detailed flora and fauna wrapping around scrollwork. She smothered the hearth with her magic, careful not to extinguish the crackling flame with so much magic.

…am ready…

There was the voice again. But it wasn't coming from the hearth itself; it was coming from within. Eira dragged her fingers over the stone carvings by the mantle, searching for some kind of hidden panel or door.

"Where are you?" Doubt crept into her mind, bringing along

its friend: panic. What if the echoes were all in her mind? What if her obsession with Ferro had turned into—

Her finger caught on a metal latch and she pulled, revealing a small recess hidden in the carvings of the mantle.

"Oh, thank the Mother." Eira heaved a sigh of relief. Inside the hidden compartment was an ornate, golden dagger, sheathed in a bejeweled scabbard. She grabbed it, shut the door firmly once more, and then retreated to her room before anyone could find her missing.

Safe and alone, Eira held the dagger before her, allowing her magic to pool invisibly around it. The weapon was covered in a bubble that only she could see and feel. It was swimming in so much of her power that, with a flick of her fingers, the air would turn to water.

"Now, speak," Eira commanded, inviting that man's voice back into her mind.

I've been waiting for you, a disembodied Ferro from some distant time repeated. He was clear and sharp, as though he were standing right next to her. This must have been the source of the majority of the echoes she'd heard.

You know I can't move freely, a man's voice answered. Eira didn't recognize it. The voice was deep, weathered with age or trauma, and carried a haunting weight.

I know, that's why I was worried. I thought you might have lost your way out.

They are none the wiser of my movements, or our plans.

What are my orders?

Always so eager, the haunting voice almost purred. *Let me just look at you a moment; it's not often I get to see my son.* Son... Now that Eira had heard the word, she couldn't unhear the familial resemblance in their voices. The disembodied man continued, *You are growing up strong and capable. You will be worthy, when the time comes.*

I pray I shall be.

That time draws near.

Ferro snarled softly. *Lumeria's ambition will be her demise. She ignores the evil that threatens to consume us all. We are the only ones who can save this land.*

We alone shall stand against the darkness, the man agreed. There was a long pause. Then, Ferro let out a soft gasp.

Father, are you sure?

Yes. We must implement our plans.

I am ready.

You know what to do with this.

I will bring it to her. The mysterious "her" was clearly someone Ferro had strong opinions about. Just the way he said it, filled with such longing and bitterness at the same time, told Eira as much.

Then you shall go and collect the Ash of Yargen and begin unraveling Lumeria's deal with the heretics, the man commanded. *Once we possess the four relics, we will reignite the flame that guides this world.*

And when that happens, you will rule.

And you will ascend. You will...

Scratching at her door scattered Eira's focus. Her magic collapsed in on itself. Water crashed down and pooled at her feet. She dismissed it hastily as she heard the scratching again.

Opening the door, Eira poked her nose into the main room. Upon seeing no one, her gaze dropped to the source of a soft squeaking at her feet. There was a sort of badger-like mole. Its chin had long tendrils dangling off of it—flaps of skin that swayed slightly as it turned its head this way and that. Its tiny claws were no doubt the source of the scratching.

"Don't tell me this place has rats," Eira said, deadpan. Out of all the things that could've interrupted her…this was it.

The tiny beast turned up its nose at her, fur covering where its eyes might have been, as if to say, *How dare you call me a rat.*

"Shoo. Shoo. I'm busy." Eira waved it away and closed her door. The scratching started again almost immediately. "What do you want, rat?"

Indignant squeaking and then the little creature scampered through the common room. Eira sighed and shut the door again.

More scratching.

"Wha—" Eira stopped herself as the creature had already scampered halfway across the room upon her opening the door. It halted to give her a pointed look and a jerk of its tiny head. Eira blinked several times. "Do you want me to follow?"

More squeaking, as if it had *understood* her.

"Are you my guide?"

Silence and then the creature dipped its nose, almost like a nod.

Eira took a deep breath. She was really about to follow a strange mole creature, and if anyone saw her, she'd have to claim the stomach pains had turned into full-blown hallucinations to explain this away. Eira shoved the dagger under her belt. "All right, lead on."

The mole dashed toward the fireplace and wormed into a tiny opening where the carved mantle met the paneling of the wall. Eira crouched down by it.

"I'm sorry, but I can't squeeze into a hole that small."

Scratching at her right was the only response. Eira stared at the wall, reminded of the secret room she'd found in the Tower— of the hidden cubby just on the other side of the mantle. Eira ran her fingers along the wood paneling. She dug her nails into the grooves in search of some kind of hidden lever. Her pinky brushed against the mantle as she followed one particularly deep crack.

There was a carved loop of a lion's mane that didn't seem completely attached to the rest of the sculpture, vaguely reminiscent of the other latch she'd found. Eira tried pushing it first. Nothing. Then pulling. Then she twisted and the wall at her right clicked softly, the groove she'd been inspecting splitting away.

Eira pulled at the door to the secret passage, heart racing in equal parts anxiety and excitement. It was even better hidden than Adela's secret room in the Tower. Its hinges were flush with the corner of the wall. The other edges were uneven—that way the knots of the wood blended together.

The mole was waiting for her on the other side. It hovered a moment before racing into the darkness. Eira quickly followed, pulling the door closed and plunging herself into pitch blackness.

"I can't see!" she called, trying to keep her voice down as it trembled with the edge of panic.

Distant squeaking was her reply. She wondered if the creature was saying, *I don't care, figure it out.*

Pursing her lips, Eira exhaled her frustration and fear, then pressed her hands against the door she'd just closed. Timidly, she reached out, brushing against the other wall instantly. The passage was barely wide enough for her to not have to sidestep. Pressing against the walls for support, she bit back the taste of bile that singed her throat.

Darkness all around her, as dark and consuming as those frigid waters. Eira squeezed her eyes closed but it made no difference. The passage was horribly silent. No voices came to her. As quiet as a tomb.

All the while, the scurrying of the mole was growing more and more distant.

She had to keep moving. She had to do this. This was how she would avenge her brother. If she didn't move now, she might as well let Ferro run free for good.

Move, Eira! she mentally screamed at herself. Her feet inched forward. *Move!*

If she could carry her brother through the frost and snow, if she could somehow subdue Ferro, if she could make it all the way back to Solarin after…she could walk through a dark passage. She wanted to meet the Court of Shadows. What did she think? They met in sunlit rooms and well-kept patios? No, this was what she had signed up for and she needed to—

Eira let out a gasp as her foot plunged through where she expected the ground to be. It slipped off the edge of a stair and she pressed her hands into the walls, trying to keep her balance and utterly failing. Luckily, she fell backward. Eira landed hard and clenched her teeth to keep in a shout as her tailbone sang. Her other foot slipped and she pushed out her magic before she began tumbling down the stairs.

Ice spread all around her, rooting her to the stairwell. She took a moment to catch her breath and closed her eyes once more. *Ice.* She could feel the room around her through her magic. It was a strange and incomplete picture, hard to focus on any one thing. But if she kept the frost crackling just ahead of her, she could actually walk down the stairs, able to tell when she'd reached the bottom. At the very least, the ice anchoring her would keep her from slipping again.

The creature continued to lead her deeper and deeper down the passage, past another door that Eira fumbled her way through, and down a long hall. When a faint flicker of light cut through the darkness, she blinked several times, trying to convince herself she wasn't hallucinating.

In the distance was a doorway lit by a single sconce. The magic flame illuminated the large hall she'd ended up in—a passageway that connected at least fifteen other smaller walkways like the one Eira had entered from.

The door at the end was unadorned, a blank, iron medallion on its surface above the knob at its center. In the knob was a keyhole. The mole came to a stop before the door, waiting expectantly.

Eira reached for the door with trembling fingers. They closed around the cool iron of the knob. It was too large for her hand. She couldn't seem to quite grasp it in a way that felt comfortable.

Was she reaching for too much? She had just arrived on Meru and she was already seeking out a secret society. This wasn't her. It hadn't ever been her. These were the actions of someone bolder, stronger, braver, someone more like—the frozen ship disappearing among dark waters like a ghost drifted through her mind—*someone more like Adela.*

If she did this, was it a sign there really could be a kinship between her and the pirate queen?

Eira stared at the iron medallion. It was polished into a black mirror, reflecting the shadows that rode on the currents deep within her own darkness. Behind this door she'd ultimately find the truth. Behind this door was vengeance. This was her last chance to back away. Even Eira could tell that once she chose this path, there was no going back.

The mole began scratching impatiently.

"I'm having a moment here." Eira glared at the creature. It stared up at her blindly, immune to her expression. "Just…give me a second, please."

The creature stilled, waiting patiently by her feet. As if, somehow, it understood the choices she was weighing. As if it knew the mental war she was waging.

One more breath. Inhale. Exhale.

For Marcus.

Eira turned the knob and entered the Court of Shadows.

THE DOOR REVEALED a cavern deep below the streets of Risen. Fires glowed and bounced off the soaring buttresses that supported a rough-hewn ceiling. Large sailcloths were suspended by ropes overhead like trophies. Huts made of wood and earth were erected around several communal hearths. The court bustled like a small town, at least fifty people milling about.

There were men throwing knives into wooden dummies. Women sparred with rapiers. An older man taught a young girl card tricks on a low table. Their clothes were all different. Some had clean hair and scrubbed faces, others hadn't bathed in weeks. They were mostly elfin, but Eira saw a few round-eared humans, the glowing dots of the morphi, and a few creatures in the back who had longer, snout-like noses and slitted eyes—as though they possessed some kind of reptilian heritage.

No one seemed to notice, or care, that she had just entered among them. Eira looked to the mole, about to ask where to next, when the air around the creature rippled. She saw the same pulsating magic that Ducot had used earlier, agitating the air, until the mole was gone in a blink, and the man himself stepped between the pulses.

Eira's back slammed into the door behind her as she jumped, startled. It felt like a thousand tiny daggers pricked her skin and she immediately straightened. The other side of the door to the Court of Shadows had a massive lock on it, the pins and grips taking up the whole back of it.

"Now that you're here, we'll need to lock that." Ducot stepped around her and produced a length of iron from his pocket. Magic charged around it, transforming the metal into a key that he inserted into the center of the ancient lock. As he turned it, levers were pulled by gears, magical script flared with power, bolts clicked into place, and the part of her mind that was linked to survival became keenly aware that there was no escaping now.

Struggling to find her words, Eira opened and shut her mouth several times, staring at Ducot. "You…were a mole?"

"Are a mole. Both, neither? Technically?" He grinned at her.

"Can you change at any time?" She rubbed her back and checked to make sure she wasn't bleeding from slamming into the lock mechanism.

"Yes." Ducot put the key away, a pulse of magic turning it back into an iron bar that fit once more into his pocket.

"So why did you have me fumbling through the dark?" She balked. "Why not just come to my room as…yourself?"

"I am myself as the mole." He folded his arms.

She put her hands on her hips. "As a *person*, then?"

"Consider it part of your initiation." He grinned. "Things are rarely as they seem, especially down here. You always have to be looking for what someone or something *is*, rather than what they *appear to be*." Ducot brushed past her, walking with confidence down the pathway. "Now, come along. You don't want to keep the Specters waiting."

"Specters?" Eira murmured, mostly to herself. She didn't expect Ducot to answer. Which was good, because he didn't.

They ambled down the pathway and through the hovels. More than one person glanced her way. The sensation of eyes on her was suddenly oppressive. She didn't know how she hadn't noticed when she'd first walked in. But stares and glances were everywhere now.

Men and women lounged in the rafters, half-hidden by the sailcloths, loaded crossbows in their hands. With a turn of their wrists, the men throwing daggers could skewer her through. The women practicing with their rapiers didn't bother stepping aside as she passed, their movements nearly nicking Eira's sleeve.

Everyone was aware of her presence, and they were *tolerating her for now*. That was the message she heard loud and clear from all of them. She had no doubt that if that message had reason to change, she'd never see daylight again.

Magic whispered from unseen mouths grazed her ears. Eira worked to keep her powers bundled and close, never letting them linger on any surface or object for too long. She needed to keep her focus and, moreover, wasn't sure if she wanted *all* the information this place held. She might hear a few things that would only make the darkness within her all the more thick.

The hall sloped down in the back, the buttresses connecting into archways that grew smaller and smaller like the ribs of a mighty beast until they trailed down a tunnel Eira imagined as the throat of the proverbial monster that was the Court of Shadows. She wondered what awaited her at its head.

At the end of the tunnel was another door, this one also locked. But Ducot didn't take out his iron bar. This time, he lifted the simple knocker, striking three times slowly, then two fast.

"A special knock," Eira whispered, her chest suddenly aching. She'd never hear Marcus's knock thrumming against her door again.

"Yes. It changes frequently, so don't bother memorizing it. If you're initiated then we'll let you know it…when we feel like it."

"I get it. My brother and I had one." The words slipped from her mouth before she could think better of them. They did nothing to alleviate the ache she felt. If anything, they made it worse.

Ducot arched his brow at her.

"A secret knock…so we'd always know it was us."

He pursed his lips. Eira regretted telling him instantly. She should have kept her mouth shut. Luckily, the conversation ended there as the door opened and revealed another one of the lizard-like men Eira had seen in the main room.

"Bring her in," the man said with a soft and surprisingly high-pitched voice.

The room beyond was what she could best describe as a war room. Three large tables were filled with all manner of notes, parchment, and papers. The center one had a map of Risen spread across it. Small figurines were positioned at various points. Notes had been scribbled directly onto the map.

Compared to the main hall, this room was almost blindingly bright. A chandelier glowed overhead, illuminating the six people already gathered. Eira only recognized one—Deneya.

"Seconds, leave us. Ducot, you may stay," she said with an air of authority. Three of the people shuffled out, leaving just Eira, Ducot, Deneya, another elfin man, and a morphi woman. Deneya waited until the door was shut to speak, a grin curling her lips. "Welcome to the Court of Shadows, Eira. Is it everything you hoped for?"

"And then some," Eira admitted. "It's a much larger organization than I imagined."

"You can trust everyone here with your life." Deneya picked up on Eira's unspoken worry. "So long as you're willing to give them yours."

"We'll see about that." The woman to Deneya's right snorted and tucked a lock of amber hair behind her ear.

"Not like she has a choice." The man at Deneya's left picked dirt out from under his nails with a knife. He looked at Eira through his dark eyelashes. "One way or another, now that you've seen this place, you're giving us your life."

"I knew that before I came." Eira focused on Deneya. "Good thing I didn't come empty-handed." Eira took the dagger and laid it on the papers covering the table between her and the three Specters.

"We have daggers plenty." The man rolled his eyes.

"This one spoke."

"A talking dagger?" he quipped. "Now I've seen everything."

Eira continued to speak only to Deneya. "It spoke with Ferro's voice."

The air shifted. The man slowly lowered his hand and returned the knife to a hidden sheathe on a bracer he wore. The woman glanced between Deneya and Eira.

"This is the power you told us about?" she asked.

"Yes." Deneya nodded, holding Eira's eyes with hers. "Eira, at my right hand is Rebec. Lorn is at my left. We are the Specters of the Court of Shadows, the overseers, keepers of the keys, lords and ladies of secrets for Meru."

"You make us sound so fancy when you speak like that." Lorn raised the back of his hand to his forehead dramatically. "I love it when you talk royal."

Deneya ignored him. "We'll be the ones who decide if you live with our secret, or die."

"I didn't know I was going to be tested." Eira glanced between them.

"You don't think we let just anyone in, do you?" Rebec smiled almost sweetly.

Eira had thought that Deneya's word would be enough. She'd thought that she and Deneya were on the same page with everything. She'd assumed too much.

"What do I need to do to prove I'm serious?" Eira had survived four trials to get this far. Turned out her fifth was waiting on the Crescent Continent.

"We'll send you the details of it when we're ready." Rebec seemed to enjoy withholding the information a little too much. Eira fortified her mental walls, determined not to let them see anything but cool calm. "Foremost, I want to see this magic of yours that Deneya has told us so much about." Rebec went to the back of the room, retrieved a box, set it on the table between them, and opened it to reveal an iron disk, reminiscent of what Eira had seen on the first door. "Go ahead, use your listening magic—the echoes Deneya has told us of."

Eira focused on the disk, visualizing her magic swirling around it. It sank into her ocean, becoming part of her consciousness. The more she practiced listening to objects, the easier it became. Voices came to her, sharp and clear.

If you really hear this, tell Lorn that he needs to wash his socks, the echo of Rebec said. Then, silence.

Eira hummed and shifted her attention from the medallion to Lorn. "Rebec wants you to know you need to wash your socks."

Lorn shot Rebec a glare. "My socks are fine! How dare—" He stilled, realizing Rebec was staring slack-jawed at Eira. That brought Lorn's eyes back to her. "It's true…you really can hear echoes."

"Yes, and now that's settled"—Eira motioned to the dagger—"would you like to know what Ferro said?"

"Go ahead," Deneya said.

Eira focused on the blade, bringing out the voices once more. Ferro's words were still a searing hot needle between her eyes, uncomfortable to say the least. But it was easier to endure when she was expecting it and the voice didn't come by surprise. Eira repeated the conversation she heard word for word as it played out in her mind. Like the last time, the voices stopped, whatever Ferro and the man had said clipped short.

"So he really does have a father." Lorn's gaze had turned serious. The previously joking man suddenly had a dangerous air about him. The shadows seemed to harden the soft curves of his face. "How did none of us know this? How did he keep up his orphan story?"

"Something to discuss with your seconds." Rebec gave him a sidelong glance.

"Do you really think he is related to the Pillars?" Lorn ignored Rebec's accusatory look and turned to Deneya.

"I can't see any other explanation. There's clearly been a plot Ferro has long been involved in, and now that Adela is also at play there are few others who have motivation and means like the Pillars." Deneya tapped her fingers lightly on the table, focusing on the dagger.

"What are the relics?" Eira asked. "He—his father—mentioned collecting the relics. Something about the Ash of Yargen?"

Deneya looked to Lorn and said, "I want you to see if you can find information."

Her stomach turned to lead. If they had any idea what Ferro

was talking about, Deneya wouldn't be sending Lorn away for more information. Eira had come into the Court of Shadows hoping they had all the answers and she was leaving with nothing but more questions.

"Have there been any leads on Ferro's whereabouts?" Eira asked. *Tell me you at least have information on that much*, she wanted to say.

"That's not for you to know." Rebec turned her annoyance on Eira.

"How is it not for me to know?" Eira leaned forward, placing her palm on the table. "I'm here to help, aren't I?"

"So is everyone else." Rebec rolled her eyes.

"I brought you the dagger and good information with it, didn't I?"

"Want a medal?" Rebec shrugged. Her careless and cutting nature was beginning to grate Eira in all the wrong places.

"He killed my brother and tried to kill me, too. I deserve to know."

Rebec's eyes flicked over Eira's shoulder to where Ducot was still standing. He'd been as silent as a statue the entire time. Then, the morphi woman leaned forward, resting her hands on the table. The swoop of her long bangs on otherwise short-cropped hair cast dark shadows over her eyes.

"You think you're the only one here who's lost something? Who's been hurt? People don't come to the court by choice. They come here because they have nowhere else to turn, because the world of order and justice failed them. They come here because these dark halls are the only place they can fit in anymore or have any hope of settling their scores."

"Enough, Rebec." Deneya sighed. She looked to Eira with a softer, but not entirely kind stare. "People know things as they need to know them here. The more people who know secrets—pieces to a whole truth—the easier it becomes for that truth to come out."

"But—"

"Follow our orders and you'll do fine," Lorn said. "We'll send them through Ducot. He'll be your contact through the lead-up to and during the tournament."

"I'm to have another caretaker?" Eira arched her eyebrows, glancing back at Ducot. He had the makings of a smug smirk she didn't appreciate.

"Think of me more as messenger and assassin. Which you get is up to how you act," Ducot said.

"Fine, I understand." Eira eased away from the table. Trying to force her way into this group wasn't going to work to her benefit. For all she wanted to lead the hunt for Ferro, she was getting nowhere pressing the matter.

"Good, we should get you back before the dinner wraps up," Deneya said.

"You didn't answer my question." Eira met Deneya's eyes. "Have there been any leads on Ferro?" Rebec looked like she was ready to explode when Eira insisted on asking again.

Deneya shook her head slowly. "Not yet. But we will find something soon."

Eira could only nod. Ferro had slipped their grasp. Her brother's killer was still on the loose. And possible accomplices were a large void, lacking information.

"And the *Stormfrost*?" Eira asked.

"Also unknown. Our last report had placed Adela off the northern coast, by the Empire of Carasovia. But it's been some time since she was last sighted, and the *Stormfrost* is a fast ship."

"Right." So Ferro *and* pirates were at play and unaccounted for. Eira bit back remarking on how good the Court of Shadows could actually be if they lost track of a whole ship.

"Come on, let's go." Ducot started for the door.

"Thank you for allowing me to be here." Eira gave a dip of her chin.

"Thank us by proving your worth," Lorn said ominously.

"We'll be in touch soon. Be ready." Deneya looked back to

the dagger, turning it over in her hands as Eira followed Ducot out the door.

Just before the door closed, she heard Rebec say, "You're right, her likeness with Adela is uncanny. We'll need to watch…"

The door to the Specters' war room shut on the dark currents churning white, icy foam within Eira. People here knew what Adela looked like. She wondered how many of the other members of the Court of Shadows saw Adela in her. How many held on tighter to their weapons because of it? How many feared her just for a similarity in appearance?

Adela might be her mother. She might not be. Frost coated Eira's fingertips. If the similarities struck fear in her enemies and allies alike, then Eira would leverage it with reckless abandon regardless of the truth of her parentage.

She would do anything and stop at nothing until Ferro paid for what he'd done.

FIVE

"I HAVE TO ASK, is it true?" Ducot closed the main door to the court behind them, locking it with a pulse of magic and his iron key.

"Is what true?"

"Are you really Adela's daughter?"

"I don't know," Eira answered honestly. She was still figuring out how close Ducot was to the Specters and where he stood in the court. He was of high enough rank that Deneya didn't immediately send him away during their discussions in the war room. But that could have more to do with him now being Eira's keeper. "Obviously people think I look like her."

"I wouldn't know." Ducot grinned in his lopsided way.

"Right, sorry." Eira glanced askance, avoiding his milky eyes.

"I don't know because I've never met Adela. What, did you think I didn't know because I'm blind?" He grinned as wide as the scars on his face would allow.

The momentary guilt vanished at his levity. "You can't see it, but I'm rolling my eyes at you."

"Oh, I can hear it well enough in your voice." He began strolling down the main tunnel that led to the court. The light of the single torch faded behind them. "My eyes and scars truly don't bother you?"

"Should they?" Eira arched her eyebrows.

"Most find them creepy at best, horrifying at worst."

"I guarantee the people who find you unbecoming on the outside are far uglier within," Eira said thoughtfully. "I'm surprised you'd care what I think. You don't really seem like the type to concern yourself with what others think."

"I try not to. Sometimes I'm even successful." Raw honesty was woven through his words, a sound that harmonized with a very wounded hum deep within her.

"It's hard not to. I can relate," she said softly.

"Can you?"

"You wear your scars on the outside. I wear mine inside. I can't know your pain…but I can attempt to empathize to some level based on the cruelty I've experienced in my own time." Her thoughts wandered to all the people and their judgmental eyes when they'd learned of the voices.

Ducot slowed to a stop before the dark tunnel that would lead them back to the holding house for competitors. The darkness shrouded him, save for the five faintly glowing dots across his brow. Even though he wasn't looking directly at her, she could feel all of his attention on her.

"You didn't even ask how I could see," he said thoughtfully. "How I manage to get around. Most people have a dozen things they must immediately inquire about."

"You seem to get around just fine. And why would any of it be my business?" Eira shrugged. "My uncle lost his arm in the fall of the Mad King. He uses an arm of ice now when he needs it and gets around without issue. He certainly doesn't want anyone treating him differently." The thought of Grahm filled her with a dull ache. He had been one of the three who'd bid her farewell. Even though he oozed disappointment with her choice to leave, he'd still held her tightly. "I assume you have your own tactics—magical or otherwise—to navigate the world."

"You're right; it's a number of things, some magical, some not." Ducot nodded. "You weren't what I expected for a Dark Isle dweller."

"I didn't expect to meet someone on Meru who could turn into a mole." Eira grinned slightly.

Ducot chuckled and started into the passage. The faint glow of the dots on his face gave her the slightest bit of light to follow. Not enough to properly see by, but enough to not be completely submerged in the total darkness that delighted in playing games with her mind. She pushed magic out from her feet again, frost coating her boots so there'd be no more tripping.

"Ducot, may I ask you something?"

"Ha! I knew the questions would come," he quipped. "How did I get this roguishly handsome? I was born with that, too."

She laughed softly. "What are the 'Pillars'?"

He stopped, feet split between stairs. Eira couldn't see his expression, but she could make out the way his chin dipped slightly and his shoulders hunched. She could feel the tension the mere mention of them put in him.

"The Pillars of Truth, Justice, and Light, is their full moniker," he said, finally. "That's a mouthful, so everyone refers to them as the Pillars." Ducot trailed off, thinking for a moment. Then he turned, placed his back against one of the walls, and crossed his arms, wearing an intense expression. "How much do you know about Meru's history?"

"I'd say a surprising amount for someone from the Dark Isle."

"Do you know about the Voice of Yargen and Swords of Light?"

"The Voice of Yargen is some kind of religious leader—Taavin. He's engaged to our crown princess, Vi Solaris."

"Yeah, that's him."

Eira couldn't tell from those few words if Ducot liked Taavin or not. "The Swords of Light are under the Voice. They're like the strong arm of the Faithful of Yargen, right?"

"You *do* know a surprising amount for someone from the Dark Isle. Are you sure you're not secretly from Meru?"

"I've wondered that myself at times." A bitter smile spread across her lips as she thought back to the discovery of the unknowns of her parentage. "I hear Adela is half elfin, so who knows."

"Right…" Ducot shrugged away the notion of her being Adela's spawn. He clearly didn't want to think about the implications. "Almost twenty-five years ago, the former leader of the Swords of Light, a man named Ulvarth, was imprisoned for killing the Voice before Taavin and extinguishing the Flame of Yargen."

"He assassinated the Voice, extinguished the flame, and was only imprisoned?" If that was how justice was handled on Meru, Eira suddenly had a dark hope that Ferro would be slain before he could be brought before the queen.

"He has friends in very high places, contacts that looked out for him. Plus, Lumeria was afraid that by killing him she'd make him into a martyr. Muddying things further, he didn't exactly assassinate the last Voice."

"How do you not 'exactly' assassinate someone?"

Ducot sighed and collected his thoughts. "He killed the Voice, claiming the Voice had allowed thieves to infiltrate the Archives and steal the Flame of Yargen. But Deneya later discovered that Ulvarth had been the one to steal the flame and framed the Voice for it. When he killed the Voice, everyone thought it was noble. They *cheered* for him." Ducot grimaced.

"I see…" The story was becoming more convoluted by the moment. Why would Ulvarth steal the Flame of Yargen—a sacred relic as far as Eira understood—that he was sworn to protect? And even if he stole the flame, why would he extinguish it? And how had Deneya uncovered the truth? Something wasn't adding up, but Eira kept her mouth shut on it, for now.

"Ulvarth ultimately claimed he was the one framed, and that he was innocent. He said he had nothing to do with the theft of the flame or it being extinguished. He was a raving lunatic, speaking madness about Deneya, Taavin, the Dark Isle, and some grand conspiracy to frame him." Ducot shook his head. "He even claimed that he was the Champion of Yargen come again."

"Champion of Yargen?"

"A legendary warrior destined to save the world, if you believe all the myths about our world and great battles of good and evil." Ducot shrugged.

"Which is why Queen Lumeria was afraid of turning him into a martyr," Eira pieced together.

Ducot nodded. "In any case, Ulvarth is locked away, and his most loyal generals and supplicants that weren't imprisoned or killed split off from the Swords of Light and the whole Faithful of Yargen underneath the Voice. They formed their own organization—"

"The Pillars of Truth, Justice, and Light," Eira finished. "Does the group want to free Ulvarth?"

"Who knows what the group wants. They say they're the last pillars upholding the moral fabric of Meru, but their demands and declarations seem to change by the hour." A deep frown crossed Ducot's lips. "They're butchers wearing the shrouds of holy men who just want one thing—power. If you're ever unlucky enough to come across one, avoid them at all costs."

"I appreciate the warning."

"Warning and a history lesson, see how nice I am." Ducot pushed away from the wall. "Now, we really must be getting back."

"Thank you for answering my questions," Eira expanded on her gratitude as they started up the stairs once more.

"Well, thank you for not meeting the worst of my expectations," Ducot replied, equally sincere.

Eira wore a small smile the rest of the way back to the Solaris chambers. Dangers might lurk in every corner. But the faster she learned about Meru and its undercurrents, the sooner she could traverse them with ease.

***

Dawn broke the same on Meru as it had in Solaris. Eira woke to a gray haze and low rumbling that heralded a storm in the distance. The first thing she did was open her window to stare out at the quiet city.

There were a few small vessels on the river, making their way out to the bay and perhaps the sea of Meru for what looked to be fishing—based on their rigging. But, for the most part, the air was still and quiet. No one walked along the riverbank on the far side. The windows of every building were shut tight and curtains drawn closed. Yes, it was early. But there was the same heaviness to the air as there had been during their walk through the city yesterday.

Risen was a city under siege. Held hostage by one man who seemed to be at the center of more than she could've imagined.

Eira performed a quick search of her room when she woke, looking for some kind of message or communication from the court. When she found none, she dressed and went to check on Alyss. Unsurprisingly, the woman was unresponsive to Eira's soft knocks, so Eira went downstairs to the main common area alone.

A woman with silver hair and soft lilac eyes was just finishing laying out a yet untouched spread of food. She startled at Eira's presence. "Oh, good morning, I was just finishing."

"Thank you for breakfast," Eira said as the woman bustled toward a back door.

"Certainly, it's my job." She ducked her head and quickly left before Eira could get in another word.

Eira had seen how the palace staff would go about their business, determined to be an invisible support for the royalty and other nobility. It appeared the expectations of servants on Meru were similar. Eira perused the glistening breads and foreign fruits, eventually settling on a boiled egg, a pastry filled with what appeared to be sauteed edible flowers, and a wedge of melon that was stripped red and white on the inside. She was just finishing her meal when the sounds of a commotion upstairs had her dashing to the main atrium.

"I am not about to be sequestered in here!" a man shouted with a growl. "I am the son of King Tortium, heir to the skies, and I fear no man or woman."

"Your Highness, there is credible reason to believe that

someone might try and take action against those involved with the tournament." Eira recognized the second voice as Deneya's and slowed up the steps. "Until this potential threat is uncovered, or otherwise nullified—"

"Elfin are just like humans." The man snorted in disgust. "Soft and weak. I'm not afraid of any threat here in Risen. I survived the culling at just twelve years old."

Eira halted, gripping the stair rail and clenching her jaw. *Soft and weak.* Her brother's face flashed before her eyes. His panic. His serene state after his spirit had departed for the Father's realms. Eira pressed her eyes closed and drew a steadying breath in and out through her nose. She didn't dare open her mouth. She couldn't trust what she might say if she did.

"I assure you there is every cause for concern but that Queen Lumeria has a handle on the situation," Deneya said. "Now, please follow me, your chambers will be on the fourth floor."

Fourth floor was where the draconi were staying. Eira eased her grip and stalked up the remaining stairs to the atrium. She caught a glimpse of the group—five of the lizard-like people she'd seen the night before in the court. None of them noticed her.

She trailed behind, hovering outside of the entry to the Solaris common area on the second floor landing, pacing while she waited for Deneya to return. It took a good ten minutes, but the woman descended blessedly alone.

Deneya's eyebrows shot upward in a look that Eira read as her being surprised or impressed. She gave a tilt of her head and Eira followed wordlessly down and back to the common area. Deneya didn't say anything until she had loaded a plate for herself and they were seated at a table positioned by one of the archways overlooking the river.

"I doubt we have very long to speak freely." Deneya dug into her food with a haste that matched her words. "Our connection is tangential. It's known, but only as a loose, professional relationship through my function as a queen's guard." Even though Deneya wasn't wearing the same plate as the honor guard from the day before, she did have a cape of red pinned at her shoulders. "I've no intention of showing you any favoritism that could potentially link us as more than that."

"Understood."

"Good." Deneya glanced up from her food. "I suppose you want your test from the court?"

"I do." Eira didn't see the point in trying to hide it.

"New shadows are always so eager at the start," Deneya murmured to herself with a chuckle. Eira didn't remark. She *was* eager—eager to see Ferro brought to a swift and harsh justice. "It's been arranged for you to go to the Archives of Yargen this afternoon, a bit of sightseeing."

"I get to go to the Archives?" Eira whispered in excitement.

Deneya nodded. "You and the other competitors from Solaris. As well as Levit and the senators." Her brief grimace told Eira that the senators hadn't been any less demanding after they'd been escorted to their accommodations. "Naturally, this will not just be a pleasure trip for you."

"Naturally."

"Listen closely." Deneya leaned forward. "At the entrance to the Larks' halls there is a particularly large bookcase. At its edge is a hidden panel. Go up the passage and meet with the man at the top of the last ladder. Take what he gives you, and bring it back to the court tomorrow night. Ducot will escort you again."

Larks' halls. Secret passage. And meeting with an unknown man. Even though she had a thousand questions about the details, Eira committed what little information Deneya had given her to memory and tried to limit her inquiry to only what was essential.

"How will I know if I have the right passage?"

"You'll figure it out." Deneya wiped her mouth with her napkin and stood.

"How will I step away from the group without arousing suspicion?"

"I'm sure you'll figure that out, too." A smirk slid across her lips. "You were the one who wanted to be a part of the Court of Shadows."

"Yes, but—"

"No buts," Deneya interrupted. "You thrive in this life, or you die trying. Good luck."

With that, Deneya departed, leaving Eira with her table scraps for company and just a few hours to figure out some kind of plan.

· CHAPTER ·

SIX

"WHEN DID YOU get up?" Cullen jostled Eira from her thoughts. She didn't know how long she'd been staring at the empty plate.

"A while ago, not long after dawn."

"Are you usually an early riser?" Cullen glanced over his shoulder as he began to fill up his own plate of food.

"It varies." Eira shrugged. "I think most of the time, yes. Alyss would say so. But sometimes I stay up too late and then can't wake."

"You did have an early night." He paused at the chair Deneya had been seated in…not long ago. An hour ago? Eira couldn't tell beyond the morning was brighter than it had been when Deneya had left. She'd been utterly lost in thought since then. "Mind if I sit with you?"

She hummed, making a show of considering his question. "I think it'd be better if you sat awkwardly somewhere else and we didn't talk to each other, even though we're the only two people here and know each other well."

"You're likely right." Cullen was fighting a grin and losing. "Wouldn't want to act like normal friends or anything."

Normal friends…was that what they were? The words didn't fit right. They hung between them like a poorly fitted dress—too large in some places and too small in others, too much yet somehow not enough. Eira bit her lip. Cullen had been there at every consequential turn over the past four months. She could almost still taste his lips on hers from their first day at court. She could still feel his arms when he'd been her source of stability after the revelation, and later when hoisted her from the brink of death as she struggled to get Marcus back to Solarin.

No, "normal friends" wasn't what they were. But Eira couldn't put her finger on a better description. Cullen's jovial expression began to fall as she stared at him, lower lip worried between her teeth.

"You know what?" she said hastily, before her knack for genuinely making things awkward kicked in. "We wouldn't want it to be uncomfortable for anyone else if they come down. I think we should make the sacrifice and sit together."

He gave her a smile, but it didn't quite reach his eyes. Questions hovered in the air around him as he took the seat. Eira looked out the archway as he dug into his food, not wanting to stare while he ate. But her effort to not be awkward only made her feel all the more so. Were her hands better on her lap? Or the table? If she kept swapping them he was going to notice.

"How do you feel?"

"Pardon?"

"Your stomach. It looks like you managed to eat this morning." Cullen motioned toward Deneya's cleaned plate. "I was worried about you."

"Worried?" Eira folded and unfolded her hands in her lap.

"Well, yes, Levit was right…your ailments must've been serious for you to miss the opportunity to dine with elfin and morphi on the first night."

"You don't need to worry about me," Eira said softly.

"I've already told you I do."

"But—"

"You asking me not to will do no good. If I could stop worrying about you, I would've. Just like if I could stop thinking about you, or trying to find ways to spend time with you, or catch a word with you, or steal a smile that—" Cullen stopped himself. A scarlet flush streaked across his cheeks and he busied his mouth with a pastry as Eira looked away, fighting a blush of her own.

Steal a smile… The words were a searing hot needle, piercing the cool waters and ice she'd been trying to use to keep others away. It wasn't enough to fracture the thick barrier…just enough to puncture, to get something warm and genuine through and remind her just how cold she had become.

"I should go," Eira said, pushing away from the table and the uncomfortable sensations of someone being too close.

"Eira, I didn't mean to upset you."

"I'm not upset." She stood. "I'm going upstairs to get a book on Meru." And hopefully find Alyss. "I hoped to read a chapter before I met any elfin. I don't want to put my foot in my mouth."

"They're lovely people, very understanding. I doubt you would," Cullen said hastily.

"I want to be sure. And I should let Alyss know I'm feeling better." Eira cursed inwardly. She'd been intending to possibly use not feeling well as an excuse later to step away at the Archives. Something about Cullen was turning her thoughts to mush.

"I'm glad you're feeling better." An air of disappointment was beginning to collect around him. "I really didn't mean—"

"It's fine, Cullen." Eira forced a smile. "I'll see you later."

She retreated up the stairs, chest tight. She was avoiding him. But she didn't fully understand why.

He's a distraction, that's why. No matter how she felt about him, no matter what he'd been intending to say to her, he was going to be a distraction if the current constriction of her ribs on her heart was any indication. Plus, if he got too close to her, she risked him finding out something about the Court of Shadows, or noticing what she was doing. Eira already had to navigate around Alyss. Cullen was a risk she just couldn't take.

Still, even as she entered into the Solaris common room to find Alyss, even as she sat on Alyss's bed while her friend got dressed and ready for the day, her mind wandered back to him. She spent every spare moment trying to scrub Cullen from her thoughts up until the Swords of Light arrived at the manor to escort them to the Archives of Yargen.

***

The walk through the city was filled with more of the same pregnant silence from the day before. The only sounds were the soft clanking of their guards' swords in their scabbards and their boots on the ground. Twice, they saw patrols of queen's knights marching through the city. There were a few couriers conducting business as well. But everyone who was out and about had a bright red ribbon pinned to their chest with a number stamped on it. Eira didn't know the meaning, but she surmised it was some kind of permission to be out in the streets, since the knights only stopped people who weren't wearing them.

Ambassador Cordon and the senators were in another manor, higher up the ridge from them. They joined the group without fuss, shepherded from a group of red-caped knights to the purple-sashed Swords of Light. Yemir went immediately to his son, pulled him to the edge of the group, and promptly began speaking in hushed tones that Eira found herself straining to listen to.

"How are your accommodations?" Yemir asked.

"They're very nice; the queen is generous. And yours?" Cullen answered dutifully. It sounded almost like a script.

"Very nice as well." Yemir glanced around as if looking for who might be listening. Eira kept her eyes forward as his gaze grazed over her. When he spoke again she could only make out every few words. "…of the remaining delegates…dinner…but I will…if you can…someone…meet…"

"You don't have to do that," Cullen murmured, agitation made it loud enough for Eira to hear.

"Nonsense, you should be there, not with the rabble," Yemir hissed. Even Noelle could hear the conversation now, judging from the disapproving glare she gave the senator's back. Luckily, she kept her mouth shut so she and Eira could both continue listening in.

"We'll see," Cullen said mildly.

They continued their hushed conversation all the way to the

Archives. But Eira was soon too distracted to care about what was said.

The Archives of Yargen loomed over all of Risen, stretching to the sky as if to kiss the clouds. Triangular buildings were positioned around it, connected by floating archways topped with glass that glittered in the late morning's light.

"Have you ever seen anything so tall?" Alyss whispered.

"No." Eira tipped her head back, trying to see the whole building at once. But it was impossible. The structure was far too large.

"Just wait until you see inside," one of the guards said proudly. "Whenever you're ready."

Yemir decided to speak for all of them. "Let's continue."

"I *so* appreciate the senator asking if we were done out here," Noelle muttered.

Eira gave her a small dip of her head. Noelle rolled her eyes at Yemir's back. For Noelle, Yemir was an exasperating inconvenience. For Eira, he was a threat. She'd never forget he'd tried to put her behind bars…*twice*.

Inside, the tower was lined with bookcases that were built into every wall and available nook and cranny. Rings of walkways— connected by stairways and ladders—were spread at varying intervals all the way to the top. At the summit, an unlit brazier was suspended over the center of the room with several archways supporting the large chains it was hung from.

Noelle let out a low whistle. "Now, *this* is impressive." Her eyes dropped to the floor. "What's the symbol mean?"

"I've seen it in the North," Alyss murmured.

"It's the symbol of Yargen," Eira said. Three interlocking circles connected by a vertical line were inlaid on an intricate mosaic. "Each circle represents the past, present, and future, overlapping. And the center line is Yargen, connecting all of them."

"Very astute of you," a weathered voice said before Eira could get out another word. "I'm pleased to see that a young one from the Dark Isle knows enough to recognize Yargen's mark." He wore plain robes of a deep sunset-red hue, tied at the waist with a wide, golden sash that the tendrils of his beard nearly reached. "I am Kindred Allan, and I will be your guide through the Archives today."

Allan led them around the base of the main tower, explaining how the books were organized and kept. There were over two thousand years of history contained in this building. Even older tomes were locked away for safekeeping. The people responsible for maintaining the books—cataloging them, checking their binding, and recording new history—were the Larks. As soon as Eira heard the name, her ears perked up.

The Faithful of Yargen were divided into three main subsets— the Larks, the Swords, and laymen. The Larks had their own triangular building connected by one of the glass-topped archways that Eira had seen outside. Allan escorted them from the main tower to the halls of the Larks.

When everyone else had their eyes on him, Eira focused on the edges of the bookcases they passed. She repeated Deneya's words in her mind. *The entrance to the Larks' halls, a particularly large bookcase, hidden panel.* But Eira saw nothing that would indicate a secret passage. Though, she only had a few seconds to look.

She had to find a way to get back to that bookcase, alone. Her thoughts were consumed by how she was going to steal away, rather than focusing on Allan as he explained the details of the Larks' order. A month ago, she would've focused on nothing but him. But now, there were higher callings she had to heed—Ferro was still out there. Free. While her brother was dead. What was the point of her breathing if not to avenge him?

They wrapped up their tour where they started, at the ground level of the main atrium. Allan thanked them for their time and the Swords of Light began to coalesce around the group to escort them back to the manors.

"Kindred Allan," Eira said quickly. Senator Yemir shot her an ugly look, no doubt upset that she would speak out of turn. But Eira had no trouble ignoring him. "I was wondering…might it be possible for us to linger for a bit longer and explore the Archives? You said the books were open to the public and there's a great many things I'd like to read."

The elderly man considered this, leaning on his cane.

"Kindred, we were told to bring them right back to the manor," one of the Swords said.

"Yes, but I would assume that was intended to mean no other stops between here and there. Not immediately after the tour was over." He stroked his beard.

"Sir, please ignore this girl; she asks far too much," Yemir said, trying to smooth over wrinkles in the interaction that Eira didn't think were actually there.

"I just want to read," Eira said defensively. "I won't take too long."

"Quiet now," Yemir part growled at her. "You should be grateful you're here at all after—"

"Father," Cullen interrupted sharply.

After what? After you tried to implicate me in the murder of my brother? Eira bit back the angry words.

"Kindred, Eira is one of the best students in Solaris. She's sincere in her honest and good-natured interest in your culture and histories." Mister Levit jumped into the verbal fray and his words sank like rocks within her, settling in the deep sediment of guilt. She bit her cheeks to stop herself from contradicting him. She needed to stay, she needed time in the Archives, but not to read. And that suddenly felt like a betrayal of all the trust he'd ever placed in her.

"It's all right," Kindred Allan luckily continued before anything could escalate further among the group. He chuckled, a raspy and breathy sound. "I don't think it would be an issue if you stayed a bit longer."

"But, sir—" the Sword from earlier attempted to object.

"Just see they're back before nightfall." Kindred Allan began to hobble away.

"Great," Noelle grumbled, and gave Eira a glare. "Now I'm stuck here all day."

"I had other meetings to attend to as well." Yemir adjusted his coat haughtily.

"I know," Levit said, tapping his fist into his opposite palm. "Let's split. Those interested in staying can remain until sunset. Those who want to leave will go now." He looked to the Sword. "That shouldn't be an issue, should it?"

The Sword of Light sighed heavily. "This is already not according to plan, so what's one more change? I'm sure we can accommodate it."

"Then I'll stay with Eira and…" Levit turned to Alyss expectantly.

"You know I go wherever Eira goes." Alyss linked her elbow with Eira's.

"Anyone else?" Levit looked to the group.

"I'd like to stay," Cullen said.

"Son, there are matters which we must discuss." Yemir folded his arms.

"This is an essential opportunity for me to learn more of Meru," Cullen said lightly. But Eira saw the edges of worry in his eyes. Why didn't he want to go with his father?

"You'll come with me back to the manor."

"Then, it's just the three of us in the Archives," Mister Levit said with forced ease, clearly trying to cut through the collecting tension.

"Works for me." Alyss shrugged.

"Me too." Eira's focus snagged on Cullen as he left with his father. Their eyes met for a brief second.

He's not your concern, she reminded herself. But Eira couldn't deny there was a part of her that was curious. She wondered if what he had to speak about with his father related back to the secret she knew he was guarding on behalf of his family.

Not your concern! she repeated, louder.

"I'm going to explore," Eira announced.

"I'll come with," Alyss said.

"I'll be around." Levit chuckled. "You ladies enjoy the Archives."

"What are you going to read first?" Alyss asked as they started up one of the staircases that ringed the bookshelves. "Is this everything you ever dreamed?"

"And more." Eira glanced toward the entrance to the Larks' halls. There were a few hours still until sundown. But she didn't know how long the mysterious man she was meeting would wait. She had to free herself of Alyss first though, possibly the hardest task of them all. "Do you think there's any romance novels in here?"

"You know I'm going to check." Alyss grinned. "I'm hoping for something really weird and juicy. Something that's going to make me question my moral compass."

Eira blurted laughter. "You are too much."

"I'm just enough to make you smile." Alyss nudged Eira's shoulder with her own. "I've been worried about you."

"The stomach issue passed."

"That's not what I meant and you know it," Alyss scolded lightly. "It hasn't been that long since—"

"Don't," Eira said gently. She dropped her arm and Alyss's hand slid down so Eira could lace her fingers with her friend's. "I don't want to talk about it."

Alyss frowned. "You haven't talked with *anyone* about it, and you need to."

Eira wanted to be invisible, submerged in the dark water rising up from her feet. It was rushing toward her head. Soon, she would be pulled under, she would be back in that dark, cold place where Marcus died.

She shook her head, trying to scare away the ghosts, only mildly successful. "I'm fine, I don't need to talk about it."

"Eira—"

"I said I'm fine." She jerked her hand away from Alyss. "If I say I'm fine then I mean it. If you're really my friend that'll be good enough for you."

The remark wounded Alyss. Her friend tried not to show it. But Eira had known her long enough, and well enough, to know a forced smile when she saw one. It was thinner, weaker, and didn't even come close to touching Alyss's eyes. Eyes that were now steeped in hurt.

"You know I'm your friend. That's why I'm worrying about you."

"I know. I…I'm sorry." Eira shook her head and put her back to Alyss. "I need some space, please."

Alyss didn't follow her down the walkway.

It hadn't been how Eira had intended to lose Alyss and break away on her own. But it was effective. She should be happy; she had the time and space now to find this hidden passage. However, the guilt Mister Levit's kind words had put in her now had company with how she'd treated Alyss.

Eira stalked up the stairs, walking as silently as possible. She clung to the bookcases, out of sight of those below. She paused at the entrance to the Larks' wing, listening closely. The air was still and the only sounds were the occasional clanking of armor as the Swords patrolled the lower floors.

With a wave of her hand, Eira summoned a curtain of illusion and drew it around her. If anyone looked on, all they would see was the bookshelf, Eira rendered invisible. She held the illusion in place with her right hand and pressed her left against the wood. A crackle of frost raced out from between her fingers and Eira closed her eyes.

She should thank Ducot. Without him forcing her to walk in the dark, she wouldn't have uncovered this little trick with her magic. Eira felt *through* the ice. She felt its broad plane and where it seeped into a crack, curving around to the backside of the bookcase. Sure enough, it was hollow.

Pulling her hand and her magic back, Eira pressed on the

wood, feeling for grooves. It popped open under her fingers. She quickly scrambled inside, closing it behind her with a fraying leather strap.

Plunged into darkness, Eira immediately pressed a hand over her mouth as a wave of nausea assaulted her. Shudders wracked her body as the walls threatened to close around her. At least last night she'd had Ducot. Even in mole form, he'd been encouraging her onward.

Now, she was stuck in place. She was drowning while gasping lungfuls of air. It was Alyss's fault. Eira cursed under her breath. Alyss had been the one who put these thoughts in her mind. She'd been the one who dredged up thoughts of Marcus from the abyss. Now those memories threatened to pull her under.

Violently shaking her head, Eira pressed her hand against the wall and pushed herself up. She had to keep moving. She was doing this, all of this, for her brother—to avenge him. She'd let him down in that lake. She couldn't let him down now. He was counting on her.

Eira made her way slowly upward. She wondered if the early members of the Court of Shadows had helped build this structure and knew to hide passages. How far back did the influence of the organization reach? What else did they have their hand in?

Eventually, after what felt like hours of climbing up and up in the darkness, Eira reached a ladder. With frost-covered fingers, she climbed, slowly feeling the passage narrow around her before opening again to a small landing. Pale light filtered in through a doorway.

A man stood alone in an empty room, his back to the door, hands folded behind him. Yet, she knew him from the wave of his hair. The way he held himself. The way the whole world seemed to hold its breath for him and only him. As if fate itself hovered in the air over his shoulder.

"It's you," Eira whispered, and he turned, meeting her with brilliant emerald eyes Eira had last seen in her dreams.

· CHAPTER ·

SEVEN

TWO YEARS AGO, Eira's uncles had dared to take her into "polite society." It had only been a year since the incident, so the memories of what she'd done were fresh in the minds of the nobles and the senators who'd tried to lock her away. But it was a risk they'd decided to take nevertheless. She had been "very good" and "very remorseful" for that first year. She had done everything they'd asked, just like she had always been taught—as had always been expected of her. It had been her birthday. She'd just turned fifteen.

They'd made the rules very clear…and they'd brought her to a winter's ball to see the announcement of the crown princess's engagement to the Voice of Yargen.

That night, she'd laid eyes on Taavin for the first time. He was the first elfin she'd ever seen. Perhaps she did have girlish fantasies surrounding him for a time following. But, more than that, when she had laid eyes on him she had immediately known she was destined to leave Solaris. Meeting him, even if for just a few brief seconds, had forever changed the course of her life.

Now, she stood before him again.

"You must be the new shadow," he said with a sigh of relief. "I was worried you wouldn't be able to make it. The Head Specter said you were still learning how to navigate Risen."

The Head Specter was Deneya. New shadow? Did that mean she was already in the Court of Shadows? Likely not. Deneya had probably not wanted to admit that she was sending an initiate to perform such an important task as meeting in secret with the Voice of Yargen.

"I-I am," she stammered. Just like the last time she'd seen him, all words failed her.

"Here, I don't have much time. They'll begin wondering if I don't get back soon." Taavin crossed the room and held out a small, wrapped parcel. It wasn't much larger than her palm and Eira took it reverently with both hands. Underneath the parchment was some kind of sturdy box. But what it contained was clearly not meant for her eyes. He hesitated, not letting go. "You're human…and you're wearing clothes in Solaris fashion."

"I'm from the Solaris Empire," Eira blurted. A grin crept across his lips, eliciting a flush that rose up her neck. "I shouldn't have said that, huh?"

"No, you shouldn't have. Shadows should be like their namesake—known but not heeded, clinging to corners, as unidentifiable as the last, and silent." The words could've been scolding, yet he wore a smile. "Luckily, I'm a friend, and, don't worry, I won't tell."

"Thank you," she mumbled as Taavin released the package.

"I'm pleased to see the Head Specter recruited someone from Solaris. I know my betrothed will be delighted by this turn. She had hopes that our lands could work together at every level possible." He stepped around her, starting for the door, but stopped just before leaving. "If I might give you a word of advice, new shadow?" Eira faced him and nodded. She'd take any wisdom he'd bestow on her. "You might not always understand the Head Specter's methods…but she's been to the precipice of the end of the world and back. She's dined with the divine. Nothing will stun her, and very little gets by her. So put all of your trust in her."

Eira didn't know the meaning of all the strange Meru phrasing, so she merely said, "I already trust her with my life."

"Good. I am—" He didn't get to finish whatever he'd been about to say next as a nearby explosion rattled the foundation of the Archives.

Eira let out a shout in surprise, hearing as much as feeling the earth groan. Her ears rang and she blinked. Taavin was much faster recovering and he raced to one of the windows. A plume of black smoke rose up to the gray sky.

"What—"

"We need to go, *now*." Taavin ushered her toward the door with a palm between her shoulder blades. "Come, follow me."

He descended the ladder into the darkness and Eira was quick behind him. Taavin ignored the pathway she'd come in through, heading for a ramp opposite the ladder. He reached up, pulling on a trapdoor that rolled on silent casters.

"Keep this entrance safe and secret. Get the parcel back to the Specters," he whispered. "Good luck, shadow."

With a gentle push, Taavin urged her onto the ramp and slid the trapdoor closed behind her. Eira scrambled up and found herself on the walkway of the uppermost level of the Archives. She blinked at the large, empty basin suspended in the air before her.

"Eira!" Levit called from below.

"Eira!" Alyss shouted.

Staying crouched and unseen, Eira quickly unbuttoned her shirt. She'd worn a belt under her loose-fitting clothes today, in preparation to carry something back to the safe house. She cinched the package underneath the belt and quickly buttoned her shirt back up to her neck.

"Eira where are you?" Alyss called again.

Eira patted the parcel, making sure it was secure, then stood, and ran over to the railing. "I'm up here!"

Alyss's face appeared over the railing about halfway down the spire. "What're you doing up there?"

"Both of you come down!" Mister Levit shouted, louder than Eira had thought him capable.

Eira scrambled down the stairways and ladders of the circular walkways of the Archives. Alyss beat her by a wide margin and when Eira arrived she was breathless. She pressed a hand into her side, subtly adjusting the parcel and making sure it hadn't slipped out from the belt. It was still cinched tightly against her skin. It hadn't moved the slightest bit.

"Where were you?" Alyss asked, grabbing her shoulder. Concern marred her friend's face.

"I was at the top, reading."

"I didn't see you go up there." A frown crossed Alyss's lips. "And why didn't you come when the explosion—"

"Enough, ladies, we need to go back to the manor, now." Levit turned to face one of the Swords of Light. "Sir, if you would—"

"The safest place for you is here in the Archives," the man responded. "Please, for now, just stay put."

More shouting was rising from outside. Eira heard barked orders to the Swords of Light, men and women in purple sashes running by the open doors. Other knights streamed in and out of the Archives, coming from the Swords' barracks that Allan had pointed to earlier.

"What do you think is happening?" Eira whispered to Alyss.

"I don't know. All I heard was an explosion, then screaming." She shuddered and took a step closer to Eira. Her voice was even more hushed. "You don't think that—"

"Stop him!" a man shouted in the square at the front of the Archives. "Stop him!"

Eira watched as another man dashed by—little more than a blur. Her eyes widened, trying to make out every detail. He was just a streak, but that deep green hair had been unmistakable.

"It's Ferro," Eira breathed. Magic flared around her. Glyphs ignited in the square beyond.

"Wait—Eira, stop!" Alyss shouted.

"What is she—Eira, get back here!" Levit called.

Eira ignored them both. She sprinted toward the open doors of the Archives, squeezing out before the two Swords shut them tight. Others were shouting—at her? Around her? Eira didn't know. Her heart was racing and it drowned out every word of the people in the square along with every shred of her better sense.

Ferro was here. She'd seen him. Her brother's murderer was close.

He vaulted over a low wall at the edge of the square, one that promptly exploded with a hail of dust and rock as a Lightspinning glyph constricted on it with a flash. Eira began running after him. Two Swords tried to stop her, but she dodged out of their grasps.

The mere sight of Ferro had frozen every last drop of blood in her. The dark waters within her churned, tunneling her vision and making him her only focus. This was the man who tried to kill her—who killed her brother. She would hunt him down, no matter what the cost, and make him *pay*.

Eira leapt over the rubble of the wall. Her stomach shot into her head as she fell. Sticking out her heels, she pushed her magic under her feet, making a ramp of ice that she slid down, scrambling and pushing off against the walls of the buildings that made up the alleyway she was now in. Her eyes caught his heel as he rounded the corner.

"You won't escape that easily," Eira growled, sprinting after him.

When she turned the corner, a flash of light caught her off guard. Eira dodged on instinct, and the glyph exploded right where her neck had been a moment ago. Pinwheeling her arms, Eira struggled to right herself but fell hard.

He was ahead of her in the alleyway, about to make another turn.

"No!" she part snarled, part shouted. Eira slammed her fist into the ground and ice shot forth, covering the buildings and street. It was faster than he could run and closed off the exit.

He stumbled, trying to stop himself, nearly smashing into her wall. Eira wished darkly he'd broken his nose on it.

"*Juth calt*," he snarled. A glyph appeared in her ice, exploding. But as soon as the ice was damaged, it repaired itself. "*Juth calt*!" He tried again, but to no avail.

"You're not going anywhere." Eira stood. Frost was thickening in the air. Rain turned into snow as water was beginning to rush out from around her feet.

How will you do it? a wicked and cold voice whispered from the most sinister recesses of her mind. *Freeze him? Drown him like he did Marcus? Whatever you do...don't make it too fast. Make him panic like Marcus did. Make him suffer as you have.*

The man turned and the dark thoughts evaporated, Eira's frost nearly vanishing with them. She should have noticed when he spoke—this was not Ferro. The man had amber eyes and a crooked nose. He snarled at her, readying another attack.

Eira waved her hand numbly and a gag of ice covered his lips, as she'd done to Ferro in the forest. But unlike with Ferro, this gag continued to spread across his face. Eira could feel it as her frost sank into him, under his flesh. She could feel his heart slowing and his body going numb.

Soon, he was a statue of ice—not quite alive, not quite dead. Eira held him in stasis just like the journal she'd read months ago had said was possible. Slowly, she approached, staring into his unseeing eyes.

"Do you know I'm here? Or will this all be a dream when I let you thaw?" Eira held the magic in place with an iron fist. He wore plain, cream-colored robes. Her eyes dropped to the satchel he was carrying. Three vertical scars had been etched onto the back of his hand. "What do you have here?"

As Eira reached for his hip, the frost retreated just enough for her to open the bag. Inside was a scroll case and a small pouch with strange markings. She took both, beginning to inspect them when barked orders could be heard on the other side of her ice walls.

Eira quickly turned away from the man—not risking him being conscious still—and unbuttoned her shirt, shoving both scroll case and pouch under her belt next to the box Taavin had given her. By the time she was decent, a Lightspinning glyph attacked her barrier from the other side.

Careful not to release her prisoner, Eira relaxed her magic and watched as the ice evaporated into the air. The snow in the alley quickly warmed, turning into rain.

A line of Swords of Light stood waiting on the other side of the wall, weapons and magic at the ready.

"Here." Eira motioned to the man she still held in stasis. "I believe this is the one you're looking for."

EIGHT

"WHAT WERE YOU thinking?" Mister Levit stopped mid-pace the moment the door to the Solaris common area opened, revealing Eira. "How dare you run off like that. How dare you ignore my orders. How dare—" He paused, looking back at the Swords of Light who delivered her back to the manor following their initial questioning. "Thank you for returning her. I'll take it from here," Levit said, jarringly sweet compared to his previous rage.

The Swords exchanged a look and gave a nod, clearly more than happy to escape the reprimanding she was already getting from Levit. As soon as the doors shut behind her, he started up again. He didn't care that Alyss, Noelle, and Cullen were in the common room as well. Her punishment might as well be an example for them.

"I'm sorry," Eira muttered. She had every intention of retreating to her room.

Levit stepped in front of her, blocking her way. "'Sorry' isn't going to cut it. You risked not only your place in the tournament, but your fellow competitors' places as well. You could've had *them* disqualified with your actions."

"They weren't—"

"What you do reflects on *all* of Solaris." He wasn't going to let her get a word in. "When you step out of line, it reflects poorly on all of us. We are here on Queen Lumeria's blessing. We have this house because of Queen Lumeria's blessing. What do you think she might do if you interfere with her knight's investigations? Do you really want to find out at what point her kindness expires?"

"I would never let any of you take the fall for my actions,"

Eira said, mostly to her peers sitting behind Mister Levit. Alyss and Cullen shared a worried expression, but Noelle didn't seem bothered in the slightest; she wore an amused grin.

"That might not be your choice and, moreover—" Levit rested his hands on her shoulders, his face was twisted with worry "—you could've risked your *life*, Eira."

"My life was at risk the moment Ferro attacked me. It was at risk the moment he escaped." She jerked away from her teacher and mentor. "I thought it was him in the courtyard." Her hands were shaking, voice trembling. "I thought I was chasing Ferro. I thought I could capture the man who murdered my brother!"

Her voice seemed to echo in the silence that followed.

Levit's expression softened. "Eira," he started.

"I wanted… I wanted…" Her shoulders tightened at the words she was holding back. *I wanted to kill him.* She had wanted to make him pay. She had felt every dark emotion that the incident three years ago had unearthed, in triplicate. *I'm not a murderer*, a voice in her whispered, weaker than she'd like. "I want to be alone."

Eira brushed past Levit and this time he didn't stop her. She slipped into her room, closing the door with a sigh. Eira didn't even make it to her bed before her legs gave out and her knees hit the floor. She curled in on herself, burying her face in her hands, drawing gasping breaths.

If it had been Ferro, what would she have done to him? How far would she have gone to try and rattle the restless, relentless need for blood as payment for Marcus's life?

A soft knock jolted her from her thoughts. Eira turned as the door was eased open despite her silence. Alyss stepped in.

"I know you said you wanted to be alone but—"

"Get out, Alyss." Eira didn't even look at her friend.

"I don't think—"

"Get out!" Eira shouted.

Alyss didn't put up a fight and left.

Eira stayed on the floor until the shadows were long and

the light had turned to gold. Her body ached from the hunched position she sat in. Her legs had gone numb. But Eira couldn't find the strength to move.

Over and over she replayed the Swords' looks of horror as she slowly released her frosty hold on her captive. She heard their whispers as they brought her back to the manor, all surrounding the name, *Adela*. Over and over she repeated the words she'd heard so clearly in her mind, so full of malice and vengeance—words spoken by a girl abandoned on a cold night, who knew only of the world's brutality and harshness.

If it had been Ferro… Would she have really been able to kill him? If she had, would she have felt guilty? How ghastly would her actions have been?

Deep down, was she the murderer half of Solaris had seen her as for years?

She didn't have answers to those questions and that shook her to her core. Was she any better than Ferro if she could act with such callous disregard for life? Did it make any difference that he was the one to kill Marcus? Or would she be a murderer, through and through, if she chased this goal relentlessly?

Every time she began to feel guilty for thinking of Ferro's death, Marcus's face, cold and lifeless, flashed before her eyes, steeling her resolve into something harder and colder than any ice she could ever make. By the time there was a soft knock on her door, almost all the light had left the sky.

Eira opened the door and found herself face-to-face with Ducot.

"Let's go." His expression was unreadable.

She merely nodded, and followed him back to the Court of Shadows in silence.

The court had a different atmosphere this evening. There were fewer people, for starters. But the shadows who were there regarded her with closed-off gazes. If they did show emotion, it was a wariness and skepticism.

Every stare wordlessly told Eira what they thought of her

actions today. But if she had any doubt as to the court's general disapproval, it was put to rest the moment she entered the Specter's chambers.

"Eira, as requested," Ducot announced. The three Specters looked up from the center table.

"Close the door," Deneya commanded. Ducot did as he was told and Eira hovered, waiting for whatever judgment they wanted to reap on her. Deneya's attention finally landed on Eira. "Well?"

"Here." Eira crossed and dropped the parcel Taavin gave her. "I brought what you asked."

"You did a lot more than that," Rebec half snarled. "You want to be a shadow, but at the first possible moment you run headfirst into danger, put all the attention on yourself, and risk your whole operation."

"I had it under control."

"Not according to the guard records." Rebec took a step forward, looming over Eira.

"I had him frozen but not dead, what more control do you want?"

"How about you don't shout to the world that you're Adela's spawn?" Rebec hummed.

A frown pulled on Eira's lips. "I didn't—"

"But you did," Deneya interrupted with a sigh. "The magic you used has Adela written all over it. It's more damning than you making a trident of ice in Solaris. Whispers that you might be Adela's acolyte have already reached the queen's inner circles and I am helpless to stop them."

"Or that you might even be Adela herself, reborn with some dark power," Lorn added. "Given how you look."

Eira kept forgetting that to the people on Meru, Adela was more than a myth. She was flesh and blood. She was death given cold shape. Eira could get away with using the magic she'd read in the journals more on Solaris than she could on Meru.

"Well, I come bearing gifts again, at least." Eira sought to divert the topic, reaching into her satchel. "I lifted these off the man before the Swords of Light saw." She placed the scroll case and the small bag next to the parcel.

"What're they?" Lorn asked, leaning in for a closer look.

"I don't know, I didn't examine them at all. I figured I'd wait for orders before doing anything with them."

Rebec snorted. "Don't act like you suddenly give a scrap about our orders."

"I—"

Eira was cut off by Deneya taking the scroll case and twisting open one end. She turned it over, tapping lightly to loosen a curled piece of paper. Deneya unfurled it, Lorn and Rebec reading over her shoulders as Deneya slowly and purposefully read aloud.

"Order is secure. Payment in full. You have three days."

Deneya opened the bag next. Dark beads rolled out, matte against the sheen of the table stain. They were smaller than marbles, unassuming, but Rebec let out a gasp and Lorn stepped away. Clearly, they knew something Eira didn't.

"I thought so," Deneya grumbled. "Bloody Pillars."

"Do you think they're really working with Carsovia?" Rebec asked her leader.

"How else would they get explosives? The Carsovian Empire has the beads under tight control."

"Explosives?" Eira asked no one in particular.

Ducot was the one to answer. "Those little black things are called flash beads." He motioned to the dark granules. "It's a rare mineral, mined and processed in the Empire of Carsovia."

"The Empire of Carsovia?"

"Here." Deneya moved back to the central table and Eira followed. The head Specter rolled a small map over one corner of the massive, detailed map of Risen that dominated the table's surface. "Solaris, Meru." Deneya moved her finger, corresponding with the different locations. "The Kingdom of the Draconi is on the island of Dolarian here, and the Twilight Kingdom is in this forest to the northeast of Risen. This little peninsula down south is the Republic of Qwint. They broke off from Carsovia, hence why they're so eager to work with us and expand their bargaining power through a treaty."

"Then this is Carsovia?" Eira asked, motioning to the land by Qwint.

"Yes…and this, and this, and this, too. All of it is Carsovia."

"Is this map to scale?" Eira whispered.

"Unfortunately, yes." Deneya pursed her lips.

"It's massive." Meru was about double, nearly triple the size of Solaris. Carsovia was at least double the size of Meru…and that was based only on what Eira could see drawn out. Carsovia's borders spilled off the edge.

"It is. And what you see is only about half of it."

How could one empire be so large? Solaris had nearly ripped at the seams trying to unify four small kingdoms. What was Carsovia like? Was it a monstrous, unified force? Or was it riddled with infighting? Constantly tearing apart and stitching back together?

"Is Meru at war with Carsovia?" Eira asked.

"No, and it is Queen Lumeria's fervent wish that we never be. Alliances are tenuous between Meru and Carsovia, but as long as Lumeria lives, they exist. It was part of the motivation behind the Treaty of Five Kingdoms—we're stronger together. Carsovia is a beast none of us want to wake." Deneya rolled up the map.

"Do the Pillars share these sentiments?" Ducot asked.

Deneya's face tightened into a pained expression. All she could do was sigh. "Let's hope the Pillars are not working with the empire and, at best, are getting these flash beads from a rogue operator."

"A rogue operator like Adela?" Lorn folded his arms and leaned against the table. "My whisperers tell me that she's peddled flash beads in the past five years. She could have an inside man at the mines."

"We could make a targeted strike against her," Rebec offered eagerly. "Give me several good bladed shadows and we will take the *Stormfrost* once and for all."

"If Adela could be taken down by several good bladed shadows then she wouldn't still be alive." Deneya stole Eira's thought right from her mind. "Foremost, Eira, can you give the scroll case and pouch a listen? See if you hear anything."

"Sure." Eira focused on the scroll case first.

There were only a few whispered words for her to hear. She relayed each of them, but knew they wouldn't be useful. The discussion was brief and transactional. There wasn't any kind of hint as to whom the Pillar had been speaking to and they gleaned nothing from it that they didn't already know.

She focused on the pouch next. Distant cries hovered on an unseen breeze, fading in and out. A whip cracked, sharp and brutal. *Fill it up*, a gruff voice said. *Back to work*. The mutterings of a woman, her mind clearly half gone.

Her magic scraped for every sound, but there were no more to be found. Those lost screams echoed in her mind long after her magic retreated. Eira relayed what she heard with as level a voice as possible.

"I think you heard the flash mines of Carsovia." Lorn stared at the floor as he spoke. An invisible weight pulled on his shoulders.

"As if we needed any more evidence of how they treat the people sent there." Rebec grimaced at the pouch, as though the horrible sounds Eira heard were the bag's fault.

"The Empire of Carsovia sends their prisoners to work in the mines," Deneya said for Eira's benefit. "They claim it's only the worst offenders that toil. But we have reason to suspect far more than that end up in those torturous mazes of rock and fire."

Eira swallowed thickly. "I see."

"In any case, we have a lead." Deneya straightened away from the scroll case, picked up the box Taavin had given Eira, and handed it to Lorn. "Per your request. Once you and your whispering shadows have figured out where their next recruitment meeting is happening, I want to know. Judging by this, I think we have an idea of when it will be. Rebec, I'm going to ask you to figure out a route in and out of the location and have bladed shadows monitoring every hour."

"Should I just kill whoever shows up?" Rebec asked a little too gleefully. Eira couldn't help but wonder how someone could treat murder so casually. She was destroyed all afternoon for merely considering it.

"Not everything is fixed with a dagger between the ribs." Lorn rolled his eyes.

"But so, so many things are."

"Don't kill them, for now. I want to keep this clean. I don't want the Pillars to know we're on to them—perhaps we'll be able to find out who's supplying the flash beads to see how deep a potential alliance runs. But if it does come to a fight, I want people who can make it out alive."

"Fine, we'll keep the stabbing to a minimum." Rebec let out a slow, pained sigh.

Eira didn't bother asking for information on the meeting. She knew they wouldn't proffer it anyway. Instead, she asked, "What did they blow up today?"

A heavy silence settled over the room. Lorn focused on his feet. Rebec cast a sad gaze toward Deneya and then looked away. Ducot remained his silent self, hovering just over Eira's shoulder.

"A city barracks," Deneya said, finally. She stared down at the map of Risen. It was then that Eira noticed a red X inside a square near the Archives. "Likely just a test run of the flash beads… making sure they're the real deal, before the Pillars use them for whatever true wickedness they have planned."

"I'm sorry," Eira said softly. By day, Deneya was one of the Queen's Guard. She could only assume that Deneya knew a few people who had been killed.

Deneya lifted her eyes to meet Eira's. Somehow, with a gaze alone, Eira felt small. "I know why you ran after that man today."

Eira glanced askance. She didn't even ask how Deneya knew.

It was likely obvious to everyone. Well, everyone but Mister Levit.

"But, you *must understand* that you're not the only person here who's lost something." Deneya's words weren't harsh or berating. They weren't even disappointed. Yet, somehow, Eira felt all the worse hearing them. "Every shadow has lost and given up more to be here. You will be called to sacrifice even more if you stay."

"I can do that," Eira said hastily.

"Can you?" Deneya fired back. Eira's retort stuck in her throat as she stared into the woman's intense eyes. "Marcus might be only the beginning. Can you follow our orders without question even if everything crumbles around you? Are you ready to lose even more for the sake of your justice?"

She swallowed once, twice, three times. Why was one word so hard to say? "Yes," Eira finally managed.

"We'll see." Deneya sighed and placed her hands on her hips. "For now, go back and await our next order."

"What am I going to do in the meantime?" Eira asked.

"Live as a competitor, try not to raise any suspicion, and, Yargen bless, stay out of trouble."

NINE

N O ONE CAME to get her for breakfast the next morning.

Eira was awake when her friends and fellow competitors began to rise. She heard muffled talking through her door and the opening and closing of the main entry to the Solaris common area. But no one even made the attempt to check on her.

She lay on her back, staring at the ceiling as dawn's light glowed across it. Ducot hadn't said much to her on their way back last night, leaving Eira to run through the conversation and information she'd found again and again. There was going to be a meeting of the Pillars in three days to discuss the flash beads. But the shadows didn't know where yet.

Pushing up, Eira swung her feet off the bed and stared out the window. There were no boats on the river today. After the explosion, she had no doubt that the lockdown on Risen had only increased. She wondered what the knights were telling the citizenry. How much was known at this point? If only she could ask the court and get a straight answer. Though she suspected there wasn't much chance of that anytime soon.

Sighing, Eira stood and dressed. Her grumbling stomach wasn't going to allow her to spend all morning in her room alone, musing. So she headed downstairs, and arrived in a very full common area.

The morphi sat in their own cluster between the elfin and draconi teams. There was still no sign of the competitors from Qwint and a sickening feeling silenced the growling of her stomach. What if something had happened to them on the way?

Eira's gaze breezed over her friends and tutor as she went to the food. The same woman with graying hair as the first morning—Mistress Harrot, she presumed—bustled about, checking on the food that was out. Eira greeted her placidly, and made herself a small plate. Rather than sitting with her companions, she strolled through the archways and headed toward the riverbank to claim one of the benches. Drawing up her feet onto the stone bench, Eira pulled her knees to her chest and began to pick at the food at her side.

Ferro was out there. If she were him, what would she do next? Was he involved with the flash beads? That might explain why Adela was the one to free him… Every time Eira could think of a theory, another bloomed. He was a roach she couldn't take her eyes off for an instant. The second she did, he'd scuttle even deeper into the crevices of the world and further from her retribution.

"May I sit here?" Her thoughts were interrupted by Alyss.

"I suppose."

"You suppose?" Alyss arched her eyebrows.

"You know it's fine," Eira mumbled and shifted to give Alyss enough room.

Her friend sat, pulling a piece of stone from the bag at her thigh. It hovered over her palm, changing shape magically as Alyss worked it into her latest creation.

Eira had three more bites of food before she managed to say, "I'm sorry."

"For what?" Alyss asked without looking at her.

"For yelling at you and sending you away." Eira tore off a piece of a flaky roll she'd covered in a sweet but spicy jam that tasted like the striped melon she'd eaten the day before.

"I'm just trying to help."

"I know."

"It's hard to see you like this."

"I know."

"And I don't know what else to do."

Eira sighed heavily. "I don't know what to do either." But she had decided that killing Ferro would help. A lot.

"Stay safe and look after your mental and emotional wellbeing," Alyss said firmly. Her rock was beginning to take the shape of a seal. "That's all you need to do."

Eira snorted softly, staring out over the river. If Alyss only knew what she was up to… Eira wiped her hands on her trousers and gripped the bench.

"You know I can be reckless."

"And impulsive," Alyss added a bit too readily. "And you can let the tides of a moment carry you."

"Yeah…" Eira sighed. She had hidden too many secrets from her friend. The longer she kept them, the deeper the chasm became. She had to let something out or the damage might be irreversible when the inevitable exposure came to pass. "I broke my promise to you."

"What?" Alyss looked up from her seal.

"I promised you, months ago, that I wouldn't go back to that secret room in the Tower alone."

"But you did," Alyss finished after a long silence.

"Yeah, I did." Eira hung her head, unable to bear Alyss's look of disappointment.

"You know I'm just trying to look out for you, right? That room worried me. I'm not trying to be mean or imposing or controlling."

"Marcus was trying to look out for me, too. And where did that land him?" Eira murmured.

"Eira—"

"Dead," Eira answered her own question.

Alyss grabbed her hand tightly, sculpture forgotten. "He died because of the actions of a wicked, evil man. Not because of you. You can't blame yourself."

Eira stared at the sunlight shimmering off the river. In a blink, her mind was under that water, trapped, pulled down by invisible hands. She was back in that night. She would escape, but Marcus wouldn't. He would be claimed by those depths.

"It was more my fault than you know," Eira said softly. She could think of about a thousand things she wished she'd done differently. Any of them might have resulted in Marcus being alive.

"Stop saying that; it's not good for you."

Eira shook her head and stood. "I'm going back to my room."

"You're here to be a competitor." Alyss stood as well, stepping in her way. "You fought to be here. Marcus would want you to seize this opportunity—a chance you've dreamed about for years. Speak with the elfin. Learn about the land of the draconi. Don't waste this whole time before the tournament starts holing up in your room."

"Thanks, Alyss. I'll think about all that." Eira just patted her friend's shoulder and retreated, determined to ignore everything Alyss had just said.

***

The next day, just before dinner, there was a knock on her door. Eira sighed and stood from the bed. She'd been hoping they would leave without her, then Ducot would show up, and they'd have some kind of lead from the Court of Shadows. It had barely been two whole days since Deneya had put her on standby, and waiting for orders was already beginning to drive her mad.

Eira expected Alyss to be waiting on her, but found Cullen instead.

"May I come in?"

"Sure." She shrugged and stepped aside. But what she really wanted to do was stand in the doorway and demand, *What do you want?*

"Alyss is worried about you." He didn't waste any time.

Eira resisted rolling her eyes. "I'm certain you're all finding things to occupy your days with rather than just wallowing in worry for me."

"We are capable of both worrying about you *and* occupying our hours with more than shutting ourselves in our room." He grinned briefly, and then his mouth tugged into a frown again. "Eira… *I'm* worried about you."

"So you've said." Eira wrapped her arms around herself and crossed to her window. "I'm fine, really."

"I don't believe that." The severity of his voice gave it a low rumble that made her ache. But Eira didn't know what she was aching for. The security of his arms once more? Since when did Cullen occupy that place in her mind as someone safe? As someone she wanted to seek out?

Eira bit her lip, grateful that he couldn't see her expression.

"Why do you doubt me so much?" His voice grew louder as he approached. The air itself was different around him. The currents his magic rode on could be felt, projected into the world, whereas her currents lived within her. Drowning her with power that had no outlet. "You've been distant since the moment we left Solarin."

"I have not."

He came to a stop just behind her. "Every time I draw near, you creep farther away."

"No, I don't." The lie was weak and she knew it.

"And yet, when you retreat… I see you look back across the distance and I can't help but feel like you don't want to pull away."

She couldn't look at him. How had he seen truths that even she had been ignoring?

"Eira…" His fingers closed around her upper arm. "Look at me." He tugged lightly and Eira obliged, tilting her chin up to meet his eyes. "Look me in the eyes and tell me that you're all right."

"I—" She choked on her words. But he didn't give her a reprieve.

"Look me in the eyes and tell me you aren't haunted every day by the things you've seen—by the things you've done."

Eira pursed her lips together, feeling her lower one quivering slightly. He had no idea of the half of what she had done and what she was prepared to do, and that made her sick. What would Cullen think of her when he knew? His grip tightened slightly as he lifted his other hand. Cullen's fingertip brushed against her brow as he tucked a wayward bit of hair behind her ear. The sunlight illuminated his eyes, turning them almost golden.

"It's all right to hurt and share in that hurt," he whispered. "Holding it in will only make it worse. Believe me, I know."

"How could you know? How could you, of all people, possibly understand?"

"Because I—"

"Good evening, Levit. I'm here for my son." Yemir's voice brought Cullen to a halt. He glanced over his shoulder at the door, his face a mix of panic and frustration.

"Come with me tonight, Eira," he whispered quickly. His eyes were ablaze for reasons she no longer understood.

"What? Where?"

"Agree to be my guest."

"Guest?" Eira tried to piece together the information he was leaving out in his haste.

There was a dull banging noise, followed by, "Cullen? Are you in there?"

"You'll love it, I'm sure. Plus, it'll get you out of here. You've hardly left for the past day." Cullen grabbed her fingers, pulling her toward the door.

"Wait, I—"

"I'm here, Father," Cullen announced, stepping out.

Yemir's eyes darted between Eira and his son, skeptical. "And just what were you doing in there?"

Noelle was perched on one of the sofas. Yemir's back was to her, so luckily the senator missed her cat-like expression of glee at this twist of events. Eira briefly gave her a look. But it only made Noelle smirk more and mouth the word, *scandalous*.

"I was inviting Eira to the state dinner tonight," Cullen announced. Yemir blinked several times over, clearly struggling to process this information with decorum. Cullen continued before his father could muster words. "You said that several competitors would be there. I thought it appropriate that Solaris be represented by more than one individual."

"Good thinking, my boy," Yemir said with a very forced smile. His gaze dipped to Noelle. "Though you have already invited Eira, *twice*, to court. Why don't we bring Noelle instead? I wouldn't want your fellow competitors to get jealous."

"Don't you worry your little senator head about me. I am incapable of being jealous of Eira—or anyone, for that matter," Noelle proclaimed.

Eira wasn't sure if she should laugh or be offended. A soft snort seemed like a good middle ground.

"Your uncle is a Western lord, isn't he? Surely you are accustomed to formal dinners?"

"You said this was a casual gathering," Cullen countered.

"I *am* accustomed to formal dinners," Noelle said, rising to her feet with a flip of her hair. "And I can't stand them. Such a bore." She yawned. Yemir's scowl deepened. "So while I do *so* appreciate the invitation, Senator, I'm afraid I cannot. Especially because I already promised to have dinner with the morphi out on the terrace and it would be terribly rude if I didn't show up."

Noelle was mingling with the morphi? Eira didn't know which way was up for a moment. She didn't think Noelle, of all people, would go out of her way to get to know their competitors from across the world. What had she been missing while she'd holed up waiting for a lead on Ferro?

"Have fun, you two." Noelle moved behind Yemir to give Eira a wink before sauntering to her room. However, she paused in the doorway. "Oh, and before you ask, Senator, I haven't seen

Alyss for hours. So you'd have to hunt her down if you're still desperately searching for another option."

Eira had expected, at best, to *tolerate* Noelle throughout the tournament. But after the past minute, the Firebearer might just be Eira's new favorite person. Eira was taking notes on how effortlessly Noelle could dance around Yemir.

"Then, I think this is all settled," Cullen decreed.

"Are you sure you'd like to come? As your friend said, it's going to be very boring," Yemir said sternly to Eira.

"I'd love to." While she was mildly annoyed at Cullen for maneuvering her into this situation, Eira gleaned the most enjoyment she'd had in the past day from Yemir's agitation.

"Excellent, I'll quickly get dressed." Cullen rested a hand on her shoulder. "Wear something nice, but don't worry about being too fancy," he instructed and then started for his room.

"A word." His father was quick to chase after him, leaving Eira reeling and debating just what she should wear to a state dinner with representatives from nations she'd hardly even known about months ago.

***

The manor the delegates were staying in was a four-story building. Similar to the competitor's accommodations, every state was given their own private retreats—though smaller, since each state only had two to four delegates currently. The other main difference was the balconies, jutting from the sides of the building in a way that reminded Eira vaguely of mushrooms on a stump. And, in place of terraces down to the river, the house boasted a sweeping veranda that had a stunning view of the castle of Meru on its distant hilltop.

Which was where dinner was served.

The initial introductions were an endless revolution of names that Eira was already forgetting. She stayed by Cullen's side, wondering constantly just what she was doing there. Coming for the purpose of agitating Yemir suddenly seemed foolish when she was sitting across from a draconi prince and a morphi princess—warrior? Knight? Eira wasn't quite sure. She was the daughter of the king, but that didn't seem to make her the princess in their kingdom. Her title was something like Eighth Royal Guard of the Twilight Kingdom.

Luckily, Cullen was seated next to her, serving as both a barrier to Yemir and as a cover to any gaps in her diplomatic knowledge. A forgotten corner of her screamed, raging at how little she had done so far to learn about Meru and its surrounding peoples. But the words of the woman she had once been were muffled. The hunger for knowledge she'd once possessed had been lost, too, sunken alongside Marcus.

"What do you think?" Cullen whispered with a lean toward her. The proximity pulled Eira from the depths.

"The food is very good." She pressed her lips into a smile.

"It is, but I didn't bring you here for the food." He shifted, facing her a bit more. His knee brushed hers underneath the table, sending a jolt straight up her spine. He didn't break the contact.

"What did you bring me here for?" Her attention dropped to his mouth. The soft, coy curve of his lips was more inviting than she ever wanted to admit.

"Isn't this what you dreamed of? Seeing Risen, meeting its people? It'd be a shame if you spent the whole time in your room."

Eira shifted, suddenly uncomfortable in her chair. Somehow it made her *more* aware of their contact. This whole affair was awkward. But it had come from a good place. Her knuckles brushed his and the rusty dusk colored his cheeks slightly. Neither of them moved, knee and knuckles touching. How did such a small expanse of skin set her whole body ablaze with a fire her magic could never hope to douse?

What are you doing to me, Cullen Drowel? The question burned her lips.

"Cullen," Yemir said, a little too loud. They were both jolted back to reality. "How are you finding your course?"

"Delicious, Father." Cullen picked up his silverware, leaving the skin on the back of Eira's hand suddenly frigid. But his knee still didn't leave hers.

Eira didn't move either as the conversation shifted throughout dinner. She listened for anything interesting, and for anything she might be able to take back to the Court of Shadows as a possible lead on the Pillars. But when there was none to be had, she forced herself to be fascinated by every bit of insight she could gain on their different states and cultures. Cullen was right. Every moment was an opportunity of some kind. It wasn't until dessert was served—berry compote on meringue—that the conversation shifted in a manner that had Eira intently focused.

"Jahran, has there been any word on when the tournament might actually begin?" Alvstar asked. He was the most recent addition from the Republic of Qwint, arriving just an hour before this dinner. Sure enough, the delegation from Qwint had been delayed due to security precautions.

"Queen Lumeria will set an opening date in conjunction with all four other nations when she is confident that the tournament and all its attendees and competitors will be safe." Jahran was "Lumeria's Quill"—a diplomat, policymaker, and the queen's right hand as far as Eira had gathered.

"So you've said." Alvstar suppressed a yawn. He'd said at the start he'd had a long journey and begged forgiveness for any lethargy. "But what I suppose I am unclear on is what threat, exactly, Lumeria is afraid of."

Cullen glanced in Eira's direction and she pursed her lips, quickly turning back to her food. Yemir didn't say anything either. Ferro's crimes in Solaris were still being kept secret, for now. It would look bad for the queen if knowledge of his escape became public.

"If Lumeria needs assistance in securing her cities, I am sure my father would be happy to send his armies," Harkor said, leaning back in his chair and picking at his teeth with a chicken bone. The draconi prince had been the one she'd overheard speaking with Deneya on his arrival—the one who'd called humans and elfin "soft and weak."

"You can send word to King Tortium that Lumeria is grateful for his willingness to assist. But marching his armies to Meru isn't necessary at this time." Jahran smiled thinly.

"One needs to first know whom they're fighting to launch an effective counter-attack," the morphi sitting across from Eira— Arwin—murmured into her wine glass.

She knows something. The hair on the back of Eira's neck stood straight up as she met Arwin's eyes. The woman had the smallest of smirks.

Judging from Jahran's expression, Lumeria's Quill had clearly heard Arwin's remark, but he didn't rise to the bait. Instead, he said, "Friends and allies. Why don't we adjourn from the table and enjoy the last of the sunset over Risen with a nightcap?"

Cullen leaned in as they all began to stand, moving to accept drinks from waiting staff. "Well? Did you enjoy it?"

"I did," she said honestly. "It's incredible to think that we're all so very different and yet somehow share the same world."

"If I've learned anything from the past few years, it's that we're not as far apart as we might think." Cullen flashed her a dazzling smile, one that made Eira's breath hitch and her knees weak. "I'm glad you enjoyed yourself. You needed to get out of your room."

"Yes, well, thank you." Awkwardness consumed her and Eira averted her gaze to smooth her hands over her skirt, trying to work out the wrinkles from sitting for a two-hour dinner. He'd been right, as had Alyss. She'd needed to do something other than occupy herself with thoughts of Ferro. Eira owed her friend another apology. Or at least an attempt at an explanation of the roiling emotions that relentlessly crashed on the beaches of her mind. Eira looked back up at Cullen, remembering their conversation earlier. "You said you knew…"

Pain flashed across his eyes. "Not here," he whispered. "I'll tell you, but not here."

That only made Eira more curious. But she couldn't press because, yet again, they were interrupted by Yemir. "I hope I'm not interrupting."

"Of course not." Eira forced a smile as Cullen echoed a similar sentiment.

"Good. Cullen, I want to introduce you to Alvstar's daughter, Lavette. They're just over there. She's another competitor and I think you two will get along famously."

"Certainly." Cullen's face became expressionless. It was the void mask Eira had first known him to wear as the "Prince of the Tower." Long before she'd ever managed a glimpse of the real Cullen underneath. "I'll catch up with you soon, Eira."

"Enjoy yourself." Eira smiled and wasted no time breaking for the veranda's railing. She rested her elbows on it and looked out over the city, catching her breath. Here was where she'd always dreamed of being. Yet she still felt like she didn't quite…fit. Her heart ached as she stared toward the line where sky met earth, wondering if the place she was truly meant to be was just over the ridges of the rolling hills that surrounded Risen. Wondering if home was out there…just a little farther past the horizon.

"Sunsets are better enjoyed with a drink in hand."

Jolted from her thoughts, Eira straightened quickly, blinking at the morphi who'd materialized at her side. Arwin held out a flute with an amber, bubbling liquid. Eira accepted it with mumbled thanks.

Arwin pinned her with a hard stare. "You're not who you're pretending to be."

TEN

"PARDON?" EIRA GLANCED over at the woman, trying not to let panic seep into her expression. Had she somehow outed herself through the course of dinner as working for the Court of Shadows?

"You're not made for all this politicking and drinking and arse kissing." Arwin had long, blonde hair pulled back into a tight bun, not unlike what Eira had seen Deneya wearing. Tiny curls escaped around her ears.

Eira concealed a sigh of relief with a sip from her flute. The tangy flavors of apple and ginger were effervescent on her tongue. "Well, the drinking isn't bad."

"I suppose it's not. The elfin could always manage a decent concoction." Arwin glanced behind her, prompting Eira to do the same. Everyone had begun to cluster in small groups and they were left mostly alone. "Ducot has mentioned you."

"Oh?" Eira kept staring forward so her expression didn't betray anything.

"Only in passing." Arwin wore a sly smile. "Just that you weren't what he'd been expecting of someone from Solaris."

"He mentioned that to me as well."

"I'm glad to hear that your people have been kind to him. I was worried. He's a good man who's lived a hard life."

"Oh?" Something clicked in Eira's mind. "Were you the princess he saved from the bear?"

Arwin let out a soft sigh, prompting Eira's attention to shift solely back on her. She stared out at the city skyline with a distant and somewhat sad expression. "He's still using that story, *hmm*?"

"Apparently." Eira took another sip of her drink. Now that

she thought about it, she should have known it was a lie. "What really happened?"

"That's not my place to say." Arwin shook her head and banished the darkness collecting in her steely eyes. The furrow between the glowing dots on her brow relaxed. "Don't mention to him or anyone else I indicated otherwise."

"My lips are sealed."

"Good." Arwin's gaze drifted over Eira's shoulder and promptly returned. "Look after him, all right? I shouldn't ask this of his competition, but I worry for him. Given how the city is, I'm afraid of what prompted him to agree to come to Risen."

"What do you think prompted him to agree?"

"He's out for blood," Arwin murmured so faintly that Eira was left to wonder if she realized she had spoken the thought aloud.

"For blo—" Eira didn't get a chance to finish; a hand closing around her shoulder interrupted her.

Cullen was at her side again. "Sorry to interrupt, Lady Arwin." He bowed his head and looked to Eira. "It's time for us to go."

"I didn't think they were taking the competitors back for another hour?" Arwin arched her brows.

"We have some business with the other Solaris competitors that almost slipped our minds. Please excuse us." Cullen grabbed her hand and tugged her away, barely giving Eira a chance to set down her flute and say goodbye to Arwin. Two knights were waiting for them at the entrance to the veranda.

"I wasn't done speaking with her," Eira whispered. She'd been hoping to get more information on Ducot.

"I'm sorry, but I have to get out of here and the only way to do it was to make it sound like all the competitors for Solaris had to be there." Panic was wrought on his face.

"What—"

"Cullen—" Yemir blocked their path "—I'm certain, whatever this is, that exceptions can be made."

"I'm sorry, Father. But I'm afraid Levit needed us all there to go over some important matters about the upcoming training for competitors, when the city is deemed safe."

"I can speak to Levit." Yemir frowned.

"He was rather insistent earlier," Eira said hastily.

"The training grounds won't be opened for some time yet. This cannot be urgent," Yemir grumbled.

Senator Henri crossed over before anything else could be said. "Yemir—sorry to interrupt—Jahran would like a word with us."

"We were just leaving. Take care, Father, Henri." Cullen seized the opportunity and stepped toward the knights with a nod. In less than five minutes, they had escaped the candlelit glow of the veranda and emerged into the relative darkness of the city. Cullen exhaled a monumental sigh as they started away from the manor. "Thanks for covering for me."

"Sure." Eira tucked some of her hair behind her ears. "Want to tell me what that was really about?"

He groaned. "You wouldn't understand."

"Weren't you one of the people earlier trying to tell me I needed to open up more or something?"

"Don't use my words against me." He gave her a mock scowl. The expression elicited a soft laugh from her. "My father can be...exhausting."

"Most parents can be." Eira's gaze drifted up to the sky and her mind wandered briefly to the beaches of Oparium. Memories of strolling late at night with her father, watching him chronicle the stars—teaching her how to find her way should she ever be lost. Those memories were like shards of glass now. Incomplete, fragile, and too painful as she held onto them despite herself.

She'd never received word from her parents before she'd left. They showed up for Marcus's Rite of Sunset and didn't even so much as leave a note for her. Now, with Risen locked down and travel times between Meru and Solaris as long as they were, Eira suspected she wouldn't hear from them until she returned from the tournament.

If she returned from the tournament.

Perhaps she'd make a life for herself here after Ferro was brought to justice. Perhaps she'd go to the Twilight Kingdom and see Ducot and Arwin's homeland. Perhaps when all this was over she'd get on a boat and keep sailing and never look back, chasing after the *Stormfrost* for the rest of her days.

"At least your parents love you," she whispered to the same stars she'd once gazed at with her father.

"Yours do, too. You know they do."

"I don't." Eira shook her head. "They didn't even come to see if I was all right after Marcus's death. Not one word." Cullen was notably silent as he chewed over that information. The only sounds were the knight's scabbards clanking softly as they escorted them. "It's fine."

"It's not. I wish you could've spoken to them properly."

"I wish a lot of things."

His knuckles brushed against the back of her hand like they had underneath the table. Once and it seemed like an accident. Twice and she knew it was on purpose. The third time, his fingers slid around her palm and laced with hers. Eira was very aware of how close he was standing. Every brush of his shoulder, the warmth of his palm, it was all cataloged. She savored the comfortable silence steeped in a security she'd begun to associate only with Cullen.

They arrived back at the manor. The knights escorted them to the front gate, disappearing as the heavy iron was shut. Eira could see the guards still patrolling the outer wall that boxed in the manor and the rooftop.

"My father," Cullen began softly, his pace slowing. Eira matched him until they hovered in the walkway that led to the great front doors of the manor. "He's an ambitious man. He always has been, I think, but it manifested differently when I was younger."

Eira shifted to face him, keeping silent as Cullen spoke, not wanting to interrupt or rush him in any way.

"First, he wanted to provide for my mother and I. But, then, after my Awakening…everything changed."

"What happened with your Awakening that made things change?" she probed gently when his hesitation dragged on. Cullen looked at her with wary eyes. "You don't have to say if you don't want to," she added hastily.

"I want to," he murmured. "I've just never told anyone before." The way he said that made Eira go from intrigued to insatiably curious. "You're not the only one who's hurt someone with your magic."

"What?" Eira blinked. What was he implying? This was Cullen, Prince of the Tower, ascended lord, noble family, the first Windwalker since the Empress. Perfect in every way.

If the truth ever got out, my family would be ruined… The echo of Cullen she'd heard in the Tower months ago returned to her. Was this the secret he'd meant?

"When I… When my powers were first manifesting, my mother tried to keep them secret. We lived in the rural East and the instincts to hide Windwalkers are still very much alive in the people—in her."

Eira knew that Windwalkers were once hunted by King Jadar in the West during the Burning Times. It was a stain on the history of the Solaris Continent that could never be expunged and should never be forgotten. That dark time prompted what many thought was the end of the Windwalkers—until Vhalla Yarl. Then, it came to light that Windwalkers hadn't truly been extinct, just extremely rare and carefully hidden.

"Your mother didn't want you to go to the Tower?" Eira asked.

"No. But my father insisted it'd be for the best, that my doing so could even give us all a better life. But she was insistent. All the while, my powers continued to grow."

"What happened?" Eira could tell by the slump to Cullen's shoulders and the way he kept raking his fingers through his hair, it wasn't good.

"My father took me to the coast, determined to deliver me

to the Tower himself. My mother chased after us. They argued and…I…I just wanted—" He sighed. "What I wanted doesn't matter anymore. What matters is I summoned a windstorm. It destroyed the entire port they were building north of Hastan."

"I heard about this," she breathed. The incident had been the talk of the docks for weeks in her hometown. "It was going to be a ferry stop from Oparium up to the North via the rivers." He nodded wearily. "But they said it was just a freak tempest that swept in from the sea?"

"No, the tempest was me."

"But… I've never…" She was trying to make sense of what Cullen was saying and the news she'd been given by the sailors as a child.

Cullen swayed, staggered over to a nearby bench, and sat. "The Empire covered it up."

"But there must've been—"

"Dozens of people? Yes, there were. They were coerced, paid, and bribed to keep their mouths shut, if they knew anything about the truth at all. My powers were secret, so some people really did think it was a freak storm." Cullen stared up at her with hollow eyes. He could still see that storm. He was watching it now. Eira didn't need him to tell her because she'd seen that expression in herself countless times.

She sat next to him, their thighs and shoulders touching. Eira wondered if, for once, she was the stable one. If he'd never told anyone before her then she couldn't imagine what he was feeling finally sharing this burden. Her magical incident had never had the hope of being secret.

"Did you kill anyone?" she whispered.

"I don't know." He buried his face in his hands. "I don't know, Eira, and it haunts me. But every day I have to sit, and smile, and preen, and be the golden child that everyone expects of the first Windwalker after Vhalla Yarl. *That's* why they covered it up. Because the Empire couldn't let the first Windwalker after Vhalla be a murderer and a herald of destruction. The reputation of the

Windwalkers was already so fragile and the East already had too many reasons to hide us."

Eira grabbed his wrists and gently pulled his hands from his face. She ducked down, low enough to look him in the eyes. "You're none of those things. You were young. You didn't mean to do it." Mother above, she sounded like Aunt Gwen.

"Neither did you," he whispered. The words struck a chord that resonated so loudly in her that Eira felt numb. "I'm so sorry I never said anything to you. I'm sorry I wasn't kinder. Our pasts… I could've been so much better to you. I could've lightened your burden by sharing in it sooner. I'm sorry I—"

"Stop." Eira shook her head. A trickle of laughter escaped her. "It's insane to think, this whole time you knew what I felt."

"And now you hate me for keeping it from you."

"I'm *relieved*." Eira looked him back in the eyes. "Cullen this is the first time that I—" Her throat closed over the words.

Cullen's hands shifted, fingers lacing with hers as he faced her. "That you don't feel so alone?" he finished for her.

Eira studied his face. Everything in her screamed for her to escape this moment. She had promised herself she'd guard her heart. After Ferro, no one could be trusted. She couldn't do this. She couldn't lean in, no matter how tempting it was, and kiss his mouth. She couldn't ask him to hold her as he once had…no, hold her even tighter.

"That I don't feel like such a freak." Eira pulled her hands away and forced a smile as Cullen's expression fell.

"You're anything but a freak." He reached for her again, but Eira stood.

"I promise I'll keep your secret," Eira said without looking at him.

"Eira—"

"I have to go." Eira shook her head and went to go inside.

"Don't do this." He was on his feet. "I know you're afraid but—"

"Don't presume you know what I think." She was at the door.

"I know more than you give me credit for."

"Goodnight, Cullen." Eira slipped inside and headed halfway downstairs quickly, rather than up. She pressed herself against the wall, listening to Cullen's footsteps racing upward, no doubt thinking she had gone for her room. Hopefully he thought she'd locked herself within as he knocked. Hopefully no one was in the common area to direct him downstairs.

With a sigh, she descended the rest of the way to the first floor. The curtains danced with the moonlight in the archways. Eira slowly walked over to lean against one of the pillars. She hugged herself, shivering against the night. The air wasn't cold. It was her core that was frigid.

She could never allow herself to feel deeply again—to love as a friend or as a woman. Doing so would either hurt the people she cared for, or they would betray her. No matter what, life had taught her that love ended in pain.

Eira pressed her eyes closed and sighed. But when she opened them, a dark streak across the grounds distracted her. A strange-looking mole creature raced between the hedges of the terraces leading down to the river.

Ducot? Eira pushed off the pillar and watched as the morphi headed for the wall. He disappeared under a hedge and when he didn't reappear, Eira crossed over. Sure enough, there was a small crack in the wall, just large enough for a mole to fit through.

Where was he going? Eira wondered. Then it struck her.

The note she'd stolen from the Pillars' courier had said three days—which would be up tomorrow. That could mean the Pillars would be meeting tonight. And if that were the case, there was no way Eira was going to let herself be left behind. Not when Ferro was still out there. Nothing else mattered.

· CHAPTER ·

ELEVEN

E IRA WALKED NONCHALANTLY back toward the manor. She kept her face down, but her eyes straining up toward the archer circling the rooftop on their nightly patrol. As soon as the archer turned their back to the terraced gardens, Eira spun on her heel and waved her hand through the air. Water shimmered, refracting the moonlight around her in a near-perfect illusion. Illusions at night were always easier to make appear realistic. People were more ready to believe that the shifting shadows were playing tricks on their eyes.

She sprinted to the wall, leaping toward it and planting her toe against it. Ice shot out underneath the ball of her foot, giving her a platform to scramble up from. Two more ridges of ice grew, ready for her hands to close around. She scaled the wall just like she had in the second trial back in Solaris, tipping over and casting aside her magic with a wave just as the archer was rounding the building.

Wedged with the wall at her back and another wall in front of her, Eira sidestepped. Rounding the corner with a breath of relief, she saw a small shadow dart across the moonlit street. She hadn't lost him.

Always two steps behind, Eira followed Ducot through the empty city. She clung to shadows and bounced on the balls of her feet, trying to keep the formal boots she'd decided to wear to the dinner from making too much noise. When Ducot rounded a building and into an alleyway, Eira charged into the shadows after him. But as soon as she crossed out of the moonlight there was a pulse of magic at her side.

Ducot materialized out of ripples in the air. He unsheathed

a dagger at his hip, reaching for her with his free hand. Eira fought against every instinct to retaliate as he pushed her roughly against the wall, dagger at her throat. Ducot paused, his milky eyes scanning the air beneath her chin as though reading some kind of unseen text.

"Eira?" he whispered.

"Sorry to startle you," she breathed, trying to keep her neck from moving so the blade didn't nick her.

"What in Yargen's name are you doing here?" Ducot pulled away, sheathing his dagger. But, for a second, he looked as if he were seriously considering otherwise. "They didn't tell me you were on this job." *Job*. She had been right.

"I…" Eira swallowed her hesitation and better sense with it. "Last minute change."

"Was it?" He frowned. "Or did you lie about not taking a peek at the package you brought to the court?"

So the bundle she'd delivered from Taavin must have led to some kind of information about wherever Ducot was going. "I didn't look, I swear."

He seemed skeptical but ultimately sighed and cursed under his breath. "Fine, let's go then. We're running out of time before it starts."

Eira nodded. She didn't know if he could see her in the darkness, or sense her movement, or if he was just done with the whole interruption, because Ducot moved on her cue. He went back to the alleyway's opening, pausing and looking around before continuing on. Eira followed wordlessly.

Where were they going? And what was the "job"? She wanted to ask, but she couldn't figure out how she might be able to phrase a question that wouldn't give away her deception.

Ducot stopped and swept his arm out, blocking her just before a street corner. He leaned forward, whispering in her ear, "A patrol. Make yourself unseen."

"Got it."

A pulse of magic and he was a mole once more. Eira pressed

herself against the building and waved her hands through the air. A blanket of illusion covered her as two of the queen's knights strolled by. One held a torch, and Eira worried the jarring difference of moonlight and firelight would expose her illusion. But they must've been too blinded by the halo of light to notice.

Ducot waited a good five minutes that felt like an hour before shifting back into his morphi form. "What did you do?"

"An illusion. It's a Waterrunner skill."

"So you can make yourself invisible?"

"I can do almost anything with it." Eira tried to frame it in terms of Meru's magics. "Think of it like *durroe watt*—if you're familiar with Lightspinning."

"If I'm familiar." Ducot snorted softly. "You say it as if I didn't have fear of Lightspinners and the Faithful instilled in me from a young age."

"Fear?"

"No time to talk now." He turned back to the street, a little too eager to walk away from her question. "We only have an hour before the meeting begins."

"Right, let's keep moving."

"Try and keep up, Waterrunner." Ducot started off once more with a smirk on his lips and a little bit faster than before. Eira couldn't suppress the feeling that he was testing her. And she was going to rise to the challenge.

They came across two more patrols on their way through the city before halting at a bridge that crossed from their side of Risen—the Archives' side—over to the side the castle was on. Ducot hesitated and Eira stayed silent, trying to still her ragged breaths. She wasn't used to running so much and her shoes definitely weren't made for it. They were biting into her heels with every step now. But at least she'd worn a looser skirt to the soiree tonight.

"Now," Ducot said without warning and dashed across the bridge. Eira followed closely behind, illusioning a blur of fog around them that she slowly dissipated on an unfelt breeze long after they were on the other side.

Eira hadn't been in this area of town yet. While the architecture was mostly the same, the first floors and building fronts seemed to be used for more official purposes. The towering facades had square columns that rose between dark windows like bars. The glass glinted in the moonlight like eyes staring down at them and, for the first time, Eira had the distinct feeling she was being watched.

They finally came to a stop in an alleyway near one of the buildings. Ducot shifted back into his morphi form, looking up and around. Eira could feel tiny pulses of magic rippling through the air, originating from him.

"There's some kind of ladder here, right?" He pointed above his head.

"Yes… It looks like some kind of escape access?" Eira guessed.

"Will it lead to a second-floor window with a pane of glass missing?"

Eira scanned the building. "Yes, back by the street. But—"

"Then this is it."

"We'll have to walk along the narrowest ridge to get to it," Eira pointed out, hoping she didn't offend him by saying something he already knew.

"Afraid?" Ducot grinned.

"Worried for you is all." She grinned back. "Want me to get the ladder down?"

"If you don't mind."

There was a latch on the side of the ladder that looked to be holding up the rusted, iron access. She drew her hand across her chest, sending a whip of water to smack against it. As soon as the latch was undone, the ladder fell freely, grinding against itself. Eira reached out her other hand, stopping it with a cube of ice just before the metal slammed into the stone below and woke up half the city. Ice hadn't been the best choice either, as it still sang on impact.

Ducot cringed. "Thanks for alerting them to our location," he said after the sound of ringing metal had finished its long, horrible resonance.

"They might not think it's anything." Eira wondered who "they" were. Though she had her suspicions.

"*Sure* they won't." Ducot rolled his milky eyes and started up the ladder. Eira followed behind him. When they were both poised on the small platform at the top, Ducot turned toward the ladder. His magic pulsed around it. Eira blinked and the ladder was up and locked once more.

"How did you do that?" she whispered.

"The shift is making what is what could be," he reminded her. "Though, I can't be certain that latch will work. It's not like I ever saw it in the first place." Ducot knelt down by the edge of the iron ledge. Eira could feel his magic pulsing out once more. It was some kind of echolocation—she presumed—that allowed him to sense the world around him. "I'm going to tackle this as a mole; it'll be easier for me that way. Will you be all right?"

"Now you're worrying about me? How sweet!"

Ducot snorted. "Tease me and I'll never do it again."

Before she could say anything else, Ducot's magic rippled around him. As a mole, he had no problem scurrying down to the window with the missing pane. He charged headfirst through the parchment loosely tacked up around it. Eira pointed down the ledge and a path of ice extended off of it, wide enough for her to walk normally. By the time she made it to the window, Ducot was already back in human form and holding it open for her.

"I hear people coming," he whispered. "Get in quickly."

Eira did as he said, evaporating her magic and leaning against the wall to the side of the window. Ducot had just eased it shut when two knights rounded the corner of the building. She yanked him out of sight. They both watched, holding their breath, but neither knight seemed to notice the small, broken pane of glass or the two people lurking in the darkness above them.

Breathing a sigh of relief, Eira turned her attention inside and tried to get her bearings. She stood in a room with several desks lined up in two neat rows. Each desk was set up in a way that was unique to its user, personal effects strewn across their tops.

"Where are we?" Eira kept her voice low.

"It's a building for the attendants to the queen, I think."

"So this is part of the castle?"

"No." Ducot started weaving through the desks, heading for a door in the far corner. "This is just where people who work for the queen work. And live?"

"Live?"

"Not sure." Ducot hovered by the door. "We should be quiet as we cut through, just in case."

She followed his lead and moved as stealthily as possible. After she almost tripped due to the pain in her ankles from her shoes, Eira coated her feet in a thin layer of ice—something she should have done from the start. They went down a dark hallway and along a corridor that led to a grand stairwell. Back on the first floor, Ducot led them through another side entry and along a hall, before stopping at a back door that overlooked a courtyard.

"Please be unlocked," he murmured as he turned the knob. The door opened effortlessly. "Thank their sunny goddess."

"I take it there's a shadow who works for the queen?"

"You think? Just one?" Ducot threw a smirk over his shoulder.

She ignored the jab and seized the opening to ask, "How many shadows are there in the court?"

"I think the Specters are the only ones who really know. More than two hundred? If I had to guess." Ducot hunched over a sewer grate, opening it with a heave. "Get in."

"Right." Eira hesitated at the edge, said a prayer for her skirts, and then descended into what—luckily—seemed to be only rainwater. "How much farther is it?"

"Not too much. We're taking the indirect route so they don't see us coming."

"Naturally." Eira coated the outsides of her boots in ice, trying to numb the ache.

After several lefts and rights, Ducot came to a stop just at the edge of moonlight streaming through the bars of another grate above.

"Wh—"

He covered her mouth with a hand and shook his head slowly. Eira nodded and stayed silent as he pulled away. It was then that she finally heard the voices.

"…an honor to have you worship with us tonight."

"It is an honor to be here. I've not paid my respects to Her in far too long. I no longer find the Archives to be a suitable place of worship."

"Truly a shame what the heretics have done to Her hallowed ground," the first man said. "But we will soon recover and restore it to its former glory."

Shadows blotted out the moonlight. Three knocks rumbled an unseen doorway and Eira strained her hearing.

"Why do you come on this long dark night?" a third man asked.

"To seek Her light," the two men said in unison. The door squealed softly as it swung open.

"Truly impressive, the level of security you have here," the second man said.

"We cannot take any chances. The Swords of Light and Queen Lumeria's Knights are trying with all their might to thwart us."

"They shall not—" The rest of the sentence was cut off by the door closing.

"We need to get up there, the meeting is starting soon," Ducot whispered in her ear. Her suspicions had been right. Ducot had been sent to stake out a Pillar meeting.

"You tell me when you think it's time for us to make our move," Eira said.

"I hear another coming, then we should go for it. Can you use one of your illusions again?"

"I can make a sudden, dense fog," she offered.

"Better than nothing." He shrugged. They waited as another person passed overhead and then Ducot went for the sewer hatch.

Eira rolled her hands, weaving together her magic with rainwater in the sewer. It rose up like a tamed serpent of fog, dancing before her, slithering through the sewer grate. Ducot paused as the mist rolled over his skin, glancing back at her. Whatever he thought of the sensation of her magic, he kept to himself.

Pushing the grate open, he hoisted himself through, pausing and listening. Then he reached a hand down for her. "Come on," Ducot whispered. Eira took his help getting up.

They had emerged into a courtyard wedged between four buildings. More windows stared down, accusatory. But unlike the dark windows of the queen's assistants, these windows had small, glowing motes hovering through them, illuminating people. Eira grabbed Ducot's hand and yanked him against the wall by the doorway, underneath the awning overhead.

"Wha—"

"There are people in the windows over us," she whispered into his ear.

"Tell me when they've passed."

Eira watched as the two men—perhaps the men she'd heard from the sewers—strolled along the windowed hall. She clutched Ducot's hand tightly and held her breath, praying they wouldn't look down. Just as they were nearing the final window, talking could be heard in the distance.

"We have to move," he hissed.

"Now." Eira adjusted her illusion, thickening the fog slightly as Ducot tugged her toward the back side of the courtyard. He pulled her into a statue's alcove, clutching her close. Just as they darted into concealment, two more people arrived at the other side of a barred gate that separated this courtyard from another beyond.

"Damn sewers," the woman mumbled as she unlocked the gate. "Always like this after rain."

"At least it can help conceal our faces should any knight see us," the man who was with her offered.

"And it filters the infernal moonlight of Raspian."

Raspian. She'd heard that name before, hadn't she? Eira remembered a firelit night with Ferro. He had referred to the moonlight as "infernal," too. Eira had little doubt he was one of the Pillars before, but now she was certain.

The two people entered the doorway, and Eira slowly relaxed her illusion, trying to make the fog look as though it were dissipating on the wind.

"I'm glad the Specters sent you." Ducot eased his hold on her. The sentiment sounded like a confession. "I shouldn't have offered to do this alone… It's good to have an ally with working eyes now and then."

"Your magic? The pulses?" Eira asked.

"It can be distorted by walls and glass. And my hearing does little for me in a situation like this." He shook his head. "I got proud. Deneya must've known it and sent you after me."

The thought alleviated some of her guilt for lying to him. If she'd proved her use, when it inevitably came out that she'd lied about being sent, he'd forgive her. Right? "Without me you'd just turn into a mole."

"True. Maybe I should take back what I said. You're a liability." His face tightened into his lopsided grin.

"Thanks," Eira said dryly. "Now what?"

"We have to get inside. See a way in?"

Eira scanned the area. Her eyes snagged on a low, rectangular window—access to some kind of basement. "I think so, hold on." Glancing up and around, and seeing no one above, Eira ventured out of the safety of the alcove and over to the window. She focused on the other side of the glass, collecting water in the air and condensing it into ice that pushed against the latch.

The window swung open effortlessly.

"In here."

Ducot dashed ahead of her in his mole form, leaving Eira to scramble down after him. Luckily, there was a workbench underneath the window. Otherwise she would've ended up falling very ungracefully to the hard floor below.

"Nice work," he praised, a man once more.

"Told you I wouldn't be a liability," she whispered back, easing the window closed.

"I'm going to go ahead. I need you to stay here and keep a lookout and our escape route secure."

"*What*? I didn't come all this way to—"

"Their meeting is starting soon," he hissed. "I can safely go as a mole. You stay here." Ducot didn't give her another chance to object, shifting into his animal form and dashing up the stairway.

Eira grumbled under her breath, hoping he heard.

Time turned into molasses. The minutes were as slow as hours and the boredom was mind-numbing. Eira jumped at every creak of the floorboards overhead, every squeak in the shadowed corners of the room, and every sigh of the building settling. The only light she had to see by was the moonlight streaming over her shoulders from the small window.

She sat in its small square, holding herself as the night began to come alive. Hands of pure shadow reached out for her. The dark floor swirled with currents that threatened to pull her under. Eira squeezed her eyes closed, but Marcus was waiting behind her lids.

What if Ferro was here, right now?

The thought had her staring, suddenly wide-eyed, at the door Ducot had left from. What if Ferro was overhead, sitting smugly at a meeting of the Pillars? She had come for him and he might now be in her grasp. The invisible hands were around her ankles, trying to yank her underwater at the thought of Ferro.

Stay here, Eira commanded herself, closing her eyes and trying to shut out the dangerous thoughts. She'd already lied to come this far. She was out of her depth. *Stay here.*

If you stay here, you're letting your brother's killer walk free…

Eira dug her nails into her arms and hung her head, drawing slow, ragged breaths. Nightmares lived in the darkness, thrived in it. She couldn't be afraid. She couldn't hesitate. She couldn't let them win.

He might not even be there tonight. Who knew where Ferro was. But she'd hesitated once, and it had led to Ferro walking free. Killing him would be relief. Killing him would put an end to the torture every night brought—to the guilt.

You let him walk free.

Avenge me, Eira, the disembodied voice of her brother commanded menacingly from the recesses of her mind.

Her eyes snapped open.

Eira crept up the stairs, easing the door slowly open. A sliver of golden light hit her face and she flinched, only to relax when the glow turned into nothing more than candlelight. Slipping through the door and weaving an illusion around her at the same time, Eira crept through the hall that connected to an empty dining room.

There were voices overhead, muffled and indiscernible. She had to get higher. Eira sneaked up a staircase, hovering at the top landing and straining her ears. A thin line of firelight flickered underneath a stately door at the end of the hall.

Where was Ducot? Had something happened to him? It had to have been at least three hours since he left, right? She had to make sure he was safe. Yes, that was why she was on the move— merely worry for Ducot.

Eira crept forward, sliding the ball of her foot along the floorboard and then easing down her heel—just like she would on the second floor of her house when she'd sneak out in the wintertime to have moonlight snowball fights on the beach with Marcus.

Crouching on the other side of the iron-banded door, Eira pressed her ear to it.

The conversation within had something to do with a grand plan for the rebirth of Risen. They kept talking about the great ascension to come following something the Pillars kept referring to as the "severing" of old ways. She heard the terms "packed flash beads" and "our contacts" more than once, peppered between the ravings of zealots upset about problems with "transport."

It shifted to focus on a discussion of the "four relics." She'd heard Ferro and the strange man mention something about a dagger. One of the relics "was missing," it seemed.

Eira tried to commit everything she heard to memory, but there was so much of it. She needed to bring along a notebook if she was going to be working as a shadow. Then again, if she were here on official Court of Shadow business, she likely would've been given a heads up as to what supplies she should consider.

The speaking came to a sudden hush following the slam of a door.

"This place has been infiltrated by shadows," Ferro snarled, his voice unmistakable. Her blood ran cold. *"Find them."*

TWELVE

*W*HAT HAPPENED TO *Ducot?* was Eira's first thought. Followed immediately by, *Worry about yourself!*

She scrambled away from the door. Eira tried to shift her weight slowly. But speed and stealth were enemies. The boards beneath her creaked loudly under her panicked, clumsy steps—a sound she could feel in her chest with bodily horror. Rumbling rose behind her.

Eira broke into a run. She sprinted down the hall and rounded the stairs as the door slammed open. Pillars rushed out.

"I saw someone, there!" a woman shouted.

"Where did she go?"

"The stairwell!"

Eira bounded down the stairs, taking them two at a time, four at a time at the end. She landed awkwardly, ankle rolling thanks to her poor choice of shoes. A cry of pain she couldn't conceal escaped her.

Clumsy, she was clumsy and foolish for thinking she had been ready for any of this. She wasn't a shadow, not really, not yet, maybe not ever at this rate. Eira pushed herself up as the thundering on the stairs grew louder. She dashed down the hall and to the door that led to the basement workshop. Not thinking about who might hear, or how close her pursuers might be, Eira slammed the door shut and slapped it with her palm. Ice shot out in all directions, lining the doorjamb and covering the plane of the door and the wall.

The ice crackled behind her as she descended the stairs, spinning in the dark room.

"Ducot?" she whispered. "Ducot?"

Her reply came not from her ally, but in the form of a dull thud against the door. Eira looked back to see her ice creeping halfway down the stairs. No doubt it was growing on the other side of the door, too. She might as well have made an ice sculpture pointing to where she was.

"*Damn it.*" She let out a panicked whine. Did she stay and look for Ducot? Or go? Eira bounced from foot to foot, ignoring the shooting pain in her ankle.

If the Pillars had him, then she couldn't do anything for him. But the Court of Shadows? She'd bet they could. And to get their help, someone had to escape and alert them. She had to tell them what happened. Eira scrambled onto the table as there was another thud on the door.

"Get out of the way!"

Eira froze. *That's Ferro.* She slowly eased away from the window. A dagger of ice appeared in her hand.

"I'm sorry…Ducot," she whispered. Eira walked over to the bottom of the stairs. The darkness blanketed her, consumed her. She stopped fighting it, allowing the night to eat her heart piece by piece. She could get one shot at him. She hadn't come here to right the nuances of Meru's politics. She wasn't here to pick a side in a religious war.

All that mattered was Ferro. If she killed her brother's killer, then—

"*Juth calt!*"

A glyph spun into existence, shattering the door. Eira shielded herself with one hand. The dagger of ice hovered over the other. Squinting, Eira stared up at Ferro, haloed by the light of several glowing orbs.

"You?" He snarled the word, but his mouth curled into a grin. "Isn't this a delightful surprise?"

Eira didn't respond. She was overwhelmed by staring up at her brother's murderer—at the man who would have killed her if she'd given him the chance. She was back in the woods, wounded, beaten within an inch of her life. The darkness was so thick it was hard to breathe and in the moment she needed it most, she couldn't be the killer she wanted to be—that the world had always seen her as. Not even when one flick of the wrist was all it would take to end him.

Do it! the wretched voice, born of hatred and sorrow, screamed within her, *Kill him and end this!*

Yet one second of hesitation was all it took. Ferro had always been the better killer.

"*Loft not*," Ferro whispered with an amused edge.

Eira's eyelids were suddenly heavy. The world spun and she fell to the ground in a deep, unnatural sleep.

***

She woke to a burning world.

The room—no, cell—she was in was made of searing hot stone. Deep trenches had been carved along every soot-stained wall. Curtains of fire burned in these trenches, raged upward on three walls, heating the room to a dizzying degree. A smaller trench of fire burned in front of steel bars—the same steel as the shackles currently singeing her wrists.

Eira tried to stand, but doing so proved hard. Her head throbbed and the side of her face was coated with something thick and sticky—something more than sweat. Dipping her head down, she reached a hand up, feeling hair matted with blood. She must've hit her head when she'd fallen unconscious thanks to Ferro's Lightspinning.

The thought of Ferro gave her a chill that was almost cold enough to make the room comfortable. She'd had him. She'd stared him down. And when the time had come…she failed.

"I'm sorry, Marcus," she rasped with a dry throat. "I'm sorry."

After about thirty minutes, a woman appeared. She startled at the sight of Eira sitting upright and promptly dashed off. The next person to arrive was the man of her nightmares.

"Hello, Eira," Ferro almost purred. "I didn't think we'd meet again so soon."

She pressed her lips together hard, her teeth clenched. Her barely concealed rage only made him more gleeful.

"You want to kill me, don't you? So why didn't you? *Hmm?* Why didn't you that night in the forest after you finished wailing over your dead br—"

"Don't!" Eira shouted, lunging. The steel shackles, chained to the center of the floor, kept her in place like a dog on a leash. Her magic sparked in the air around her, instantly evaporating. Eira let out a yelp of pain as her skin suddenly burned, followed quickly by a cooling sensation. Her magic was keeping her from burning up in this room of eternal flame. If she used it for anything else, she'd be dead.

"I see you've figured out the nuances of our cell. All the fire is a bit tricky to maintain. But, lucky for you, we were prepared for someone of your ilk. We'd been intending to hold Adela's first mate behind these bars as collateral. But her bastard daughter might be even better." Collateral for Adela? Did that mean she wasn't working with the Pillars? Eira stored the information away to bring to Deneya, should she make it out with her life. "Miraculous, really, all the ways I've been able to use the information you gave me."

Those late nights, all his inquiries about the history of Solaris, the mountains around the capital, and the magic of Waterrunners… she was always the orchestrator of her own demise.

"I doubt I'm Adela's child."

"We'll find out soon enough. The pirate queen is hard to clamp down, but we'll get word to her. If you are, you'll be just the thing we need to get her to agree to work with us."

Further proof Adela wasn't on their retainer. So, if not, then how did they get the flash beads? And who freed Ferro?

"If you're not, then all we wasted was some time and magic keeping you alive." The fires glittered in his violet eyes like a raging dawn. "Really, you should be thanking me. I lived up to my end of the bargain, didn't I? I'm helping you find your mother."

"You can rot!" she seethed.

"I see whatever infatuation you had with me has cooled." Ferro swept a hand through his hair. "I did so enjoy playing into every sad, longing emotion you had. Poor Eira, alone in the world, so ready to see herself without anyone, practically begging someone—anyone—to sweep her into their arms and tell her she belonged. Tell her they wanted her. You made it so easy."

Her mind, and heart, betrayed her. Cullen was in the forefront of her memories. *He'd* been the one who'd held her when she'd needed it most. He'd been there after the revelation, after Marcus. He'd laid himself bare last night—two days ago? *How much time had passed since she was knocked out?* And she'd run away from him. She'd never be able to thank him for all he'd done. Never able to tell him how she really felt.

Now she never might have the chance.

"However, if you can realize that I am still on your side, that I alone am your chance to mean something to someone in this world...I could be inclined to let you out of this cell."

"What?" Eira didn't believe him for a second. But she'd hear him out. It was her turn to try and make him talk. Maybe, this time, she would be the one to weave his words into his downfall. "Why would you do that?"

"It pains me to see you in here." He put his hand over his heart, gripping his shirt. "Your beauty—your *power*—is wasted in this cell."

His compliments grated against her ears, but she worked to keep her face passive. How did he want her to react? Once she figured that out, she'd use it to play him.

"Were you pained when you tried to kill me?" she asked, the quiet question barely audible over the crackling fire.

"Circumstances were different then." His mouth tensed into a hard line, but relaxed again quickly. "You were a liability and a loose end. But things changed and I adapted...now you could be an asset to us if you came to the light." Ferro approached the bars, stopping a step back from their immense radiant heat. "The current vote is to kill you if you can't be used as leverage with Adela. But I think I could sway my peers into reconsidering, given your other *unique abilities.*"

"You mean the echoes."

"Yes." The air between them shifted. His eyes held glittering malice in contrast to the almost sweet smile across his lips. "And how you can steal people's magic."

Steal people's magic? What in the Mother's name was he talking about? Eira pursed her lips.

"Keep your secrets, for now. But I know what you did that night. And if you consider sharing that skill for the glory of Yargen…" He shook his head and his whole expression shifted. It was uncanny how he could slip into a look of earnest compassion after giving the appearance of wanting to skin her alive. "After all, I can give you everything you ever wanted."

"What I wanted?" she whispered, trying to sound hopeful, trying to sound like she was actually considering his insanity. Her empty stomach churned at the thought of even pretending to work with him. But she had to survive this somehow. And getting out of this inferno of a cell was a good first step.

"Yes, to come to Meru, to find your place—*your destiny*—here among us." Sweat dripped off his nose as he spoke. Everything handsome about him was melting off like a lady's cheap powder in the afternoon sun, exposing true ugliness beneath. How had she ever found him attractive? "You have a chance to make a difference. Show the Pillars that you can be one of us, that you can serve our causes. Your gifts are surely Yargen designed. I can make the rest of them see that if you swear to use them to glorify her."

She was worth more to them alive—at least that's what Ferro thought. Her ability to listen to vessels and whatever other gifts he *thought* she possessed were clearly prized if he was willing to risk letting her out of the cell. Or, maybe he underestimated her. Maybe he thought she was that same ignorant, meek young woman sneaking off in the night to meet with him, thrilled by mere glances and hand kisses. That her heart was still that open, that weak. *Fickle.*

Eira tried to embody what she thought she had been like then. She tried to find the naivety she'd known living under Marcus's shadow and protection.

"But I sneaked into your group's hideout. I listened in on your meeting. They will never trust me."

"These things can be forgiven, depending on your intentions… Why did you come to our meeting that night?" His eyes bored holes into her skull.

Eira chose her next words carefully, wishing she could think about them longer without raising suspicion. "I was looking for you." She started by skimming off the top of the truth. "After what you did to Marcus, I…I thought I wanted to kill you."

"You *thought*?"

"I don't know anymore." She widened her eyes to the point that they began to water. "I'm so confused, Ferro. Meru is everything I wanted but also, nothing I expected." Eira shook her head. "I loved you! Why did you do it? Why did you attack us?"

"Because Solaris is a blight on the world—a festering wound that must be cut out from the roots." He spoke so plainly about killing everyone and everything she'd ever loved. It was so chilling his words almost made the room feel cold. "I know it might be a shock to you, but that's only because you grew up being fed their propaganda. Your mind was filled with false tales of their righteousness and goodness. But, Eira, the very Emperor and Empress whom you lived under were the ones to set Yargen's antithesis, her mortal enemy, Raspian, free with the destruction of the Crystal Caverns."

There was the name Raspian again. So the Pillars perceived the Crystal Caverns as having some connection to this evil god and thus used their destruction as proof that the Solaris Empire was on the god's side because he was "set free." It undoubtedly also explained part of the motivation for attacking Solaris's candidates. The last people the Pillars would want to see Meru aligning with were the perceived acolytes of an evil god.

"You told me about Raspian once," Eira murmured, trying to keep up her act. "One of the nights…"

"I was trying to warn you. It pains me to see you like this. Someone with so much promise still within their veins should not be relegated to the depths; let me lift you up. Yargen spared you that night. She revealed your powers to me and gave me a revelation—a path forward that I set into motion before I even left your shores." He had been captive. How could he have… unless he had people even in Solaris working with him, for him. Eira was beginning to get a sense of just how deep the Pillar's influence ran. "You can be of use to the Pillars. You will have a place here, people who care about you, people who will want to elevate you—not tear you down." He was trying to play to every insecurity she'd ever shared with him.

"Like a family?" She made her voice quiver on the last word.

"Yes, we will be your family," he soothed. "So long as you love us like your family. Are loyal to us like family."

"What if Adela is my family?" The words were a monumental effort for her to say. This whole conversation had sweat streaming down her neck and back, but not from the heat. Her hands trembled, though not from the weight of the shackles. These words dredged up genuine fears and insecurities Eira hadn't fully confronted. She didn't want to tackle them, not here and now. But Ferro seemed to feed on the vulnerability they wrought in her. So she didn't push them back underneath the deep waters. She swam in the emotions.

She had to be vulnerable to this horrible creature to survive.

"Your family is who you choose. Will you choose the parents who didn't even bother to see you off? Who so clearly blame you for your brother's death? Or will you choose us? And in doing so, I'll free you from this place. You will mean something to a new family."

"All right," she croaked. How did he know about her parents? He had been watching her the entire time she thought he was the one trapped. "I will put myself in your care. Help me, Ferro."

"I'll see what I can do." He eased away from the bars with a satisfied smirk and, before she could say anything else, disappeared down the hall.

They kept her there for another day. At least, it felt like another day. There was no way to know without windows or natural light.

She lay on the floor in a ring of fire, her magic thin and straining to protect her against the heat. Eira rasped softly, the air thick and hard to breathe. Had she played the wrong hand? Did Ferro suspect her still? Even if he did, she was still valuable to them as long as they thought they could use her as leverage over Adela.

After that…it depended on her acting.

Eira kept her eyes closed, for the most part. The fire was too bright, and they kept drying out. She would give anything for water. Her whole body was wrung out and dried up. She'd long since stopped sweating.

Then, without warning, darkness.

The walls popped and hissed as they began to cool. Eira sat up, blinking. The faint glow of one of the Lightspinner's orbs appeared, bobbing behind Ferro and another woman she didn't recognize. The woman glanced warily at Ferro, who just gave her a nod.

She inserted a key into the lock, using mitts to protect her from the radiant heat of the metal. Ferro approached Eira like a predator stalking its prey. He knelt down before her, producing a waterskin.

"Be reborn, Eira. Wash away the sins of your forefathers," he whispered and poured the water over her head. She couldn't resist the urge to tip her head back, mouth open. It was the sweetest thing she'd ever tasted. Steam hissed all around her as the water met the hot stone. "Now come with me, my pet," he cooed like a lover as the waterskin emptied.

His arms wrapped around her and Eira barely resisted the urge to push him away. The woman still wore a skeptical look, but said nothing. Eira had more than just Ferro to win over.

"Where are we going?" Her voice cracked. She could drink two more full waterskins before the day was done.

"To your new room."

· CHAPTER ·

THIRTEEN

HERE WERE FOUR other holding cells, Eira learned. The two others she saw on her way out were empty. She couldn't tell if the rustling she heard in the fourth was rats, or another person.

Ducot? Eira wondered. Had he been captured, too? She had to find out. But first, she had to keep focused on saving her own skin. She wouldn't be helping anyone if she was dead.

The cells were expectedly in a basement. Ferro helped her up the stairs. Her knees were weak and her head was spinning. For all she loathed his touch, she might not have made it without his sturdy hands.

There was a hall behind the first locked door. At the end of the hall was a second locked door. The woman stopped and produced a blindfold, holding it to Eira.

"What?" Eira glanced between her and Ferro.

"It's for security." Ferro took the blindfold and stood behind her.

"But I'm one of you, aren't I?"

"Far from it," the woman said coolly.

"Soon enough." Ferro chuckled as he lifted the blindfold to her eyes. "But you must pass your initiation before you're truly one of us." Eira doubted she would. Hopefully she would be free of this wretched place before then.

They led her blindfolded through the door. There was the sound of scraping and grunting. More walking. Eira tried to listen for echoes with her magic, but it was too thin and weak.

"Stairs, careful now," Ferro said softly into her ear.

She could hear the footsteps of others passing by her. How

many were there? Five? Ten? Twenty? It was more than five… less than twelve, from what she thought she could hear. If only she had Ducot's keen senses.

They finally came to a stop.

"Leave us," Ferro commanded.

"Sir—"

"That's an order."

"Very well." The woman's acquiescence was followed by the click of a door.

The blindfold was removed and Eira opened her eyes, facing Ferro. He pocketed the fabric and settled his hands back on her shoulders. "I have something I want to show you," he whispered softly.

"Yes?"

He spun her and Eira inhaled sharply. She stumbled over to the bay window of the bedroom. "Where…where are we?"

Outside wasn't the city of Risen. Rolling hills spilled into dense trees. Mountains in the distance were purple with the fading light of sunset.

"The Pillars' stronghold." Ferro's hands were back on her shoulders, smoothing down her arms. "You're far from anyone who might hurt you. Don't worry about them any longer. We will be all you need," he said, but what Eira heard was, *far from anyone who could free you.*

How long had she been out for? The hills looked like the ones that were on the outskirts of Risen. Perhaps the city was just on the other side of this towering estate? The side she couldn't see.

"I'm safe here?"

He turned her once more, his hands slipping upward this time, from her shoulders to her cheeks. Eira resisted the urge to bite at his fingers and kick him in the groin. She had to be strategic if she wanted to make it out alive. Survival was the only thing fueling her right now.

"You are safe with me. No one else," he said solemnly. "Do not show anyone your powers without me present. Do not use them without my permission." His fingers began to dig painfully around her face and into her neck. "If you do, I can't promise your safety. Do you understand?"

"I understand." Eira tried not to wince.

"Good." His grip relaxed and he smiled unnervingly widely. "I can give you everything you dreamed of, Eira. A family, a home, a purpose. Let me fill the void that has been made in you."

"That is all I ever wanted." Funny how a remark could be both truth and lie at the same time. Every moment, every word of this game had to be calculated like her life depended on it.

"Excellent." He stared as if intent on consuming her with his eyes. How was her face not showing her disgust? Maybe she was a better actress than she'd ever thought. "Be my good girl, and you shall be rewarded." Ferro released her and left.

After he was gone, Eira sunk into the seat and gripped the cushions tightly, shivers wracking her body. She grabbed at her arms, at her face, at everywhere he'd touched her. In her frantic movements, she glanced out the window once more and stilled.

What had she gotten herself into?

Eira grabbed one of the pillows from the seat and pressed it against her face to muffle her screams.

***

She had exchanged one prison for another.

For two days, they didn't let her out of her room. A servant wearing a tabard emblazoned with three vertical lines, the same as the man's scars that she'd frozen in the alleyway, brought her food twice a day—once at dawn and once at dusk. It was the same young morphi man attending her, time and again, but he never said anything. On the night of the second day, Eira tried to speak with him.

He gave her a glare and vanished.

If he wasn't going to help her, Eira was determined to help herself. But when she made an attempt to listen to the room, there was nothing of note to be heard. Just prayers, and murmurings, and the ravings of madmen.

She was waiting for breakfast on her window seat when the door opened and finally revealed Ferro. He spoke in that same sickly-sweet tone as before and Eira had to pretend to lap it up like nectar. He gave her new clothes—similar to what the young morphi wore—and told her to make herself clean before noon.

Thankfully, he didn't stay to ensure the task was done. But Eira followed the instructions to the letter. The way he spoke made it sound like she might be getting out of her room, and that would be the first step to planning some kind of an escape. Or maybe just trying to get word out that she was trapped here.

Eira adjusted the tabard on her shoulders and tightened the belt. She stared at herself in the mirror, not recognizing the young woman staring back. She looked like one of them—a zealot. Eira practiced making faces of wonder, horror, and her best attempts at pious up until the moment Ferro arrived.

"Come to me, pet," he said gently.

Eira bit back a demand that he never refer to her as such again. But instead her face fell into a trained look of relief. "I couldn't wait to see you again. It's been so lonely."

"I know, but this is what we all must endure. The seclusion is what breaks your ties with the old world that misguided you and filled you with evil." He stroked her hair as one would an animal. Eira suppressed a shudder. "But you are taking this first step with grace. Now it is time to take another." He held out a blindfold and Eira didn't bother objecting.

They made a right out the door, thirty paces, then a left, fifteen paces, through another door, forty paces… Eira tried to keep track of the route they took. She didn't know where they were going yet, and it was likely they'd end up somewhere she didn't *want* to return. But beginning to try to map out the estate felt like she was doing something. Eira needed every little bit of potential hope to help her maintain her resolve.

A heavy knocker thudded, startling Eira from her repetition of their walking path. She heard the grinding of metal on metal and a chain clanking. There was a *whoosh* of air and the temperature rose slightly.

"Head up, come along," Ferro whispered to her and pulled her forward into the warm room—thankfully not nearly as hot as her cell. Eira heard a heavy clank behind her as Ferro undid the blindfold.

She was in some kind of audience chamber. The hall was taller than it was wide, pointing at the apex. Before her was a raised platform with three large basins, burning brightly with fire. In front of these stone firepits was an ornate throne. A woman sculpted in gold loomed over the chair, her arms reaching down as if to embrace the seated elfin man.

He had a beak-like nose and short, cropped black hair that was pulled tightly against his head. His golden armor blended in with the throne, making him look like a living statue. His plate was embellished with mother-of-pearl and intricately carved with squiggles and lines like lightspinning glyphs. The man's blue eyes were a colder shade than even Eira's, looking more like steel than water or ice.

A robed Pillar walked toward the edge of the stage, stopping and shouting, "Eira Landan, you come before the Chosen One, the Champion of Yargen, the man who is destined to restore Her goodness and order to our world. The man who is the rock of the Pillars, our base, our foundation of righteousness."

"Kneel before your leader, commander, and rightful ruler of Meru," Ferro hissed into her ear.

Eira did as commanded. She initially kept her gaze on the floor out of habit drilled into her for how to approach royal meetings. But her eyes began to wander, running down the lines of more robed Pillars along the walls on either side of her.

"Ferro, you have brought before me a new supplicant," the man who had been the Champion of Yargen said after a long stretch of silence.

"May she be worthy," the Pillars chanted. Eira lifted her eyes to the Champion. It was impossible to tell how old he was by appearance alone—as was the case with most elfin. But he didn't seem as young as Ferro. Though Eira couldn't tell if that made him fifty, eighty, or one hundred.

"I do not think she is worthy yet, Your Grace, but should Yargen find purpose for her, then may she wash away the evil marks her forefathers imprinted on her soul." Ferro said the words as if he were reading from a script. Eira was clearly not the first person he had brought forward in this way.

"And what sins they are." Their leader hummed. "A human, from the isle of Solaris."

"The isle of the evil one. The isle of the evil god Raspian's former tomb," the Pillars chanted.

It was little wonder Ferro was driven to murder if this was the world he'd grown up in—how he was taught to think about her home. But the realization didn't garner him much sympathy from Eira. Her brother was still dead. Her fellow apprentices of the Tower were still dead. Understanding his actions wouldn't bring them back, but it might help her out-maneuver him and the rest of them.

"Do you think you are worthy of serving me—Yargen's Chosen?" the man asked her. He didn't seem to have a name beyond "Champion" or "Chosen."

"I—I don't know." Eira hung her head as though she were ashamed. The curtain of her hair gave her a moment to collect herself and smother the disgust growing within her for what she was about to say and do. "I have been told my people were responsible for a great evil, but I don't understand."

"Of course you wouldn't, child," the Champion said sweetly, his manner almost fatherly. The tone made her bristle. "Would you like to learn?"

"Very much." Eira brought her eyes back to his.

"Long ago, the goddess of light, and life, and all that is good in this world, Yargen, sealed away an evil god, Raspian. She cast his tomb out to sea and guarded it with her very essence.

You know this tomb as the Crystal Caverns. When they were destroyed, his evil returned to the world. The Night-Noon Day twenty-four years ago signified his return."

Eira had heard the sailors in Oparium talking about a day when the sun was blotted from the sky. Was that the Night-Noon Day? It was mysterious, certainly. But nothing bad—as far as everyone Eira had spoken to was aware—had happened.

"It was shortly after that wretched day that my standing, my purpose, was stripped from me by Queen Lumeria—"

"Bring down the queen with the evil heart. Topple the corrupt government that spreads Raspian's evil," the Pillars intoned at the mere mention of Lumeria. There were trigger words that seemed to prompt replies. Perhaps this whole meeting was scripted, and every new recruit heard the same speech. It was slightly less terrifying when she thought of it more like a performance than being surrounded by madmen.

"—Raspian sank his claws into the land of Meru and its people. The Flame of Yargen was extinguished and without its guiding light, the citizenry turns from Yargen. Their leaders look to make deals with those born on the land of Raspian's tomb. Even the Voice has been corrupted."

"There is only one true Voice, Chosen of Yargen, Champion of Yargen."

Eira barely refrained from rolling her eyes at the chanting this time.

"But we work tirelessly in secret, Eira. To shun Raspian and his ways. To bring about a new age where her holy fire burns once more and all know of Yargen's glory—where all respect, revere, and *fear her.*"

And, fear you, too, as her Champion, right? Eira wanted to say. Instead she inhaled slowly and summoned the helplessness and turmoil she had felt as Marcus was pulled deeper and deeper. Fear and reverence, those were the emotions she wanted to invoke with the arch of her brows, the parting of her lips, and the widening of her eyes—make it look just like she'd practiced in the mirror.

"I fear and revere her," Eira whispered.

"Respect, revere, fear." They all chanted in reply to *her* this time. The sound felt like she was sinking into the embrace of some thick, cold, slimy substance. This wasn't like the pure waters of her powers, or the dark waters that churned from Marcus's death. This whole place was tainted. Rotted. Festering.

"Good." The Champion clapped his hands together. "If you truly fear and revere, then you will also seek to serve. To be made worthy in her eyes. For as you are now, kneeling in the dirt, you are undeserving of her soon-to-be-rekindled light."

Eira's gaze drifted to Ferro, finding him staring down at her. He wore a small smile on his face—like the look of someone gazing at a beloved dog, or prized hog. Ferro looked back to the man and his expression shifted to pure admiration. He really believed every word of this, they all did.

The sickening sense of dread only grew.

Zealots couldn't be reasoned with because they didn't want reason. They wanted blind faith. It was their way, their faction, or nothing. Everything that disagreed or opposed them would be cast on the "holy" fires burning behind the man they saw as their savior. They looked at him as if he were a god made flesh.

"Do you wish to be made worthy?" The Champion leaned forward as Eira's attention returned to him.

She wished to go back to Risen and lie in the comfortable safety of the manor. She had been missing now for two or three days, hadn't she? Surely they'd sent out search parties? But she wasn't in Risen any longer. She couldn't count on anyone finding her. And some part of her hoped they didn't go looking. She had put herself in this mess and didn't want anyone else risking their life for her stupid mistakes.

She could only count on herself.

"I do." Her safety was guaranteed as long as they thought she was sincere. *Keep playing along, Eira, keep the fear and*

*reverence on your face like your life depends on it—because it
likely does.*

"Good." A wicked smile curled the Champion's lips and he
looked far closer to the evil god he'd described than the serene
and kind goddess that stretched over his throne. "To prove you
are worthy of the light, you must first yearn for it."

"What?" Eira breathed, but no one heard.

"Take her to the pit."

FOURTEEN

"WHERE ARE WE going?" Eira dared to whisper to Ferro as they walked away from the throne room. She was blindfolded once more and too frantic to think about counting her steps or their turns. The events that transpired with the Champion had erased her mental record of their path from earlier anyway. Another one for the list of reasons why she was a terrible shadow.

"Don't worry." Ferro patted her forearm. Their elbows were linked. "Everyone must endure the pit. It is the test to become one of us."

"What is the pit?" She didn't know if she wanted the answer.

"You'll find out soon."

They descended two staircases and then a third that seemingly didn't end. Eira heard the clanking of metal and a heavy door swinging open. She walked with Ferro, feeling the breath of nearby people chanting softly as she passed. It sounded like prayers for strength and protection.

Eira hoped someone above was listening. She could use some strength.

"Stay here, and when I tell you, you may take off your blindfold."

"All right." Eira's voice quivered despite her best effort. Her knees shook as Ferro left her side. She loathed the man. But at least he was offering her some measure of protection here. Or… she thought he was.

There was more clanking. Eira felt the sound of a lock engaging in her chest as much as she heard it. Footsteps retreated and then, silence. Silence stretched on endlessly.

"You may remove the blindfold." Ferro's voice echoed to her from far away.

Eira did as instructed. But was met with a darkness somehow even more complete than behind the cloth. Eira slowly raised her hands to her face, touching the corners of her eyes, tapping lightly underneath her lower lids to verify they were, indeed, open.

"F-Ferro?" she called out.

"Learn to love the light. Seek it within."

"Ferro?" Eira held out her hands, shuffling in the darkness. She wandered aimlessly until she ran into a cool, damp stone wall. "Ferro?" she cried. "Ferro!" Her scream reverberated all around her, whispering in the silence that underscored just how alone she was.

***

Darkness surrounded her. Cold, as cold as the water was that night. Tighter and tighter it swaddled her—smothered her.

She shook violently, clutching herself, curled in a ball. In the first day, Eira had learned that the void had shades to it. There were creatures that lived in the impenetrable ink that she breathed hour over hour. They flooded her system like the water she should have inhaled.

It should have been me who died. This is my punishment.

There was no sense of day or night in this horrible place. But Eira knew she slept because there were hours where Marcus was still alive.

He swam toward her, pushed away by the relentless current. She stretched out her hand with all her might. Come to me, *Eira wanted to scream. She would save him this time. She would reach.*

But then she watched his eyes go wide. She watched him choke and die.

She shivered, in a different position than she last remembered. "Awake," Eira muttered into the darkness. "I'm awake. I'm here.

Marcus is dead. I'm in the Pillars' stronghold. Marcus is dead and Ferro is here…"

He had died because of her. Because she wasn't fast enough. Because she couldn't break the shield.

Her fault.

She deserved this.

No, Eira, the disembodied voice of her brother whispered to her like a hug from the void. *It wasn't your fault.*

"My… My…" Her thoughts were breaking down, as if the darkness were some parasitic being that was gnawing through them, through her, from the inside out. There was no escaping it. No reprieve. Darkness and silence and—

Light.

Eira blinked several times, certain she imagined it. The light grew brighter and began to illuminate the prison she'd been left in. It was nothing more than a stone room, circular, with a staircase that ended at a locked iron door. The light chased away the shadows that she'd allowed to torment her. The darkness that had seemed so alive and threatening mere minutes ago.

The haunted thoughts scuttled into the corners of her mind as Eira pushed herself to her feet, scampering over to the door, desperate for the sanity the light brought. Booted feet appeared and Eira followed them up the tabard to the face of the young man who had brought her food in her room. A task he seemed responsible for yet again.

He stopped right before the bars, judging her. Eira gripped the iron so tightly the skin on the back of her knuckles split. She inhaled, suddenly breathless. Anxiety wormed its way up her chest, into her throat, nearly making her gag.

Let me out, she wanted to say. The words burned her lungs as she held her breath. If she breathed, she'd say them. She'd beg for reprieve. They would know they were winning. But Eira had enough strength left not to allow that to happen.

Luckily, the young man spoke first. "You might be drenched

in the evil one, but the Champion has deemed you worthy of a meal. Bless his goodness."

Eira held out her hand expectantly, but the Pillar didn't move. He kept holding the loaf of bread with both hands. He seemed to be waiting for something.

"Bless his goodness," he repeated.

"B… Bless his goodness," Eira echoed.

The man smiled serenely. He looked like a statue of temperance and charity as he passed her the loaf. Eira snatched it between the bars, bringing it to her chest as though he would take it from her again.

Wordlessly, he spun, and started up the stairs. The glowing orb of light that hovered over his shoulder retreated with him.

"Wait," Eira rasped. "How much longer?" The bread slipped through her fingers, falling to the floor. "How much longer do I have to be in here?" She shook the bars. "How long will you leave me here?" she screamed.

Her shouts echoed without response.

***

"I'm awake. I'm here. Marcus is dead. I'm in the Pillars' stronghold. Marcus is dead and Ferro is here. I am awake. I'm here…" Over and over, she muttered the words as she lay with the cool stone on her cheek.

The bread had been gone a day ago and her stomach was now trying to eat itself. Luckily, she could summon water from the damp walls to drink. They didn't seem to be bringing her anything else. Did they intend to kill her here? Had she already failed? She was certainly the worst spy there had ever been.

Eira shifted, curling into the fetal position. "I'm tired, Marcus. I'm so tired…and I'm so sorry."

That night replayed over and over again in her mind, relentless and horrible. How many times would she have to relive his death before it was enough? How much longer would she endure this until her sanity gave up?

Eira blinked into the void.

The light had returned.

The young man was back again with another loaf of bread, the dots along his brow shining softly. They did the same dance. He judged her, said she had been deemed worthy of food.

"Bless his goodness," Eira repeated.

She got food and was left in the darkness.

Over and over, time after time. How many days had it been now? Did her friends think she was dead? Had the city guards and shadows given up looking? Or had it merely been hours since she left Risen? Time had expanded and contracted to the point that it was no longer something she could comprehend.

Eira closed her eyes, welcoming the thoughts of Marcus. It was the only way she slept. But this time, her thoughts continued beyond weeping over his body in the moonlight. They continued to her fight with Ferro.

He should have killed her, too.

She shouldn't be alive. Not because of just punishment for Marcus's death. Ferro was strong and had no problem subduing her. Why hadn't he that night?

She *should* be dead.

Eira blinked, as if suddenly seeing clearly. Somehow, she had finally suffered through the memories of Marcus's death enough to see them with some level of objectivity.

Ferro should *have killed her*. He'd tried. He'd wanted to. But he couldn't. She'd overpowered him against all odds. There was no reason why she should have won.

The memory replayed for her—his flickering glyphs, fading and weak. No matter how many times he repeated the words of power, he couldn't summon strength. That was when she'd overtaken him.

Had he been merely exhausted? Or was it something more? The glyph on the lake had vanished, too, when he had never seemed to have a problem controlling his magic prior. It had been the end of a long and bloody night for him.

And how you can steal people's magic, Ferro had said to her.

Is that what he thought she did? Eira touched the pads of her fingers together lightly in thought. She could almost see the glyphs Ferro tried to summon.

Eira had never heard of a Waterrunner being able to steal someone's magic. But she had heard of Waterrunners being able to eradicate other sorcerers—to put a block in the channel that connected a sorcerer with their power. It was difficult to do, however, and usually required a great deal of focus and time. She couldn't have done it without meaning to. She couldn't do it at all.

But what if you could? Marcus's disembodied ghost had returned, whispering from the corner of her cell.

"I can't."

Are you sure?

Eira turned to face him, imagining his silhouette cutting against the void.

You said that unintentional vessels were more common than anyone thought. Even when everyone said otherwise, you persevered. You knew the truth—your truth—and with it, you proved everyone wrong.

"This isn't the same," she whispered.

How do you know? Have you tried?

"I haven't tried very hard at anything since you left," Eira admitted. The only times she'd been spurred to action were at the idea of hunting down his killer. Otherwise, what had she done? Retreated from the world? Lay in bed?

You promised me we would fight together.

"I did." She hiccupped softly, suddenly choking on emotion. "But you were supposed to be with me at the very end."

His ghost smiled tenderly at her. *I'll always be with you, Eira.*

She cried.

She wailed into the darkness and poured out her soul as

sound and tears. She had mourned Marcus that cold night, and then retreated to numbness. These were the first tears she shed for him in months. These were the tears she should have wept weeks ago—the ones Alyss, and Cullen, and even Noelle with her sidelong glances knew Eira had been holding back.

If she ever got back to her friends, she would simultaneously apologize and thank them. Her brother was gone from this world—resigned to look after her from the Father's realms—but her friends were still here. They were still fighting for her. They were trying to get to her right now. She had to believe that was true. She knew it in her bones.

And if they would fight, so would she. Not just for Marcus's vengeance, but to honor his life and the promises she'd made to him. She would fight for everything she could still yet become.

When the light appeared again, Eira was upright, waiting. She didn't launch to her feet, lunging for the door like a ravenous beast; even though she salivated at the mere sight of the crusted loaf, she remained seated, calm, tranquil.

The young man approached the door and tilted his head one way, then the other, clearly unsure how to process this shift in her demeanor. Eira stared back at him, waiting for him to start his part of the speech. She didn't beg or grovel today. She merely waited.

"You might be drenched in the evil one, but the Champion has deemed you worthy of a meal. Bless his goodness."

"Bless his goodness," Eira repeated, as she knew he would want. But when he held out the bread through the bars, she didn't move. The man frowned slightly, eyes narrowing. After being alone for so long, void of sensation, she could almost *feel* the magic in the air around him, rising like the tides, steeping with power ready to be unleashed should she attack.

"He has deemed you worthy of a meal. *Bless his goodness.*"

"Bless his goodness; but I do not want a meal." Eira looked the young man right in the eyes, mentally commanding him to be her messenger. "Tell the Champion I want the light. I will live by it or am willing to die here in this pit."

She'd drawn her line in the sand and made her play. The man slowly retracted his arm and passed the loaf of bread from hand to hand. He clearly didn't know how to process her ultimatum. Finally, wordlessly, he retreated up the stairs. Luckily, Eira's stomach didn't growl until after he was well out of earshot.

Now, she'd wait and see what their reply was to her demands. Would they let her starve to death? Or they would make the mistake of setting her free?

FIFTEEN

FERRO CAME ALONE to collect her from the pit. He coddled and cooed over her as he helped her up the stairs—blindfolded again. He praised her for her perseverance while simultaneously reassuring her not to worry about how wretched she looked, how bad she smelled, how much she trembled.

"We all were like this after the pit," he said gently. "Wear it like a badge of honor."

"I will," Eira said softly, looking up at him as though the sun rose from his ass. She clutched his arm tighter, intentionally stumbling on the last step to her room. Ferro pulled her upright. "Thank you."

Let them think you're helpless. They wanted to beat her down. But all they had done was hammer her into a harder metal. Ever since leaving the pit Eira could feel the world in ways she had never thought possible. Tiny currents of magic, trembling in the air around everyone, were suddenly perceptible. Almost loud with their vibrations.

"Of course." He smiled thinly.

"Not just for that." Eira shook her head. "For speaking on my behalf to the Champion, for giving me an opportunity for my eyes to be opened."

"And are your eyes open?" The question was guarded. Eira couldn't be sure what he wanted to hear.

"I see the light, everywhere, and from within," she said, trying to evoke the emotionless hollow that the other Pillars' voices echoed from. "I have known the darkness, and now I wish to eradicate it from our world. I have shaken Raspian's hold on me."

"I believe you." Ferro placed his hands on her cheeks. Eira resisted the urge to spit in his face with a smile. "But you will still need to prove yourself to others, and to our Champion."

"Bless his goodness."

Ferro laughed with relief at her intoning the words. "Bless his goodness, indeed. Now, carry on, we're almost to your room. Tonight, a good night's rest. Tomorrow, recovery. And then we will begin showing the Pillars the blessings Yargen has given you in your magic."

The hours passed just as he had instructed. Ferro left her to freshen up and the young Pillar brought her food. Eira made an attempt at getting his name, but the man ignored her. She might have Ferro's confidence, but it seemed the rest of the Pillars were still skeptical of her.

That night, the bed was too soft and the pale moonlight that streamed through her window was too bright for her to sleep. It felt like she had been sleeping for days, weeks even—one long, horrible nightmare that she had finally woken from. That nightmare had started back on Solaris, the night Marcus died.

Now she was awake, and sleeping felt like wasting more time. Eira stared out her window down at the grounds. She never saw anyone walking the lavish gardens below, or on the hills beyond. No animals…not even a bird.

Eira spent the whole night staring out the window. Twice the moon dipped behind the clouds and the world seemed to blur a moment. Eira blinked, rubbed her eyes, and kept watching. Was she just tired? Or…

When the dawn rose, she put her hand on the glass. Even though the sunlight streamed through the window, brightening her room, the glass didn't warm. She moved her hand from pane to pane. The metal was icy to the touch. It should be warming due to sunlight.

What she saw wasn't real. The scenery beyond her room was some kind of intricate illusion. She laced her fingers and held her hands together tightly to keep herself from smashing the glass to confirm her theory. If the scene beyond was fake then she could be anywhere.

I could still be in Risen.

Closing her eyes, she tried to grab onto the sharpened sense of magic she'd had since leaving the pit. She could feel *something* vibrating behind the glass. Her brow knit with focus. She focused on that thrumming sensation that hovered around her. She was learning magic was an almost sentient thing. It lived in stone, water, fire, and in the air itself; it had been strung throughout their world and sorcerers merely tugged on the threads.

Eira slowly opened her lids and stared at the illusion. She imagined a dozen invisible, magic hands stretching from her back. The unreal fingers knotted in the magic. Pull? Tug? What did she do now? Was any of this real or was it all in her head?

Sweat rolled down her neck.

She made the mistake of blinking. For a second, just as her eyes were about to close, there was a wobble. There was a stone wall where the green pastures had once been. But when Eira opened her eyes again, it was gone.

Her second attempt was interrupted by the door to her room opening for Ferro.

"Oh, good, you're already awake, my dear."

I'm not "your dear;" I'm your undoing. The smile she plastered on her face was the antithesis to the cutting thought.

"I was so excited to work with you today—to prove myself to the Champion—that I couldn't sleep." She motioned to the window. "Plus, I wanted to wake with the dawn."

"And what a lovely dawn it is."

"Indeed. I think the sun shines brighter on Meru." Eira stood. "Are we far from Risen? The air seems fresher and crisper here."

His smile thinned and panic settled into her gut. Had she overstepped? Did he now know she was onto them?

"I think you are simply correct in that Yargen shines her light brighter on her chosen land. Even our air is better for it."

Ferro crossed to her, resting a hand on her shoulder. "Come, I've arranged an important meeting for you today."

"Oh?"

"You'll see when we arrive."

Ferro escorted her out, blindfolded, of course, and through the halls. They went down two flights of stairs and then through what Eira suspected was a long tunnel. The top of her head kept brushing against the ceiling and the walls were so close that Ferro's side pressed against hers. Eira imagined the long, skinny tunnels she and Ducot traversed to get to the home of the Court of Shadows. Were the Pillars operating much like the shadows? Eira imagined layers of webs suspended at different levels underneath the streets of Risen. The city was ancient. It had been built on itself for years. Fathoming that there might be cities underneath cities wasn't all that difficult and she felt foolish for not thinking of it sooner. Yet another useful piece of information to take back to the Specters.

Up a small flight of stairs, Eira could feel the shift of the air as the space opened. They finally came to a stop and Ferro removed her blindfold. They were in an empty room, save for three men.

One was the Champion, and he was flanked by two other Pillars Eira didn't recognize.

"It is good to see you again, Eira," the Champion said with that unnerving fatherly smile of his.

Eira dropped to her knee and put on her most pious voice. "I am not worthy of being before you, Your Grace."

"You are not," the light-haired elfin to the Champion's right sneered.

"But her recognizing such speaks volumes to the progress she's made," the Champion said. "Stand, Eira. You are here to demonstrate the powers my son has told me so much about."

Son? Eira looked between the Champion and Ferro in shock. Ferro was the Champion's son.

"Forgive me, darling." Ferro just kept giving her new pet names, as though he were in a competition with himself to find out what she hated most. Darling was slightly better than pet. But she'd love to punch in his teeth for either. "I lied to you. But only because you couldn't understand the glory of my parentage. No one could know."

"No one should know," the light-haired man mumbled under his breath. He kept shooting her skeptical looks. Eira knew he'd be the hardest to win over.

She smiled warmly at Ferro. "I understand completely. I was not worthy then." She bowed her head and Ferro hooked her jaw.

"But you will work to become worthy now?"

"With all my might."

"Good, pet. I need you to show them how you can hear voices."

"All right." Eira nodded.

"This is what you will listen to." The man to the left of the Champion stepped forward, holding out a golden medallion. Eira was once more reminded of the uncanny similarities between the Pillars and shadows. Both operated in the underbelly of Risen. Both were outside the law. And both wanted to test her with a stupid piece of metal.

Eira looked at the medallion, connecting with it easily. The senses surrounding her magic had definitely been sharpened by the pit. What sounded like a prayer began to echo in her ears and Eira repeated it word for word, even the parts about beseeching Yargen to rain fire down on her enemies and the heretics and apostates born from Raspian's tomb.

"It's true, then," the blond whispered. "You can hear the words of those who came before."

"She can hear the echoes of time in Yargen's ears," the Champion said in a way that sounded a lot like a decree.

"It is a gift," Ferro said on her behalf.

The man holding the medallion was silent, staring in awe. Eira thought she should be tired of people's stunned silence by now… but she wasn't. Maybe it was just these men—her captors—being in awe of her that gave her a sense of power.

"She could do it," the man holding the medallion whispered, glancing to the Champion. "She could absolve you."

Absolve him? Absolve the Champion of what? Certainly the Pillars weren't well loved in Risen. Did they mean some kind of religious absolution?

"These powers, who else recognizes them?" the Champion asked Ferro, speaking as though she was no longer there.

"She displayed them during the third trial on the Dark Isle. The Emperor and Empress of Solaris recognized them."

"You would have us use *their* word?" The blond seemed appalled.

"I would have us use the allying of Solaris and Meru against both parties." Ferro held out his arms. A crazed look had overtaken his face. "Think about it. Meru—Lumeria—has made the decision to connect herself with the offspring of Raspian in this foolish treaty of hers. We will use it against her. If she has convinced the people that the Solaris government is legitimate then she cannot refute their recognition of Eira's powers."

"How do we know the Emperor and Empress won't go back on recognizing Eira's abilities?" the man to the left of the Champion asked. "We can't trust anyone from the Dark Isle."

"The trial was public. Too many people saw the Empress recognize her for them to back down now." Ferro stepped forward, speaking just to his father. "This will work. Then all of Risen will be forced to reconcile the lies they've been served. They will rejoice your return to status. They will see you as their Champion—as you were meant to be seen. And when you reignite the Flame—"

"Enough." The Champion raised his hand, stopping Ferro. "You've given me much to think on." His eyes darted between them. "You're both dismissed."

Ferro blindfolded her once more and escorted her back. Eira remained silent the entire way. Her time with the Pillars was forcing her to learn strategic silence was often best. It gave her an opportunity to think through, and carefully structure, her questions and statements. Moreover, the Pillars seemed like a silent bunch. She could be passing through a room with twenty of them and not know it.

Eira let out a sigh of relief when he removed the blindfold. For good measure, she clutched her chest as if she was fighting back nerves.

"Are you all right?" Ferro wrapped an arm around her, resting both his hands on her shoulders.

"Yes, I'm sorry." Eira shook her head. "Standing before the Champion of Yargen, chosen by the goddess herself..." She staggered out of his embrace toward the window seat, sitting heavily. "The weight of his presence is too much for a mere mortal like me. After the pit, he...he looked glorious." Eira looked up at Ferro, widening her eyes slightly. "And you—you're—"

"Forgive me." Ferro sat next to her, scooping up her hands. "I wanted to tell you, Eira, I did. But it wasn't the time. And I..."

"Yes?" she pressed when his thought trailed off.

"I didn't know how much you would mean to me—to all of us."

"To you?" she repeated softly, eyes darting between their laced fingers and his face.

"I knew you loved me then."

The words hurt more than Eira wanted them to. She hated the sting they left in the still festering wound Ferro had created in her. First Adam, then Ferro... She knew how to pick men who would inevitably hurt her.

But where did that leave Cullen?

She could feel her face softening at the thought of Cullen and banished the mere idea of him. This wasn't a place for thinking of him. What Eira was called to do—who she had to be to survive right now—wasn't meant for Cullen and his tenderness. Who she was becoming might not ever be meant for such delicate and loving hands.

"But I admit, back then, I only saw you as someone to be used to bring about the glory of Yargen," Ferro continued, oblivious.

"*Back then*; what about now?" She was safe as long as she was useful to him. That much was clear. And if she was going to keep manipulating him successfully she needed to know where she stood and what he wanted from her at all times.

"Now…" His fingers tightened. "Think about it, Eira. You and I…ushering in her glory. All of Solaris will look to you as one of their own who has seen the light—who has been blessed by her love. By *my* love." Ferro exhaled with a small smile. He almost looked sincere. The expression made her hate him all the more. He wasn't a man *capable* of love.

Yet the mention of love brought Cullen to the fore once again. No matter how hard she tried, she couldn't escape him. The thought of him pressing her against the wall at court, the feeling of his fingers in her hair. If she made it out of this alive…she'd kiss him like that again at least once. She'd not waste another moment with him or any of her friends.

"I want to be useful to you," Eira said as delicately as possible.

Ferro tilted his head, clearly assessing her as a sinister grin slithered on his lips. He radiated a horrible smugness. "*How* do you want to be 'useful' to me?"

The implication had Eira biting back bile. She had to put a stop to his more sensual implications that she'd been ignoring until now. He could think of her as his pet, his student, a means to his ends. But she wasn't going to let him think of her as an object of desire. Eira swallowed the bitter taste in her mouth and spoke with words with more ease than she would've been able to a week ago, given the rising panic within her.

"I want to bring about Yargen's glory." Eira wore a placid, awestruck expression. She looked at him as though he were a sculpture of the divine and not a man. Not someone that her mortal hands could or should touch. Not that she would ever even want to. "Once, I might have been a foolish girl and thought that the best way to do that would be to *serve you*." She allowed a lustful tone to hover in the last two words. Hoping her intent was clear. Hoping he followed along. "But now I see there are far greater ways I can contribute. I was a foolish, confused little girl. But no longer. My eyes have been opened. I see the light and now I think I know how best I can bring about the Pillars'—and your—glory. It is with my magic and my adoration for your righteousness. It is by following your orders and wishes as a soldier should. Not by any girlish infatuations that are long gone."

Recalculation shifted in his expressions. There was a sort of recalibration he went through as she spoke, no doubt reassessing how he could manipulate her. Ferro eased away from her and the atmosphere thinned.

"Go on. Tell me how you think you can be an effective tool for me."

She would be a tool over his object of desire any day. "There's something the Champion needs me to do—to listen to—right?"

Ferro nodded cautiously, prompting her to continue.

Eira drew a quivering breath, knowing what she was about to ask. If there was ever a moment she would overplay her hand, this was it. "I can find it."

"How?" He narrowed his eyes slightly, no doubt putting together what she intended.

"Let me go back to Risen. I'll make up a story about kidnappers I escaped from. They'll see me as a competitor who fought and won to return. I'll be celebrated and trusted."

"But it will also stoke suspicion of the Pillars." Ferro frowned.

She was in too deep; she couldn't back down now. "Perhaps. But I can make up a story that will throw them off the trail of the Pillars. Risen is a large city. Cutthroats must be common enough and as a competitor I am already in the spotlight. If the Pillars are worried…send a ransom note ahead that corroborates this claim before I embark on my mission."

Ferro seemed to be considering it.

"They won't suspect me," she continued. "They've already let me move freely in the Archives, even. I could find a way to get whatever you need, I'm sure of it."

"They let you roam free in the Archives?" he questioned with an arch of his eyebrow.

"Yes."

"Truly?"

"Yes." Eira leaned forward. "I can do this for you. This is my destiny—why Yargen blessed me with this power."

"You could get it and we could expose their lies at the competitor's gala," he murmured. "We could sacrifice some of the young ones to be the thieves. They would be happy to die for the Champion…" Ferro shook his head. "No, it's too much of a risk."

"I can do it," Eira insisted. His attention slowly wandered to her. She searched his eyes, trying to ooze sincerity. "Let me."

He stood, back to her. "It's too risky."

Eira watched as her chances for escape began to slip through her fingers. She'd find another way out, eventually. But how long would *eventually* take? Far too long. She didn't want to wait here to find out how many more disturbing tests they'd force her to endure before they'd trust her to even walk around unsupervised.

She rose and declared, "My magic is yours." He glanced back at her, clearly startled by the sudden proclamation. "You are a man of action, a man of power." He so clearly craved power in all things. The more Ferro tried to look tough, the more she saw a sad little boy, begging to be noticed. Eira wondered if that was how she looked when she'd insisted on competing in the trials. Regardless, she played into that desire. "You said it yourself, you have a tool in me. Why are you acting afraid to use it?"

"I am never afraid." He let out a low growl, prowling back to her. His hand was at her throat, fingers tightening to the point that she wheezed for air. "Would you die for me?"

"If you asked it of me," Eira gasped.

His hand continued to constrict around her windpipe. Eira struggled to remain calm. She balled her fists into the fabric of her clothes, preventing them from reaching up and gripping his forearms. As the air thinned and her vision tunneled, the room faded into the darkness of the pit…of that night underneath the water. He had tried to steal her air then, but couldn't.

And he couldn't now, either.

Ferro released her with a light shove. Eira collapsed back onto the bench, gasping and massaging her throat. But when she looked up at him and saw that smug smile, she knew she'd won.

"I'll see what I can do. You've given me a lot to think about, pet." He patted the top of her head twice and left.

Eira counted to ten before collapsing on the bench, throat aching and bruised. She'd now bet the ultimate wager—her life. And all too soon she'd find out if it paid off.

NOTHER DAY PASSED without word, and Eira grew more anxious by the hour. The longer they waited, the more time search parties had to look for her. The deeper the Pillars would go into hiding and the harder they might be to convince to set her free. Or, perhaps, her suggestion would look more appealing by the minute. The Pillars could agree to her plan to get the pressure off them.

That assumed people were still looking for her at all.

She wrung her fingers and paced her room, waiting for word. Waiting for *something*. When the young man who delivered her food finally arrived, Eira had to evaporate a dagger of ice quickly to prevent herself from holding it against his throat and demanding that he tell her what was going on. It likely wouldn't have worked. The zealot would be all too happy to die for his "noble cause" and Eira's hope of ever escaping would be lost.

"The Champion has summoned you," the man said casually as he set down her platter of gruel. "Wash and dress in this." He motioned to the clothes neatly folded beside the bowl on the platter and left.

Eira ate the tasteless mush dutifully. She had to keep up her strength. The Champion summoning her following her last interaction with Ferro had to mean *something*. The weight of her gamble was on her shoulders and already the oats were coagulating into a brick in the pit of her stomach.

She ignored the clothes for most of her meal, afraid to find out what they would put her in. But as soon as her fingers brushed over the fabrics, she recognized them. It was the skirt and blouse she'd worn to the dinner with Cullen. The hem of her skirts was muddied and stained from the tunnels she'd traversed with Ducot. Her boots were bloodied from where they'd cut her ankles while running through the city. There were rips in the blouse that Eira didn't recognize.

An odd sense of familiarity overtook her as she dressed. It wasn't because she was finally back in *her* clothes after dressing like a Pillar for over a week. It wasn't because those clothes were filthy and unwashed.

This feeling… She knew it from the revelation of her parentage that had followed the second trial. Yet again, the remnants of her old life didn't quite fit as they once had. Every stitch fell in the same place; *she* was what didn't fit. Eira stared at herself in the mirror. Yes, this feeling was similar to back then.

Furrowing her brow, Eira stared at herself with intensity, feeling power simmer underneath her skin. The ocean within her was white-capped and raging, ready to be unleashed. If the Champion wasn't summoning her to set her free, she was ready to fight her way out or die trying.

"Eira?" Ferro didn't even knock when he entered.

The expression fell off her face instantly and Eira spun away from the mirror, sprinting over to him. She gripped his arms, frantic. "Ferro, my lord, my guide through this dark world, what have I done?" Eira blinked several times, trying to summon tears. It was harder to cry on command than she would've thought. A little bit of magic summoned water on her lower eyelids. "Why has the light forsaken me? I only wanted—I only wished—I—"

"Pull yourself together." He slapped her across the face. The pain was numbed by shock. It seemed he was taking his "ownership" of her life and wellbeing to heart. "What has upset you to hysterics this morning?"

"These clothes." Eira stepped back and held out her skirts. She didn't fuss over the stinging in her cheek. Something told her that if she did, it'd only make things worse. "They are from before my eyes were opened—before I knew the truth. But I'm being forced to wear them again. Am I being cast out? Did I say too much? I cannot go before the Champion of Yargen in these pathetic rags of the Dark Isle! I will not—"

"Calm yourself." Ferro grabbed her shoulders, scowling. "What will truly embarrass you is going before the Champion as a shrieking harpy."

"All I want to do is please the Champion." She hiccupped and composed herself at his command. An easy enough task when her "hysterics" were superficial.

"And you will."

"What we talked about yesterday…" Her voice dropped to a whisper. "Is that why he's summoning me?"

Even though they were alone, Ferro glanced around as if someone might be listening. "Yes." A smile snaked across his lips. "You will have a chance to prove to my father how much you love Yargen and are loyal to our cause."

"I live to serve."

"And you live to bring me glory."

"Yes. So he agreed to let me go?" She hoped she didn't sound too eager.

"You'll see soon enough."

The entire blindfolded walk to the throne room, Eira played out situations in her mind. If they let her go, she would have to find a way to get back to the Court of Shadows first thing and report on her discoveries…and apologize to Ducot…if he was still alive. The thought made her chest tighten with guilt. Death haunted her wherever she went, but it didn't turn its immortal gaze on her. No, death hunted the people who were foolish enough to ally themselves with her. They paid the price of her actions.

If the Pillars refused to let her go—which she had to admit was the most likely—they would probably do one of two things. They would either throw another messed-up test of loyalty to them and to Yargen to prove that her suggestion wasn't a desperate attempt to flee. Or, they would kill her on the spot. If that was what they chose, then she wouldn't go without taking Ferro with her.

She'd find the courage and iron will to murder him where

he stood for Marcus. There would be no more hesitation if the moment presented itself. But for now, she'd keep him alive. His existence was still serving her.

The heat of the throne room was familiar. Even though she'd only been here once before, Eira would recognize that distinct warmth for the rest of her life. Ferro removed her blindfold and went to stand at her side.

Pillars were lined up, flanking her, but fewer than last time. Were the others off on some kind of mission? Or were they not privy to what was about to happen?

"Eira Landan, you come before the Chosen One, the Champion of Yargen, the man who is destined to restore Her goodness and order to our world," a Pillar announced. "The man who is the rock of the pillars, our base, our foundation of goodness and righteousness."

"May I be worthy of his righteousness." Eira knelt before the man on the throne.

The Champion was silent for a long time, staring down at her with perfectly still composure. Finally, when the silence was so tight that it nearly thrummed in the air like a string under tension, he spoke.

"I have received the wisdom of Yargen and have decided to give you a mission." The Champion stood. "You are to return to the world of heretics and apostates. You will go back to the Archives, Her most holy site, now violated, and use a secret passage underneath the bookcase at the very top of the spire to access a hidden room that was once the chambers of the Voice."

That was the room she'd met with Taavin in.

"There, you will seek out a token that carries words from the altercation that happened in that room. You will take this token, and deliver it to Ferro in two weeks at the tournament ball that will soon be announced."

Soon be announced stuck out to Eira foremost. If this ball wasn't announced yet, then they must have people on the inside of Lumeria's court. Eira imagined a shadow and a Pillar, unknowingly working side by side in that room of desks she and Ducot had sneaked through.

"What does the token look like?"

"Whatever you can find that contains the words. If your powers are truly ordained by the goddess—as my reign is—then you will have no problem finding something to our satisfaction."

"Of course," Eira said with a blissful smile. "And…what altercation am I listening for?"

His eyes narrowed slightly and the Champion seemed to debate telling her. "You will likely hear mention of the name Deneya. That should be all you need to know. Let your faith guide you to the rest."

Deneya? How was Deneya involved in all this? Eira worked to keep the peaceful smile slung across her cheeks.

"I understand. My faith will guide me."

"Good. Because if you fail, we will be forced to exact Her righteous justice on you."

"I will not fail."

"And if you should attempt to tell anyone of our organization… The punishment will not only fall on your head. The other Solaris competitors will also suffer for your betrayal."

They're not part of this! Eira wanted to scream. Instead, she said, "I understand."

"I hope you do, Eira. We are putting a great deal of faith in you. But it is a risk we take knowingly. The Pillars are the foundation of Risen. We are found in every house, every organization, every order of knights, and every *manor*."

The competitors' manor wasn't as safe as everyone thought. At least, that's what Eira heard him say underneath his words.

"I will not betray your trust. I have seen the light and never wish to return to the darkness."

"And will you do anything to be worthy?"

"Anything."

"Good." The Champion sat on his throne. "Soon, you will sleep, Eira. And when you wake, this will be nothing more than a dream. Your truth will be that you were taken captive by two morphi who lured you away. They wished to give their competitors an advantage by demanding that Solaris be out of the competition."

Even in her cover story, the Pillars were trying to break apart the treaty by sowing doubt between the kingdoms.

"Now, you must look as though you have been captive, and not living in our generous safety and hospitality." The Champion lifted a hand and flicked his wrist.

The motion was a cue to the other Pillars in the room. They descended on her swiftly, closing in on all sides. Ferro was the first to strike. He kicked at her side without warning. Eira smashed against the ground. Dazed, she blinked, Ferro's face hovering in her vision.

"Don't make a sound," he whispered with a smile. "If you do, we'll know the limits of what you can endure for your goddess."

Eira pressed her lips together as he caressed her cheek.

"Yes, that's it…good girl." His fingers knotted in her hair and he jerked upward, slamming her face against the ground.

Everything went dark.

***

Eira woke with a groan. Her head ached all the way down her spine. Her ribs were bruised and it hurt to breathe. The world was blurry and dim, taking far too long to come into focus. She licked her cracked lips, tasting blood.

Panic set in when she tried to move and discovered she couldn't. At first, she thought they'd broken bones, or worse. But as sensation returned to her body, she could feel the binding on her wrists and ankles.

She had been tied with rope and left in some kind of warehouse. Around her were the makings of a hideout—food, bed rolls, clothes. But there was no one around.

Inhaling slowly, Eira brought her magic around her wrists and ankles. The ropes strained against the ice, fraying and breaking the second she pushed spears through them. Just that effort left her breathless. Her head throbbed with every movement.

The moment she stood, she was on her knees again, retching. The process made her ribs scream and the pain blinded her as stars popped behind her eyes. Eira wiped her mouth with the back of her hand, stifling sobs. She couldn't cry. It physically hurt too much to do so right now.

Trying again, Eira made it to her feet this time. One ankle barely supported her and she had to hobble out, using crates and trunks for stability. She was on the highest floor of the building. Eira stood at the top of the stairs, swaying. If she tried to walk down them, she'd trip and snap her neck.

Instead, she sat, using what strength she could muster to summon a slide of frost. Her first attempt was too fast and Eira smashed against the landing hard enough to leave her dazed and breathless. Her second attempt was better. She managed to summon a snowbank for her third.

She was on the second floor catching her breath, clinging to the wall for support, when the sight of a queen's knight patrol caught her eye. Eira didn't hesitate to smash the glass of the window. The commotion caught their attention and Eira leaned out, broken glass and all, shouting, "Help! Help me please!"

SEVENTEEN

APH—THE LIGHTSPINNING WORD to block pain. *Halleth, ruta, sot, toff,* all healing words. *Loft not…*to sleep. At least as far as Eira could figure, since those seemed to be the last two words she heard before falling into a deep and dreamless slumber.

Eira spent her first few hours after being recovered by the soldiers in a state of mental transience. Some things were too painful to remember accurately. Other hours were spent sleeping and waking up to different healers attending her.

This time, however, she woke and felt surprisingly good—comparatively, at least. The familiar ceiling of her room at the competitors' manor came into focus, moonlight turning it silver. The weight of the blanket on top of her, the scenery outside her window…it was enough to have her choking on emotion and blinking away tears.

Yet, between the shuttering of her lids, she transitioned in and out of where she was and where she had been. One moment, her window showed the river winding through Risen. The next, like a flash of lightning across a dark sky, she saw that horrible illusion they'd plastered in front of her for days in the Pillars' stronghold.

Muffled speaking from outside the door distracted her from the oscillating distortions. Eira sat, her head swaying slightly but eventually coming to a stop with the world right-side-up. Her stomach stayed in place, her vision didn't blur. The healers of Meru had done wonders to patch her broken body back together in what seemed like record time.

Pushing her blanket aside, Eira padded over to the door. As she rested her hand on the latch, she took a steadying breath. *This was real.* She had made it out. Yet a creeping terror overwhelmed her that she would open the door and find herself back in the Pillars' halls, back in the dark pit that would always be a part of her.

Amber light from the fire crackling happily in the hearth spread across her as she entered the room beyond. Its warmth tingled up her exposed legs and arms, seeping through the sleeping gown she'd been put into. Alyss, Cullen, and Noelle all sat in a collection of chairs between the fireplace and windows, their heads turning to face her.

"Eira," Cullen breathed with wide eyes.

"Eira!" Alyss barely kept her squeal at a low level. She leapt from the sofa, rushing over to Eira and slamming into her with a heavy *thud*.

"Alyss." Eira tried to hold her friend as tightly as she could— which wasn't very tight. The muscles in her arms didn't seem quite as strong as they once were. But her friend was as sturdy as a rock, compensating for whatever weakness was there.

"I was so worried—" Alyss choked on her sobs. "—You—You disappeared. We didn't know. Then they found you and…and…" Alyss pulled away, rivers streaming down her cheeks. "They brought you in, I'd never seen so much blood. They said you'd been conscious when they found you but none of us believed it."

"You were basically pulp." Noelle glanced over her shoulder. Despite her dry remarks, Eira thought she saw real relief in the woman's eyes. "Shocking they could put your face back together even halfway decent after all that."

"Your face is fine." Alyss wiped her cheeks.

"You look beautiful, as always." Cullen was on his feet, but he had yet to make his way to her. Eira could see him holding himself back. The barrier of everything still unsaid was between them. The wounds that she'd no doubt made with her reaction to the vulnerability he'd shown her were healing ugly, fusing him a few steps away from her. A distance Eira wasn't sure she wanted any longer.

"Calm down, lover-boy." Noelle rolled her eyes.

"Excuse me?" Cullen balked.

"Please, spare me your mock surprise, or offense, or whatever that was supposed to be." Noelle shifted back in her seat.

"We were all so scared. I'm so glad you're okay." Alyss hooked her elbow with Eira's, guiding her back toward the sofa. Eira was sure her friend could see how unsteady she still was on her feet.

"Who's going to get Levit and the knights?" Noelle asked as Eira and Alyss sat. Cullen had moved onto the same sofa as Noelle to give them room. "They want to question you."

Alyss turned into a mother hen. "She just woke up, give her a moment."

"I'll talk with them soon… But I would like a moment with the three of you alone." Eira laced her fingers with Alyss's, looking at how the firelight played on her friend's cheek. She tucked her head in the crook of Alyss's neck and shoulder, breathing a sigh of relief. They were all right. The Pillars hadn't done anything to harm them…yet.

But the Champion's words thrummed in her, his threat turning her throat to ash and her stomach to bile.

"What in the Mother's name happened to you?" Noelle leaned forward, resting her elbows on her knees.

"She's going to have to tell Levit and the knights; don't make her do it twice," Cullen said.

"Levit and the guards might not give us all the details." Noelle shot him a look and then turned back to Eira, eyes on fire. "With how much you worried us, you owe us all an explanation."

Eira laughed softly, uneasily.

"You don't have to say anything, if you're not ready." Alyss rubbed her shoulder.

"Thank you, but Noelle is right. I owe you all a lot of things…" Eira looked between her fellow competitors. "Like an apology for starters."

"For worrying the pants off us? Apology accepted," Noelle said.

"Is that why you're wearing a skirt for once?" Eira couldn't stop herself from quipping.

"Oh, *har har*, if you're well enough for jokes, you're well enough to spill *all* the details." Noelle smirked.

Eira straightened off Alyss's shoulder. She stared at her hands, thinking of her time with the Pillars, of their threat. Eira drew a deep breath, tried to find the right words, failed, and then exhaled with a long sigh.

The Pillars had made it clear that if she told anyone *anything* about her time with them, her friends would also suffer the consequences. But because her friends would suffer the consequences, didn't she owe them the truth of what happened?

"Well?" Noelle pressed.

Cullen elbowed her in the side. "Give Eira a minute. She's clearly been through a lot."

"Okay, I'll spare your lady." Noelle rolled her eyes.

"She's not 'my lady,'" Cullen mumbled. His eyes flicked to Eira then quickly away. The hesitance, uncertainty, and trace of longing Eira saw filled her with a strange hope and excitement.

Alyss held her tighter. "You really don't have to…"

"No, I do." Eira gripped her knees and took a steadying breath. "First, are the other competitors all right?" She couldn't ask for Ducot by name. "Is anyone else missing?"

"No, just you," Alyss said and Eira breathed a monumental sigh of relief.

Ducot had escaped. Whomever the Pillars had in that cell wasn't him——if they'd had anyone at all. She'd been in a broken-down state at that point and Eira wouldn't be shocked if she'd imagined the sounds entirely. Relieved that Ducot was safe, she leaned forward, keeping her voice as low as possible. The three had to lean in as well to hear her.

"I'm going to give you all the choice…you are in grave danger, and the more you know, the more danger you're in. But, because you're in danger, I feel you have a right to the truth."

"I'm not afraid," Noelle readily proclaimed.

"I'd like to know," Alyss said.

"Me too," Cullen added.

One by one, Eira locked eyes with them, seeking hesitation. Finding none, she drew a trembling breath. But the words locked up, her throat becoming a vault. Where would she start? Where could she? What if someone was listening now?

"Are you sure you want to tell us?" Alyss whispered.

"I need to," Eira decided. "I've kept too much from you all… I should have opened up to you long ago about Marcus, about everything. And I didn't. Holding in my emotions—my truths— was part of how I ended up in this mess."

"It's not your fault." Alyss rested a hand on her back.

"Thank you for saying so, but it is." If Eira had made peace with Marcus's death earlier, she might not have run off after Ducot. She might not have been so reckless in her pursuit of Ferro. "I was thinking only about myself and revenge before. And now, because of that, you're all in danger."

"So you've told us." Noelle's voice had become heavier. The gravity of the situation was slowly seeping into her.

"Have any of you heard of the Pillars yet?"

Alyss and Noelle shook their heads no.

"I heard something," Cullen whispered. "In that, I overheard the name mentioned at one of my father's stupid dinners after you'd gone missing." He looked guilty for dining while she was captive. As if she didn't full well know how Yemir was.

"You didn't have a choice," Eira breathed, resting her fingers lightly on his hand.

"Still…" He seemed to readily accept that she'd accurately surmised his thoughts. "But it was just a mention. No details."

"The first thing you all have to know is that the Pillars are ready to do anything to undermine Lumeria…" Eira began telling them everything she knew about the Pillars, stopping when her throat was hoarse and Alyss bounced up to fetch her water.

"You came to all these realizations when you were kidnapped?" Cullen's brow furrowed.

"More or less…" Eira had been debating how much to tell them about the Court of Shadows. They were already targeted by the Pillars. But joining the court should be their choice. Yet, how could she give them that choice without going back on her word to the court and exposing them? No, them joining the court or not wasn't her choice, it was Deneya's and the other Specters'.

Biting her lip, Eira hoped they would understand her cageyness. "There are some things I can't tell you just yet. For your safety and the safety of others… I hope you can all accept that."

"Just what did you get yourself into?" Alyss whispered. Eira gave her a tired smile.

"The night that I disappeared, I wasn't kidnapped from the manor… I sneaked out to chase after the Pillars. I had reason to believe I knew of a meeting. Something I, *uh*, heard in the Archives." The lie stung a bit. But she'd drawn the line at keeping her word to the Court of Shadows and keeping her dealings with them a secret. Besides, it wasn't the court threatening her friends. "I had reason to believe that Ferro would be at this meeting, and I was right."

Alyss let out a soft gasp. Cullen met Eira's eyes with a mix of hurt and rage. He knew what Ferro had done in extreme detail. He wanted revenge as badly as she did.

"But I was captured…"

It must have taken an hour for her to tell them everything that transpired. Even skipping over some of the harder parts, or glossing over some of the uglier bits, the tale seemed to drag on forever. Eira could feel the darkness closing in around her as she told them about the pit. Her words were shakier, messier, when she spoke about Ferro. She went into the least amount of detail there.

A slimy shame coated her skin at the mere mention of Ferro's name. Now freed, what she had to do and say to escape seemed too extreme. *There had to have been another way*, a part of her mind insisted, *but instead you allowed that wretched man to think he owns you.* Eira smothered the internal voice. She had done what it took to survive. She was strong enough to live with the consequences.

"…and so, come morning, I'll have to blame the morphi and keep the appearance the Pillars want me to. Otherwise you're all in grave danger. That's why I had to tell you the truth now. I owed it to you all."

Alyss was crying again. Noelle seemed shaken to her very core. Cullen's face had started out horrified and shifted to rage; now his expression was cold and stony. Eira waited for someone to say something.

Had she just condemned her friends to their deaths by trying to lean on them when she hadn't in months?

"I hope…you all don't hate me now," she said finally.

"I'm glad you told us." Noelle folded her arms. "These scum are still out there and we need to be ready for them."

Eira ran a hand through her hair. "I'm so sorry, for everything."

"You can't change what's been done." Cullen leaned forward. Without hesitation, he placed his fingers on the back of her hand resting on her knee. "But we'll be here for you going forward. Thank you for telling us."

"And for Mother's sake, listen to me for once in your life and stop being so reckless." Alyss gave her a squeeze. "But yes, we're here for you. We'll make sure we all stay safe."

"Thank you," Eira murmured, leaning into her friends as her fingers moved against Cullen's. He pulled away the second she began to take his hand, staring out the window with that same dark and guarded expression. The movement was a strike to her gut. There was clearly much more left to be said between them.

"You should go back to bed," Alyss instructed. "You'll have a long day tomorrow, no doubt, and you'll need your strength."

Eira allowed Alyss to help her back into bed. Cullen and

Noelle bid their good nights and retreated to their rooms. Eira sank into her sheets as Alyss pulled the duvet up to her chin.

"Alyss," Eira murmured.

"What do you need?"

"Stay with me tonight? I don't want to be alone…"

"Of course."

Alyss walked around the bed and slid between the sheets next to Eira. On occasion, they would have sleepovers in the Tower, cramming into one bed, or one of them sleeping on the floor. Alyss was always fast to fall asleep and her familiar, soft snoring was just what Eira needed to close her eyes.

She was among friends. She was safe, for now. But she'd have to fight to preserve that safety, starting first thing in the morning by finding Ducot.

· CHAPTER ·

EIGHTEEN

THE NEXT MORNING was a blur. Eira woke to an attentive Alyss, who insisted on checking over her status before Meru's clerics. "They're very good," Alyss admitted, "But I'll feel better if I have a hand in your care." Eira was too grateful to have her friend's concern to fight against her persistence.

When Alyss was satisfied, she went to get Levit and the healers. Eira's room became a revolving door. Levit was first in, alone, to express his worries and apologies for not keeping her safe. Eira wasn't sure what he was apologizing for…she was the one who had run off. She tried to assuage him, but he'd hear none of it and her guilt was a heavy burden as Levit's eyes filled with tears. He refused to let her out of his sight even when the clerics entered.

After being poked, prodded, healed, and healed some more, the clerics were finally satisfied. Eira thought that might have been the end of it, but then a whole patrol of the city guard, Swords of Light, and queen's knights entered. She was surprised Deneya wasn't among them. But Eira remembered what Deneya had said—if they appeared too close, it'd draw too many questions. And if there was one thing she knew about Deneya, it was that the woman would find Eira when she was ready for her.

Eira told the story the Pillars had instructed her to say. As she spun the tale, she looked each of the soldiers in their eyes, wondering if one of them was a Pillar in disguise, here to make sure she did as told. She wished she'd had more opportunities to get better looks at the Pillars' faces. But between the blindfold and trauma, their features were murky in her memory.

How deep did their infiltration run? Not knowing meant

everyone was a suspect. Ferro had been the one to first teach her how dangerous trust was. Now she needed that lesson more than ever.

"I'm sorry," Eira said, voice cracking from overuse. "I've told you everything I know and remember."

"You're certain it was only two morphi men?" the knight who had been interrogating her questioned for what felt like the hundredth time.

"I don't know much about this world, but morphi are distinct with their glowing dots instead of eyebrows." Eira looked to Levit for relief. "May I have some water, please?"

"Of course." Levit went over to a basin and pitcher the clerics had left. As he filled a cup and brought it back to her, he spoke. "I think this has been more than enough."

"We're trying to get every bit of information we can. Even something that seems insignificant can help find the perpetrators." The knight closed the small journal he'd been taking notes in. "If you remember anything else, no matter how small, tell it to one of the guards stationed here at the manor."

"Of course."

"After being taken from the safety of these walls, I know you might not believe me, but this place is secure. We have doubled down on our patrols," he said.

All Eira heard was that it'd be harder than ever to sneak away if she needed. Though, after her last nighttime venture, Eira had no plans on escaping anytime soon. "Thank you. I'll do my best."

"Then, for now, we'll take our leave." The knight nodded, motioned to the soldiers, and they all filtered out of her room. Levit followed behind them and Eira was alone. The endless barrage of healers and knights had taken most of the day. Her friends brought her dinner and they ate together in the Solaris common area before Eira went back to bed to continue her recovery. While part of her had been hoping to report to the shadows, the other part was grateful to have the night to rest. The shadows would come for her when they were ready.

The next morning, she rose late and felt almost completely back to normal. As she dressed, her thoughts kept drifting over to where she'd found the dagger containing Ferro's voice. How had it ended up hidden in the mantle? She knew the Pillars had infiltrated this place. Eira shuddered, thinking of Ferro wandering the rooms before the competitors arrived, thinking of traps he could lay, wondering where she might be staying.

If she could just get her hands on the dagger again, perhaps she could listen more closely for any other words that could be locked within it. Her magic still felt sharp and potent, ever since the pit. If she tried to listen again, she was sure she could—

A knock interrupted her thoughts.

"Come in," Eira said, tugging on her clothes to make sure they were all in place.

"Oh, sorry to intrude." A kind woman with graying hair and lilac eyes poked in her nose.

Eira bristled instantly. The first time she'd seen the woman laying out breakfast, Eira hadn't made the connection. Neither had she the next time. But now, seeing those eyes so close after seeing Ferro…

"I thought you'd already stepped out for the day." She smiled, genuine and sage, and Eira's worries evaporated. She was being paranoid. On closer inspection, the woman's eyes weren't much like Ferro's at all.

"I was just about to. Is there something I can help you with?"

"No, I wanted to make sure you didn't need anything."

"You came because you thought I stepped out…but also wanted to make sure I didn't need anything?" The worried feeling was creeping back.

The woman chuckled softly, lines wrinkling around the corners of her eyes. "Apologies. I know you've been through a lot; I shouldn't have confused you further."

"I'm not confus—"

"I'm Mistress Harrot." The woman bowed her head, bringing

a hand over her chest. "I oversee this manor and its occupants on behalf of Queen Lumeria."

Lumeria's ranks had been infiltrated. "Levit mentioned you. So how might I help you again?"

"Even though I thought you stepped out for the day and it was futile, I still thought I would try and catch you to see if you needed anything. My duties kept me busy until now. But as the keeper of the house, I'd feel wretched if I wasn't attentive to my guest's needs."

"I'm fine, thank you." Eira forced a smile. Part of her felt guilty for being suspicious of everyone. Part of her had learned better. "If you'll excuse me."

"Yes, of course." The woman retreated and Eira brushed past her, shutting her door and wishing she could lock it. But she wasn't in possession of anything secret, was she? Her heart was racing as she scoured her memories of the things she'd had in her room. There were Adela's journals, hidden under her bed. But everyone already expected her to be Adela's spawn. And she could always feign ignorance as to their author, if it came to that.

"If you need anything, you just let me know." Mistress Harrot departed.

Eira tried to shake the unsettled feeling and was only mildly successful. But suspicions could wait. Food was the more pressing matter. Food, and Ducot.

With her heart thundering in her throat, Eira opened the main door of the Solaris common area. There was no sign of where Harrot had gone off to. A bored-looking soldier straightened at her presence. He wasn't one of the people who had been interrogating her yesterday. Eira didn't recognize him as one of the Pillars, either.

There were more soldiers placed at every door along the stairs and two at the main entry. She wound down to the common areas that overlooked the river. It was noisier than she expected and Eira hesitated on the stairs. If she could face Ferro, the Pillars, and their Champion and live to tell the tale, she could survive facing the competitors at large after what happened.

The moment she came into view, every conversation hushed and every eye was on her. The competitors sat in groups according to the nation they belonged to. Eira's eyes grazed over the draconi, elfin, and humans that must be from the Republic of Qwint, to land on the group of morphi. She knew her gaze lingered for a fraction too long, but Eira couldn't help it. The relief she felt at seeing Ducot, even if his face was expressionless at her presence, was too overwhelming. Eira quickly averted her eyes before anyone would think to question why she was so focused on a random morphi she'd only spoken to a handful of times.

Eira crossed to the table of food, pretending not to notice them all still staring. Taking a plate, she began to fill it generously. Her hand hovered over the stone-cut oatmeal, trembling slightly. It looked a little too much like the gruel she'd been served by the Pillars.

That room flashed before her eyes and, for a moment, she hadn't escaped. Eira pressed her lids shut and blinked with purpose, dislodging the thought. For months, she'd been haunted by the darkness that Marcus had never surfaced from. The last thing she was about to do was allow the Pillars to smother her again.

"Would someone like to fill the blind man in on why no one is saying anything?" Ducot asked dryly, the words shattering the tension.

The morphi competitors snorted and then burst out laughing.

"Eira is back," Graff said, finally.

"Didn't we already know she was back?" Ducot shoved a hunk of bread into his mouth. "What's the big deal?"

"It's the first time we're seeing her?" Graff shrugged.

"*Ah.* Seeing. No wonder I don't get it." Ducot snickered. "Welcome back, Eira." The words sounded almost bored, but Eira knew they were meant sincerely.

"Thanks, Ducot," Eira said with a small smile. "It's good to be back."

"Good to have you."

"Welcome back."

"Welcome back…"

The other competitors stood from their chairs, coming over to her, introducing themselves, asking how she felt, and wishing her well. A few were brave enough to ask her for an account of her experiences. Cullen and Alyss jumped up almost at the same time as the inquiry.

"She needs to sit and get some food so she can regain her strength." Alyss seemed like she was ready to beat the other competitors away with a stick.

Cullen, ever the diplomat's son, was more tactful in his approach. "We are all grateful for your concern. It speaks to the spirit of this competition—what brought us all together, the Treaty of Five Kingdoms. Now is truly a monument to—"

"No one cares, Cullen. Spare us your speech," Noelle drawled, not looking up from the papers she was reading. "Come and finish your breakfast."

Cullen glanced between Eira, Alyss, Noelle, and everyone else. Eira had never seen him look so shocked. A snort escaped her and it was the sound of the floodgates opening for laughter. Before she knew it, Cullen and everyone else were laughing along with her as well.

Except for the draconi.

Eira couldn't help but notice that none of their party had come up to greet her. They regarded her warily and whispered among themselves. A wicked smirk slithered across Prince Harkor's face. Unease coursed through her at the expression, but Eira worked to ignore it. She had other things to worry about. Whatever game Harkor was playing would show itself as a concern or not in its own time.

"Did you really need to embarrass me like that?" Cullen asked Noelle as he sat.

"I didn't embarrass you, I saved you from yourself. You're welcome." Noelle flipped over one of the papers. It seemed to be a collection of information—news organized underneath bolded type. Such things were becoming popular in Solaris following the introduction of the press from Meru, but they were still reserved for the wealthy. Eira scanned the writing curiously. "No one cares about your political speeches; they don't win anyone over."

"Don't let my father hear you say that."

"Your father wants so desperately for you to get in my pants I doubt he'd care what I say to you." Noelle gave Cullen a smile that was more like a sneer.

Eira coughed into her drink, and it wasn't just because the juice was uncomfortably thicker than she was expecting. "I'm sorry?"

"Oh, don't worry about me. I'm not a threat to you. Cullen isn't my type." Noelle gave her a look.

"I'm not—why would I? What's your—Cullen and I aren't—"

"*Mmhmm.*" Noelle rolled her eyes and returned to the paper. Cullen's face was scarlet.

Alyss leaned forward eagerly. "And just what is your type, Noelle?"

"Why would I tell you that?"

"I know a lot about romance so maybe I could help you find the perfect person." Alyss waggled her eyebrows.

Eira resisted pointing out that she doubted Noelle would count reading a bunch of romance novels as "knowing a lot."

"Says the woman who has never been with a man in her life." Noelle rolled her eyes.

"By *choice*," Alyss insisted. "Every young man in the Tower I was interested in seemed to only care about *one thing*. And when I told them that I did not care in the slightest for it, they were turned away from me. So I'm waiting to find someone either like me, or someone who loves me so much it doesn't matter to them."

Noelle was intrigued enough to put down her paper. "When you say 'like you' and 'cares about one thing' you mean…"

"The 'one thing' is the bedroom dance between the sheets," Alyss clarified. "All matters of the carnal nature."

"And you don't want such things?"

"No."

"At all?" Noelle leaned forward, obviously fascinated. "Ever?"

"Never, not even a little."

Eira fought a grin and slid the paper to face her as the conversation continued. She'd had a similar discussion with Alyss long ago and knew Noelle's next question before it was asked.

"But you read so many romance novels."

"I like romance—I *want* romance. I'm on a quest to find a great love story. But not sex. They're not the same thing, you know. I mean, they can overlap. But it's possible to want one and not the other. I want the romance and not all the touching bits."

"Huh." Noelle folded her arms and leaned back in her chair. "I suppose that makes sense."

"Of course it does, I said it, after all." Alyss preened.

"What the…" Eira whispered, lifting the paper. Her shock silenced the table.

"What is it?" Cullen asked.

"They already found the kidnappers." Eira pointed at the headline; it read: TWO MORPHI APPREHENDED FOR KIDNAPPING. "They're going to put them to death in the Queen's Square later today."

Silence fell across the table as they all stared at the ink. The paper was suddenly as heavy as a tombstone in Eira's hands. For some reason, she couldn't stop thinking about the young man who had been attending her during her time with the Pillars. He'd joined their group of his own accord, right? He hadn't been forced, coerced, or brainwashed? Who were the two morphi that the Pillars had chosen as lambs for the slaughter?

"You're happy, right?" Noelle said, somewhat forcefully. "These are the people who kidnapped you."

Eira pried her eyes away and struggled to find words. Noelle stared at her with severity, as though she were trying to remind Eira with a look alone what was at stake—that Eira still had a role to play. Eira swallowed thickly and forced a nod.

People were watching and every action was a performance.

"Yes, of course. I merely didn't expect for them to be found so soon." She folded over the paper, unable to read the rest. She likely should. A good shadow would stay informed. But Eira didn't have the will. Her gaze drifted beyond the wafting curtains of the archways and past the guards positioned throughout the terraced gardens. "I think I need to go to the square and see it," she whispered.

"What?" Alyss said with a gasp. "Are you sure that's a good idea?"

Eira nodded.

"There's no way they're going to let you leave." Cullen frowned.

"I'll explain it to them." Eira took a deep breath. "I need it as closure. These individuals wronged me. I want to be there when they are brought to justice. I deserve that much." What Eira really wanted to say was: the plan she pitched to the Pillars would cause two men to be put to death. Not looking away when the time came was the right thing to do.

Her friends all exchanged glances. Finally, Cullen spoke in what sounded like a consensus they'd wordlessly reached. "Fine, but if you're going, we're going with you."

Alyss nodded aggressively. "Strength in numbers."

"I'm morbidly curious." Noelle took a sip of her tea. "I want to see who we're up against." The sentiment was met with noises of agreement.

"It's settled then. I'll talk with Levit and get it sorted," Eira decreed. She'd succeeded in confirming Ducot was alive. But the manor was clearly too crowded between all the competitors and guards for them to get in a word now. She trusted he would come to her when the time was right. So, for now, she'd head to the Queen's Square.

NINETEEN

I T WAS EASIER than she'd expected to convince Levit to let her go to the Queen's Square. When Eira had made it clear she wanted to travel with all her friends, plus him, plus whatever knights needed to come, *plus* the senators, it was difficult for him to argue on the grounds of safety concerns. Moreover, he reasoned the square would be closely monitored by a strong military presence. His only rule before they left was that she had to stay close to him and the rest of their party.

It was clear that it was a well-thought command when they stepped into the city.

After seeing Risen dormant since her arrival, Eira was caught off guard by just how alive it now was. People, mounts, and carriages had flooded the streets. Men and women strolled arm in arm, laughing underneath the shade of parasols. Lightspinning sparked in every direction, hovering over the backs of elfin's hands, on their fingers like rings, even around some of their necks.

This was the Meru she'd dreamed of. A place alive with culture and magic and people that had been previously relegated to the pages of loaned tomes from Levit and her fantasies. Unfortunately, Eira couldn't summon joy for any of it. These people carried on as though everything was fine. The world had returned to normal for them. The people acting against the competitors had been captured—Lumeria clearly had no publicly justifiable reason to keep the city under lockdown anymore. They didn't know about the forces seeking to upend their pleasant lives lurking just underneath the surface of Meru's carefully mortared streets.

"Is the city no longer under restrictions?" Eira asked one of the guards escorting them.

"No, much to the relief of a restless populace, they were lifted this morning. Your kidnappers were the ones who had made direct threats to the competitors," the knight confirmed her suspicions. "Now that they have been brought to justice, the citizenry is free to roam."

"Are you sure it was only the two of them?"

The guard arched his eyebrows at her. "You had said there were only two, and we didn't see signs of others at their hideout. Unless you have other information?"

"No, of course not," Eira mumbled. Alyss grabbed her hand and Cullen gave her a look from the corner of his eye.

They knew as well as she did the Pillars were still out there. Eira glanced around, searching for a face she might have seen in the Champion's throne room. Of course, she didn't recognize anyone, but the feeling of walking among her former captors— among the people who still held her by an invisible leash—made it hard to breathe throughout the entire trek to the Queen's Square.

The castle of Meru was on the hilltop opposite the Archives of Yargen. Eira had seen its silhouette against the night sky when she'd sneaked through the city with Ducot. But seeing it in the daylight was an altogether different experience. Luckily, Eira could take in the majesty of the building without the memories of her night with Ducot haunting her too viciously since they'd come up to the castle on a different route.

Noelle let out a low whistle, tilting her head back. "That is *almost* as impressive as the castle in Norin."

"Did we see the same castle when we left? Because this is easily at least twice as impressive," Cullen said with a grin.

"I'm surprised you're so uncultured for a lord." Noelle rolled her eyes.

"It's almost the height of the great trees of Soricium," Alyss murmured. "But those ancient trees are naturally growing. It's incredible to think this was made by the hands of men."

None of the paintings or black and white drawings Eira had seen in books could have done the castle justice. Sheer walls stretched up into a jagged line of spires and turrets, creating an imposing facade. The central keep had two wings stretching out from either side that split into a T shape capped by rounded towers. Those outer towers connected to a thick wall that ringed the entire hilltop.

They crossed underneath the main gate and into a courtyard where others had come to a stop. The courtyard was bisected by another wall, a heavy portcullis shut tight. In the center of the square was a raised platform, vacant…for now.

As the crowd grew, the knights who had been their escort pulled in tighter. Eira was wedged between Cullen and Alyss, and she reached out instinctively with both hands. Her palm clasped around Alyss's. Her fingers laced against Cullen's, drawing her attention to him. His lips were slightly parted, as if in surprise. The expression, filled with longing, reminded Eira she had so much still that she wanted to say to him.

"Cullen."

"Eira," he breathed in reply, her name barely audible over the din of the crowd.

"I want—"

"Look, they're competitors!" an elfin interrupted, far too eager.

"Competitors?"

"Where from?" another asked.

"We are from the Solaris Empire," Yemir declared, too loudly for Eira's taste.

"Father," Cullen hissed.

"Stand tall," Yemir whispered back in harsh reply. His eyes darted to their laced fingers. While waving to some of the elfin onlookers, he slapped at their hands. "And don't engage in anything that could draw too many questions," he said, mostly to Cullen, but his glare ended on her.

Eira unlaced her fingers. Cullen tried to hold fast, but she wouldn't let him. She was not interested in having this battle, not here, and not now. She had other fights to engage in and other matters to be concerned over. Yemir was suddenly the least of her worries.

"An honor to meet you," an elfin said, stepping forward.

"I've never met one of Solaris," someone else said. "Of course I've seen your princess, but—"

"We're excited for the tournament."

"Wasn't one of you the one who was kidnapped? Dastardly plot that was."

"So glad to see all four of you here."

"Is it true that you are charged by the magic of Raspian?" a woman asked, causing Eira to cringe.

On and on their questions went. The crowd seemed to close in on them and Eira pulled Alyss closer. Cullen and Noelle took defensive positions as well, guarding Eira from the relentless inquiries. Levit and Yemir tried to take the lead, but it was impossible to hear and answer everyone at once.

Then, horns blared, and a hush overtook the crowd.

With the attention off of them, Eira could breathe easier. She turned her own focus to the portcullis as it slowly ground open with the cries of metal on metal and the grunting of men pulling heavy levers.

Behind the portcullis was a legion of queen's knights. They marched forward, slowly. In their captivity were two young men, both morphi, bound and gagged. Eira didn't know if the gags made any difference for the morphi's ability to shift. But they looked imposing and forceful.

After the prisoners and knights was another honor guard. And behind them were two people Eira had seen only a few times before—the crown princess, Vi Solaris, and her betrothed, Taavin, the Voice of Yargen. Vi stood tall, as a crown princess should. On her brow was a golden crown that looked like a miniature version of the sun crown the Emperor wore. Fiery tongues stretched toward the sky. Taavin was dressed in the regalia of the Faithful—clothing that matched Solaris' nobility impeccably with all its whites and golds.

Behind them, after another line of guards, was the queen herself. Eira suppressed a gasp as she laid eyes on the woman who ruled Meru. Well, she didn't *quite* lay eyes on her. Lumeria was covered from head to toe in layers of sheer fabrics, their weightless movements on the breezes like a haze of living smoke that covered the queen. The cloth obscured her face and body, reducing her to a silhouette—at best. But she wore an ornate crown of woven silver and gold that left no question as to who she was and what her position meant.

Every elfin dropped to their knee as the queen passed. They bowed their heads in subservience. Eira felt a tingle rush across her flesh as Lumeria's head twisted and she took in the gathered crowd. Even if she was just one of hundreds, Lumeria had seen her, more or less.

Behind Lumeria were the morphi, led up onto the platform in shackles. The knights manhandled them to their knees in the center of the stage. Lumeria stood before them. Taavin and Vi were off to the side. A row of knights closed in around them.

Eira couldn't take her eyes off one of the young men. Sure enough, she recognized him. They'd hardly exchanged more than a few words. He hadn't exactly been friendly to her. But he hadn't been cruel either when he could've been.

She didn't care about him. He had made his choices and they led him to this moment. She couldn't feel sympathy for the Pillars. These were the people who had killed her brother.

But nights with Ferro whispered across her memories. He had taken her in with little more than smiles, looks, and charming words. He had made her feel wanted and special in a way no one else had. That had been enough to make her loyal to him and blind to all his faults. What were these young men's stories? How had the world treated them? Had they suffered a life of torment until the moment the Pillars took them in with their serene smiles and promises of belonging?

"Eira?" Alyss whispered. "Are you all right?"

"Yes, fine, why?" Eira pushed the words past a tight chest.

"You're crushing my hand."

Eira looked down at their hands, still clutched tight. "Sorry." She tried to release her fingers but Alyss wouldn't let her. Her friend held fast.

"Don't apologize. We can go if you need to."

Noelle and Cullen were noticing their conversation. They both gave Eira concerned glances.

"I'm fine, really." Eira looked to the stage with determination. If these men were going to die because of a plot she concocted then she needed to be here to witness it.

"Are those the men?" Levit asked.

Eira could only nod. She was certain there were Pillars all around her. Perhaps it was a Pillar that pointed out her presence to begin with as a test.

Lumeria raised her hand, a curtain of fabric catching on the breeze with the motion. The crowd fell into an even deeper thrall. No one said a word.

"You have acted against the crown—my own and the crown of Solaris," Lumeria said softly. Her voice was like the whispering of wind through willow branches, as cold as moonlight, as hard as steel. "You have conspired to act against the Treaty of Five Kingdoms by endangering our revered guests from Solaris. For these crimes, it has been decreed you shall be put to death. Do you have any last words?"

The two men continued to look skyward, straight into the sun, smiling in an unnerving, placid way.

"Her light warms," one of them finally said. "Yargen shines down upon us. Even when we have forsaken her ways, her goodness does not abandon us." His eyes dropped from the sky and onto the crown princess, Vi Solaris. For her part, the princess didn't even flinch, but Eira's stomach clenched on her behalf. The man had a slightly murderous, unhinged glint to his eye. "You are the true agent of Raspian and your roots run deep. Beware…

Beware to you and to everyone who aligns themselves with you. Her holy fire is coming, and only those who stand on the pillars of truth, justice, and light will be spared."

The crowd looked on in stunned silence. Lumeria turned her head to the crown princess and gave a small nod. Vi stepped forward.

"I am not afraid of fire." As she spoke, flames danced up her bare arms for emphasis. They ringed her neck and tangled in her hair like a lover. Vi Solaris moved with the same grace and power as her father.

"She truly has the blood of Fiera within her," Noelle breathed in awe. Fiera Ci'Dan was Vi's grandmother, and argued to be the greatest Firebearer to ever live.

"Your people were the ones wronged," Lumeria said to Vi. "Justice falls to you."

The crown princess wore an emotionless mask as she lifted a hand and two columns of fire engulfed the men. Their screams echoed across the square. The stench of burning flesh singed everyone's noses, causing most to turn away and some to gag. None from Solaris averted their eyes.

Eira watched as the silhouettes of the men burned away and, when the fire vanished, there was nothing left but ash.

E IRA SAT UP in her room long after everyone else had gone to bed. She'd told Alyss she'd join her if she couldn't sleep, or was plagued by nightmares. But sleep was still far from her.

Ducot would come to her tonight, she was certain of it. The Court of Shadows would want to see her sooner rather than later, and it had already been a day and then some since her return. But while she waited, she stared out the window, perched on the edge of her bed, and looked past the glass and back to the events of the day. She saw the men as they burned; their screams filled her ears. Yet, within her chest was the void of the pit. The darkness that had encapsulated that night with Marcus, hardened by the Pillars into something so unfeeling that Eira was certain a corner of her had broken beyond repair.

Whenever she needed to, she could retreat there. She had turned the solitude and darkness into her weapon. If necessary it could numb and harden her more than ice could ever hope to do. It could hone her magic and make her powers sharper than any blade they could ever wield against her.

Holding up her hand, Eira envisioned her magic pooling in her palm. It tipped back and forth as she twisted her wrist—a little ocean of her own making. Yes, magic had been *different* since the pit. She'd tapped into something there that the Pillars hadn't been intending for her to find.

Or…maybe they had. Ferro had thought she could take powers away and that was part of what made her useful to him.

"Steal magic," Eira murmured, and reached under her bed, relieved to find the journals just as she'd left them. She knew she had seen something jotted down about closing a sorcerer's channel. "Here it is. Closing a sorcerer's channel..." Eira skimmed the page, beginning to learn magic her uncles would've never taught.

A soft scratching finally broke her from her reading. Eira was faced with a familiar mole when she opened the door. Ducot barely glanced at her before dashing off, disappearing behind the mantle. Eira moved silently through the moonlit room. She waved a hand, summoned an illusion around her, released the latch, and stepped into the hidden passage.

They made their way between the walls. Eira pushed her magic through her feet, using her ice to help guide the way so she didn't trip and fall. When they had finally descended underneath the manor, a pulse of magic surrounded the mole and Ducot—the man—stood before her.

He rounded on her. Eira jumped back, startled. His face was twisted in anger; his scars accented by the pale light of the glowing dots on his forehead. He gripped her collar, yanking her toward him.

"You *lying* little Dark Isle dweller. It's because of people like you that those of us on Meru are skeptical if you even know *how* to keep your word," he snarled.

Eira pursed her lips. He clearly had more to say. She was right.

"Because of you, the whole mission was compromised. More than that, the court's entire operations were compromised."

"They were alerted to your presence before mine."

"But *I* could give them the slip, unlike your clumsy human feet. If you had just waited like you were supposed to..." He yanked her closer, both hands now at her throat. Oddly, for all his rage, Eira didn't feel threatened by him in the slightest. Not because Ducot couldn't hurt her. But, for some reason, she truly believed he wouldn't. It was nothing like when Ferro's hands were at her neck and she could envision him just continuing to *squeeze*. "Do you know how long it took for us to find the information on that safe house of theirs? Do you have any idea how long it might take for us to relocate them? Do you have any idea how many shadows lost their lives to make that mission possible and you just come waltzing in at the end, deliver an item, and think you're entitled to go because of some foolish vendetta?"

"Avenging my brother isn't foolish," she snarled, defensive even though she knew he was right about everything else.

"You're not the only one who wants vengeance!" His milky eyes were wide and shining. Ducot hung his head in the wake of her silence. His fingers loosened, some, but didn't leave her throat. "That was *my* chance," he whispered. "You…you ruined it."

"What?"

Ducot lifted his face, staring at her for a long moment. "You want to know how my face was scarred? Really?"

"I'm guessing it wasn't from saving a princess?" Eira arched her eyebrows.

Ducot shook his head.

"Then only if you *want* to tell me the truth."

He chuckled darkly. "You think you can handle the truth? It's darker than you could imagine."

Eira snorted.

"Really? You scoff at me?" His fingers tightened.

"I'm not afraid of darkness. Not anymore. Not after the pit. Not after I watched my brother die at Ferro's hands."

Something about her stone-cold tone, her stare, finally had his fingers unraveling. Ducot stepped away, straightening and looking somewhat apologetic. And, for what might be the first time, Eira felt like they were on equal footing. He might not like her, not anymore. Or agree with her. But maybe they were beginning to at least understand each other a little better.

"Those of the Dark Isle aren't the only ones that the Faithful so readily associate with Raspian." Ducot leaned against the wall, staring at nothing. "The morphi and draconi also have that esteemed privilege and, for hundreds of years, it meant we were hunted. We didn't have the benefit of a small sea and barrier isles.

It was why we retreated into the Twilight Forest. Why the then king used the royal shift to pull our city outside of this world—but not quite into the next—to create a haven for us where we couldn't be found."

Eira didn't quite understand what he meant by "royal shift," or how a city could be between worlds. She was still grasping how the shift worked in general. Some things on Meru were best to take at someone's word and figure out later. Now wasn't the time to inquire about magical logistics.

"Ulvarth, the man who then led the Swords of Light, started a campaign against the morphi, claiming the woman who was the Voice at that time had decreed it as Yargen's holy order." Ducot lifted his hand, touching his scars lightly. "They came for us with their swords and Lightspinning. They hunted us, tortured us. I was helpless as my family, friends, everyone who had dared make a settlement in the forest on the outskirts of the Twilight Kingdom died around me."

"How did you survive?" Eira whispered.

"Barely." He chuckled darkly. "I should have died. They left me for dead. But life clung to me stubbornly until Rebec found me."

"Rebec?" Eira remembered the female morphi who had been introduced as Deneya's right hand and one of the three Specters of the Court of Shadows.

"She had been trailing the Swords of Light. Lumeria had known of their treachery and had sent Rebec to warn King Noct. But it all happened a little too slowly, and a little too late."

"So you vowed vengeance and joined the Court of Shadows then and there," Eira reasoned. Ducot nodded. She chuckled softly.

"Something funny?"

"You and I…we're very similar, aren't we?"

"Deneya said so when she informed me we would be working closely together as competitors."

"Ferro killed my brother."

"So you've mentioned."

"He tried to kill me, too." Eira sighed heavily. Ducot pushed away from the wall as if sensing her change in demeanor, now listening more attentively. Eira met his eyes, though she wasn't sure if he could see the motion or not. "Even still, and most importantly, you're right...I endangered you and disrespected the other shadows with what I did. All I was thinking about was killing Ferro with my own two hands and avenging my brother. It was selfish of me."

"Did you?" Ducot whispered.

Eira laughed bitterly and shook her head. "When I had him...I couldn't."

"It's hard to kill a man."

"I've killed someone before." Eira wasn't sure why she was trying to defend herself or point out that part of her history. She was far from proud of it. "But...it was an accident," she clarified.

"*Ah*. Killing with intent, as you know now, is something very different."

"Are you going to tell me not to when the time presents itself again?"

Ducot shook his head. "No, I'm not sure if you'd even listen if I did. So I'm going to tell you to be ready next time. Because if you endanger my life again, and the Court of Shadows, *and* don't even get your mark... The Pillars will be the least of your worries."

"I came out of this with information for the court, at least. I might not have killed Ferro. But I did get *something*."

"Let's hope it's good, for your sake. The Specters will be a lot harder to subdue than me." Ducot put his hands in his pockets and started down the stairs. "Oddly enough, I'm beginning to like you. It'd be a real shame if I had to kill you." He sounded sincere, even though he'd just been at her throat. It felt as if the air had been cleared between them, the pressure valve released, and there was no need to linger.

Eira snorted. She really shouldn't find her own death so darkly amusing. "You're beginning to like a woman who nearly got you killed?"

"I have shit taste in women. That's been long established."

Her laughter echoed in the halls around them, quieting long before they reached the heavy, locked door to the Court of Shadows.

Ducot escorted her inside. The court was alarmingly empty. Only a few shadows were visible in the roosts high above, where the sailcloths were suspended from. They looked down on her both literally and figuratively. She saw one spit as she passed.

Eira brought her eyes forward and passed through the tunnel that led straight into the Specters' war room.

"Shut the door," Deneya said without turning. Lorn and Rebec stood on the opposite side of the table, facing them. Rebec wore an expression of disgust. Lorn's face was blank, and somehow Eira found that more unnerving than outright anger.

The closing of the heavy door was as solemn as a bell tolling.

"I'd ask what you were thinking, but I know you weren't." Deneya straightened away from the table with a sigh. She didn't sound angry; she sounded disappointed, and that was far worse. "You have no idea what your antics cost us."

"The Champion—the leader of the Pillars—wants me to find something in the Voice's room at the top of the Archives that mentions *you*." Eira wasted no time.

Deneya turned, brow furrowed. Eira could see her breathing shallow. "Excuse me?"

"You saw the Champion?" Lorn asked skeptically.

"He's real?" Rebec picked her nails with the point of a dagger.

"They took me to what I think is their base of operations— their equivalent of the Court of Shadows."

"And you lived to tell the tale." Rebec sheathed her dagger and folded her arms, suddenly looking impressed, albeit begrudgingly so. "So I suggest you start talking."

Eira looked to Deneya, who gave a nod. Taking a deep breath, Eira began her story with what she'd overheard at the Pillars' meeting, her sorry attempt at fleeing, her captivity, the pit, Ferro, the Champion, and everything between. She didn't have to dance around certain topics like she had with her friends. The Court of Shadows got the unfiltered truth. Ducot was right, she'd endangered many, and baring her ugly truths to them would be a good start at making amends.

When she finished, the four others in the room stood in silence, processing the information.

Ducot was the one to finally break that silence. "Do you think the Champion is *him*?"

"It can't be," Rebec answered sharply. "He's under tight, constant surveillance."

"If he moved, we would know," Lorn added.

"I check on him personally." Deneya got the harsh, final word.

"Who is 'he'?" Eira asked, reminding them she was present and still new enough to not have all the details.

"The man who murdered my kin and scarred my face. The former head of the Swords of Light, Ulvarth." Ducot took a step forward. "I saw him that day and the description matches him perfectly."

"And maybe it's someone using his name and face," Lorn countered sharply. "Ulvarth is no longer a concern."

"Wasn't Ulvarth imprisoned for killing the last Voice and extinguishing the Flame of Yargen?" Eira asked, seeing if her memory served her. Ducot nodded. "And that he claimed he was the Champion of Yargen come again?"

"Exactly, so—"

"So why can't it be him?" Eira looked from Ducot to the Specters. "Surely, all this can't just be coincidence? How can he not be a concern?"

"He had high enough friends to keep him off the executioner's block." Ducot pointed to the ground. "Because of him, the Pillars were spawned in the first place. Of course he would be the one to lead them. He must be—"

"Ulvarth is *dead*," Deneya blurted suddenly, ungraceful

compared to her usual tactfulness. The word seemed to echo in the cavernous space. Ducot staggered backward, as though he'd been struck by it.

"You…he…"

"I killed him myself and disposed of the body," Deneya finished, glancing back at the table, as though she were talking about the weather.

Ducot looked between Lorn and Rebec. Neither of the other Specters seemed surprised in the slightest. His attention landed solely on Rebec. "You…you knew."

"It is one of the most closely guarded secrets of Meru. If word of Ulvarth's death got out—especially given that it would be considered an unjust murder under Lumeria's imprisonment—it would only spur the Pillars on more," Rebec said. "It could cause others to flock to them."

"Unjust?" Ducot's voice rose. "He… He murdered babes in their bed. He slaughtered the last Voice."

"And yet the mere *idea* of him unjustly imprisoned spurred zealots to action," Deneya said with disgust. "Just think of what the Pillars would do if they found out he'd been made a martyr." She listlessly moved the tokens spread about the map of Risen. "Yet, we also couldn't leave him as a loose end."

"Unless they did find out," Eira said softly. All eyes were on her. "A Champion chosen by the goddess's hand is a powerful motivator, a martyr of said Champion even more so… Just think of how it might embolden and empower them if they think they have a Champion martyred and reborn?"

"You don't think…" Rebec whispered, looking between Eira and Deneya.

"You said it yourself, the leader of the Pillars might be someone masquerading as Ulvarth." Eira kept her focus on Deneya, whose usually guarded expression was crumbling.

"Damn it all." Deneya cursed several times under her breath and looked away.

There was a long and heavy silence. All eyes were on the Head

Specter, who was now hunched over the table. Eira could feel the grief and hesitation unfurling like dark wings from Deneya's shoulders.

"What are your orders?" Lorn finally said.

Deneya took a deep breath. "We get Eira to the Archives and she finds something that they might believe has this conversation they're looking for. We follow the Pillars every movement, as they follow her. We use the information Eira has given to us to guide our shadows and see if we can smoke them out before the gala. And we gather our forces in case we can't. Lumeria will announce the pre-tournament ball tomorrow and the Pillars will not be the only ones who will attend ready for battle."

· CHAPTER ·

TWENTY-ONE

HER EYELIDS WERE drooping by the time she returned to the manor. Ducot had other business to attend to, so he'd led her to the main tunnel and trusted her to find her way back. Eira decided to take it as a good sign—that he trusted her to do that much still. The secret passage clicked shut behind her and Eira released the illusion she'd summoned.

The moon hung low in the sky and the shadows were long as she dragged her tired feet across the plush carpets back toward her room. She would get a few hours of sleep, and then wake as refreshed as she could be to start the training Ducot had mentioned the competitors were going to begin engaging in. The city thought everything was fine. Lumeria couldn't keep things locked down forever without arousing too much suspicion. And Adela hadn't been sighted again…

Eira was so lost in her thoughts that she didn't notice the shadowed figure, still as a statue, until he stood from the sofa.

She spun, heart racing. A dagger of ice was in her palm, more magic tangling in her free fingers. A breeze pushed lightly against her hand, holding back the dagger like an invisible palm before she could swing. The man came into focus.

"Cullen?" Eira breathed.

"Sorry for startling you, but I didn't want to wake up everyone by announcing myself," he whispered, barely audible. His eyes held an intensity she hadn't seen from him before, brow slightly furrowed, lips pursed. "Let's step into your room?"

Eira gave a small nod and led the way. As she banished the dagger into the air, he closed the door. Cullen stood, back to her, shoulders pulled up to his ears.

"Is that how you escaped before?"

"What?"

"That passage?"

Eira inhaled slowly. "What passage?"

"Don't play dumb."

"I think you're tired and—"

"I know what I saw." He turned, staring down at her. "I felt your magic when you summoned the illusion from the other side. Waterrunner illusions are only good when the air is still, or they can account for breezes." Cullen twirled his fingers and Eira felt breezes spinning around them. "As soon as I sensed your magic, I summoned just enough to distort the illusion. I saw you."

Eira wasn't sure if she should be flattered that he knew her magic well enough to sense it. Or if she should be bothered by the fact that *she* hadn't sensed *his* magic. Sneaking around just might not be her strong suit and if she didn't learn quickly, the weak links in her skills would kill her.

"Where were you?" Cullen took a step forward.

"Why were you awake?"

"Because I…" He faltered and frowned slightly. "I asked you first."

"I can't tell you," Eira said weakly.

"Enough secrets." He grabbed her shoulders. Eira tried to step away but the backs of her legs hit the footboard of the poster bed. "Your secrets got you taken away. Every night you were gone I dreamed of them torturing you only to find out that there was truth in my worst nightmares." He shook her lightly. "Stop taking risks. Stop sneaking off. You can't—I can't—"

"Can't what?" She stared up at him. Shadows and moonlight clung to the edges of his handsome face—the curve of his strong jaw, the faint stubble that lined his chin.

"I can't spend another night worrying about what might happen to you. I can't knock on your door again to have no answer, to have my panic force me to peek in—just in case—and find your bed empty. I can't sit, debating if it is more of a risk to you to sound the alarm of your absence or to wait and see if you return from whatever it is you've gone off to do."

"If it wasn't important I wouldn't go." Eira grabbed his arms behind his elbows. She felt the tension rippling in his muscles. "You have to believe me."

"I do. But share this burden like you did the Pillars. You don't have to bear it alone."

"They're not my secrets to tell."

"Let me in," he pleaded.

"Cullen—"

"Eira, please, I love you."

Three words, and the world halted. Three magic words and he stole the air from the room, leaving her breathless. Her chest tightened and her eyes burned. She hadn't realized how badly she wanted to hear him say that until he had. Neither did she realize just how terrified it made her.

"I… I'm sorry for springing it on you. I know you have a lot to worry about and I am the last thing you need." How wrong he was. "But I can't spend another night tortured thinking I will never have the chance to tell you."

She was back with the Pillars, sitting on the window bench and swearing to herself that she would work up the nerve to tell him when she returned. She imagined them doing the same thing—staring out different windows—and vowing to make their feelings known when they next had the chance because who knew if it might be their last.

He misinterpreted her silence. "If I have read this wrong… then please, tell me you don't love me. If you won't let me into your heart, then do me the courtesy of giving back the piece of mine you've taken. Because seeing you and wondering is torture. Being around you without you knowing how I feel has been agony. Having you within my grasp but not touching you is like dying a beautiful, horrible death…yet all I want is for you to slay me time and again."

As he spoke, his fingers trailed up her neck. His palms landed on her cheeks and his hands cupped her face. Eira was unable to suppress a shiver at the phantom memory of his fingers tangling in her hair. He was as close as he had been that day at court.

"Do you love me?"

"I…"

"Tell me you don't and I will walk away to repair my heart. But I will still hold you in nothing but esteem," he said, his voice husky and deep.

Ferro told you he loved you as well. Adam told you he loved you. And we both know how well they worked out. Eira pressed her eyes shut, trying to block out the bitter words of her past self. In the darkness, she found the same truth she'd discovered during her time in the pit. She had made a promise to herself. Now was the time to make good on it.

"I don't want to hurt you." Her fingertips danced over his bare arms, feeling the curve of his biceps, hooking and twisting his sleeve.

"You couldn't."

"I am death and danger to everyone close to me. Misfortune might be in my blood." *Absolve me of the pain I might cause you,* she wanted to say, *because it might end up being too much for me to bear.*

"You are everything I could ever want, nothing more or less."

"Cullen—"

"Tell me you don't love me, and you will be free of me. Come dawn, this night can be a forgotten dream, and I will be nothing more than a loyal friend."

She opened her eyes, meeting his. Cullen's nose was almost touching hers. His eyes searched her, wanting, seeking.

"I should," she murmured.

"Only if it's true," he breathed. "Don't break my heart for misplaced good intentions. The only thing I want from you is the truth."

"Don't break *my* heart." Eira met his eyes. "I won't survive it shattering a third time."

"I will never hurt you," he swore to her. "I love you too much to even dream of it."

She looked at him through lashes and heavy lids and found nothing but truth. He had been there when she had been fighting to be a competitor, she had been his support in court when he didn't want to face his father alone, he had been hers after her brother had died. Even after she had tried pushing everyone away, he remained.

"I don't deserve you."

He let out a huff of amusement. "Funny. I think the same of you every day."

"Cullen, I love you," Eira finally admitted. Shivers coursed through her like lightning dancing under her flesh with excited pops and flares. "But I—"

She didn't get a chance to warn him that she was likely destined to bring him heartache. She wasn't able to tell him that she had no hope for them. That there were a million reasons why they were a bad idea.

Cullen's lips pressed against hers lightly, so terribly gentle that it almost elicited a whine from her. She wasn't made for such tenderness any longer. She could hardly recognize it. He took a half step forward, closing the gap between them. His hand shifted. There were the nails brushing against her scalp that she'd been secretly yearning for.

Eira's hands moved up his arms, to his shoulders, and down the wide muscles of his sides. They landed on his waist, pulling him to her. He had been right in that tonight would be a dream. Though it would not be forgotten.

He shifted, parting his lips and deepening the kiss. His tongue slid against hers and Eira moaned ever so softly into his mouth. A chuckle rumbled in the back of his throat, all gravel and sensuality that she had only fantasized he might possess.

When he broke away, it was only for a second before returning his mouth to hers. They kissed until her knees were weak, his face was flushed, and they were both left breathless. He rubbed the tip of his nose against hers, releasing a groan that shot pure heat right down her center.

"I can't tell you how long I've been wanting to do that again," he murmured, kissing both her cheeks. "When I kissed you that day at court…it was the rawest form of magic I've ever known. All I've wanted is to see if the power you had over me could be replicated."

"And was it?"

"In triplicate." His hands had fallen to her hips and they tensed slightly, the pads of his fingers sinking into her flesh before he made lazy circles with his thumbs.

"You know this is a bad idea, don't you?" Eira smoothed her palms over his chest, thinking about pushing him away. She didn't have the strength to. She never would. "You're already at risk because of me. You don't even have any idea of everything I've done…"

"I don't care." Cullen pulled on her slightly, jostling her from her thoughts. "Look at me." She did. "I don't care. I love you, all of you. I want you, all of you. Not just the parts you think are lovely…because I think *all* of you is the most beautiful person— inside and out—that I've ever laid eyes on."

Eira closed her eyes and pressed her forehead against his. Her arms wrapped around his neck and she held herself against his lean and sturdy form. "What about your parents?" she whispered. "Your father will have something to say about us."

"Several things, I imagine. But leave him to me. This isn't his choice to make."

"I don't think it'll be so simple. I don't think any of this will be simple."

"If I wanted simple I wouldn't want you." He chuckled.

The sentiment brought a bitter smile to her face. "I suppose that's true."

"Just promise me you won't leave me in the dark anymore."

"It's for your safety."

"Let me worry about my safety." He pulled away, running a

hand through her hair. There was so much love and adoration in his eyes. Love Eira didn't know if she was worthy of after all she'd done and all that had transpired because of her. "Share your burdens with me. Let me lighten the load."

"There's a group of people," Eira started carefully, "who are working against the Pillars. I'm helping them. If I tell you too much, you might have to be involved with them and listen—please—" she tried to speak over his hasty objections "—this is a group that I involved myself with knowingly. They're good people. But once you know of them, you're a part of them, forever."

"Why do you give me more reasons to worry for you?" He sighed.

"Don't blame me. You're the one who decided to fall in love with me." Just saying so aloud sent shivers up her arms. He was a streak of sunlight breaking through the grime and hardship her world was coated in. Eira was still certain she didn't deserve him. But having him in her arms somehow made everything better, if only slightly.

"You have me there." He grinned and planted a firm kiss on her mouth. "So this group you're involved with, those are the ones you sneaked out to meet?"

"Yes."

"Because of them you were kidnapped?"

"No, that was my own stupidity," Eira said firmly. "I rushed in when I shouldn't have. *I* was the one who risked *their* safety. Not the other way around."

He sighed but seemed to believe her. "Tell me how I can help you?"

Eira made a show of mulling over the question. "Keep my secrets," she started. "Continue helping me as you're able, as I ask."

"My heart and magic are yours."

"Be an ear and a confidant."

"Done and done." He kissed her twice, once on each word.

"Two more things."

"More?" He chuckled.

Eira pressed on, keeping the tone serious. "Firstly, I want you to keep us a secret."

"What?" He narrowed his eyes slightly.

"For your safety," she said. He went to object; she stopped him. "I know you can look after yourself. But you were already a target by being my *friend*. I don't want to think of what threats the Pillars might make if they know I love you. Don't make me even have to hear them." Eira's hands balled in his clothes. The mere idea of the Pillars threatening Cullen twice over because she'd dared to love him was unbearable. "And your father... I believe you when you say you'll handle him and his reactions. But we—I, if I may be selfish—have enough to worry about right now. Let's cross that bridge when we have to and hopefully when our very lives aren't hanging in the balance?"

He relented. "Very well. For the time being, we will keep our involvement with each other a secret. But as soon as all this business with these Pillars is settled, I will tackle my father and the world will know you are mine."

There was a defensive and needy edge to the way he said the word "mine" that had Eira shifting in place and savoring the way their bodies brushed against each other.

"What's the final thing?" he asked.

"Kiss me again." She looked him in the eyes as she made her demand. "Kiss me until I'm breathless. Kiss me until we forget the lips of every other man and woman we've ever kissed." *Kiss me until I can wholly believe that you, magnificent creature, love me.*

"That would be my supreme delight."

This time, when he kissed her, it was clear he had abandoned anything that had been holding him back. Cullen kissed her as though he were trying to consume her. As though she would vanish if he didn't kiss her hard enough, long enough.

Eira returned his fervor. He smelled of warmth, sunlight, and everything she'd ever associated with home and goodness in this world. He was everything she'd given up on ever having. But he illuminated the hope she'd lost. His touch made her feel more alive than she had in years.

Y THE TIME the sun rose, Eira had only dozed for an hour or two. The covers were bundled around her, a honey haze dripping from every corner of the room with the first morning's light and the memories of the previous night. She raised two fingers, touching them gently to her still-tender lips. Who knew kissing someone could feel so good? Or that it was possible to do it for so long without tiring of it?

Rolling over, Eira stared at the other half of her bed, trying to imagine what it might feel like to see Cullen on the pillow next to her. Knowing him, he was as handsome asleep as he was awake. The perfect statuesque figure of a man in slumber.

Eira rolled her eyes and smiled. Her "Prince of the Tower" hardly ever had a hair out of place—unless it was from her fingers raking through it.

Hers.

The thought simmered in her, rolling on a warm tide. Eira liked the idea of him being hers. She liked the idea of him in general. But something about knowing that he desired her, of all people, was supremely delicious. Knowing he had sworn himself to her, time and again last night, between eager kisses…made thoughts of him the sweetest sort of torture now.

How was she ever going to pretend that nothing had happened? Eira groaned. The right decisions were always the hardest ones.

She lingered as long as she could in her tired, satisfied haze. But, eventually, the room had brightened to the point that Eira could no longer ignore the time and she pulled herself from the warmth of her covers to dress and start her day. When she emerged, she'd expected to find the common area empty, given the relative silence. But Cullen sat in the same spot as the night before, a journal perched on his knee.

His eyes drew up to hers immediately on her arrival. One corner of his lips quirked upward in a slightly smug expression that Eira had a hard time resisting kissing off.

"I didn't know you journaled."

"Sometimes it's journaling, sometimes it's short stories, sometimes it's notes." He shrugged, put his quill in the crack of the page, closed the journal on it, and wrapped a length of cord around it.

"What was it this morning?"

"Wouldn't you like to know?" He stood, still smirking.

"Fine." Eira shrugged, acting like she hardly cared, when she cared very much about everything he did. "Don't tell me. Keep your secrets."

"I'm not the only one who has them." The statement could've been a jab, but it came out somewhere between playful and a harmless observance. "Are you headed down for breakfast? I'll put this away and then join you."

"Sure." It wasn't suspicious if they went down to breakfast together, right? She was certainly going to be overthinking everything for a while when it came to him.

"Oh, that reminds me; I have something for you."

"You do?" Eira arched her eyebrows.

"Yes, in here." He motioned for her to follow. Doing so was certainly a bad idea. But Eira did so anyway.

"What is it?" Eira asked as she crossed the threshold.

The moment she cleared the door, Cullen shut it quickly behind her and yanked her to him. Eira let out a surprised chirp. Her weight pushed his back to the door, and Eira's hands landed on his chest for balance. His fingers were back in her hair, his mouth on hers. Returning his kiss, deepening it, devolving into a chorus of content sighs, it was all already instinct for her.

Cullen kissed her as though they had never kissed before. She kissed him like she intended to devour him whole. Nothing had ever felt so good, or so right. Nothing smoothed over the anger, hurt, and pain the world around her blazed with. He was so immensely soothing.

He would also be her downfall if she couldn't get herself under control and keep her head around him.

They broke apart and Cullen gave her a satisfied smirk, trailing a finger down her spine. Eira shivered, pressing her eyes closed and laying a few light pecks along the edge of his jaw.

"Is that all you wanted me for?" she asked softly.

"I want you in far more ways than merely that," he growled.

Eira looked at him in surprise. She'd never heard Cullen make a noise like that before. She certainly would be all right with him making it again.

Awareness of what he'd said—what he'd *implied*—dawned on him and a scarlet flush spread across his tan cheeks. "I meant to say—" He cleared his throat.

"I know exactly what you meant to say." Eira grabbed his collar and pulled his mouth to hers one last time. "But anything of that nature is going to have to wait." She couldn't risk it with Ferro out there. They were already struggling to keep things a secret a mere few hours into whatever this was.

"Of course." He gave her a light squeeze and they parted. "We should go, before anyone else wakes."

Eira nodded and stepped away so he could open the door. They'd just tiptoed out when a snicker could be heard. They turned slowly to see Noelle closing her own door with a smug smile.

"Oh, don't mind me. I know how to be discreet." She grinned and Eira's chest tightened. They'd hardly made it a night before rumors would start flying.

"It's not what you think," Eira said hastily.

"I honestly, truly—and let me make this *abundantly* clear to you both—do not care about what you do. If one of the competitions in the tournament was caring less about you two,

I would lose because it is impossible for me. I cannot think of anything more—"

"I think we get it," Cullen interrupted with a sigh. "We're heading to breakfast before today's training begins."

"Oh, good, me too." Noelle looked to Alyss's room. "Should we wake her up?"

"I'll do it and catch up with you both in a bit," Eira offered.

"Suit yourself." Noelle shrugged and started for the door.

"I can wait." Cullen lingered.

"You go ahead," Eira encouraged. "I'd like a bit of time with Alyss."

"Of course." Cullen squeezed her hand. "See you soon."

Eira knocked lightly on Alyss's door and was greeted with expected silence. She slowly eased the door open, poking her nose in and whispering, "Alyss?" The mound of covers on the bed stirring slightly was the only sign of life. Eira crept through the twilight room; the dawn was shuttered out by heavy curtains. Crawling into the bed, Eira hooked an arm around her friend.

"No," Alyss groaned. "It's too early."

"It's not."

"Damn you morning people."

"You don't mean that."

"I *do* mean that," Alyss grumbled. She still had yet to surface for air and presently appeared as a talking duvet. "You are criminally insane for trying to function at this hour; go back to bed."

Eira leaned over, whispering where she presumed Alyss's ear to be, "I kissed Cullen."

The covers were in the air. In a flurry of movement Alyss was upright, staring at Eira with wide eyes.

"*Imsorryyoudidwhat*?" The words blurred together in Alyss's excitement. Eira grinned sheepishly. Her friend grabbed both her shoulders, shaking with reckless abandon. "Details. Details! Now!"

"I'll tell you as you get dressed and come down to breakfast with me."

Alyss paused, eyes narrowing. "You drive a hard bargain."

"I know."

"Fine." Alyss released her and swung her legs off the bed. "I'm up, now start talking. I want every juicy detail."

"Last night, we, well, I couldn't sleep—"

"I was wondering if you were going to join me. I expected you to come if you needed me, but I guess you found someone else." Alyss waggled her eyebrows as she started her morning ablutions.

Eira couldn't hold back a laugh. There was a simmering guilt at feeling so happy. So much of the world was still at risk. There was so much she had yet to do. But she could enjoy herself for a few minutes. Eira glanced toward the window.

The Pillars had been right about something, Eira realized. The more she knew darkness, the more she appreciated the light.

"*Well?*" Alyss pressed. "Stop thinking about kissing him and *tell* me about it."

"I ran into him last night and…how did it happen? I—we—we got to talking and it sort of came out that he had feelings for me."

"And you told him the same, right?" Alyss pulled back her braids with a length of cord.

Eira nodded.

"And then you kissed?"

Another nod, met this time by a squeal from Alyss.

"This is *everything*! You deserve a good guy. You deserve happiness." She twirled and flopped back on the bed, giving Eira a dazzling smile.

Eira chuckled softly and squeezed her friend's hand. "Thanks. So do you."

"Unlike you, I've never doubted that. I've just had trouble finding said 'good guy.'" Alyss stuck out her tongue, prompting Eira to roll her eyes.

"Well, now that you know, and you're dressed, let's go to

breakfast. I want time to eat before this training—whatever it is—starts."

"You're right, we should."

They headed for the door and Eira paused. "One more thing."

"What?"

"Cullen and I… We're keeping it a secret for now," Eira said.

Alyss let out another squeal, grabbed both of Eira's hands, and jumped up and down with excitement.

"What has you so excited?"

"This is exactly like the plot of one of my favorite novels."

"It is not."

"Yes, it is," Alyss insisted. "Two competitors in a foreign land, embarking on a quest for glory, danger lurking behind every corner, the fate of nations hanging in the balance, an evil to vanquish, and a secret romance on top of it all! Okay, you're right, it's not exactly like one of my favorite novels. It's *better*."

Eira rolled her eyes. "Fine. Just, keep it a secret for now?"

"You know you can trust me." Alyss slung her bag over her shoulder. "Oh, do you know his favorite animal?"

"*Um*, no, why?"

"I'm going to make him something." Alyss patted her bag. "As a thank you for being interested in you."

"You make me sound like a charity case." Eira cringed.

"You said it, not me."

"How dare you!" Eira said with mock offense. "That's it, I'm leaving."

"Not without me!" Alyss squeezed through the door at her side. It was too small for them both and they stumbled through with a fit of giggles.

"Never," Eira wheezed. Her face hurt from smiling so much. "Never without you."

***

Breakfast went well, as far as Eira was concerned. The sight of Cullen filled her with effervescent excitement that threatened to bubble over at any second. They exchanged small glances and smiles, as though conversing in a new language all their own. Every movement he made held weight now. The tilts of his head, the arches of his brows, the way his eyes scrunched slightly when he laughed…Eira had permission to enjoy them all in a way she'd never let herself before.

When the competitors were finished eating, servants entered to clear away the remaining platters of food, all directed by Mistress Harrot. Guards trudged down the stairs in a pack that parted to make way for Deneya. She wore her usual plate of the queen's knights, and her palm rested lightly on the pommel of her sword.

"Finish up, wash up if you need to, and meet in the front gardens in ten minutes," she declared. "We'll head to the training arena as a group."

Levit had instructed them the night before to dress in their competitor regalia, so the four of them didn't have much to do but wait. Most of the other competitors went off to change, returning in an array of attire. The morphi wore fitted clothing with lightweight leather armor on top. The elfin were in looser styles of flowing silken robes and layered chiffons that were clearly inspired by Lumeria. Those from the Republic of Qwint looked the most like their Solaris counterparts in simple leggings and utilitarian tunics emblazoned in the green, blue, and white of their nation's checkered flag. The draconi were the most different, scantily clad in tight leather clothing, their tough and almost scale-like skin on display.

The competitors were arranged in four columns, each nation having its own row. Soldiers flanked them on both sides and behind. Deneya led at the front with knights on either side of her. They were escorted out the gates and into the city, met instantly by applause and cheers.

"This must be the parade we were promised when we first arrived," Cullen murmured.

"Make sure you smile and wave. I bet your father is positively tickled it's finally happening," Noelle said from his right.

"I bet he is," Cullen said under his breath.

The mention of Yemir sobered the glee Eira had felt all morning. Suddenly, the cheers of the crowd were muted, the excitement dulled. Yemir and Patrice had made it perfectly clear that they would never see Eira as someone worthy of their son. But what did that matter, anyway? Cullen was a grown man and Eira was a grown woman. They could make their own choices, couldn't they?

She glanced at Cullen from the corner of her eye. No, there was no way he'd ever forsake his father and his family like that. Not after what she'd learned about all they'd been through.

So where did that leave their love?

The thoughts followed her every step through the streets of Risen until they arrived at the training arena. The arena reminded Eira vaguely of a ring where horses were ridden, and she wondered if the space had been repurposed. If that was the case, the Queen of Meru had gone to great lengths to give them a practice area that could contain everything they'd need. On the packed earth of the arena's floor were all manner of weapon, practice dummy, rings, weights, and more. Spectators sat in a few rows of seats that ringed and overlooked the entire arena.

"Are we certain the tournament hasn't begun yet?" Alyss did a turn, looking at everyone gathered. "Seems like a lot of people."

"If you think this is a lot of people, just wait until you see the coliseum the queen is building on the outer hills," a female elfin competitor said over her shoulder with a proud smile. "It's unlike anything you've ever seen before. The greatest arena ever constructed."

"A coliseum?" Alyss asked on all their behalf.

"Think of it like this place," a man at the woman's right said, motioning around them. "But about ten times the scale."

"Ten times," Eira repeated softly, having a hard time imagining it.

"You'll see when you get there." The man gave her a wink and headed toward the other side of the arena with his fellow competitors.

A sudden hush fell over the masses followed by a ripple of murmuring spreading across the arena. On a platform at one end of the oval, a woman covered completely in layers of silken fabrics floated to the edge of the balcony. Queen Lumeria lifted her hands.

"Good competitors, gathered from states across the seas. You have come here as a show of faith from your homelands. You have come to take place in what will hopefully become a tournament for the ages. A new tradition to celebrate our unity." Polite applause as Lumeria took a breath. "Every day, from now until the tournament's start in two weeks, you will have an opportunity to practice here. Heed the advice and insights of my knights to better prepare yourselves. Five kingdoms look on you with fondness—we can't wait to see what you can do."

More applause, louder this time.

"We know that your arrival was less than conventional. All of Meru wanted to cheer for you from the moment you landed on our shores. But now that those who would threaten you have been thwarted, we look forward to the tournament and all its celebrations before, during, and after."

"*Thwarted*," Cullen scoffed under his breath. Eira shot him a look. He pursed his lips and gave a small nod. The Pillars might be the worst-kept secret in all of Risen. But the queen was clearly trying to avoid giving them any further opportunity to gain ground in public consciousness by pretending they didn't exist in the first place.

"To that end, it is my pleasure to announce that I will be opening the doors of my castle to all of you, your dignitaries, and my esteemed friends the night before the tournament's start for a ball."

The crowd cheered as Lumeria stepped away. The masses acted as though they were all going to be invited. Of course, maybe they were. Lumeria's castle was certainly large enough and impressive enough to house hundreds of revelers.

But revelry seemed far from the competitors' minds. They regarded each other warily. For the first time, it began to sink in that they were each other's competition. The atmosphere at the manor had been friendly enough, but here it was already becoming thick with critical looks and assessing glances. Even if the tournament was intended to inspire goodwill, it was clear that they were all here to win and bring glory back to their homelands. Who knew what every competitor really had at stake?

"So we're supposed to train now?" Alyss asked.

"I guess so?" Eira shrugged.

"I'm not some trained dog that's going to perform magic for spectators like tricks for—" Noelle didn't get to finish.

There was a wheeze, and a murmur of anticipation rippled through the crowd. The four of them looked over in time to see Harkor, the draconi prince, let out a mighty roar toward the heavens. Sound became flame as he breathed fire.

"I cannot wait to dominate the tournament!" Harkor declared with a shout. "The draconi will show every kingdom our might." His fellow competitors punctuated the declaration by slapping the centers of their chests twice and letting out guttural noises of agreement.

"Am I supposed to be impressed by him spitting fire?" Noelle folded her arms and stuck out her tongue, a flash of fire curling off its tip.

"Let's keep to ourselves," Cullen suggested. "This is just day one and we have two weeks before the tournament even begins. It might be prudent to pull our punches a bit and hold back from showing what we can really do."

The four of them continued to watch as the other groups of competitors settled into their corners of the arena. Magic pulsed off the morphi, shifting swords into roses and changing their bodies into beasts and birds. The elfin moved with glyphs of light. The other humans from Qwint spun tiny bracelets around their wrists that conjured sparks, flames, and wind gusts not unlike the elemental affinities of Solaris.

"Eira." Deneya's voice broke their silent assessment of their competition. She hadn't even heard Deneya approach. "Can you come with me? I have a matter pertaining to your kidnapping that I need to discuss."

"Of course. I'll be back soon, everyone."

Eira followed Deneya into one of the two tunnels that led in and out of the arena. Deneya glanced over her shoulder, looking around quickly before grabbing Eira's hand.

"*Durroe watt radia. Durroe sallvas tempre,*" she whispered quickly. Glyphs surrounded their locked hands. "We don't have very long and we have a lot of ground to cover."

Eira remained silent, listening closely as Deneya gave her orders.

"If *they* ask, you'll tell them that you gave me the slip and sneaked away during training. But let's hope you don't spend enough time with them again for them to have the chance to inquire."

Eira nodded as they crossed out of the pathway and into the square the competitors had been escorted through not even an hour ago. She didn't have to ask who Deneya meant by "they." It was clear she meant the Pillars.

"Are we headed to the Archives?" Eira asked.

"Where else?" Deneya gave her an agitated glance. "Let's find you a stupid rock."

CHAPTER

TWENTY-THREE

DENEYA LED HER down an alleyway and through a door she unlocked with a key on her belt. The passage was wedged between at least four buildings, the mortar and stone changing in style as they carried on. At the end was a small room—supply closet, more like. Deneya pointed to a change of clothes that was reminiscent of the flowing styles the elfin wore.

"Change quickly." Deneya put her back to Eira.

She did as commanded, stripping out of her competitor's clothing and putting on the simple dress and jacket. There was a wide-brimmed, floppy hat, adorned with flowers, that finished the ensemble. "Done."

"Good." Deneya grabbed a cloak off a peg on the wall, slinging it around her shoulders. "Now you're slightly less recognizable. I'm going to step out first. I'll knock and then you count to twenty before leaving. Head left—you'll see the Archives and can work your way there by sight."

"You're not coming with me?" The thought of being in the city alone for the first time since her captivity had her tight-chested and breathless.

"Of course I am. I'm going to trail behind. You might not see me, but I'll be there."

"I'd feel safer if—"

"If any Pillars are watching you, they'll get suspicious if they see you too close to me." Deneya locked eyes with Eira in an intense stare. "Listen to me—you'll be safe. If I say you are, then you will be. Do as I say and trust me."

Eira bit back a remark that Deneya had said the manor would be safe…only to discover that enemies were lurking in their midst. But the Pillars hadn't made a move against Eira until Eira had been the one to stick her neck out. And she had vowed to follow Deneya's orders; it was time to prove that she could.

"Understood," Eira said, putting all her faith in the Head Specter.

"Good." There were no further words of encouragement. Deneya slipped out the door and left Eira alone. After about a minute there was the expected knock. Eira counted slowly to twenty, stepped out, and headed left.

The street was quiet and she kept her head down, resisting the urge to look behind her for Deneya. Imaginary enemies lurked behind every column of the arcade she walked in. They lounged in the sunken doorways of closed shops and shuttered inns. This must not be the "nice" area of Risen. This forgotten corner of the city looked just as much like the underbelly of Solarin, even Oparium. Poverty was universal.

She stepped into the sunlight at the end of the street and glanced upward. Sure enough, the Archives were visible, but farther than she would've expected—or hoped. She didn't know how much time Deneya had bought them, but Eira had the keen sense that haste would be her friend. Picking a street that seemed to go in the rough direction of up and toward the large spire, Eira began to make her way through Risen.

Twice she thought she caught a glimpse of Deneya from the corner of her eye, but she never looked long enough to be sure. Once, she thought she recognized a man's face as one of the Pillars. The familiarity nearly made her come to a sudden halt. But the man passed without so much as a glance her way and Eira kept her head high and eyes forward, ignoring the frantic beating of her heart.

She arrived at the Archives unharmed, albeit mildly winded from her aggressive pace and the long progression of stairs that her path had necessitated. Swords of Light patrolled the large square in front of the Archives and two were posted on either side of the doors. But none of them stopped her as she entered.

"This way," Deneya murmured, brushing past her. Eira nearly jumped out of her skin. She hadn't realized Deneya had come to her side. The woman could move more silently than Ducot in mole form.

Deneya led them up a side stair, beginning to wrap around the circular tower of the Archives, higher and higher.

"That's where the Flame of Yargen was before it was extinguished, wasn't it?" Eira murmured, mostly to herself as the realization settled on her.

Deneya paused, looking over at the giant, unlit brazier. There was a sad sort of longing in her eyes, emotions that had been steeping too long unattended in the ocean of time. "Yes, a long, long time ago."

"Didn't Ulv—" Deneya shot her a glare and Eira rephrased "—wasn't it extinguished more recently? In the past thirty years?"

"The real flame was," Deneya said finally and started forward again. "But the real flame hadn't been burning in that basin for a long time."

"What?"

"The flame Risen saw was an illusion…nothing more. The real flame had been weakened to the point that it was kept hidden away." Deneya spoke without looking back. Eira had to stay within mere inches to hear her soft words.

Eira waited to ask her next question until Deneya opened the trapdoor in the floor and they were back in the passages that led toward the final ladder and the room she had last met Taavin in. "Did *he* really extinguish the real flame?"

Deneya didn't answer until they were both up on the platform at the top of the ladder. She stared at the empty room, seeing things that Eira couldn't even imagine. There was a history here that Eira had only begun to piece together. A history that Deneya, Taavin, and Ulvarth were woven into.

"The truth of what happened to the Flame of Yargen is too difficult to tell. It's not made for mortal minds."

"But—"

Deneya turned to face Eira, her blue eyes shining almost purple in the low light. "Don't ask questions when you're not prepared for the answers. And trust me: you're *not* prepared. If you thought you were already at risk for what you know, you have no idea what this line of questioning will yield."

Eira closed her mouth on all objections and gave a small nod.

"Good, now let's find you a talking rock to convince them you were here." Deneya led the way into the room, Eira following two steps behind.

The place was barren, just like the last time she was here. But this time Eira wasn't hopelessly distracted by Taavin. This time she could explore the room at her leisure. The ghostly outlines of portraits once hung on the walls were burned into the plaster from years of sunlight. There were still the footprints of trinkets on the shelves in the dust that had collected around them.

The room was in the shape of an octagon with four doors. One was where she'd entered from; another was a washroom; a completely vacant room was the third; but behind the fourth door was a strange, absolutely dark room that beckoned to her with gentle caresses of a magic so potent that Eira had no idea how she hadn't felt it the first time she was here.

Unlike the rest of the quarters, this room was unadorned—there were no delicate patterns of swords, birds, and suns. It was empty save for a single pedestal. The stone column had a divot in its top. Collected in the empty basin was the power that had drawn her in. She could almost see it swirling, overflowing down the edges of the pedestal. The magic was like a beacon—a light in the darkness—calling to her. Beckoning. It was as potent as the first magic she felt after leaving the pit.

Eira couldn't stop her magic from unraveling from her to greet it. Her powers sank into the pores of the stone and ignited words trapped within the fragments of the magic. They were splinters, said again and again by different people, yet also the same. She knew the voices, and yet couldn't quite place them. These were unlike any other echoes she'd ever heard.

This is—isn't—real flame?
Yes—legendary flame of—left of it.
I know—our destiny.
Thrumsana.
—do now?
I heard the goddess.
I wanted—everything you desired—only way.
Thrumsana.
Whenever—ready.
Thrumsana. Thrumsana.

The words continued, disjointed and broken. Segments of conversations flickered like a candle in a breeze, casting haunting shadows on the walls. They seemed to spin through her mind like a vortex, faster and faster, trapping her in a rising torrent of sound. Two voices, three voices, six. All the same people. All familiar. All different. It made no sense. It would tear her apart.

Give me the flame. Deneya's voice. *It is—commands it.*
—will be killed.
Death comes for us all.
Thrumsana.

Where is it? a masculine voice roared. The sound was horribly familiar. It was different than the whispering tones she'd last heard it as. This was the voice of the man they had called Champion. *What have you—ruined—kill you.*

Thrumsana. Thrumsana. Thrumsana. Thrumsana. Thrum—

The noise reached a crescendo of a hundred voices screaming all at once. Eira's head sang in horrible harmony, and she let out a shout and clutched her skull.

"Make it stop," she pleaded, withdrawing her magic. "Make it stop!" She was shaking. She was being shaken.

"Eira, look at me. Eira, *look.*"

Eira peeled open her eyes to stare up at Deneya. The woman had her hands on Eira's arms, clutching her so tightly that her fingers would no doubt leave bruises. Eira panted, breathless. Her head was splitting open with unbearable pain.

"What did you hear?" Deneya growled.

"I...too much." Eira shook her head.

"You weren't supposed to actually listen to anything here. I told you not to go asking questions."

But it was too late now. The voices had been unleashed, and the room was suddenly alive with them. Eira heard conversations between Ulvarth and the last Voice of Yargen—the woman who held the position before Taavin. She heard Deneya and the same woman, as Deneya asked the former Voice for the flame. She heard Vi and Taavin's voices in conversations that made no sense. The stones practically screamed for her to listen, as though they were trying to unload a thousand years of untold secrets and stories.

Deneya's voice from long ago came back into clarity. An altercation had happened here between her and Ulvarth. Ulvarth's rough tones accused Deneya of undermining him, of framing him. They lingered against the words Eira had heard in the Pillars' hideaway.

"You...you took it," Eira whispered, eyes darting between the room, Deneya, the column, and back. There was too much, but she could make sense of that little. "You were the one who took the Flame of Yargen. Then you blamed Ulvarth for it. You were the one who had him locked away, who brought the knights here to take him."

Deneya's expression twisted with horror and disgust. "Stop."

"If not for you, the Pillars wouldn't exist. *You* were the one who gave them their Champion unjustly condemned...who gave them motivation."

"Enough!" Deneya shouted at her, shaking her twice. "Did I not warn you that there are some truths you should never uncover? Did I not tell you that some stones shouldn't be upturned or, in your case, listened to?"

Half of Deneya's face was illuminated by the bright sunlight let in by the large windows of the main room. The other half was cast in intense shadows from the dark place that once housed the Flame of Yargen. In this moment, Deneya looked capable of great good and great evil and Eira wasn't quite certain what side she would ultimately be resigned to.

"My magic acted on its own." It wasn't entirely true.

"You've said you have control."

"I usually do but that pedestal…" Eira trailed off, staring at the offending object. It looked so innocuous. "There's a fearsome intensity to it. Frightening, even. I wish I hadn't heard it."

"You'll wish that more if you don't keep what you heard to yourself," Deneya cautioned and finally released her. Disapproval—maybe even disgust—radiated off the woman, and Deneya could no longer look Eira in the eyes. "Come over here. I think I found something that might work."

Eira diligently followed behind to a far corner of the room. There was a crack in the plaster that Deneya wedged a pocket knife into. She stabbed around the plaster, perforating it to the point that a hunk the size of Eira's palm came loose.

"It has the painting of this room, so they'll be certain to recognize it."

"Good thinking." Eira took the token, slipping it into one of the deep pockets of the loose-fitting trousers she wore.

"You should go. Do you remember how to get back to the passage where your clothes are?"

"I think so."

"All right. I have some other business to attend to," Deneya said dismissively.

"You're not going to watch me and make sure I make it safely?" Eira patted her pocket. "They might abduct me just because they know I have this now."

"Don't get caught then."

Deneya was disappointed in what Eira had discovered and was punishing her for it. Eira had seen the emotion from her family enough times to know it well. It was the same look Marcus had given her when Eira had discovered one summer that he was sneaking out to see a lover at the beach.

"You have to manage as a shadow sometime," Deneya continued. "Use your illusions. When you get to the door, use the combination 0-1-5."

"Very well." There was little point in arguing. It wouldn't go over well and, even though fear was already tugging at her hems with every step, Eira was certain she'd be all right. She had to keep believing that—no matter how foolish it was—to keep existing in this world.

Eira started for the door but paused, glancing over her shoulder. The Head Specter leaned against the wall, arms folded, a scowl across her face as she stared out the window at Risen below. Eira ran her fingers over the hunk of plaster, resisting the urge to give it a listen…for now.

"Deneya," Eira said softly. If her companion didn't hear her, then she'd leave.

But Deneya turned, and Eira was committed. "You're still here?"

Eira ignored the curt remark. "You took the post of looking after Ulvarth yourself because you felt guilty for what you did, right?" Deneya merely grunted at her. Eira continued, "You're *certain* Ulvarth is dead, right?"

Deneya locked eyes with her and Eira could hear unspoken warnings. Eira saw the bitter and hardened expression Deneya had worn the night Ferro had slipped from their grasp. She saw everything she'd been hoping not to.

"I was there the night he fell from the tower we were keeping him in. He took his own life rather than live in captivity. There was no way he could've survived." Deneya looked out the window again. But even in profile, Eira didn't miss the doubt that twisted her face.

Deneya was Head Specter for a reason—she had her secrets. However, despite being new to this world, Eira was already beginning to unravel them. And if she could see the hidden threads stitching the fragile peace of Meru together, it wouldn't be long until others could see them as well. Once they were visible, nothing would stop the dangerous forces at play from snipping and pulling at them until the whole order of the world unraveled.

• CHAPTER •

TWENTY-FOUR

EIRA MADE IT back to the arena without issue. Her friends questioned what had taken so long, but that seemed to be the extent of anyone's suspicions. Most of the interest today was on the sorcerers from the Republic and their strange rune-covered bracelets. No one paid much notice to Eira disappearing for almost two whole hours.

Cullen stayed close to her for most of the day. He was the only one who seemed skeptical of the story she'd sold. But he kept any questions he might have to himself, focusing instead on running sword drills with Noelle. Meanwhile, Eira pulled Alyss aside to focus on practicing her ability to sense magic. It was still a basic skill. But Eira was committed to learning just how it might be able to serve her. After the events in the Archives, Eira was more convinced than ever that her senses had heightened to new levels.

For the majority of dinner, Eira kept to herself. She must've been more aloof than she'd thought because Cullen and Alyss both made determined efforts to strike up conversation. Eira played along, eventually underscoring that she was merely tired and had a lot to think about for the upcoming tournament. When she told them that by morning she would be back to normal, they seemed to believe her.

Excusing herself from dinner early, Eira retreated to her room, hoping to get a few moments alone to work through her thoughts—and nearly knocking down Mistress Harrot on entry.

"Apologies, dear!" The lady of the house stumbled backward, gripping her chest with a laugh. "You gave me quite the startle."

"Sorry," Eira murmured, eyes darting around. There was still something about the woman that left Eira unsettled. "Is there something I can help you with?"

Mistress Harrot ignored her question. "You're back from dinner early."

Eira glanced at the feather duster in the woman's hands. "Do you usually dust in the evenings when people are at dinner?"

"I take care of all the rooms in the manor." Harrot stepped around her and out the door. "It's a time-consuming job, so I do what I can, when I can."

Eira watched her leave, debating if she should inquire further about what the woman was doing. If she'd had doubts about Harrot working for the Pillars before, they were completely gone now. Harrot was watching her. Eira would bet her life on it. So she just had to make sure Harrot didn't find anything of note to report back. She did a turn about the common area and her room, trying to figure out what Harrot might have been searching for, but came up empty-handed.

Still unable to shake the slimy feeling of the idea of someone searching through her things, Eira hunted through her room for a better hiding place for Adela's journals and the stone. She had to keep the piece of plaster she'd taken from the Archives from falling into the Pillars' hands before she intended it to. She had value to the Pillars because of this rock and her magic. And her magic seemed to only have value as long as Ferro vouched for her.

"I have to keep it safe," Eira murmured, looking around her room. But where could she keep it that no one would think to look? Mistress Harrot no doubt knew every corner of the manor. Except—

Eira rushed to her bag and grabbed a leaf of paper. She had originally intended to scribble a note to Ducot explaining the small stack of books and plaster, but quickly abandoned the idea, realizing it futile. She'd just explain it the next time she saw him.

Before the others returned, she opened up the passage to the Court of Shadows. If anywhere was safe from Harrot's prying eyes, it was here. Because if Harrot knew about this passage, they all had larger concerns. Eira put her things to the left of the door, where they would hopefully be out of the way, and then shut it, retreating to her room.

The dusk bled out into night and the stars found her still awake. Eira paced the room for what must've been the hundredth time. Deneya, Harrot, Pillars, shadows, they were all connected. If Deneya had been the one to take the Flame and frame Ulvarth, where was it now? Extinguished, yes, that much seemed true, but…

Her restlessness promised no sleep anytime soon. Sneaking out of her room, Eira treaded lightly over to the main door of the Solaris accommodations and slipped out. She didn't know where she was going, but her brain was too full to rest. Downstairs, Eira stepped out onto the terraced gardens. Two knights patrolled them in addition to two more posted on the rooftop. Eira gave them a nod in acknowledgment and they did the same. They didn't stop or question her as she made her way down to the river, leaning against the railing and staring out over Risen. Though, she could feel their attention on her, tracking her every movement.

No one wanted to be on duty the night another competitor slipped away. It was only natural for them to watch her like hawks.

A shadow grew near, heralding the presence of a man. Eira straightened from the railing and said, "I'll go back in soon. I just couldn't sleep."

"Glad to know it's not just me."

"Ducot? I wasn't expecting you," Eira said, surprised.

One side of his mouth pulled into a wide grin. "You come here often? Can't say I've seen you around these parts before," he said with a flirtatious edge.

Eira burst out laughing. It released some of the tension that she'd been steeping in. "I don't come here regularly, no. You come here often looking for women?"

"Only the sort with loose morals and a penchant for scarred, blind men who will most certainly be gone by morning." He still wore a grin as he spoke. But there was a lingering self-depreciation in his words that was a little too real.

"How's the hunt for said women going for you?"

"Not well." He snorted. "Mind if I join you instead?"

"Oh, I think I've reserved this entire stretch of railing for the night. Sorry," she said with an extra sarcastic note.

"And what will I do now that I can't stare out and admire the visual beauty of Risen's skyline glittering on the far bank?"

Eira laughed again. "Of course you can join me."

He rested his elbows on the railing and stared out, as though he really could see the skyline.

"What're you looking at?" she couldn't resist asking.

"Not much of anything right now. I'm completely blind at night." He shrugged. "But…I can *feel* a lot."

"Like what?"

"Like the subtle shifts in the air between breezes, or the way the moonlight is broken by clouds drifting across the sky. Or how I feel moisture condensing in the air for rain—or fog, maybe. I can hear the boats clanking over there—" he pointed "—their ropes straining softly. I can smell the river water—fresh, but with a nasty tang from the sewers that dump into it." He glanced her way. "The world doesn't stop existing for me because I'm blind. It just exists differently."

"Seeing differently…" Eira stared at her palm, recalling training with Alyss and trying to sense even the slightest fluctuations in her power. "How did you learn how to do that?"

"I don't remember." He shrugged. "Asking me that is like me asking you, how did you learn how to see? You've always just done it, right? I was born this way, I never knew anything different."

Eira hummed and a brief silence passed between them like the fog that, sure enough, crept across the river as Ducot predicted. Maybe, eventually, she'd ask him if the morphi understood channels in the same way Solaris sorcerers did. When that day came, he might even be able to help her explore or harness whatever abilities she had…*if* she had them.

"You disappeared today." He disrupted her thoughts. "I was worried about you."

"Deneya was the one to take me; I was fine."

"I know. I still worried about you."

"*Aww*, are we close friends now?" Eira said the words like a tease, but they carried the weight of sincerity.

"Not in the slightest."

"You wound me." Though Eira couldn't blame him.

"But I suppose we're headed in that direction."

A tired smile crossed her lips. "Well, I consider you a friend."

"Such a privilege. If risking my life is a show of how you treat your friends, I can't wait to see how you treat your enemies." Once more, a sarcastic remark with the underpinning of sincerity. Perhaps it was natural among people who regularly risked their lives to find flexibility when it came to moving past such concerns in their line of work.

"Ducot…" Eira hesitated, glancing around. Her voice dropped even lower. "Do you think it's safe to talk here?"

"Nowhere is safe. But…" Magic pulsed out from him. Ducot continued to stare forward, but Eira got the sensation that he was suddenly, somehow, looking everywhere at once. "If you mean can anyone hear us? I don't think so."

"I hid something in the hallway." She trusted him to know which one she spoke of. "It's out of the way. But so you know it's there."

"Understood." She appreciated that he didn't pry as to what it was or why. Ducot was clearly accustomed to only receiving the bare minimum of information. "Though I don't think that's what you *really* wanted to tell me."

Eira ran her fingers over the railing. "I'm jumping at shadows."

"You should be the shadow the world jumps at."

She snorted softly and came clean with what was on her mind—what had been on her mind the entire day since her encounter with Deneya. "I'm worried that the inspiration for *that group* is still alive." She didn't dare say "Pillars" or "Ulvarth" outright.

"If she says he's dead, then he is." Yet even as Ducot spoke those words, his mouth pressed into a firm line. Eira couldn't quite read the severe expression.

"You have your doubts."

"I'm not in a place to have doubts."

"But what if my suspicions are founded and he is alive?"

"Don't go there," Ducot cautioned.

"What if he's out there? I—" Eira stopped short, thinking back to the voices she'd heard earlier and Deneya's confessions tied tightly with warnings.

"You what?"

"I have a feeling is all," she murmured. "I'm worried he's not as dead as she thinks."

"If he is alive…" Ducot sighed heavily. His hands wrapped around the railing so tightly his knuckles turned paper-white. "If he is then all the better. Then I'll get to kill him myself."

"Don't do anything rash."

"You're one to talk." Ducot snorted. Eira should be embarrassed, but she ended up smirking, an expression Ducot shared briefly before turning serious. "If he is alive, I want to hunt him down."

"I think all of us do."

Ducot shifted to face her. "You owe me. Because of me you got to the man you were hunting. If you know anything about my mark, then you tell me. Deal?"

"Deal," Eira said easily. Keeping Ducot as her ally had far more perks than downsides.

"Good." He yawned and stretched. "I think I'm going to try and head back to bed. You should do the same. Another big day of training tomorrow. The competition is less than two weeks away now and we have to survive whatever games both Lumeria and the Pillars will have us playing."

"Yeah, I think I'll go in, too," Eira said, following behind him.

She went back to her room, but couldn't seem to quite find a position she was comfortable enough in to fall asleep. Instead, she spent most of the night thinking about the golden dagger that was in the hands of the Specters, unable to shake the nagging feeling that there was more to it than any of them suspected.

***

Three long, sweaty days passed.

Levit took turns with the senators in overseeing their drills. Only competitors were allowed in the arena. But their overseers could perch on the lowest row of seats above them, barking orders.

Eira had never run, jumped, or swung a sword so much in her life. If she thought the training she'd done with Alyss for the trials had been bad, this was worse times a thousand. She was stiff and everything ached on the second morning. By the third morning she could hardly sit without every muscle in her body nearly giving up in agony.

Alyss helped her that night—she helped all of them—using her healing abilities. Eira woke up on the morning of the fourth day and could actually sit in bed without collapsing. She could stand without her knees wobbling. Progress.

"It's not like me to be up before you," Alyss said when Eira emerged from her room. Her friend was seated on one of the chairs by the hearth, working on a sculpture of a noru cat—Cullen's favorite animal, apparently. "You've been sleeping in later these days. Something…or should I say, *someone* keeping you up at night?" Alyss cackled as Eira sank heavily into the chair opposite her.

"Oh, by the Mother, Alyss," Eira groaned. "As if I've had the energy to even *think* about anything other than sleep." Her relationship with Cullen had been put on an unspoken and hopefully temporary hold as they focused on surviving their new training regimens. But if there was one blessing that came of being so tired, it was that Eira couldn't keep herself up with endless worrying at night.

Alyss laughed. "I figured, I'm just teasing you." She set the small statue down on the table next to her. The bits of clay and dust floated magically off her fingers, collecting in a small pile by the statuette. Alyss motioned to the floor in front of her chair. "Sit."

Knowing what Alyss was about to do, Eira was eager to allow it. She sat on the floor in front of her friend as Alyss sank her fingers into the muscles of Eira's shoulders. Pulses of magic rippled through her, teasing out the knots of her muscles, mending the small tears brought on by training the day before. Alyss always had a detailed explanation for how her magical healing worked. All Eira needed to know was that she always felt amazing when Alyss was done.

"I'm next," Noelle declared. Eira cracked open her eyes; she hadn't even realized she'd shut them.

"I'm almost done," Alyss said, finishing up with a light squeeze and three ripples of magic. "All right, your turn."

Eira and Noelle swapped places. Leaning forward, Eira rested her elbows on her knees. It was strange to think she was here with Noelle—that they had somehow become *friends*. Despite her better judgment, Eira tried to remember the details of Noelle's face that night with Adam. How she looked when she sneered and threw her verbal jabs. But the memory had become somewhat hazy. It was hard to imagine Noelle was the same person now as the girl that night. They'd all grown.

"*What?*" Noelle asked, forcing Eira to realize she'd been staring at the woman.

"Oh, nothing. I was thinking about how far we've come."

"Indeed...to a whole new land." Noelle glanced out the windows thoughtfully. "Do either of you ever miss home?"

"Sometimes," Alyss said softly. "But I've been in the South

for so long… Here or in Solarin, either way I'm not with my family in the North."

"I suppose that makes sense," Noelle murmured.

"Aren't your parents some Western nobles? Don't they still live out West?" Eira asked. Many nobles had relocated to Solarin, where the true court met.

"Yes, they are and they do." Noelle puffed her chest a little that Eira would remember such a detail. "But they do come to Solarin often to attend court. So I see them regularly." Her attention shifted to Eira. "What about your parents?"

It was Eira's turn to look out the windows.

Her mind wandered as far from that room as she could get. But doing so betrayed her. It wandered right back to the small home she'd grown up in. She remembered the smell of the hearth, the way everything was perpetually covered in soot in the winter months. There was the feeling of the salt air in her hair, tamped down by the weight of her father's hand when he patted her head and told her she'd done a good job on their first fishing trip together.

Every memory was so fragile that even thinking them made them shatter. The pieces were coated in a thick, grimy film, making them impossible to recall perfectly once more. Even her happiest days as a child had been tainted. The more time that passed, the more Eira wondered if any of them had even been real. Perhaps she'd just fabricated those pleasant hours to fill in the gaps of things she hadn't wanted to see as a child.

"Eira—" Alyss started, painfully gentle.

"My parents don't care I'm gone. They don't care about me at all," Eira said softly.

"That's not true," Alyss protested.

"Because of me, their son died."

"Marcus's death wasn't because of you."

Eira was too tired to argue the point. It didn't matter anymore. Marcus was gone, and she'd come to terms with it in her own way. "Even if that were the case…I went against their wishes by competing. They didn't come and visit me when Marcus died."

"Weren't you in jail?" Noelle asked, cringing as she did, as though she realized how terrible a thing it was to point out.

Eira glanced at her from the corner of her eye. "They didn't even leave a note for me with my uncle."

A heavy silence settled between them. Alyss's hands had stilled on Noelle's shoulders. Eira sighed. She'd blow away the tension if she could.

"It's all right. I'm bad luck for people to be around. This just frees my parents of having to deal with me."

"I don't think they want that," Alyss said firmly.

The conversation ended abruptly when Cullen emerged from his room.

"Ah, good morning, everyone."

They all greeted him as he approached.

"How are you all this fine day?" He flashed Eira a dazzling smile, one she forced herself to return.

"We're good."

"I was just working on Eira's and Noelle's muscles. Would you like some help?" Alyss asked, wiggling her fingers.

"I'd never refuse that." Cullen took Noelle's place and Eira returned to staring out the window as the three struck up a conversation without her.

The mention of her parents had stirred up all the thoughts she'd been trying to bury. She might have found a tentative peace with herself when it came to Marcus's death. But the relationship between her and her living family was something else entirely.

Then, there was the mystery of her birth mother. Could her mother really be Adela? Was there any way Eira would ever find out? If anywhere had the information, it was the Archives. Eira kept coming back to that. But when would she have time?

"Good morning, Solaris competitors!" the perpetually cheerful Mister Levit chimed as he opened the door to his room. "Good to see you're all up and dressed."

"We're up and dressed every day." Noelle gave him a dumb look that just slid right off Levit's cheer.

"But today you're going to get undressed!"

"Pardon?" Noelle raised her eyebrows.

Levit cleared his throat, the natural brown of his skin turning a ruddy shade with a fearsome blush. "To get re-dressed, in something better." He pinched his nose and sighed. "I have not had tea yet and it is early. You're all going to the tailor today to get fitted for gowns for the pre-tournament ball! And a suit, in your case, Cullen."

"And here I wanted to wear a gown." Cullen lounged back in the chair with a lazy smirk.

"If you want to wear a gown, I won't stop you." Levit shrugged. "But the senators will have final approval on your attire to make sure you 'properly represent Solaris.' So it'd be your father you have to convince."

Noelle groaned. "Yemir has the *worst* fashion sense." She glanced sideways. "No offense, Cullen."

"None taken." Cullen shrugged, as if the fact was well known.

"We'll leave shortly after breakfast," Levit decreed. "So be ready to be made into your best selves."

· CHAPTER ·

TWENTY-FIVE

THE TAILOR WAS a posh spot called LOOM AND WREN. Bolts of fabric were stacked against every wall and sumptuous materials stretched across tables and chairs down the long shop. The seamstress was a morphi woman named Estal. Her hair was woven into intricate braids that were piled atop her head like an upside-down basket. She took great pride in the style, proclaiming she'd worn it thusly in honor of her Solaris guests. "After all," she'd said, "The Crown Princess Solaris always has her hair pinned in such beautiful braids."

There were two fitting rooms in the back of the store. In the middle were two pedestals flanked by mirrors. Noelle and Cullen went first. As Eira and Alyss waited up front, getting lost in the seemingly endless depths of fabrics in every color and texture, the other two were taken back to the fitting rooms. They emerged and were promptly placed on the pedestals for review.

"How did you…" Alyss murmured, rounding Noelle. "How did you make a dress in a mere fifteen minutes?"

"Darling, some morphi can use the shift to make plants grow or carve stone. Some perfect their animal forms. As for me? Textiles are my muse and canvas." Estal lovingly ran her fingers along the hem of Noelle's gown. "What do you think, dear?"

The conversation faded from Eira's awareness as the whole world seemed to narrow on Cullen. On his hair, perfectly brushed to one side, messy locks insisting on framing his face in an imperfectly perfect way. They had dressed him in a deep purple, almost black. Intricate designs were woven into the fabric with golden thread that reminded Eira vaguely of the paintings she'd seen in the mysterious room at the top of the Archives. He was a blend of traditional Solaris handsome, rough around the edges in a way that only Eira could see, with elements of the fashions of Meru. As she looked on him then, she wondered how she could've ever seen any other man but him.

"Well? Am I presentable?" Cullen asked her with a small smile.

"Barely." She gave him the makings of a coy grin.

He snorted. "'Barely' is the best I can hope for most days."

"You look amazing," she said earnestly. "Like the first time we went to court. No, better."

"*You* were the one who looked amazing that day. I still cannot believe how flattering that dress was on you. I should have known I was done for then and there." He stared down at her in admiration. The way the emotions softened his expression made him raw. She hadn't kissed him for a few days now and that was a few too many.

"Sorry to make you wait." Yemir forced himself into their conversation and moment. Eira took a step away.

"It's fine, Father." Cullen brought his eyes from Yemir to her. For a second, she was worried he might say something that would betray them. But he didn't. Eira clutched her hands in front of her, trying to tighten her fingers to the point that she would have a firm grasp on her emotions as well. But a deep ache that had started this morning at the mention of her family still rode on her undercurrents.

"We'll need some adjustments to be made here…and here…" Yemir quickly dominated the conversation with tailoring talk. He'd had little to say on Noelle. But when it came to his son, Estal would need almost an entire book to record all of the senator's demands.

One of Estal's attendants saved Eira from drowning in her thoughts. "Miss, would you like to come back now? The mistress will be held up a moment, but we can start getting you situated."

"Oh, yes, sure."

Eira followed the young woman to the back corner of the

store. There was a rear door positioned between walls of curtains on either side. The attendant brought Eira into the fitting room, asked her to wait there, and left by pulling the curtain shut behind her. The heavy velvet muffled the conversations still happening in the center of the store. But Eira was certain that Yemir would keep Estal busy for a while yet. She might as well get comfortable while she waited.

Unfortunately, there was no chair in the room, just a large, gilded mirror leaning against one wall. Eira was going to sit on the floor when movement caught her eye. She hardly had time to react before a hand clamped over her mouth and the voice of her nightmares filled her ear.

"Don't shout, pet. We don't want everyone to know I've come to pay you a visit," Ferro whispered.

Eira forced her muscles to relax and Ferro released her. The room was suddenly darker, dingier. Everything beyond the curtains was gone. Had it ever really been there to begin with? Or had this whole thing been an illusion like the one outside her window in the Pillars?

Was she still in the pit?

A part of her always would be.

"You came for me." Eira forced calm serenity onto her features. She stared up at him as if he were a god. There was an unnatural sharpness to Ferro. His skin had a luster she didn't remember it having before. His hair seemed extra tousled in an intentional way. As if he had just come from the beach…or a tumble in the bedroom. The latter thought made her shudder.

"Of course I did. I always will." He grabbed her chin. "I am never far from you and your precious powers. Remember that." She nodded. "The ball is a mere week away. Have you done it? Did you get it?"

Eira wondered if this was a test. If he truly had no idea since she'd hidden the piece of plaster so well. "Yes, I got what the Champion asked of me."

A grin that showed far too much teeth spread across his face. "Good, pet. Good. Where is it?"

"I don't have it with me. I wouldn't risk—"

"I didn't ask if you had it, I asked where it was."

"Hidden safely back in the manor." She avoided being too specific.

"Good. I imagine the Raspian lovers you are forced to associate with will be held up here for a while. Maybe I should go and retrieve it."

"No!"

"No?" His grin fell, darkness shrouding his face as the shadows seemed to grow longer around him. If there was anyone who loved a dark god…it was him. "You'd dare—"

Eira grabbed his hand with both of hers. "It's too much of a risk. I'd lose my purpose if something happened to you. You are my guide and guardian."

"Oh, you sweet thing." He ran his knuckles down her cheek. "They would never catch me."

"The manor is well guarded. They've only increased the defenses since I returned." *Don't go rummaging around my room. By the love of the Mother, I don't want* you *in my room,* Eira mentally screamed. "I would be too worried if you went. Let me bring it to you."

He chuckled darkly. "I was merely testing your devotion to me. Everything is going according to plan. You'll do your part when the time comes; there's no need to rush." He had the most horrible smile. "But do not fear for me. Even if I were to go into the manor, they will never catch me, and do you want to know why?"

"Why?" Her hands were coated in a thin layer of sweat. Her pulse was racing.

Ferro leaned close to her, making her heart beat faster. "I'll let you in on a little secret… That place is part of my inheritance. I'd play there as a child."

"*What?*" Eira gasped.

"It was mine before they took everything from my family. The witch Lumeria tried to eradicate my family's name, our legacy, off this earth."

"H-How dare she!" Her voice quivered slightly. Eira hoped he didn't notice how shaken she was at the thought of him being associated with the manor she was staying in.

"Yes, but there is one thing she can't take—none of them can." His hand moved behind her head, nails digging into her scalp as he grabbed her hair and yanked her so his eyes could be level with hers. Eira stayed silent, struggling to keep her face passive as her eyes watered from the pain of her hair nearly being ripped out. "My birthright as the Champion's general, as his right hand, as the one who will bring true light to this world. And once you absolve my father, I will take you with me into the world of Her brightness. No one else shall have a right to your power but me." His words stung her face. Eira shuddered in horror as she looked up into the eyes of a madman. To think, she'd once found him desirable.

"Glory to the Champion," Eira whispered. It felt like far too much time had passed for no one to check on her. But no one had a reason to suspect she was trapped with Ferro.

"Glory, indeed," he said with a snarl and released her. "To think, when I first met you I saw you as nothing more than a silly girl to be used. Now, you will become so much more to me." He ran a finger down her cheek, trailing around her neck, and leaned forward to whisper into her ear. "Stay well, pet. Imagine my leash right here, tight around your throat. You breathe only for me. You act only for me. You are mine."

Eira inhaled sharply, and by the time she exhaled, he was gone. Only a flash of light and the rustling of velvet to betray he'd ever been there in the first place. She stumbled backward, one step, then two more. Her back hit the wall. The space was suddenly too small. Everywhere was closing in on her.

You are mine. The words were a raw and brutal form of possession. Ferro had truly taken to heart that her life was his to own—to do with as he pleased. Even if that ownership wasn't possessive, but stemmed from his lust for power…what would Ferro do if he found out about Cullen? He would no doubt see Cullen as a threat to his control.

What had she done? What danger did her love put Cullen in? His life might be the cost of indulging her fantasies.

Eira raised a hand to her mouth, fighting back the feeling of wanting to retch. She drew shuddering breaths in and out through her nose. She had to get herself under control. She had to pull herself together, and put on a brave face.

This was the gamble you made. This was the choice you made. She repeated the sentiments over and over. If she chose this then it meant she could handle it, right? The attendants would be here any moment. She had to get herself—

The curtain opened to reveal one of the smiling morphi assistants. But her expression quickly fell.

"Oh my, are you all right?" The woman rushed over to her.

"I…yes—" Eira swallowed down bile and disgust with herself "—I am. I just felt dizzy and a bit sick for a moment is all. I might have eaten something strange for breakfast." She made an attempt at a smile. Judging from the attendant's expression, she didn't do a good job of it.

"You're very pale." The attendant frowned. "Would you like me to fetch a healer?"

"No, no." Eira shook her head. "I'm feeling much better already. Just a passing moment."

"All right." The attendant stepped backward and motioned toward the center of the room in front of the mirror. "If you please."

Eira did as she was told. But her steps were still slightly disjointed, as though her spirit hadn't quite returned from that underwater place it had retreated to in the depths of her consciousness. She stared in the mirror. *That's me*, Eira told herself. *My body is mine because it still moves as I tell it. My thoughts are still my own. I am not his, not really.*

"Now, we're thinking—" The attendant stepped forward, placing her hands on Eira's hips.

"Don't touch me!" Eira wriggled away. The thought of anyone else touching her right now was utterly sickening. She needed a moment to herself—to be herself. To not be dressed up by anyone, *claimed* by anyone.

"I… I'm sorry. But for the fitting to happen, I'm going to need to drape fabrics and be able to touch you." The attendant wrung her hands, looking guilty. "I can get someone else. If I've done something to make you uncomfortable—"

"No…no, it's me." Eira shook her head. "I'm having a weird day. I'm sorry." She forced a laugh. It went over even worse than her smile.

"It's all right. I will do my best to touch you as little as possible." The attendant was true to her word. She only tapped Eira lightly with one finger when absolutely necessary to explain the cut or line of the garment they were envisioning for her.

Eira tried to follow along but kept getting distracted. She kept glancing over her shoulder, as if she'd find Ferro lurking in the corner, smirking like the fiend he was, satisfied that he held one end of her invisible leash—at the mess he had made her.

"Now, if you could undress."

"I'm sorry, what?"

"I'll need you to undress for this next part—just to your small clothes, not completely naked." The attendant smiled. "I'm going to drape you with muslin and create a rough of the design we've discussed for review." Eira honestly had no idea what that design was and the fact scared her slightly. Ferro had completely scrambled her brain, making it impossible to think or function as she knew she should. "Estal will then come in to make adjustments and render the design into the best and most flattering fabric possible."

"I can't," Eira whispered.

"Pardon?"

"I can't." Eira shook her head and staggered away. "I can't

do this right now." She had just been laid bare by Ferro's mere presence. She could smell his cologne. How could the attendant not also? How did she not see the ghost of that man lingering in every corner? How was the attendant even breathing? The air was so very thin.

"Let me assure you, this is perfectly normal in our line of work. Most young women your age have concerns about their bodies. But you are lovely. And I have the utmost respect and discretion for your modesty." The woman had a coddling smile and frustrated eyes. She was running out of patience.

"I'm sorry." Eira jerked her head from side to side. The smile fell from the assistant's face. "I'm sorry!"

Before the attendant could say anything else, Eira barged through the curtains and into a rack of fabric. She tumbled to the floor with two large bolts.

"Eira! Are you all right?" Noelle rushed over to help her up.

"What's going on?" Alyss poked her head out of her fitting room.

"Mother above, we are so sorry for her. The girl clearly was raised in a barn," Yemir apologized profusely to Estal.

All eyes were on her. Eira stared at Noelle's outstretched hand and shook her head slowly. Pushing herself off the ground, she swayed and then began running. She sprinted past Noelle's shocked expression and Yemir's shouting. She ran for the door and out into the open air.

She ran, and ran, and ran, not knowing where she was going and not caring.

Away.

She had to get away…from Ferro, from the Pillars, from *everyone.*

Chapter Twenty-Six

THEIR DAYS OF training and Alyss's skilled hand in her recovery had done more than Eira had previously realized. She ran for what seemed like hours before finally stopping, side split. Eira doubled over and vomited into a sewer grate, praying that no shadows were lurking below. With how well everything else was going, she was certain she'd just thrown up on Deneya's head.

Wiping the back of her mouth with her hand and ignoring the sideways glances from the people passing by, Eira stared upward, catching her bearings and realizing the direction she'd gone. She let out a single chuckle of bleak amusement.

"Here, again… Why must everything come back here?" she asked the Archives of Yargen towering over her.

She'd come this far. Eira continued along the last of the stairs to the main square. She strolled into the Archives and stopped, staring at the empty brazier overhead and trying to imagine an illusion flame there, like Deneya had said. A flame that was supposed to represent light, truth, and justice, and the Goddess of everything good in this world… To think it had been a fake.

No wonder the Pillars claimed that Meru's whole society was rotting from the inside out, a thin veneer of goodness and order overlaid. Deneya had made it sound like the very foundations of their core faith had been a lie for ages. What other lies had been carefully plastered over into half-truths?

"Eira, was it?" a weathered voice said from her left. Her gaze drifted, focus returning to the presence. It was the same old man who had given them the tour of the Archives her first time here.

"Kindred Allan?"

"Yes, I'm delighted you remember my name." He hobbled over to her, cane tapping against the tiled floors softly. "What are you seeking today?"

"I…" She choked on her words. It was too hard to pretend she was okay. The lies were becoming too much. She was so tired. "I just want a safe place to rest." Silent tears streamed down her face.

"Come, child, come."

Her mind shouted that he might be a Pillar. But she was tired of jumping at shadows and fighting invisible enemies. If she trusted wrongly in this…then at least it would all be over with, one way or another.

Kindred Allan guided her up the stairs and along the pathway that led to the Larks' halls. There were a few other crimson-robed men and women he greeted briefly, who cast curious glances her way but said nothing. He took her to a small lounge, shooing off the other Larks who had been occupying it. There were pillows and chairs across the entirety of the room, a low table with a game half-finished on its top.

"Please, sit. You are safe here. You look hungry and thirsty; I'll fetch you some food."

"You really don't need to—" Eira didn't get to finish before he shut the door on her.

She stared about the room, wondering just how she ended up here of all places. With a monumental sigh that turned into a high-pitched, painful whine, Eira collapsed onto the pile of pillows beneath the window. The fabrics were threadbare and moth-eaten. Their colors had lost their luster from too many days of direct sunlight. But there was a sort of worn familiarity to them. Even though it was the first time her fingers had traced the intricate patterns, many people had come here before her, seeking reprieve and a moment to catch their breath just as she was.

Eira clutched a pillow to her chest, curling into a ball and just focusing on breathing. She could feel the ice crackling beneath her skin, trying to manifest as it did the day of the revelation—

trying to numb her. Eira fought to keep it at bay. As hard as it was, she had to keep feeling. Numbness was worse, dangerous even.

The door opened again and Eira jolted up, ready to attack but instantly relaxing at the familiar faces rushing to greet her.

"Oh, thank the Mother!" Alyss threw her arms around Eira's neck. "You really are here."

"Thank you for looking after her," Noelle said to Allan.

"Alyss? Noelle?" Eira blinked. "What're you both doing here?"

"We ran after you, obviously." Noelle rolled her eyes, helping Allan settle a platter of tea and cakes on the table in the center of the room by moving aside the game pieces. "You sprinted out of there like you were possessed."

"We were so worried." Alyss grabbed her hands. "You've been acting a bit strangely since the talk of your parents earlier. We thought we upset you."

The conversation about her family…that had been today, hadn't it? It all started to blur together in Eira's mind. "No, you didn't do anything. I'm sorry for worrying you."

Noelle hummed as she sat in one of the chairs. Allan closed the door behind him, giving them privacy. "What did you tell me in the Tower forever ago?" Noelle made a show of thinking about what she was going to say, even though it was clear she already had it in mind. "That you shouldn't apologize needlessly?"

"I don't think that was quite what I said." Eira smiled weakly.

"That was what you meant." Noelle leaned forward, helping herself to a cake. "So, what happened?"

"Where's Cullen?" Eira asked the second it hit her he was absent. Her mind was already inventing a thousand reasons why he was gone…most of them involving Ferro somehow having found out about them and doing horrible things to him.

"Keeping his father at bay," Noelle answered.

"He wanted to come, truly. We could tell. But he told us to go on, that he could take care of his father and Levit to give us time," Alyss added.

"*Ah…*" Eira stared out the window. "He really shouldn't worry about me."

"That ship has sailed." Noelle snorted.

Eira scowled and snapped, "You have no idea why I say that. It's not merely worrying about our future prospects or his father." Though, those were also valid concerns.

"Why don't you enlighten us, then?" Noelle tilted her head.

"I can't." Eira's stomach rolled. She couldn't look either of them in the eye.

"Eira…" Alyss squeezed her hands. "Please… Remember when you came back from—from that place. You promised to tell us more and let us in. You said that you realized you can't do this alone."

Eira stared at her fingers intertwined with her friend's, chest aching. She hated this invasive feeling Ferro had left in her. He was like a thorny plant, rooting deeper than she ever imagined, smothering her. The only way to shake him would be to share the burden…but how could she when the disgust and frustration with herself was so strong?

"I can't." Eira shook her head.

"You need to," Noelle said firmly.

"Stop," Eira begged.

"In your own time, but…" Alyss hesitated, glancing between them. "I think Noelle is right. You should talk about this. Keeping it in clearly isn't good for you."

"We have all night." Noelle shrugged and leaned back in the chair. "No one knows we're here. Allan said he'd shelter us as long as you needed and, hey, the cakes are pretty good."

Eira snorted softly; it turned into a hiccup. Tears were falling once more, landing in heavy droplets on her and Alyss's intertwined fingers.

"Take your time," Alyss said softly.

Eira did. She stared at their clasped hands. It was real. Her friend was real. Alyss had been there through thick and thin. Through the best and the worst times. She'd remain.

Believing that gave her just enough shreds of courage to say, "I bartered my life to him."

"Who?"

"Ferro…" The words poured from her, messy and urgent. They filled the room like the tides that filled her at the mere thought of Ferro's touch. Eira told them everything she had withheld from her first summary of her time at the Pillars and didn't mince words. They listened diligently, expressions ranging across the spectrum of emotions as Eira told them everything leading up through the earlier interaction. When Eira was finished, Alyss's eyes were wide and shining. Sparks crackled around Noelle's clenched fingers.

"So, when are we killing the bastard?" Noelle finally broke the silence.

"We can't kill him yet." Eira loathed saying every word of the sentence. She hated that it was true.

"Why?" Noelle picked at her nails, and sparks flew out instead of dirt. The way the air around her teemed with pure, writhing rage had Eira wondering if Noelle had ever killed someone. Unlike Eira's previous accidental murder, Noelle was acting like she already had experience in hiding a body. A fact further emphasized when Noelle added, "No one needs to find out. Even bones turn to ash if you burn hot enough."

"You're scary and I like it," Alyss said in awe.

"Ferro is too guarded and too important to the Pillars." Eira forced herself to think like a shadow. To focus on doing what Deneya would want her to do rather than acting on instinct. She had been weaving a plan together since her time at the Pillars and the gala wasn't far. She could last until then. "If we move against him now we risk the Pillars' retaliation at best."

"How is that 'best'?" Alyss arched her brows.

"Because if they retaliate, we know where they are. At worst, they go further into hiding. As long as Ferro is interested in making me his"—Eira choked on the word—"*plaything*, we have access and insight into the Pillars. The longer I play along and the more he trusts me, the easier it'll be to maneuver not just him but that whole bloody group into a trap on the night of the ball."

"*Who cares* about these Pillars?" Noelle leaned forward. "They're Meru's problem. In case you've forgotten, we're from Solaris. We don't have Pillars there."

"But they came to our lands and killed our fellow apprentices," Eira said sharply, glaring at her friend. "A danger to Meru is a danger to Solaris." That was the whole point of the treaty, wasn't it? To show how each state was stronger together than hiding in their own corners, picked apart by vultures like Adela and the Pillars...or the looming Empire of Carsovia to the northwest of Meru. Unified, they were a force to be reckoned with.

Noelle scoffed. "You're letting your love of Meru get in the way. This man didn't just kill nameless people, he killed your brother."

"You think I don't know that?" Eira seethed. She was teetering on the edge of seeing red. Every inch of her felt as exposed and raw as the bruises Ferro had left on her skin during her time with the Pillars. Every word Noelle said was a dagger that glanced against tender flesh with brutal sharpness. "I've been picked apart too much today. I'm not going to let you flay me."

"Then do something! Don't let him get away with this!"

"I am doing something!"

"Enough, both of you." Alyss tried to see level heads prevail... and failed.

"You're letting him abuse you."

"Everything I've done has been of my own volition." Eira had locked eyes with Noelle, but the words somehow felt like they were said more to herself than the Firebearer. They were an echo of what she'd intoned to herself earlier—to remind herself that she'd had a choice somewhere in the whole situation. "I know what I did. It was my decision."

Noelle's expression darkened like the light outside the window. "I'm going to stop you right there. What you did was *not* a choice."

"I am manipulating him," Eira said defensively. She didn't want to let Noelle take this from her. The earth already felt like it was crumbling. The box she'd carefully built around her time with the Pillars…the contorted monstrosity of walls she'd tried to mentally trap her perception of Ferro in…it was all cracking by the second.

"You are *surviving*."

"I chose to—"

Noelle was off her chair. In a second she was pushing Alyss out of the way and gripping Eira's shoulders tightly. Noelle shook her gently, but firmly, as if she knew about those walls and wanted them to crumble. Wanted to see Eira break apart. It only made Eira cling to the idea of perceived strength with all the more fervor.

"If your choices are death or doing something, that's not a choice at all," Noelle said firmly. "I'm not faulting you, Eira. I'm not shaming you. But what you're doing is allowing yourself to feel guilty—to feel like you were in control of a situation you were not in control of, and that puts culpability on you that isn't fair. What he's done—is doing to your body and mind—isn't something you or anyone should ever have to endure. I don't care about 'manipulating him.' He's hurting you and it's *okay* to admit that. Just because you're strong enough to keep going doesn't mean your world hasn't been jarred beyond recognition for the time being."

Noelle kept drifting in and out of focus. Eira blinked, several times. *Oh, I'm crying again, that's why*, Eira thought vaguely. Noelle's eyes were shining too, but her mouth remained pressed in a hard line. She yanked Eira to her and held her just as fiercely as Alyss had.

"Being wounded doesn't make you weak. Admitting a transgression was made against you doesn't sap your strength," Noelle whispered. "Stop trying to shoulder this alone. You said you would let us help. Embrace that mantra and actually do it."

"Noelle is right," Alyss said softly. Her best friend wrapped her arms around both of them. "I'm sorry for what you're enduring. But we want to help. Let us help."

"All right." Eira nodded. Yet, even though she said that, Eira knew there was one major truth that she had yet to tell them—that she *couldn't* tell them.

They were already in too deep. She wouldn't involve them with the Court of Shadows.

· CHAPTER ·

TWENTY-SEVEN

THE LARKS SHARED their dinner. It was a simple meal—stew and bread—but Eira hadn't had anything taste so good in a long time. For a little while, she could sit with her friends in a safe place and they could chat and lament about things as if the world was normal. Alyss and Noelle didn't bring up anything further about Ferro and the Pillars. It didn't feel like they were trying to ignore the situation but, if anything, be respectful to Eira and allow her to bring it up if, when, and how she wanted.

Eira appreciated the confidence in her it displayed. They weren't holding her silence on those matters against her. They trusted her to bring it up as she needed. But doing so was the last thing Eira wanted. Pretending everything was fine for just a little bit was the best medicine she could find for her weary soul.

But, as stars bloomed across the sky, they all collectively agreed that their time together was nearing its end. Eira thanked Allan on their way out. She couldn't convey how much she appreciated his hospitality. He informed her that she was welcome back any time—that the Larks would always save a place for her when she needed it, which was an offer too good to not be tempted by. Promising him she'd return if ever necessary, he saw them to the end of the Larks' halls.

"What is it?" Alyss asked, noticing Eira had come to a halt in the center of the Archives. Larks had lit lamps all along the bookshelves that twinkled like the sky.

"I don't think we should leave yet." Unease had been brewing at the idea of going back to the manor as Ferro's words returned to her. That place was his family's. She had a suspicion as to how…but she couldn't rule out her own paranoia affecting her judgment. She needed proof.

"What are you thinking?" Alyss stepped forward.

"We need to look for something."

"Cullen can only stall for so long," Noelle said uncertainly. "We should get back soon."

"I'm sure we have a bit more time," Alyss insisted. "What do you need, Eira?"

"Some kind of property records, or historic maps of Risen, maybe architectural logs for famous families…" Eira wracked her brain for something that would lead them to the history of the manor they were staying in.

"This place is massive, it'll take forever," Noelle murmured.

"If we have to stay here, Allan said we were welcome."

"I am not interested in sleeping on a floor, thank you very much." Noelle scrunched her face in disgust at the mere idea.

"Then we better get looking."

"Or…" Alyss stepped away. There were a group of Larks that had just emerged from the hallways. She pulled one aside. "We're looking for old maps of Risen. Can you help us find them?"

The other Larks stalled, waiting for their friend. Eira shifted uncomfortably as their eyes darted between Alyss and her and Noelle. The company of the Larks suddenly felt slightly less safe.

"Is there something specific you're looking for?" the Lark asked. "So I can guide you to the best section?"

"It's nothing—" Eira started.

Alyss was faster. "Property records would be good, too. We're interested in the history of the manor we're staying in."

Eira cringed. She thought she kept the emotion to herself, but the expression must've crept onto her face because Noelle leaned in and whispered, "She's a little too direct, isn't she?"

"It'll be fine." Eira hoped. "Let's just see what he gives us."

The Lark took them to the middle of the Archives—three walkways up. There he pointed out an entire section that was dedicated to the construction of Risen. He said, "Most of these are on major buildings—the castle, the Archives themselves… but there are records on other smaller, prominent buildings as well. Most notable families had the same architects as the large city projects."

"Thank you so much." Alyss beamed.

"You're very welcome. The Larks are always pleased to assist in furthering someone's personal knowledge and betterment." He gave a small bow and walked away.

An invisible thread pulled on Eira, as though there was a spool at her center, spinning, unfurling the tether being yanked through her chest. Soon, that spool would be empty. It would slip between her fingers. But what was tied at the other end? Eira didn't know. She grasped the end of the thread on instinct, not ready to give up whatever fate was leading her toward.

"There's something else," she said hastily, right before the man started down the stairs. He arched an eyebrow at her. "The… The Archives have all the information in the world, right?"

He gave her a tired smile. "The Archives of Yargen are the greatest single collection of information in the world, yes… But the only one to have *all* the information in the world is Yargen herself. This is merely man's testament to her honor. To try and keep our own logs of the histories she weaves so that we might learn from them." He lifted his arms, motioning reverently around him.

"Are there records of births? Deaths?"

"Of important people."

"Can you show me them?"

"What are you thinking?" Noelle asked.

"You two look here," Eira said quickly to her friends. "I need to go check something." She darted over to the man, clutching her hands tightly together. A wave of nausea crashed down on her—Eira might not be free of that particular tide today. But this sickness stemmed solely from nerves and the vast, unknown waters that she found herself adrift in. "Please, take me to them."

The Lark did, pointing out a whole section of histories two

more rows up. There were easily thousands of books, more than she could ever check. Eira bit her lip. At least she knew where they were now in case she ever had the time…or courage.

"If that is all—"

"One last thing," Eira said with a note of apology. "I promise it's the last one." She could tell he was biting back a sigh.

"Yes?"

"Do you have any information on the pirate Adela Lagmir?"

"That would be one rung down, almost exactly beneath us. She has a small shelf dedicated to her among the nautical and wayfaring books."

"Thank you," Eira said sincerely. "We really appreciate the help."

He bowed his head, and left.

Eira stared up at the rows of books as they attempted to dwarf her with the sheer scale of information they possessed. There were too many for her to check. Eira backed away from the bookshelves, bumping into the railing behind her. She grabbed it for support and sighed. Even if she did have the time to hunt through them…it wouldn't matter.

The people who were in these books were "important people." They were no doubt kings and queens, great thinkers and poets. Perhaps…Adela's birth date was scribbled in one of them. She'd achieved enough infamy that it wouldn't surprise Eira.

But Eira's name wouldn't be anywhere within these books…

She had been a no one, abandoned. Even if Adela *was* her mother, Adela had clearly gone to great lengths to hide her. And Eira's parents had named her…not Adela, so her name had no chance to be in any of these books. Eira pushed off the railing and away from the mental void she had been teetering closer and closer to.

Just because she wasn't important enough for a Lark to transcribe didn't make her no one. It didn't make her lesser.

Heading downstairs, Eira quickly located the shelf of Adela's books below. There were about eight of them in total. An

insignificant amount considering the scale of the Archives. But…
to think Adela was so important to have *this many* dedicated to
her. She was important enough to have eight tomes when Eira—
and most other people—wouldn't even have their name scribbled
on a line in one.

Her finger hovered at a spine, trembling slightly. What if she
actually found the truth? What if she was Adela's daughter by
blood and one of these books confirmed it? What if she wasn't?
What if she still didn't know? Eira didn't know which answer
would haunt her more…but she knew that being so close and not
even trying to look was far worse.

She pulled the first book from the shelf.

Artists' renderings of the *Stormfrost* illuminated the pages.
The sketched lines brought to life the ghostly ship Eira had seen
among the dark waves weeks ago with fascinating detail. If she
hadn't seen it with her own eyes—hadn't felt the raw magic and
its blustering chill from across the ocean—she might not believe
the drawings to be anywhere near accurate. They captured the
icicles that hung from the deck rails and their brutal tips. On the
back of the ship the lines carved out the shapes of windows of
some large cabin—Adela's, Eira would bet. As fascinating as
the pictures were, however, they did little to help Eira in her
quest to find her parentage. She moved on to another book and
found nothing more than records of Adela's supposed routes and
hideaways.

The third book had information on the chronological history
of Adela. She read this one more carefully than either of the
first two. Eira's back rested against the bookshelf as she leaned,
quickly flipping the pages, searching for any clue. Her eyes
snagged on a line and she read it several times over:

*Adela has mothered no known children and, according to all
best records and accounts, has no claimed heirs to the legacy of
the* Stormfrost.

"Not that this really means anything." Eira slowly shut the book. She had already assumed her name wouldn't be in any of these tomes. Hoping otherwise had been foolish—almost as foolish as thinking she was actually Adela's daughter. Eira stared at her hand, thinking of the trident she'd summoned on instinct. It had been because she was reading Adela's journals. It wasn't some instinct in her blood. Yet... She opened the book and found the page again, running her fingers over the dry ink. "No *known* children," Eira murmured. "Could my magic really just be chance?"

Adela was the pirate queen—hunted and hated across seas and kingdoms. If she had given birth to a child, she wouldn't have wanted anyone to know. A child would be a weakness that could be used against Adela. They would be heir to the greatest pirate ship that ever existed.

Eira glanced back at the shelf, replacing the book and grabbing the second she'd previously glossed over, *Record of the Activity of the Pirate Queen*. It was more of a ledger than a book, punctuated with maps and seafaring routes, and Eira stared at the dates as she did some quick math. The Larks, naturally, kept records using the calendar of Meru, not Solaris. Fortunately, figuring out her birth date on Meru's calendar was one of the first things Eira had done for fun after realizing Meru had a slightly different way of tracking time.

Her finger hovered on a date that would correspond with about the year 350 on the Solaris calendar—*Adela sighted in the barrier islands, heading southwest*. That was five years before Eira was born. The next recorded sighting wasn't until twenty years later.

Right around the time of her birth was a giant gaping hole in the history of Adela. "Headed southwest." What did that mean? To the Republic of Qwint? To some of the southern barrier islands? Farther? Southwest from where? Depending on where the sighting was, it could've even meant Oparium.

"Spotted off the coast of Little Brother Bay," Eira read aloud.

"Where in the Mother's name is that?" She began to flip back through the pages in search of the name on one of the maps listed when a shout promptly followed by a burst of flame distracted her.

"Eira!" Alyss cried.

The book tumbled from her hands and Eira slammed into the railing, leaning over to get a view of her friends. Noelle had placed herself between Alyss and a knife-wielding man. Fire sparked between her fingers, threatening to leap forth again. Their assailant cursed, stamping out the last remnants of flames from his sleeve.

"Alyss, behind you!" Eira shouted. Alyss turned too late. Eira threw out a hand and jagged spears of ice jutted out from the metal walkway, keeping a second attacker at bay. Eira's pulse was racing. The two men were wearing Larks' clothing. Had it been the man who helped them? Had it been one of the people who stared a little too long at them? Who was the Pillar in Larks' clothing and how many more were there?

Moreover, why were they attacking Noelle and Alyss? Eira felt nauseous. She might have brought this on her friends by Alyss asking for the records. The Pillars might have seen them as getting too close to the truth and… Eira shook her head, interrupting the thoughts. There wasn't time now to worry about the answers; they had to get moving.

Taking a breath and allowing the swell of her magic to rise to new heights, Eira pushed herself over the railing. Her feet met empty air, but only for a moment. A ramp of ice suspended between where she was and Alyss and Noelle. Eira slid down, landing between them.

"Showoff," Noelle huffed, not taking her eyes off the man.

"Why are you doing this?" Alyss asked the woman who had been about to attack her. "Allan said we would be safe—"

"They're not Larks." Eira grabbed Alyss's elbow and hissed in her ear. "We have to leave, now."

The urgency in her voice seemed to shake Alyss from the

trance the shock had placed over her. She nodded. Eira yanked her toward the railing.

"I've always hated cliff jumping," Alyss growled and gave her a sidelong glance.

"You can tell me how much later." Eira hooked her elbow with Noelle's and said, "Trust me."

"Trust you as far as—"

Noelle's question was cut off by a scream as Eira pulled them both over the edge. It was too bad Cullen wasn't with them. He could make pockets of air to ease their landing. Instead, stone sprang forth from the ground far below, reaching Alyss's feet. One pillar retreated and another rose as Alyss leapt from platform to platform down.

Noelle's and Eira's pathway was less graceful. Holding tightly to her friend, Eira slid down a corkscrew of ice toward the ground, Noelle screaming in her ear the entire time. On the ground floor, they were met with a rush of Swords of Light, weapons brandished, Lightspinning shining.

"What's the meaning of this?" a Sword barked at them.

Eira dismissed her magic as she stood, the ice turning to vapor. Alyss was busy wiggling her fingers, putting the mosaic back exactly as it had been before she'd disrupted it with her magic. If her friend hadn't been so artistically inclined, they might have really left their mark on the Archives.

"We—" Eira was cut off.

"They're stealing from the Archives!" one of the Pillars in Larks' clothing shouted from over the railing. "Stop them!"

Eira cursed and waved a hand through the air. The air grew thick with water and magic as a cloud of dense fog filled the room. She grabbed her friends' hands, yanking them forward.

"We're not—"

"Don't even try, Alyss." Eira was sprinting. "We have to get out."

"The Swords will help us!" Even as Alyss countered her, she kept running, thank the Mother.

Eira couldn't count on the Swords to help them. She couldn't count on anyone to help them. They exploded out of the wall of fog and into the square of the Archives. Eira glanced around, heart beating hard in her throat, nearly making her sick from the sensation.

Where could they go? What could they do? Her instinct had been right—the Pillars were everywhere. They had infiltrated Lumeria's knights and attendants. They had infiltrated the manor and the Archives. The whole city was under the oppressive gaze of the Champion and his nameless, faceless zealots.

"Stop them!" a knight shouted from behind them.

"This way!" Eira pulled her friends as she began running again, dropping their hands so she could pump her arms, praying they could keep up.

"Where are we going?" Noelle asked as Eira leapt off the first step of a stairwell she knew all too well by now.

"The one place where that man can't see."

"What? Who? Where?" Alyss panted.

"Trust me." Eira glanced over her shoulder. "We're going to have to take the long way to lose them."

"Let me help." Alyss flicked her hand over her shoulder and bars of stone rose from the ground, blocking the end of the stairwell as their feet crossed onto the steps below.

Eira swung right, trying to keep her bearings. As long as the Archives were behind her, and the castle was in front, she was headed in the right direction. Two more turns and they were out onto a major street. The three women darted across, heading down another alleyway.

"Hold—Hold—I—" Alyss didn't get to finish. With one hand on her side and the other flat against a wall for support, she barely refrained from upending the contents of her stomach.

"Sorry for the pace," Eira said guiltily, just as breathless and body aching.

"What in the Mother's name is going on?" Alyss demanded.

"Those men were Pillars," Eira said with confidence.

"Why else would they attack us?" Noelle seemed to begrudgingly agree.

"But they—" Alyss was interrupted by a shout echoing to them from the street.

"They went that way!"

Eira cursed. "Come on, we have to keep moving."

"Where are we going?" Noelle demanded. "You said the manor's not safe. And if they're in the Archives…"

"I know somewhere we can lose them—Pillars and Swords. We can catch our breath and figure out next steps there." Eira just hoped it was empty.

As they reached quieter, more rundown streets, the three slowed their pace. It was agonizing to move slowly, but running like they had hounds on their heels only made them more conspicuous. Eira's eyes kept darting around just like when she had walked this path for the first time with Deneya. The Pillars could be anywhere—anyone.

When the doorway that connected to the secret passage between buildings was in sight, Eira heaved a sigh of relief. She skipped two steps over to the door and prayed the combination hadn't changed.

It was the same.

"In here, quickly." Eira closed the door behind Alyss, plunging them into momentary darkness.

A flame appeared over Noelle's shoulder, illuminating them with the brightness of candlelight. "What is this place?"

"I can't tell you." Eira pressed her hand into her side, massaging away the pain. Noelle gripped her shoulder.

"They're going to think we're criminals now. We ran from the law." Noelle shook her head and cursed. "Didn't we just say *no more secrets*? I think you owe us an explanation."

"You don't want to know what this place is."

"I'm with Noelle." Alyss straightened, finally catching her breath. "I'd rather know everything at this point, regardless of the danger."

"You don't know what you're saying." Eira ached all over and not just from their sprint through Risen. It hurt her to think about the web she was trapped in—that her friends were slowly but surely becoming further and further tangled in. Sooner or later, there'd be no way out for them.

"We want to know." Alyss folded her arms. "Please."

"I—" A pulse of magic distracted her. Eira glanced into the corner of the room in time to see an all-black cat stepping from the shadows through ripples of reality. Where an animal once was, an amber-haired woman now stood.

"She can't tell you, because it's not her place to tell." Rebec, Deneya's right hand and Specter of the Court of Shadows, smiled thinly. "But now that you're here, you've seen too much to leave without knowing."

"Without knowing what?" Noelle asked.

"Please, don't. They don't need to be involved," Eira beseeched on her friends' behalf.

"They already are," Rebec said sharply. "Now, come along, you three."

"Where?" Alyss asked, looking thoroughly confused.

"To the Court of Shadows."

CHAPTER TWENTY-EIGHT

THERE WAS A secret passage within the secret passage, which didn't surprise Eira in the slightest. Rebec led them through a door that was covered in blocks on one side, made to look flush with the stone walls of the passage save for a small, hidden lever.

The passage down into the depths of Risen wasn't unlike the pathway from the manor. It was several sloping halls, a couple of stairwells, and stretches that would have been in complete darkness if not for Noelle's light. Eira glanced at her friends. Alyss seemed to have a mix of awe and concern. Noelle kept her eyes on Rebec. There was a tough and brutal side to her friend that the tournament was bringing out. Eira wasn't sure if Noelle had always known it had been there. Or if it was a surprise to even her.

"We don't have to go—" Eira tried to say. Rebec cut her off with a glare. It was too late for backtracking. Alyss and Noelle had seen their secret access; they'd run into Rebec; they were in the Court of Shadows now, or dead.

And it was all Eira's fault.

The four ended up at the intricately locked door. Rebec produced the key and with a flourish of her arm announced, "Welcome, ladies, to the Court of Shadows."

"What exactly is the Court of Shadows?" Noelle asked.

Alyss stared at the caverns in silent awe.

"All will be made clear, soon enough. This way, if you please." Rebec wore a grin that said she really didn't care what they pleased. It would've been far more accurate if she'd said, *follow me or die.*

Noelle seemed to pick up on the threat and her expression continued to darken as they walked down the main path.

With every step, Eira's feet felt heavier. She was unraveling. The world was spinning out of her control and there was nothing she could do to bring it back together. The pieces of the game she'd started back in Solaris were scattered to the winds, the board flipped, and all of Risen had gone upside-down as it had fallen into the hands of the Pillars. Ferro was gaining more and more control. Secrets were budding in the most unexpected of corners. And the stakes seemed higher by the second even if Eira couldn't yet entirely fathom their depths.

Expectedly, Deneya was waiting for them.

"D-Deneya?" Alyss said, jaw nearly hitting the floor.

Deneya just folded her arms, offering no explanation as to her position or why they were here. Instead, she said simply, "What is the meaning of this?"

Rebec offered a brief explanation of Eira leading them into the secret passage, speaking over any attempt from Eira to recount events for herself.

Deneya pinched the bridge of her nose. "Word of the incident in the Archives has already reached me… If you weren't competitors, you'd be dead."

"I don't think the Pillars cared that we're competitors. They would have killed us if we hadn't fought back," Noelle said.

"Oh, I'm not talking about the Pillars in the Archives. I'd kill you myself for being here."

Eira's stomach clenched. It felt as if the organ was contorting itself, folding over countless times until it was a tiny, dense rock that sank deep into the pit of all her worst fears. She breathed in and out, trying to stop the world from spinning as Deneya turned her unnatural eyes to her.

"Care to explain yourself?"

"Ferro came to me…" Eira worked to keep her voice level as she told Deneya everything—Ferro, running to the Archives, them hunting for the records that could elaborate on his claim of owning the manor. As she spoke, Deneya's expression wavered from the blank slate she'd originally presented. There was genuine shock in her eyes at the idea that the manor was originally under Pillar control. Midway through Eira's tale, Lorn arrived and stood by Rebec, looking utterly unsurprised to see them. When she finished, Rebec leaned over, whispering in his ear what Eira assumed to be the parts he missed.

"What did you find?" Deneya looked to Alyss and Noelle.

"The manor was under the crown's purview for the past twenty-five years," Alyss reported as if she was already a shadow falling into line. "It had been donated to the crown following the death of its previous owner—a Lady Yewin Cortova."

"Cortova?" Deneya looked to Lorn. "What do we know about Cortova?"

Lorn crossed to the back of the room, where several large safes lined the wall. At the same time, Rebec went to the only entrance and exit to the Specter's hall, barring the door. Lorn shielded the safe lock from view with his body, and a soft clicking and rattling filled the air. There was a flash of light, and then he stepped back, swinging open the door. Lorn reached in, fished around, and produced a leather folio.

"What's back there?" Noelle asked.

"All the secrets ever whispered in Risen," Deneya answered.

Alyss's eyes darted to Eira. She wore an enthusiastic grin, as though she was barely holding back saying, *How exciting is this?* Eira pursed her lips slightly and Alyss picked up on the severity of their situation, her expression shifting into something more solemn.

Lorn settled the folio on the back table. Noelle took a step forward as Deneya did and Rebec grabbed her shoulder.

"They're not for your eyes," Rebec said with a note of warning.

"Here she is." Lorn held up a sheet of parchment to Deneya. "Lady Yewin Cortova…yes, now I remember her. Sad case indeed."

"Tell me," Deneya demanded as her eyes skimmed the paper.

"Mother died in childbirth. Father was a wealthy merchant, lost at sea. Pirate activity suspected…but never confirmed."

"As is too often the case," Deneya muttered. "Pirates can move too easily before we even know they're there."

Like Adela. Eira's heart thrummed. *When she dropped me off in Oparium, a place where she knew I'd be safe and hidden as the* Stormfrost's *heir.*

"Yewin was raised in the care of the Faithful, as is customary. They managed her estate until she was of age. She seemed to be a pious young woman, full of opportunity, until she became pregnant out of wedlock and was shunned by the antiquated notions of the then 'polite' society. She met her ultimate demise in childbirth like her mother."

"What happened to the child?" Deneya asked.

"Stillborn." Lorn passed another sheet of parchment. "According to the reports of the Lark healers who delivered."

"For people who supposedly uphold truth, the Pillars are certainly good at lying," Deneya growled.

"They like making us chase them." Rebec sighed. "Have us jumping at rumors all across Risen."

They certainly had Eira looking twice at every turn.

Deneya's gaze turned to her. "You were reckless once, and we forgave you, but this time—"

"When was the baby born?" Eira asked hastily. "Wait, don't tell me." She looked to Lorn, trying to find some kind of ally in the keeper of secrets. "Was the baby born the day after the Night-Noon Day?"

"Yes, how did you…"

"It's Ferro." The pieces were beginning to slot together for her so completely that Eira was shocked no one else had seen the whole picture yet. The suspicions she'd had in the Archives—all the way back to the first time she'd seen Mistress Harrot—were beginning to solidify. What had felt scattered and distorted was suddenly coming into view. "The child she had was Ferro."

"Did you not hear what the Larks reported—"

"The Larks have been infiltrated by the Pillars, clearly," Eira countered before Rebec could finish. "Moreover, this was twenty-five years ago. Was it before Ulvarth was taken captive?"

Lorn glanced down at the paper he was holding and then looked back at her. His lips were pursed so tightly that it was a wonder he managed to say, "Yes."

"Meaning, Ferro was born right before Ulvarth was arrested. He was born to a woman who grew up in the care of the Larks—under the protection of the Swords of Light and all the Faithful, groups that Ulvarth was the ultimate head of at that time. He would have had access to her, and she to him."

"You're claiming that Ferro is the bastard son of Ulvarth and Yewin…that they kept his birth a secret?" Deneya arched her eyebrows. "Why? What would their motives be?"

"There could be any possibility. You know Ulvarth far better than I. If I can imagine a few uses for a secret child, I'm certain you can as well."

All eyes were on Deneya. She tapped the table next to her, staring accusatorially at the papers spread on it, as if they dared to keep this secret from her for so long. Eira wouldn't be shocked if, before all this was over, Deneya demanded copies of the documents just so she could burn some in frustration.

"I can," Deneya admitted. "I never understood that man, but he was the secretive sort. And he suspected we might be closing in on him even then. He might have seen the boy as an opportunity to have an agent on the outside. Someone who could act in his stead and who wouldn't be questioned by his most devout followers." Deneya cursed and slammed her fist into the table. Her knuckles were bloody, but she didn't so much as wince. "We missed it. All of us."

"Every secret is usually supported by several more," Lorn said solemnly.

"We are the ones who need to know them, all the way down." Deneya inspected her knuckles, sighed, and murmured some Lightspinning. Glyphs rotated over the wounds and knitted the flesh. "So Ferro is Ulvarth's son and the manor was his home, his birthright."

"The key is to figure out what *exactly* Ferro has been working toward this whole time," Eira said, continuing to inject herself into the conversation.

"Bringing his father back to power," Rebec gave Eira a roll of her eyes. Eira resisted returning the expression.

"But *how*? Freeing Ulvarth would've been the first step." Eira spoke over Deneya's objection that Ulvarth was dead. She didn't believe it in the slightest anymore. "Then they see the treaty and the tournament as an opportunity to undermine Lumeria's rule. But they need something to justify them being ordained by the goddess. What would—"

"What are your orders?" If the sharpness of the question to Deneya was any indication, Rebec clearly had had enough of Eira's interjections.

Eira pursed her lips. She was already in trouble as it was.

"What book did you find this information in?" Deneya glanced between Alyss and Noelle. "I'll need it to report to the queen."

"I…" Noelle picked at her fingers in a guilty motion Eira had never seen from the self-assured woman. "I might have torched it."

"*What?*" Lorn's eyes were consumed by white as he stared, utterly horrified.

"It's not my fault! Everything happened so fast. The man lunged, and grabbed the book, and then I saw he had a dagger in his other hand… I acted on instinct." Noelle put her hands on her hips and regained her composure. "I defended myself and I'm not going to apologize for it. But the book was caught in the crossfire. And I am a bit sorry about that."

Deneya sighed and looked to Lorn. "You know what I'm about to ask, right?"

"I'll see if I can find another copy, or the original records, or a Lark that knows about that book and can transcribe something."

Lorn put the pages back into the folio and returned them to their safe in the back of the room.

"And me?" Rebec asked.

"You're going to turn over that manor, from top to bottom, and make sure there's no entries or passages we don't know about. I don't want a rat to shit in that place without a shadow knowing."

"Understood."

"What about people working in the manor?" Eira had yet to bring up Harrot. "I think that—"

"They've all long been vetted." Deneya brushed off the notion.

"But—"

"That is the final word on the matter." The Court of Shadows was so self-assured in their power and they had been for so long that they weren't looking at what was actually there. That power they thought was cemented was slowly slipping from their grasp, eroding away by assuming they were in control.

Eira wanted to scream. She didn't for the sake of her friends.

"What about us?" Alyss asked, motioning to her and Noelle.

The keen, horrible weight of disappointment seeped into the air from Deneya's pores at the question. Even Alyss and Noelle could feel it. But the one Deneya's stare lingered on the longest, the one it held the most weight for, was Eira.

She choked down an apology. The words wouldn't matter now. They wouldn't help Deneya sort things out. Or smooth over the messes Eira had made.

"You have done more to endanger and hinder the Court of Shadows than even our enemies of late. You're a risk we simply can no longer bear."

"But I—"

Deneya held up a hand, stopping Eira and confirming what Eira already knew. It didn't matter what she said. Deneya had already made up her mind.

"We're going to return the three of you to the manor. And on pain of death you are going to *stay there* and keep your mouths shut."

As if starting now, Alyss and Noelle nodded mutely.

"What do I do if the Pillars come to me again?" Eira asked, barely resisting adding that they were already in the manor. No matter how much the Court of Shadows wanted to be rid of her, and the Pillars loathed her, both needed her for different reasons. Until one of them was ended by the other, she was going to be stuck between.

"If you stay where you're supposed to be, the Pillars won't be able to get to you," Deneya said curtly.

"I was where I was supposed to be when Ferro cornered me," Eira countered. "'Where I'm supposed to be' is in a den previously owned by the Pillars that I think they *have infiltrated.* I think Yewin is still in that house."

"Yewin was likely a victim," Lorn said on Deneya's behalf. "Ulvarth was no doubt using her as he does everyone else. 'Died in childbirth.' I would place my bet on Ulvarth killing her to keep her quiet."

Deneya gave Lorn an approving nod.

Eira stopped herself from objecting further. No one was listening to her. What did it matter?

"I will be personally in charge of looking after the manor from here on. You'll be safe under my watchful gaze," Rebec said with a thin smile that made it clear she wasn't just watching the people outside the manor, but the people within—she was watching *them.*

"We will make sure there's no more incidents and no more opportunities for Ferro to get to you. You'll take the plaster we took from the Archives to the ball and deliver it to him as you promised. That will lure him—and hopefully a vast majority of Pillars—out into the open and the Court of Shadows will take it from there."

"And at the ball—" Eira started.

"I said that was all you needed to worry about." Deneya's whispering tones had become as sharp as daggers. "There is no 'we.' You are not one of us. You've never been. You don't have the slightest aptitude toward being a shadow."

The words wounded deeper than Eira had been prepared for. *Not one of us*. Yet again. She didn't belong. Not here. Not anywhere. She'd never be a part of a group because every time she tried she did something that endangered those around her.

Invisible waters were rising around her. She felt herself sinking, deeper and deeper, but did nothing to stop her descent. Why had she tried? Why had she dared? What good had her attempts done for anyone?

A ghostly face in the darkness of the magic within her was her reminder of why she was fighting—Marcus.

"Do you understand?" Deneya's question demanded a response.

"I'll do as you command." Eira bowed her head. "I'll stay put."

"Good. Ducot will serve as our between—"

"Ducot?" Noelle said in surprise. Deneya ignored the interjection.

"—for any messages that need to come from the Court of Shadows. After the ball and all this ugliness involving the Pillars is resolved, you are no longer needed. I strongly recommend never even *thinking* of us again." Deneya allowed her words to sink in during a long stretch of silence before ending with, "Rebec, get them out of my sight."

Twenty-Nine

"IT'S NOT YOUR fault," Alyss tried to console Eira as they walked up the stairs in the safe house. Noelle flanked Eira's other side. Rebec had dropped them back long after everyone else had gone to bed. She said they were going to have a report of them being returned in the night by guards after they were cleared of the incident in the Archives.

By the time the sun rose, everything would be "as it should be." And they were to act like good automatons, not stepping out of the lines Deneya drew for them.

"No, it is." Eira sighed and shook her head. "I keep acting like my actions only affect myself. As though I'm the only one with skin in this game. And because of that I've put so many people in danger. You two included."

"I don't feel like I'm in that much danger." Noelle shrugged. How the woman could be so blasé about whatever the world threw her way was a trait Eira was beginning to both fear and revere. Eira knew she never wanted to find out what could bring her down.

"I'm glad you don't." Eira meant it. If her friends could sleep well at night, she didn't want to take that from them. They didn't have to live with the nightmarish memories of the Pillars and the pit haunting their every waking moment.

"You only acted rashly once," Alyss pointed out. "You can't be faulted for what you did today." But they all knew Deneya already had. "Running from Ferro, getting some space, defending yourself in the Archives, any of us would've done the same."

Eira shrugged. "It doesn't matter. All that matters is the Pillars are ultimately brought to justice. If the court can do that without me, then that's fine." Though her opinion of the court was diminishing by the hour.

"It'll happen, I'm sure of it." Noelle's hand landed on the door to the Solaris chambers. "Now, it's been a long day. If you're all right…"

"I'm fine. Go to bed." Eira squeezed both her friends.

"Want to come with me?" Alyss asked as Noelle opened the door. "You don't have to be alone if you don't want to."

"Maybe… But I think I'm going to see if Cullen—"

The man in question stopped pacing mid-step, frozen as his eyes landed on them. Eira was trapped by his stare. She was made weak by the relief that flooded through her at the mere sight of him. As if just from seeing him again, the world was somehow right.

"I think we should give them some space." Noelle shared a grin with Alyss and they both retreated to their rooms before Eira could say anything else.

She was laid bare by his eyes alone, his willing captive. Eira drank him in as she submerged herself in the warm, *safe* feelings he flooded her with. In a breath, she would learn his reaction to the events of the day. In a second, they would have to confront the source of his worried look, of her frantic escape…of everything.

But for this one second, he looked at her as if the world began and ended between her right and left feet. He looked at her like she was a goddess among men. She wasn't strong enough to break that stare.

He was.

"Cullen…" she started, weakly, as he began to cross the room to her.

Wordlessly, he swept her into his arms, crushing her against him. Her hands landed on the expansive plane of muscles that made up his back as her senses were overwhelmed. The smell of citrus soap, of windswept laundry, of sun-drenched duvets and lazy days that she wanted to slip between her fingers like his hands in her hair. Cullen's fingertips grazed her cheeks, exploring tentatively, as if confirming that she was real.

"Eira." He breathed her name like pain, like ecstasy. "Thank the Mother. I was so frightened." His breath was hot on her cheeks. Or perhaps that was just the flush of guilt for worrying him. "You ran. Something was wrong. I knew it and I wanted to help you…but I couldn't follow. I should have. But my father, he—" Cullen's face twisted with agony.

"He what?"

Cullen ignored the question. "Then I heard of an incident at the Archives and you were missing again." He made a strangled, choking noise and the muscles of his throat constricted as he swallowed hard. "I thought they had you again. I thought I might have lost you for good."

"I'm here." Her hands covered his and Eira's eyes fluttered closed. She breathed so deeply her head spun. "I'm sorry for worrying you."

"Don't apologize." He sounded like Noelle. "I'm just glad you're all right."

Eira nodded and looked up at him. His expression, so vulnerable, so pure. So everything Ferro was not. Cullen was truly a balm to the scarred and tattered remains of her heart.

"What happened?"

"I…" Instinct silenced her. But the darkness of the pit lingered in the shadows of the room, reminding her how fleeting each moment was. Her time with Alyss and Noelle—their support— emboldened her. "I need to tell you something, but I'm afraid."

"Of what?"

"That you'll see me differently, or will want nothing to do with me."

"Trust me when I say, that will never be the case," he reassured her, stroking her cheeks lightly with his thumbs. "You are everything to me, Eira. *Everything.*"

Trust him, she urged herself as she drew a shaky breath. "It's about Ferro…"

Cullen's expression darkened and doubt passed through her at the sight. Was he about to back away at the mere mention of Ferro's name? How much did he know of her previous infatuations with the man?

"What did he do to you?" Cullen growled savagely. The tone might have frightened her if it was not directed at those who would harm her.

"There are some things I didn't tell you about my time with the Pillars... Things I did..." For the second time in one very long day, Eira shared the gambles she had made with Ferro. She shared every blow he had made against her body, and her mind. She laid out every insecure, ugly, vulnerable part of her at Cullen's feet and, when she was done, awaited his judgment.

As she spoke, his expression only grew more brutal. The muscles of his cheeks had turned to stone from clenching his jaw. Even though his expression remained grim, his eyes burned with a rage she hadn't thought Cullen could possess.

When she finished, he continued to stare wordlessly, looking through her as though he were glowering at the version of Ferro who existed only in her memories. Eira shifted, throat sore and uncomfortable at his nonverbal probing. Was all of this anger truly a result of Ferro alone? Had someone ever been this protective, this enraged on her behalf?

"Say something," she demanded softly as the silence dragged on.

"I am a failure."

"You are not."

"I have failed in the one thing I want to succeed in—protecting you."

Eira rasped a laugh under her breath. "The feeling is mutual... I don't know what Ferro would do if he found out about us."

"All the more reason to keep things secret." He released her and wandered over to the hearth, staring at the smoldering embers of the fire. Eira watched him, remembering how he had stopped himself short when it came to Yemir earlier.

"Did something happen with your father?"

Silence was her response.

"Cullen—"

"It's been a long night." He sighed and faced her once more. "You should get some rest."

"No." Eira crossed to him, grabbing his hand as though he had been about to run away. "I told you everything. Now it's your turn."

Cullen gave a tired, gentle smile, tucking some hair behind her ear. "I will, I promise. But not tonight. We've been through enough today. Let's talk about it in the morning."

"But—"

"It's nothing we need to worry about now. It'll keep," he reassured her. As though sealing his words with a promise, he leaned forward and placed a gentle kiss on her lips. "Go to sleep, Eira."

"And we'll talk in the morning?"

"First chance we get."

"All right." Eira released him and Cullen walked her to her door, bidding her a good night. It took every bit of control not to demand he stay with her. But for every bit of her that wanted him to stay, there was a counterweight that wanted to be alone. She felt like a wounded animal that needed space to lick her wounds.

So Eira went to bed alone. At first light, she woke to the muffled sounds of Yemir and Cullen speaking. Their conversation ended right as Eira regained awareness.

By the time she roused enough to get out of bed and dress, Cullen was already gone for the day.

***

The days became a strange kind of monotony. Yemir utterly monopolized Cullen's time. If it wasn't discussions over breakfast, it was dignitary dinners or "important matters." The only time she could manage to see him was on the training fields.

But that was not the place to have a heart-to-heart about whatever was going on between Cullen and his father. Eira knew that by Cullen's increasingly distant, haunted eyes.

The other man in her orbit was Ducot. He didn't seem to pay much attention to her. But Eira could feel his attention when he thought she was distracted.

When they weren't at the training grounds, Eira spent most of her time in the common area. She tried to get to know the draconi, but they'd have none of it. Ducot must've said something to the morphi, because they cast wary glances her way. For all Eira knew, every one of them was in the Court of Shadows. The elfin would speak with her from time to time. But it seemed all the competitors were growing ever more aware that the ball was only a week away, and that meant the competition began in earnest in just eight days.

Noelle didn't have the same poor luck that she did. Surprisingly—or perhaps not for the daughter of nobles—Noelle flowed easily from group to group. The morphi seemed to enjoy her presence and the elfin invited her regularly for dinner. She seemed closer by the day with Lavette, the daughter of one of the dignitaries from Qwint.

All this made Eira's primary company Alyss.

The two women sat in the terraced gardens on a bench down by the river. Alyss fiddled with a bit of wood, her magic bending, shaping, and smoothing it into the figure of an eagle. Eira poked at her arm, still sweat-slicked from their hours at the training grounds this afternoon. Her body had begun to change, muscle emerging in places it hadn't ever before.

"Is your arm all right?" Alyss asked without looking up.

"*Huh?* Oh yeah, fine… It's just…never looked like this before."

Alyss's eyes darted over and then returned to her work. "I believe that's called biceps."

"I know what it's called." Eira folded her arms and sank back onto the bench. The position only made her more aware of the new muscle that was there. "I'm not used to having one is all."

"You've always had one, that's how you move your arm," Alyss said dryly.

"You're in rare form today."

Her friend smirked. "Only because you're making it too easy."

"You get what I mean though."

"I get that you're discovering the wonders of a regular exercise regimen."

"Don't say that as though you're some kind of training-ground frequent." Eira stuck her tongue out at her friend. Alyss giggled.

"You're right, I'm teasing. I've noticed a difference in me, too. I guess this is what happens when we finally stop spending every waking hour in a library or classroom." Alyss paused, staring at her arms and legs. There were shadowed lines cutting across her dark skin that had never been there before. "I hope my dress for the ball will still fit when it arrives. Though the seamstress was using the magic of the morphi to make it. I think she could…" Alyss trailed off when she noticed Eira's solemn expression. "Sorry. I know you don't like thinking of that day."

"It's all right."

"It was insensitive of me." Alyss nudged her shoulder against Eira's gently. "Forgive me."

"Done well before you needlessly asked." Eira smiled at her friend, putting on a brave face in the wake of the memories of Ferro that were suddenly swimming like sharks in her inner ocean. She hadn't heard anything from him since that day. But a part of her always felt like he was watching, hovering, one step away. In a breath he'd close the gap and—

Eira looked over her shoulder, making sure no one was there. The nearest people were sitting up in the common area under the archways. Just her mind playing tricks on her…

Her eyes wandered over the manor, thinking back to what she'd discovered that day. The manor had been Ferro's mother's. She pursed her lips, wondering if Deneya's and Lorn's suspicions about Ulvarth killing Ferro's mother to keep his son a secret were founded. Or, was she correct in her theory that she'd never had a chance to say?

"What is it?" Alyss waved a hand in front of Eira's face. Eira blinked, head jerking toward her friend. "You were lost to the world for a moment there."

"Sorry, I was thinking about—" she swallowed hard "—about *him*."

"It's best not to." Alyss hooked her arm with Eira's and scooted closer, resting her head on Eira's shoulder.

"I know. But…it's hard not to when a part of me still feels like I'm sleeping under his roof."

She glanced back over her shoulder despite herself. The people who had been sitting at the table by the archway had left, and an elfin woman bustled about, cleaning up their mess. *Mistress Harrot.* Her lilac eyes darted over Eira's way, lingering for several seconds too long.

Eira quickly looked back to the river.

"What is it?" Alyss's voice was distant. She was back in the real world. Meanwhile, Eira's mind was whirring leagues away.

This house had belonged to Ferro's mother—a woman whom little was known about. A woman whom most people likely wouldn't be able to recognize because she'd spent most of her life in the care of the Larks. The manor had been taken by the crown on her death and an overseer appointed to it.

I will bring it to her. That was what Ferro had said, right? When she'd first listened to the dagger? Eira closed her eyes, struggling to remember every word of that conversation. *Her.* The word stuck out in her mind. The way Ferro had said it.

He was talking about his mother. She was certain of it. Harrot's seeming obsession with her room… What if her "dusting" incident wasn't checking in on Eira…but looking for the dagger?

What if that stupid golden weapon was more significant than any of them—even her—had thought? "Eira?" Alyss pressed again.

If she was right… That meant the golden dagger was given to Ferro by his father. Ferro had brought it to his mother—Mistress Harrot—for safekeeping while he went to Solaris to…what did the dagger say? Eira gripped the bench, trying to focus.

"Eira, you don't seem—"

"*Shh*," Eira hissed. She glanced at her friend, who looked a mixture of startled and wounded. "Sorry, Alyss, give me a moment…"

"Okay." Her friend tilted her head, looking more curious than upset.

Eira stood. The Court of Shadows might be done with her. But she wasn't done with them. And Eira was going to make *someone* listen to her before it was too late.

Alyss grabbed her hand. "You're not running off without telling me where you're going."

"I need to speak with Ducot," Eira said in a hushed whisper. "There's a missing piece to this puzzle, something they're all overlooking, and he's the only person who might hear me out."

THIRTY

Mistress Harrot was nowhere to be seen when Eira reentered the building. She kept glancing out of the corner of her eye, looking for the silent overseer of the manor. Alyss stayed close by as Eira made her way up to the third floor and knocked on the door to the Twilight Kingdom's apartments.

Griss was the one to answer. He seemed startled by her sudden appearance. Not that she could blame him.

"I need to speak to Ducot."

Griss leaned against the doorframe, blocking her entry and visibility into the room. "And what do you need to speak with him about?"

"It's personal."

"He doesn't want to speak to you."

Eira bit back pointing out that Griss hadn't even gone to ask Ducot what he'd want. She took a deep breath and reached within her for an emotion that resembled calm, or gentle. Surely something like that still existed in her seas. Or was she all chop and icy daggers now?

"Please," Eira said softly. "Just, get him? If he doesn't want to speak to me after I tell him why I'm here then I'll leave. I promise."

Griss stared down at her, head cocked, a frown on his lips.

"Eira, tell me what you want," Ducot's voice came from behind Griss. "Make it fast; and it'd better be good."

Rolling his eyes, Griss pushed open the door the rest of the way to reveal a common area much like the Solaris competitors had. Ducot sat with a morphi woman Eira had come to know as

Amlia, and the morphi trainer. The latter two stared at her with intense gazes. But Ducot didn't even turn. He kept his back to her. Yet, Eira could feel his pulses washing over her like a tiny barrage.

How could she tell him without raising everyone else's suspicion? She couldn't, Eira realized. Eira bit her lip. She was doing things all wrong again. This was exactly why the Court of Shadows had kicked her out. Or, rather, never really considered her a member in the first place.

"I… Nevermind. I'm sorry to interrupt," Eira said sincerely. "I shouldn't have barged in. If you have a moment, Ducot, I'd like to speak with you sometime tonight. You know how to find me."

"I do indeed."

Griss shut the door on her face without another word.

"How rude," Alyss mumbled.

"They hate me." Eira started down the stairs. "Not that I blame them."

"What you did really wasn't *that* bad." Alyss dropped her voice to a whisper. "The punishment isn't even close to the crime."

"I don't even care about that. There's something they need to know." Eira gripped the railing so tightly her skin squeaked as she continued to descend. "I was hoping that Ducot would at the very least listen. But I guess not."

"You never know." Alyss bumped her hip with Eira's. "He might surprise you."

"I might indeed."

Eira and Alyss turned. Ducot eased the door to the Twilight Kingdom's common area closed with a soft click.

"You… I thought you…" Eira fumbled, trying to find words and failing.

"I heard what you said."

"After the door was closed?" Alyss blinked, startled.

"Obviously." Ducot stood on the stair right above Eira,

meeting her eyes with his. She was reminded of the first night he'd taken her to the Court of Shadows. "So?"

"Not here." Eira glanced around. "Come with me." She started back for the bench she and Alyss had just occupied.

"Are you coming as well?" Ducot asked Alyss.

"She already knows everything. And I need my trusted friends," Eira said before Alyss could answer. "I can't do all this alone. Whenever I try to, I screw things up."

"At least you've finally realized it," Ducot mumbled.

"That's what I said!" Alyss beamed and the two shared a conspiratorial look that Eira wasn't entirely sure she liked.

Back at the bench, Alyss and Ducot sat while Eira stood, pacing by the river. She worked to keep her voice in check so it didn't carry up to the manor or over the water. She came to a halt, finally deciding where to begin in her explanation.

"I've been thinking about what we know—or what I believe is true—and what the Pillars want. I've come to a conclusion and I just want someone to hear it and you're the only person who will listen to me. So, please, will you hear it?"

He kept her in suspense for an agonizing moment. "Very well."

"Thank you." She heaved a sigh of relief. "We'll start with that Ulvarth was unfairly imprisoned for stealing and extinguishing the Flame."

"*Unfairly*," Ducot repeated with a snort.

Eira bit back sharing Deneya's secret. She knew, for all the wrong Ulvarth had done, that his imprisonment was unjust. But explaining why would only earn Deneya's ire and likely push Ducot away.

"Yes…well, before he was locked away, he fathered a son."

"A son?" Ducot arched the glowing dots that served as his brows.

"Ferro."

"How do you—"

"We found out this manor belonged to his mother," Alyss explained. "There was a book in the Archives."

"So this is the Archives incident." Ducot sounded almost amused.

"And Lorn had additional records on its owner, Yewin. I think Ferro is Ulvarth's son, and his mother was Yewin. Ferro was hidden away and was integral in organizing the Pillars and ultimately helping free Ulvarth because Ferro was an unknown agent, even to the Court of Shadows. He could move freely," Eira said. "The Pillars want power. And to do that they need to undermine the government and prove that they're ordained by the goddess."

"I follow." Ducot nodded. "I take it you have more?"

"Yes." Eira stopped pacing and sat, but her legs bounced with restless excitement. "Cutting down Lumeria is tied to what Ferro did in Solaris…what I'm afraid they'll do when the tournament starts."

"That's undermining the government—how will they prove they're ordained?"

"I was thinking about the conversation I heard from the dagger…something about four relics."

"And those are?" Ducot asked and Eira bit back a groan. She was hoping he'd know.

"I don't know for sure… But if I remember what I heard correctly, Ulvarth said something about them reigniting the flame that guides the world." Eira leaned in, her voice dropping further to a whisper. "I also overheard them mention a dagger at the meeting. I think it was the golden dagger. I think it's a relic along with the Ash of Yargen."

"And the other two?"

"I don't know," Eira admitted. "But I think with all of them they'll prove they were selected by the goddess, somehow."

"It's an interesting theory."

"It's more than a theory," Eira insisted. "This is right, I know it. Just like I know Ferro's mother is Mistress Harrot and that this place isn't as safe as the Specters think it is. He brought the dagger to hide right under Lumeria's nose, right where the Court of Shadows would never think to look, so it could be collected at his leisure."

"Now you're reaching."

"I found Harrot in my room one night." When Eira disclosed that piece of information, Ducot's demeanor shifted. It was slight, but Eira didn't miss it. "She was looking for it. Ducot, please, I know the court has every reason not to trust me. But the Specters won't let me get a word in. You're the only person who will listen. If I can just see the dagger again, I can try and listen further. I still think there's more to that conversation; my powers have grown since my time with the Pillars, I'm certain I could hear the rest of it now. And with that information I can figure out what it is the Pillars are trying to do with these four relics."

"*You* won't do anything," Ducot said firmly. "I think Deneya made that clear enough."

"I…" Eira sighed. "Yes, I know. But the court can take action. If the Pillars need that dagger, Harrot knows it's gone. They must be hunting for it. And I'm sure they already suspect the court." Ducot continued to stare at her with that enigmatic look. The conversation hadn't gone how she'd hoped. But it could've been worse. "I'm not going to take any action. I swear it. But thank you for listening to me. I needed you to know—as someone who considers you a friend—that this place isn't safe and to stay on guard. I leave the rest in your hands, Ducot. If you think anything of what I've said has merit, please take it to the Specters and then if they can entrust me with the dagger, even just for a few moments, they will."

"We shall see." Ducot stood and left, unreadable.

Eira looked to Alyss hopelessly. Her friend stood and gave her a squeeze.

"You did what you could," Alyss said.

"Yeah…" She watched Ducot go, resisting every urge to demand he take her to the Court of Shadows. Eira knew she could do more. She could find a way to sneak into the court. She knew the passage there and then somehow she could get to the Specter's war room. Or maybe she would corner Mistress Harrot herself and demand answers—

No. That type of thinking was what got her in trouble and put the court at risk in the first place. She would stay put and do as she was told, come what may.

***

Something hard banged against the glass of Eira's window, rattling the panes and frame. She was jolted awake with a yelp of surprise. Moonlight washed the room in silver as magic crackled under her fingertips, rising in her like a tide.

Panting softly, Eira looked around her room, and then toward the window. There, on the sill outside, was the dark outline of a bird, unmoving. A bird had flown into the glass. That's all it was. Gripping her shirt over her chest and taking a deep breath to remind herself that she wasn't under attack, Eira unlatched the lower pane and lifted it.

The bird twitched as she scooped it up, nestling it in the crook of her left arm. A knock on her door was the second startle of the night.

"Eira?" Cullen called softly. "Are you all right? I heard a shout."

"I'm fine." She opened the door, the bird almost completely forgotten for a moment as her eyes met Cullen's. The tournament was getting nearer and they were only growing farther and farther apart by the day. They hadn't even managed to steal words at night, too exhausted from training or Yemir keeping him too late. He felt like a stranger now, and that made her chest tighten and her breath hitch despite herself. "This little guy, on the other hand…" Eira brushed past Cullen, starting for Alyss's room. "He flew into my window."

"Into your—"

"What's going on?" Noelle opened her door with a yawn. Fortunately for all of them and their various late night discussions and adventures, Levit was an incredibly heavy sleeper.

"A bird flew into Eira's window," Cullen answered as Eira knocked softly on Alyss's door.

"All this fuss over a bird?" Noelle ran her fingers through her hair.

"Alyss?" Eira opened the door. If there was one person who was a heavier sleeper than Levit, it was her friend. Eira gently set the bird down on Alyss's writing desk and jostled the sleeping woman. "Alyss, I need you."

"What is it?" Alyss grumbled without opening her eyes.

"A bird flew into my window. I think it's injured." Eira noticed the specks of blood on her arm and side. "I need you to heal it or it might die."

That got Alyss up. She scrambled from bed, pushing Eira aside and rushing over to the desk Eira pointed to. Alyss sat, holding the bird with both hands.

"You poor dear," she murmured. Alyss had always possessed a soft spot for animals. "Who beat you up like this?"

"Will it be all right?" Noelle asked from the doorway. She and Cullen hovered, apparently too invested in the fate of the bird now to go back to bed.

"I think so. Eira, can you get me my box, please?" Alyss said as her magic washed over the small animal.

Eira did as she was asked. Taking the vials from the box, handing salves and herbs to Alyss so she could perform her work, Eira was transported back to the clinic. She'd always finished her duties before Alyss, as she'd never had as much to do thanks to Uncle Fritz. Sometimes, if Alyss was close to being done, Eira would lend a hand as her assistant.

How simple life was then. All Alyss had worried about was if she had enough clay on hand and when her next favorite romance novel would come out. And Eira, all she worried about was... was...

She hadn't worried about anything. Eira stared at the frail bird in Alyss's fingers. Her friend's desperate attempts fell on deaf ears as the world around her was muffled. Eira hadn't worried about much. Certainly, she'd had her interests, her trivial concerns—and how trivial they did seem now.

Trying to surpass her brother, longing to see the world, she'd wished for all of those things, and now that she had them…what she wouldn't give to go back to that simpler time. But she couldn't, no more than this little bird could've avoided her window in its swan dive from the heavens. Eira had gained direction and things to fight for and she could never be the girl she once was.

"There." Alyss leaned away. "I think that'll do it, for now at least."

"It's going to be all right?" Eira asked. The bird twitched, its head beginning to move.

"It should rest here tonight, and then we can check on it in the morning. I'm sure it'll be flying by—" Alyss didn't finish before she jumped out of her chair, nearly landing on the bed.

A pulse of magic surrounded the bird. Then, another, as the black creature flapped, righting itself. A third pulse and the creature leapt from the desk and landed as a woman with glowing dots in place of eyebrows.

Her hair had fallen in chunks of curls from the bun it had once been pulled back into. Blood was smeared across her face. Her clothes were torn in the same places that the bird's feathers had been rumpled. She looked around her, tried to lunge forward, and fell to the ground.

"Ar—" Eira wasn't fast enough recalling her name.

"Lady Arwin?" Cullen rushed over. "What happened?"

"I'm no lady," she snarled, pushing Cullen aside, using him as a prop to get herself upright. But she tipped perilously and fell into a chair that rose from the floorboards with a lift of Alyss's hands. Arwin let out a string of curses. "I have to go."

"You're not going anywhere in this state." Alyss crossed to

Arwin's side. "I healed you like I would a bird, not a person. Let me look at you."

"They're in danger," Arwin said, trying to push Alyss away, but Arwin's strength had left her.

"Who?" Eira asked, heart already racing. "Who's in danger?"

Arwin met Eira's eyes. "You…you know the way. Go."

"What?"

"The court…they're going to be attacked." Arwin grimaced as Alyss smeared a particularly potent salve into her wounds. "You have to warn them."

Heart racing, Eira spun. She'd been right. And she hated it.

Cullen caught her arm. "I'm going with you."

"You need to stay here."

"I'm coming too," Noelle declared.

"Both of you—"

"There's no time!" Arwin snapped. "*Go!*"

"I'm going to stay with her," Alyss declared. She met Cullen's eyes, and then looked to Noelle. "You two, look after Eira for me."

At least Alyss would be spared from whatever fallout Eira would have to endure from the Specters. Arwin fumbled in her shirt, producing a bar of iron. With a pulse of magic, it transformed into a key.

"Here, take it and go. Warn them. The whole court has been compromised." The statement drew a sharp inhale from Eira. Arwin nodded slowly. "They have to leave…"

"I'll do it. You recover; they need whatever information you have." Eira spun and dashed through the common area.

"Someone want to tell me what the Court of Shadows is?" Cullen asked as he followed.

"Oh right, you weren't there." Noelle cracked her knuckles, flames dancing around them. "You'll see soon enough. Just keep up."

Eira pulled on the hidden lever, opening the door. Cullen was next and Noelle closed it after her. Eira caught the confusion, fear, and touch of wonder on his face in the light cast from the mote of fire hovering over Noelle's shoulder.

"The Court of Shadows works for Lumeria," Eira said softly as they descended. "They're friends."

"And you're involved with them?" Cullen asked, worry edging into his voice. "These were the people you mentioned after you returned from the Pillars? The group you were involved with."

"Yes, I *was* involved. More or less." Eira nodded. "But not anymore."

"They were being utterly unreasonable," Noelle said. Eira focused on the path ahead, rather than objecting. But that didn't mean she didn't appreciate her friend's defense of her.

About halfway down the path, a strange echoing sound rose up to them. Eira slowed, trying to listen.

"What's that?" Noelle whispered.

Cullen pressed his eyes closed. Eira could feel his magic radiating outward from him. It floated on the air, filling the pathway, soaring ahead.

His eyes snapped open. "We…we should turn back."

"What did you hear?" Eira knew that Windwalkers had an affinity of the self that allowed them to place their consciousness beyond their bodies. She wondered if that was the magic she'd just felt.

"It's not safe."

"Of course it's not."

Cullen grabbed her by both arms. "I don't want you to keep running into danger."

"I have to see this through," she whispered. "I don't have anywhere else to go." The little wounded bird was still in Eira's mind. The feeling of living in Marcus's shadow. The girl she had been, wanting nothing, longing for everything, oblivious to the world. "I can't go back, Cullen, there's nothing there for me. The only way ahead is forward."

"Be ready, then."

Three ominous words had her magic rising as Eira charged

into the darkness. Soon, the light of Noelle's flame merged with an orange haze. Smoke plumed up along the ceiling of the tunnel. Eira stalled, reduced to a coughing fit.

Raising his hands, Cullen banished the smoke. Wind teased her hair, tangling it hopelessly. But Eira kept onward all the same. She pushed as fast as she could into the wall of heat. Into the orange-tinted nightmare that awaited her.

"No," Eira breathed as she came to a stop in the main passage.

Bodies littered the ground, charred, stabbed, mutilated. The key Arwin had given her slipped between Eira's fingers, clanging against the ground. The door to the Court of Shadows with its mighty, ancient lock had been blown clean off its hinges.

· CHAPTER ·

THIRTY-ONE

How?

How could... How did...

Her brain wasn't functioning. She blinked, several times, forcing her mind to start working again. As cohesive thoughts returned, so too did the sensations of heat, and smoke, and screams. They rose up from within the Court of Shadows as a chorus of agony.

"We have to put out the fires!" Eira shouted to her friends over the chaos. "Cullen, you help clear the smoke. There has to be some kind of venting." She was guessing, but it made sense. She'd seen fires in the Court of Shadows before. The smoke had to go somewhere. "Noelle—"

"Already on it." Noelle lifted her hands. Her fingers were rigid and claw-like. Fire of her own making swirled around her feet. It shot off her fingers like darts, mingling with the flames and granting Noelle control. The woman was the embodiment of fire and power, the orange glow highlighting her dark skin and black hair in striking detail. As she drew her fingers into fists, the flames around the entrance snuffed and Eira rushed forward.

Half of her power remained focused on herself. She wouldn't help anyone if she was burnt to a crisp. Steam billowed off her shoulders like wings as Eira pressed onward into the inferno.

The other half of her power was given to the first person she saw. It was a woman, pinned to the wall. Barely alive. But conscious enough to raise her head when she saw Eira. Drawing an arc around the woman, ice fought upward, keeping the fire at bay.

"Noelle! Over here."

"Over here? Over everywhere!" Noelle griped as she stepped into the inferno of the caverns.

Lightspinning glyphs flared in the tunnel leading to the Specters' war room. Someone was still alive back there. Eira resisted the urge to charge ahead. They had to take this slowly.

At the shadow's side, Eira crouched down, cooling her wounds with ice and water. The woman stared at her in a daze. Burns covered half of her body. The other half was coated in what looked like some kind of oil.

"They… They came… They… It's gone. It's over…" the woman murmured.

"You're all right." It was likely a lie. Eira was no healer, but she'd worked with enough of them and seen enough people on the verge of death to know what it looked like when life was leaving someone's eyes. "Stay alive. I have to go look for other survivors."

As Eira stood, Noelle shouted, "It's too much, there's no way I can get all of it under control." She still had her hands out, but sweat beaded down her face and neck. Not from heat—Firebearers couldn't feel heat in the same way other people did—but from the exertion. Noelle was nearly at her limit and they'd only carved out a small portion of the room.

"I have an idea," Cullen shouted over the flames. "But it's risky."

"Now seems like a pretty great time for risky," Noelle said.

"What is it?" Eira had rejoined them.

"Fire needs air as fuel… I can suck it all up to the ceiling. That should take enough power from the blaze that both of you should be able to get a handle on the majority."

"Air is also important for breathing," Noelle snapped.

"I said it was risky, you have a better idea?"

"We should do it," Eira decided for the three of them. There was no way they'd get the blaze under control if they didn't take the risk. And there were still flashes of Lightspinning down on the far end of the cavern. Taking the air might impair the combatants.

But at least it would impair them all equally—shadows and Pillars alike.

"On three, be ready—hold your breath," Cullen said, a look of intense focus overtaking his features. "One."

Noelle widened her stance, holding out her arms.

"Two."

Eira crouched low, ready to sprint forward. She inhaled deeply at the same time as Noelle.

"Three!"

Cullen thrust his hands upward with a grunt. A mighty rush of air roared in Eira's ears, ripping at her hair and clothes. The flames instantly diminished. They wavered, sparking, sputtering, burning through what little air still lingered on the ground of the cavern. Noelle swept her arms and legs, almost like a dance, as she sent out tongues of flame to extinguish the rest.

Eira charged forward to the back half of the caverns. The Lightspinning had stopped with Cullen's removal of air. Flinging out her arms, she sent jets of water to the smoldering embers that might flare back up when the air returned.

But the exertion was too much. Her chest burned. Her lungs screamed. And every curse word Eira knew flung across her mind as she stumbled and took a heaving breath.

It was a raspy wheeze. Eira swayed, head spinning. She tried to take another breath, but there wasn't any air.

Cullen, she mouthed. How much longer would he hold the air? Eira swayed, her knees hitting the ground as she collapsed. This was what Marcus had felt.

Keep going, Eira, her brother's voice echoed in the darkness of the cavern, the darkness behind her heavy lids.

At once, like an invisible weight crashing down on the room, the air returned. Eira pushed herself up, heaving lungfuls. Fires sparked, flaring back up. The first was extinguished by Noelle almost as quickly as it formed. The second Eira doused with a small wave fueled by rage and frustration.

Trusting the rest to her friends, Eira charged into the tunnel.

She saw men in pale robes, standing as well, swaying, rubbing their heads.

"Time to go," one of them grunted, seeing her. He didn't seem to recognize her. She was a sopping mess of soot and ash. But Eira recognized him. The man was one of the Pillars who had been with the Champion the day she'd displayed her power.

The three Pillars fled into a hole in the wall that had been blown in. They hadn't infiltrated the court through the normal passages. They'd found a way to a tunnel—or a secret passage of their own that paralleled the court—and exploded straight into the main hall. Then, they'd removed the main door, no doubt to get others through.

Eira skidded to a stop by the hole, glancing between chasing the Pillars into the hole, and the ransacked war room. When her eyes landed on the bodies of Lorn and Deneya, her choice was made. She summoned a thick sheet of ice to plug the hole in the wall and sprinted over, dropping to her knees by Lorn.

"Lorn, Lorn!" She shook him and held a hand by his face. *Still breathing.* He'd merely passed out.

She scrambled over to Deneya.

The woman was in much worse shape. Gnarly burns covered her arm and side. Her other arm was limp and flattened, as though the bones and muscles within had been shattered. She had two crossbow bolts—one in her abdomen, the other in her leg.

"D-Deneya." Eira stared at the brutality her ally had endured, at a total loss for what to do. "Deneya, wake up, please," Eira whispered.

She held a quivering hand by Deneya's nose and mouth. An inhale. An exhale. Slow and weak, but there.

Eira ran back to Lorn, flipping him over with a grunt. "Lorn, wake up!" she shouted. "You have to wake up! I don't know Lightspinning. I can't heal her!"

The puddle of blood around Deneya's body seemed to grow larger by the second. Eira's heart raced. No, this was wrong. Deneya was the strongest among them. What had Taavin said?

She'd dined with the divine. A person like that couldn't… couldn't…

"Deneya!" Eira rushed back to the woman. She was pulled back and forth by her emotions—lurching between getting help, and being at the woman's side for however many more breaths she had. "Please…"

Deneya let out a soft groan and Eira's heart skipped several beats. The woman's eyes fluttered half open. Her left eye was bloodshot and gory from the burns she'd endured.

"E… Eira…" she rasped. A small smile crossed her lips. "Didn't… Didn't I tell you not to come back?"

"I'm sorry," Eira hiccupped. "I'm bad at following orders. You know that. But the flames are under control now. It's all right. We're going to heal everyone. You're going to be all right."

Deneya winced. "The relics… They took…the dagger." Ducot must have said something. He was still on Eira's side, despite all odds.

"Save your words," Eira pleaded. She gripped Deneya's burnt hand as gently as she could. "Use them for Lightspinning. Heal yourself, please."

"You have to get…" Deneya whispered.

"Deneya, Lightspinning, now!"

She sighed and closed her eyes. "*Hal—Hall—Halleth ruta—Halleth ruta toff,*" Deneya finally managed. Her words were raspy and the sounds weren't perfect. She opened her eyes to stare up at Eira again. "I don't have the strength."

"Yes, you do," Eira insisted, trying to will it into existence. "You're the strongest person I know and you're not dying here." Eira gripped Deneya's hand harder and the woman grimaced, but Eira didn't let up. She'd pour magic into Deneya herself if she had to. "Try again."

"I can't."

"You can!" Eira pressed her eyes closed and imagined magic rising around them. She imagined the vibrating threads she felt in the Pillars' stronghold—the magic that permeated the world around them, fraying at Deneya's edges. She could stitch them back together, somehow. "Please, once more, for me."

"*Halleth—Halleth ruta toff.*" Light flickered over Deneya's chest, the outline of a glyph, incomplete but present.

"Again," Eira demanded. Magic was flaring around Deneya's body, trying to find its currents. How could she fuel it? What more could she do?

"I—"

"Again! You're not dying here. I won't let you. I refuse." Eira gazed up at the dark ceiling, soot-stained and dripping from the steam of fires being extinguished. She stared through the rock, imagining the city above, and the starlit sky beyond. If there was a goddess, *let Deneya live.*

Just once, let Eira not be the harbinger of Death. She closed her eyes and imagined the waters that filled her also lifting Deneya. Her tides could hold both of them aloft. Deneya would find the power she needed. The magic around her thrummed in harmony, every thread vibrating in time as they floated within her imaginary waters.

"*Halleth ruta toff.*" The words were strong and clear this time. Eira could almost feel the power flowing through her magic and into Deneya. Their eyes widened, meeting. Deneya felt it too. Eira wasn't imagining the sensation.

Surprise, and a touch of panic at the strange phenomena, had everything crashing down around her. The glyph guttered and vanished. Deneya's eyes closed, her body limp.

"No," Eira breathed. "No!" She held out her hands over Deneya's body. Let her actually be part elfin. Let Eira have magic unlike any other. Let one of her curses turn into a blessing just this once. "Halleth ruta toff." Nothing happened. "Halleth ruta toff. Halleth ruta toff!" she shouted.

"Eira!" Cullen and Noelle arrived. But there were more footsteps than just the two of theirs.

Standing at the entrance to the war room was a small brigade of shadows led by the Voice, Taavin, and Vi Solaris. Eira blinked, trying to make sure she wasn't hallucinating.

"Save her," Eira pleaded to any of them—all of them.

Vi Solaris, the crown princess of the Empire, was at Deneya's opposite side in a breath. She held out a hand, long fingers steady.

"Stay with me, friend," Vi commanded softly. *"Halleth ruta toff."* The words flowed from the princess's lips as though she had been born to say them. Eira watched in awe as a glyph, blue at its center, yellow at the edges, formed under her palm. It spun slowly as she moved her hand up and down Deneya's body. *"Halleth ruta sot."* Vi summoned another glyph. This one spread underneath Deneya, warm light drifting upward. "You."

"Yes?" Eira had been so mesmerized she'd forgotten herself a moment.

"Take out the crossbow bolts," the crown princess commanded. "The skin won't knit correctly if we leave them in."

Eira did as she was told, breaking the bolts and, as gently as she was able, quickly pulling them out. Deneya let out a hiss of pain. But pain was good because pain meant there was still life.

Vi continued to use Lightspinning to finish healing Deneya. When she sat back on her heels with a sigh, Deneya looked— save for her torn and dirty clothing—refreshed and perfect. The elfin sat with a mischievous grin, as if she hadn't just been on Death's doorstep.

"You always did have a knack for showing up at the last second," Deneya said to Vi.

"You're lucky I'm here at all. I was almost too late."

"People who bend fate are never late." Deneya chuckled. Vi gave a huff of amusement and shook her head.

Eira continued to stare, blinking. The crown princess had used Lightspinning. *How?* Vi Solaris was a Firebearer…wasn't she?

"Thank you, for getting the fires under control," Deneya said to Vi. "The bastards used flash beads and oil."

"That wasn't me." Vi shifted her gaze to Eira, leaving her to squirm uncomfortably under the weight of the princess's stare.

"You have these Solaris competitors to thank for quelling the fires. If not for them, I wouldn't have been able to come straight here when I arrived and you might have been dead."

Deneya's attention slowly drifted back to Eira. They shared a long stare. Every time she blinked, the Deneya who had been on the verge of death overlaid with the smiling—and slightly perturbed—woman sitting before her now.

"I guess a thank you is in order," Deneya said finally.

"I'm just glad you're okay," Eira said weakly.

"That makes two of us." Vi stood and held out a hand. The princess helped Deneya to her feet. "Because I want you to be there when we take down the bastards who did this."

THOSE STILL ALIVE were quickly patched up. In the brigade that had arrived with Vi and Taavin were about six Lightspinners. There weren't many shadows left living in the cavern. Only ten people. That meant that, total, the Court of Shadows now consisted of twenty-two people, most back in the main cavern beginning to collect the dead. Ducot had been among the brigade, but there wasn't any time for them to exchange words before he was sent to gather the dead.

Deneya leaned against the table, arms folded. Vi was at her side. Taavin and Lorn inspected the damage to the record vaults at the back of the room.

"You—" Deneya started, giving Eira a hard look.

"Arwin came to me," Eira said quickly. "I wasn't going to come. I didn't want to. I mean, I did. I didn't know what else to do. But Arwin said the Court needed to be warned and she entrusted me with the key and…" She hung her head. "I wasn't fast enough."

"No, *we* weren't smart enough." The crown princess looked to the table. Eira had seen Vi Solaris a handful of times, but never like this. She wore the clothes of a warrior in the color of night. Her hair was pulled into a simple braid and pinned at the back of her head in a bun. The crown princess had always exuded power. But this was a different sort. The deadly confidence was more like a queen or empress than the princess Eira had seen from afar. "They outmaneuvered you."

"Obviously." Deneya cursed under her breath. "The question is, how?"

"I will not rest until I find the answer," Lorn declared.

Eira resisted confirming if Ducot had told them all the details of her theories. She didn't want the inquiry to be interpreted as gloating. It didn't matter now that she was right.

"With what manpower?" Deneya looked beyond Eira, Cullen, and Noelle, down the hall and toward the cavern. "There's only twenty-two of us now."

"How many do you have topside?" Vi asked.

"Perhaps another ten to twenty."

Vi shook her head and picked through the papers on the table. "It's not enough to keep operating underground. And after this…" She motioned around the war room. "If we don't take decisive action, they're going to keep cutting us off at the knees, working their way up until slicing our throats is all too easy."

"You said the dagger was taken," Eira interjected boldly. "When you were…" she couldn't bring herself to say *dying*. "Incapacitated."

"It seems to be the only thing they took." Lorn returned to the center table, Taavin at his side. "All my records are still there."

"They're toying with us." Vi shook her head grimly. "They want us to have the information because they're so confident we won't put their plans together."

Deneya looked to Eira. "Did you hear anything else during your time with the Pillars that might be of use?"

Vi straightened from the table quickly, spinning to stare down at Eira. She'd never felt so small as she did underneath the princess's gaze. "You…you were the one who was taken to the Pillars' stronghold?"

"Yes."

"Tell me everything."

Deneya sighed at the princess, a bold move that spoke volumes of their closeness. "I already told—"

"I want to hear it from her." Vi motioned to Eira. "Speak."

Eira did as she was commanded and recounted the tale of her time with the Pillars. The words took her out of her body. She stood adjacent to the woman, recounting everything that had happened to her. That wasn't her. Not really. She had moved past those matters. She was stronger now. Yet Eira was relieved when she could shift the topic finally to her theory on the dagger and manor.

When she was finished, the crown princess had fire in her eyes and crackling around her knuckles. She took a deep breath and dismissed the power that raged right at the edge of her control.

Vi turned her eyes to Deneya. "The ball it is, then."

"That's been the plan." Deneya nodded. "But we must decide if these relics are going to come into play before then."

"It doesn't matter; it won't change anything." The crown princess skewered Eira with her stare. "I have something to ask of you. Though you might fairly hate me for doing so."

"I doubt I'd hate you, Your Highness." Though the princess's concern filled her with dread.

"You have done so much, but there is one more thing we're going to need of you. We're going to need you to be the bait at the ball."

"What?" Cullen stepped forward. "Your Highness—"

Vi ignored him, continuing to speak right to Eira alone. "Ferro is clearly obsessed with you. If you're there, *he* certainly will be. If we put you out on the dance floor, dancing with others, laughing, carrying on without him, it'll surely drive him mad. Men like that can't stand when they're not in control."

"I didn't think I had a choice in being at the ball," Eira said, weaker than she would've liked. The night was catching up with her, hitting her all at once. She was exhausted.

"You always have a choice, we are not the Pillars." Vi tapped the table. "But what I'm asking is for you to go out of your way to lure him into our trap. If he clings to the edges of the ball, in hiding, you need to do whatever it takes to draw him out."

"What're you thinking?" Taavin asked his betrothed.

"That I'm going to make an example of him. You want to kill a snake? Chop off the head. If we get Ferro publicly, then the rest of the Pillars will fall. We'll maneuver him into a compromising position and then we can take action."

"Like his father," Deneya murmured. The Specter was right. Vi's plan was alarmingly like how they handled Ulvarth. And she knew how well *that* went.

"There's also the Champion of Yargen," Eira said quickly, seizing on the opportunity to remind them of that past failure. "*He's* their leader, not Ferro." She was so tired of everyone acting like the Champion didn't really exist, like he was some imaginary enemy Eira had concocted. "Capturing or killing Ferro will only embolden them further because we've taken their right hand."

Vi let out a soft huff of amusement and shook her head. There was a distant glimmer in her eyes that looked toward a time long gone. She had a knowing smile at the mere mention of the "Champion of Yargen." It accompanied a tired stare at nothing.

"He is *not* the Champion of Yargen," Vi said softly, confidently. Then she continued, stronger, "Whoever that man is, he's just a puppet, held up by strings. The more I hear, the more I'm certain Ferro is at the center of this."

"Listen, please—"

"Eira," Deneya said with a cautionary note.

One Eira ignored. "Whoever the Champion is—Ulvarth or not—they *believe* he is the Champion."

"He's not," Vi repeated.

"It doesn't matter if he is or isn't!" Eira's voice pitched slightly as her emotions rose. "It doesn't matter what *we* think, or know, or believe. What matters is what *they* believe. Even Ferro saw him as the Champion. They want to use the relics to justify him as such. They revere him like a god and no doubt think if they can get the citizenry to do the same they will hold all the power they need. Faith is more powerful than fact."

"Trust us, we have information you don't know about. This situation is under control," Deneya said, a weary edge seeping into her voice.

"Like you had Ferro under control to begin with?" Eira spat.

"Eira…" Cullen took a step closer to her. She ignored the placating tone in his voice.

"You have it under control? Is that why you still haven't found the *Stormfrost*? Or any other signs of Adela?"

Deneya leveled her eyes with Eira's. "We have found the *Stormfrost*."

"What?" The wind left Eira's sails.

"It's running off the western regions of Meru, near Carsovia. The ship that night was merely a decoy."

"A…decoy…"

"They had multiple Waterrunners and Lightspinners on hand to perform the illusion, to keep us off their trail," Lorn confirmed.

Adela wasn't anywhere near. She'd never been. She was still half a world away—as close as Eira was to the truth of who she really was and where she came from. As close as she was to avenging her brother.

"The Pillars were using the guise of Adela to mask their movements."

"How did you find this out?" Eira whispered. It made sense. She'd pieced together that the Pillars likely weren't working with Adela during her time with them, thanks to Ferro's mentions. But so much had transpired, there were so many pieces…she'd overlooked it when she'd finally escaped.

"We don't owe you our ways." Deneya folded her arms.

"When did you know?"

"We figured it out weeks ago."

"Why didn't you tell me?" The invisible wounds Eira had endured were being cut deeper and deeper by the minute.

"Because you didn't need to know." Deneya frowned. "Because telling you might have risked you running off. Shadows only know what they have to. You're not privy to all our plans."

"Enough," Vi said firmly. The command held a royal tone, one that begged to be heeded…or else. "This squabbling is getting us nowhere. Eira, will you be our bait at the dance? If so, we will handle all the other arrangements."

"Fine." Eira folded her arms. "I'll do it. And then I'm done with all of you." She wouldn't give Deneya the opportunity to cast her out again. They just wanted to use her. "I'll help you take down Ferro, then, good or bad, I'm *never* coming back here or helping you. You're on your own."

"Very well," Deneya said coolly, as though she wasn't wounded in the slightest to agree. Eira wondered if she'd ever meant anything at all to the woman. If the mentorship she had once felt from her had been like everything else about the Court of Shadows—an act, an illusion.

"We should go back, for now." Eira went to leave. Her feet felt like dead weight, numb. "I trust you'll get word to me about what you want me to do, exactly, when the time comes."

"Are you sure about this?" Cullen asked softly, taking her hand.

Eira looked from their intertwined fingers to his face. "Of course I am."

"But—"

"I said I'm sure." Eira ripped her hand from his. "Now, let's go. We should get back before dawn and leave them to clean up this mess." She started to leave, Cullen and Noelle following.

"One more thing." Deneya halted them. Eira faced the woman, skeptical that she would say anything good. Deneya wore an unreadable expression. Whatever she felt toward Eira now, she was doing a good job of concealing. "How did you do it?"

"Do what?" Eira asked.

"We put out the fire by sucking up the air and then these two used their powers to handle the rest," Cullen answered.

"No…" Deneya continued to stare only at Eira. "How did you give me power when I had none?"

So she hadn't imagined it. Eira stared down at her empty palms. They hadn't been able to summon glyphs, but the strength that returned to Deneya hadn't been chance. Could she have really done that?

Steal people's magic… Ferro had said those words. He

thought she had the power to take magic and Eira had begun reading about closing channels. But Deneya thought she had the power to give it. What was true? Or, were they both wrong? Eira forced a blank expression on her face.

No matter what the truth was, she'd uncover it on her own. *No, not alone.* She had friends at her side now. True friends. The ones who didn't abandon her when it was convenient for them or those who saw her as nothing more than a token on their gigantic war table—someone to be maneuvered but not respected or heeded.

"I have no idea what you're talking about." Eira shook her head and blinked as though she were startled. "Giving you power?" She glanced to Cullen and then Noelle. "Either of you ever hear a Waterrunner doing something like that?"

"No." Noelle shrugged.

"Can't say I have." Cullen frowned slightly. There was a glint in his eyes that suggested he might just believe the claim. But if he did, he had the better sense not to say anything for her sake.

Eira shrugged. "Sorry."

Deneya pursed her lips slightly. "Very well. Go and—"

"Await further orders," Eira finished. "Yes, I'm familiar."

She put her back to them and left. Eira could hear them whispering. She felt a stirring of Cullen's magic.

"Don't listen," she said under her breath, glancing up at him. Vi Solaris was a Firebearer *and* had Lightspinning. They couldn't be certain a woman like that didn't have some sort of other powers that could detect magic. "It doesn't matter. Let them say what they want."

Cullen stared at her with shadowed eyes and a hard line for a mouth. He gave her a small nod and then looked forward. Eira could feel his frustration and confusion. All of this was new to him. The perfect nobleman's son, thrust into the smoky, burning underworld that she'd been dealing with for weeks.

As they passed the blown-in hole, Eira waved her hand and the ice she'd used to block the tunnel the Pillars had infiltrated from disappeared. Let the court deal with it. She was only good to them when they wanted, as they wanted.

The three Solaris competitors ascended through the main hall as a handful of shadows began to carry bodies, piling them up to be burnt. This was the last time she'd see this scarred and singed place. Even if she continued to work with the Court of Shadows, they would no doubt move hideouts.

Eira said her mental goodbyes to it all as she crossed the threshold of what was once the door. Two more nights, then the ball, and she was done with the Court of Shadows for good.

THIRTY-THREE

"EIRA," CULLEN SAID softly as they neared the end of the dark hallway that led to the Solaris chambers.

"Yes?" Eira continued walking, eyes forward.

He caught her hand. "I want a word."

Eira stopped. She had a dismissal ready. But when her eyes met his, Eira knew there wasn't any hope of it. Cullen had an intensity to his stare that assured her he wouldn't be denied. And even if Eira had wanted to…he did just risk his life for her. Hearing him out with whatever he wanted to say was the least she could do.

"All right."

"Alone." Cullen glanced up at Noelle.

"Oh, thank the Mother, I am exhausted and the last thing I want is to stand here awkwardly and witness a lovers' quarrel." Noelle dramatically heaved a sigh of relief. "I'll just see myself out then." She paused after three steps. Noelle brought up two fingers and separated them. The mote of flame that hovered over her shoulder divided into two, one hanging by the ceiling and the other remaining with her. She pointed at the one she was leaving behind. "That way you're not left completely in the dark."

"Thank you," Eira murmured.

"Don't say I never do anything nice for you both." Noelle yawned. She was doing a good job of presenting strength. But Eira could see the dark circles under the woman's eyes that hadn't been there at the start of the night and were caused by much more than a lack of sleep.

"Do you know how to get out?" Eira asked as Noelle came to a stop at the top of the walkway.

Noelle couldn't refrain from rolling her eyes before pulling the lever that released the door. She slipped out, shutting it softly behind her.

"She's nicer than she wants you to believe," Eira mused, staring at where Noelle just was. "And incredibly strong."

"She is, on both accounts," Cullen said thoughtfully before bringing his gaze to Eira. The weight of his stare settled on her shoulders. Eira took a small step back, as though she could avoid it—which was impossible in the narrow passage. They were always toe-to-toe. "You should have told me."

"I was trying to protect you. I told you. I warned you," she whispered.

"Stop shutting me out. Protecting me is not your job." His voice was low and thick with emotion. His brow was furrowed in anger or sorrow. His mouth was slightly parted. And his eyes... the dim light of Noelle's flame somehow made them glow. "I can protect myself.'"

"Stop shutting *you* out? Like you've been shutting me out for days?" Eira hadn't realized how much he'd been hurting her until that moment. She'd allowed his excuses and half-hearted explanations, smoothed over by stolen, loving glances. But there had been more festering beneath. "I told you everything about what happened with Ferro, afraid of what you might think, and then you all but disappear from my life."

"My father—"

"I know." She held up her hands. "I've reminded myself you don't have a choice when it comes to him but..."

"I should have been better." Cullen pulled her forward. Eira could have—*should have* put up a better fight against him. But she was so tired. The world was relentless and he was offering her the one thing that had smoothed over every jagged edge that cut into her flesh.

His arms encircled her, tightening. Eira pressed her face into his shoulder, her hands wrapped around him and gripping his shirt by his shoulder blades. He smelled of smoke and blood and the nightmares that would haunt her for weeks to come. But underneath all the horrors…was Cullen. That unique musk all his own. A scent that made her head spin and her knees weak.

"I'm sorry," he whispered. "Have I utterly messed this up?"

She laughed bitterly. "Not if I haven't."

"You haven't even come close."

Eira twisted to meet his eyes. "I'm afraid for us. You saw what the Pillars did. They're so strong. No matter what we do, he can get to me. This house, these halls…he might even know we're standing here now." Eira glanced around, realizing the truth in her words.

Cullen's hands settled on her shoulders. "You're safe."

"I'll never be safe. Not as long as Ferro's alive."

"You're safe," he repeated firmly. As he spoke, one hand worked its way into her hair. His fingers trailed along her jaw. His thumb caressed her cheek.

"I'm afraid he will kill you because he'll see you as a threat to his possession of me." She blinked back tears of frustration. The rage within her was desperate to escape, as screams or sobs. The hold Ferro had over her and her world was unbearable. Every day was worse than the last. "He'll find out about us, about you, and he will *kill you*."

"You are not a thing to be possessed. You are a strong, beautiful, and wicked smart woman." Cullen shook his head slowly. "I'm not afraid of him."

"You should be."

"We will be his undoing," Cullen declared with all the confidence Eira wished she could feel. Her hands tightened in his shirt. *Believe*, her heart screamed, *just believe in him.*

"I am death."

"You are my life, my love." Cullen leaned forward. He braced himself with a palm against the wall by the side of her head. Her whole world narrowed to him and him alone. "Do you believe in me?"

"I…" She ached all over. Every part of her screamed at the

same time, demanding she chart a different course—any different course than what she was doing. But her hands wouldn't listen. They smoothed down his sides, resting feather-light on his hips before tracking up his chest.

"Do you believe in us? Do you believe in our love?"

The question demanded an answer. Her throat was thick with all the words she wanted to say but didn't know how.

"Tell me true right here and now and I will never ask again. I will shatter my heart into a thousand pieces because that is what it will take to make the damn thing stop beating for you."

"I can't lose you," she repeated softly.

"That's not what I asked." He pressed his forehead against hers. "Ignore the world, Eira, and just listen to your heart, because that's all I care about."

"I love you so much it scares me," she whispered through quivering lips.

"I know." His lips crashed against hers with what felt like every emotion they had been holding back for the past week. Eira groaned softly as her body awakened to him.

Cullen cupped her cheek and held her lips to his. An arm tightened around her waist. She lost herself in his kiss—his *taste*. How she had missed him. Every inch of him pressed against her. The yearning that made her weak and left her perpetually wanting.

"You know this is a terrible idea, right?" Her slick lips glided over his. Pulling apart enough to talk was already turmoil.

"I think this is the best decision I've ever made."

Arrogant man, Eira thought almost pleasantly as he sucked her lower lip between his teeth, nipping softly. It elicited a groan from her that she didn't know she could make. Her body pressed into his and Cullen held her closer.

More. She wanted it all. She wanted to be bare and breathless before him. She wanted to shed her clothes and with them every worry, every reality that haunted her.

Cullen tipped her chin upward, kissing down and onto her

neck. He bit her lightly, responding to her groan with a low growl of his own. The sound was molten heat, shooting straight through her, incinerating every nerve. Her nails dug into his shoulders, holding him to her as she let out a gasp.

With strength she didn't know he possessed, Cullen pushed her farther up against the wall. Knowing what he desired—because her desires matched—Eira's legs wrapped around his waist. Her arms were around his neck. His hands were under her, supporting her, sending shivers up her spine with every caress.

"I love you," she rasped, pulling apart for air and pressing her nose into his. "I love you and because of it I might be your destruction."

Cullen merely looked up at her with a languid smile. He oozed delicious sensuality as he held her, pinned against the wall. Eira ran her fingers through his dark brown tresses, silky even despite the night they'd had.

"You could never be my demise," he whispered.

"But I will." She knew her fate. Her whole existence was cursed. It was her destiny to suffer and bring suffering to those around her. Be it Adela, or some other cruel jest played on her by the uncaring divine.

"Then…if you are destined to destroy me, Eira…let it be a destruction of our choosing. I come to you a willing sacrifice."

She brought her mouth back to his, hungry and yearning. He tasted of longing, of promise, of a hope she didn't want to dare allow herself to feel. Every moment she spent with him wracked her with guilt. Yet every turn of his head, every caress of his tongue, slowly eased away those concerns. Eira was lost to the bliss that was his hands, his mouth, his body. She couldn't fight it any longer. Merely trying was its own slow form of agony.

They might be headed for destruction. But they would go there together.

***

The next morning came too soon. It seemed as if Eira's head had just hit the pillow when Levit was calling for all of them to get up so they could go to the training grounds. Prying herself from the warmth of her sheets, Eira washed her face again, dressed, and stole a moment to quietly stare out at the relentless dawn.

It would all be over soon. The ball was tomorrow night and that meant she only had to endure one day more of this limbo. One day more, and Ferro would be dead.

Eira emerged to see the rest of them gathered. Her eyes went on instinct to Cullen, but he barely spared her a glance. Last night they were on fire. But today he was nothing more than a statue of cool marble. He treated her with the same breezy distance that he had been for days now. She wondered if he was making a point to prove to her that he was capable of keeping them a secret.

"Come along then." Levit started out of the room. Eira hung back, snagging Alyss's elbow.

"Any problems with our feathered friend?" she asked. Alyss had been sleeping when she and Cullen had finally emerged. No sign of Arwin.

"No. I got her mostly patched up and she insisted on leaving before dawn." Alyss grabbed Eira's hand and squeezed it tightly. "You should have woken me when you got back."

"I didn't want to disturb your sleep; it was a long night."

"It was." As if to make a point, she yawned. "I was worried. I stayed up. Luckily I caught Noelle…she was the one who told me not to stay awake any longer."

Eira pushed ice onto her cheeks to fight a scarlet blush. "Just got sidetracked is all."

Alyss hummed low.

"I said that's all." Eira shot her friend a pointed glance.

Alyss laughed softly. "I know, I know… But, for the record, I'm happy things are working out there. I've decided this pairing has my blessing."

Eira rolled her eyes and fought a smile.

Alyss apparently knew her well enough to recognize her

internal battle, because it drew a laugh from her. "Nothing to be ashamed of."

"We shouldn't talk about it," Eira reminded her.

"No one can hear us."

"Still."

Alyss fortunately dropped the subject as they joined the other competitors in the gardens out in front of the manor. The Solaris contingent emerged amid a heated discussion between Harkor, the draconi prince, and Olivin, the man who had emerged as the leader of the elfin competitors.

"Say that again," Harkor growled, stalking over to Olivin.

"Gladly. The draconi don't stand a chance in the tournament. You're all brash and brawn—not a single brain between you four." Olivin folded his arms over his chest, looking smug.

"You couldn't even survive an hour in the culling." Steam billowed from between Harkor's teeth.

"If you haven't noticed, this is not the culling. Fortunately we don't engage in such brutal practices on Meru."

"Enough, both of you." Cullen stepped forward. He was the mirror of his father in his tone and movements, enough that it had Eira sucking in air. "This tournament is about unity."

Harkor roared with laughter. "This tournament is about domination and showing that the Draconi Kingdom is not to be trifled with."

"You can't reason with a man like him." Olivin shook his head in a way that somehow managed to straddle the line of condescending and disappointed.

"Not a man, a *prince*," Harkor corrected, whirling back on Olivin.

"Oh, forgive me, Your Highness." Olivin bowed.

"Cullen is right. Enough, all of you." A man emerged from the manor, leading the competitors from the Republic of Qwint. Eira recognized him from the dinner she'd gone to with Cullen. He was Alvstar, if she remembered correctly.

"I don't answer to you." Harkor folded his arms in a way

that made his mighty chest and arms bulge. He was physically intimidating, Eira would give him that. But all she'd seen from the draconi prince so far was a lot of smoke and no real fire.

"Come back, Your Highness." One of the other draconi finally stepped forward. She cut them all a glare. "They're not worth your time."

Harkor relented, returning to his group.

"Things are getting a bit tense, aren't they?" Noelle laced her fingers and placed them behind her head. "So much for a friendly tournament."

"I'm sure it'll still manage to be friendly," Alyss said hopefully.

Eira could feel the powder keg that was the dynamics of the competitors filling to the brim. The tournament would be a spark, and who knew what the subsequent explosion would unleash. But even though she could feel the tension in the air, she was oddly immune to it.

"It seems almost trivial to be fighting about it," Eira said softly, so no one else but Alyss and Noelle would hear.

"Especially after last night," Noelle agreed under her breath.

Alvstar approached Cullen, placing a hand on his back and talking softly. Cullen's brow furrowed and he tilted his head. Eira tried not to stare as the two men spoke. After several minutes, Alvstar joined the other competitors from the Republic of Qwint and Cullen returned.

"What was that about?" Fortunately, Noelle asked the exact question Eira had been wondering but wasn't sure if she should vocalize.

Cullen stared back at Alvstar for a long moment. "Some political nonsense I need to discuss with my father."

"Political nonsense like what?" Eira asked.

"Nothing to worry about. I'll get it sorted." He dismissed her question with a smile. But the way concern lit the edges of his eyes made Eira worry all the more. Something was wrong. But she couldn't ask here and now. Not when they'd been doing such a good job of staying distant.

So she shrugged and engaged in a conversation with Alyss. When the morphi finally joined the group, they lined up, ready to march out to the training grounds. Eira tried to step over to where Alvstar and Cullen had been talking, but her attempt at seeing if any of their words had seeped into the stones at their feet was interrupted by Ducot suddenly appearing.

"Sorry I didn't have a chance to speak with you last night."

She glanced up at him. "It was hardly the time."

"Very true. In any case, thank you," he said softly as they started walking forward in a line, knights falling into step around them. The Twilight Kingdom and Solaris competitors buffered the two of them in the front and back, as if everyone knew they needed a moment alone to talk.

"I didn't do much."

"That's not what I heard." Ducot glanced her way. "Arwin told me, then I got the full story from Deneya later."

"Do you have orders for me?" Eira said under her breath. The sun was dimmer while she talked about the Court of Shadows; Risen was less glorious.

"No."

There was more to be said. She could feel it skulking in the silence that followed. So Eira waited patiently, walking in step with him as they passed by the residents of Meru.

"I don't like how Deneya is handling all this."

Eira merely hummed. Saying too much seemed ill advised. Ducot was still a shadow, last she checked, and that meant he still was loyal to Deneya first, regardless of his feelings.

"I don't think it's fair to you," he elaborated.

"I'd agree." The words burned too much to keep inside. "But I'm also biased."

He chuckled. "I do agree with her that you're reckless and have been a liability more than an asset."

"I'm not arguing that point." Eira shoved her hands in her pockets, keeping her eyes forward.

"I know. And that's part of why you're earning my respect.

Your recklessness has given us information we wouldn't have otherwise had, or would've gained long after it was too late. You were the one who put that information together, trying to warn us. And even after we ignored you…you *still* ran headfirst into danger last night. You saved Arwin and the rest." Eira glanced up at him, even though he still spoke without looking at her. "You have my respect, Eira Landan. And I owe you a debt of gratitude on Arwin's behalf."

"No, you don't. It was the right thing to do, maybe even because I'm so reckless. I owed them that much. Plus, it's not entirely selfless. I still need the court to help me take him down."

"Take my gratitude. I don't give it to many people." Ducot took a step ahead, going to rejoin his group. But he paused, adding, "I'll be there, whenever you need me. I'm on your side."

"What about *them*?" Eira whispered, not saying "the court" or "Specters" aloud.

Ducot shrugged. "I make my own judgments. If they don't like it, then they'll let me know, and I'll adjust accordingly." He flashed her a lopsided grin and returned to his friends.

Eira hung back, falling into step between Noelle and Alyss.

"He's an interesting one, isn't he?" Noelle said with a soft, intent gaze.

"He's a good one," Eira emphasized. "Definitely a friend."

"We need all the friends we can get these days," Alyss murmured.

They reached the training grounds without incident. Each group of competitors went to their respective corners and promptly began to settle in, only to be interrupted by Jahran— Lumeria's Quill and right hand. He stepped out onto the balcony that overlooked the grounds, summoning the attention of those gathered with his presence alone.

"Good day to you all!" He held out his hands, motioning to the gathered spectators in the stands as well as competitors. "While it has been delayed, we are most excited for the tournament's official start with the ball tomorrow night."

Eira's stomach twisted at the mention, reminding her she hadn't gotten up early enough to eat breakfast. Tomorrow night, she'd face Ferro again. She'd be the bait to make sure he'd be lured out…whatever it took.

"I want to inform all competitors and their dignitaries, as well as esteemed members of her court that might be present today, that her royal majesty will open her gates at sundown tomorrow. Dancing, drinking, and merriment will follow. At the end of the night, our queen herself will inform everyone of the tournament's official start and details. So train well, competitors! Your days of practice are nearing an end. Soon enough, you will be thrust into the tournament and all it holds."

"All it holds," Noelle repeated as the crowd applauded politely. "Wonder what that is, exactly."

"It can't be worse than what happened on Solaris," Alyss said hopefully.

Noelle shot her a glare and rolled her eyes. "*Please*, don't jinx us."

"They're still out there," Cullen whispered, stepping closer to the group. "Until he is dead, none of us are safe." Eira bit her lip. Cullen's attention shifted to her and, for a second, his gaze softened. "How are you hanging in there?"

"I'm fine. But there's something I want to start experimenting with. Or, I have been, with Alyss. But I think I need more help."

"What have we been doing?" Alyss blinked, startled.

"I didn't exactly tell you." Eira gave her friend a guilty glance.

Alyss huffed. "No. More. Secrets." She poked Eira with every word.

"I know, I know." She took a deep breath to gather her thoughts and courage. "It's just that…I know this will sound insane."

"Does it have anything to do with what she said last night? About you giving magic?" Noelle was sharp as ever.

Eira nodded. "She wasn't the first person to say something like that to me… *He* accused me of being able to steal people's magic." Her brow furrowed and Eira shook her head. She couldn't believe she actually said it aloud. "I know that's not something that I should be able to do, and it's silly to try, but…"

"It wouldn't be *entirely* unprecedented." Cullen tapped his chin in thought. "If you think about how a Waterrunner can make vessels, it's a form of funneling magic. Or, how they can create blocks in people's channels to eradicate magic."

"But I was never taught anything of the like. There's no way my uncles would've ever let me learn. I've only just now begun reading about it."

"You were never taught how to listen to the echoes of unintentional vessels, and you've done a great job of figuring that out along the way." Alyss nudged her.

"I only figured it out with your encouragement." Eira looked at each of her friends. "It might be nothing. But could we try? Will you help me?"

They each nodded in turn.

"You know we're here for you, always," Cullen said with a touch of pride and affection that softened Eira's nerves.

"Less tender moments, more magic." Noelle grinned. "You've been a surprising one, Eira. I'm excited to see what else you can do."

Eira nodded, determination cementing in her. "All right, let's begin."

THIRTY-FOUR

THEY PRACTICED ALL day, but they didn't manage to make any progress on Eira's alleged mysterious power. She honestly didn't know where to start in exploring it and left the training grounds feeling like she'd wasted some of their last precious hours to practice their magic for whatever the tournament might throw at them. Her friends insisted otherwise. But her ineptitude had Eira doubting all evening.

She stayed up after everyone had gone to bed. Eira scrounged up the journals she'd taken from Adela's secret room. Spreading them out across the bed, Eira flipped through them, looking for anything that might indicate Adela having some kind of power like this. If anyone did, Eira was certain it'd be the pirate queen.

The candle had burned low when a soft knock on the door startled her from her reading.

"Who is it?" she whispered, not wanting to be too loud. The door opened and Cullen poked his head around.

"Am I interrupting?"

"No, come in." Eira closed the journals, stacking them, as Cullen shut the door and lightly padded over.

"What're you reading?"

"Some journals I found in the Tower." Eira paused, her hand hovering on the stack. "I never showed you that room, did I?"

"What room?" He sat on the edge of the bed.

"I found a secret room connected to the Waterrunner's storeroom. It was Adela's."

"Really?"

Rather than answering, Eira took the top journal off the stack and flipped open to one of the less disturbing pages of Adela's magical experimentations. Cullen took it from her, skimming the tight, swirling script that danced across the page.

"So this was part of the edge you had in the trials." He smiled softly.

"Who knows?" Eira shrugged. "I've only been able to master a few of them recently. There're years of work here. I've been reading everything she wrote on sorcerer channels." She stared at the journal, willing them to impart deeper secrets than they already had. "She really was—*is* incredible. In a terrifying sort of way."

"As are you." Cullen ran a finger down her spine. Eira shivered, reminded of just how thin her sleeping shirt was. "Though less terrifying."

"I think there's quite a few people who would disagree with you on that." She gave him a tired grin.

"I think I don't care what others think," he responded, his knuckles brushing over her cheek. The way he looked at her then, with such sorrow and longing… He looked as if he was the one who was going to try to separate them now.

"What's wrong?" Eira whispered.

"Nothing."

"You're lying."

He chuckled softly. "Perhaps I am." His hand slid around the back of her neck as he met her eyes. "I love you, Eira."

"I love you too," she breathed. The words were still hard to say. She still felt as though every time they passed her lips she was doing nothing more than digging an even deeper hole for them to have to escape from.

"I want to be with you, and only you. Nothing will change that." He leaned forward. "Do you believe me?"

"Yes," she breathed. "And it *terrifies* me."

"Good, we'll be terrified together." He pressed his mouth against hers, gentle but firm. The way he kissed her, unhurried, but filled with such a deep and utter longing, had Eira's own yearning responding in kind.

Cullen continued pushing forward, causing Eira to lean back. His hand was still behind her head, now wedged between her and the pillow. Cullen shifted. The journals fell to the floor with heavy thuds that they both ignored.

"Let me stay with you tonight?" he breathed across her lips.

"I should tell you no."

"I shouldn't ask." He grinned slightly, outlined by candlelight.

"Stay with me." Eira didn't care how bad of an idea it was. There was something heady and desperate in the night air. She needed him to be here. For all Eira knew, tomorrow would be their last day alive.

With a flick of Cullen's hand, an unseen gust guttered the candle and plunged them into darkness. Moonlight streamed through her window, turning his golden outline silvery. Eira traced every edge of him with her fingers between kisses. She would learn him, commit him to memory, steal a knowledge of him that would be only hers.

His hands roved as well, leisurely exploring her sides, the plane of her stomach, her hips. Eira exhaled pent-up delight.

"I want you," she breathed into the darkness.

"And I want you."

Her hands slipped underneath his shirt, feeling the muscle she knew was there without any barriers. The sound of the clothes sliding off of him—off of her—was as sweet as a song. He was warm, almost fever-hot on her cool skin. It was as though he was the embodiment of life, and goodness, and she was a wraith in the night, thieving from him something she should never even touch, let alone take.

But Eira would pillage and steal whatever he laid bare to her. She twisted and his back pressed into the bed. Her turn to be on top and in control. Her fingers grazed over his chest, drawing goosebumps with their chill and a sharp inhale. She liked him shivering under her, yearning, gasping. Eira leaned forward, inhaling slowly, savoring every sound and scent with every part of her. Fingers splayed across his chest, she kissed down his neck, nibbling lightly on his collarbone.

Cullen groaned and the sound drove her wild. "I want your lips."

"Where?"

"Everywhere," he rasped. His thumbs dug into her hips as he grabbed them, massaging lightly. "I don't want to hold back."

"So don't." Eira nipped at his neck. His back arched. "Give yourself to me."

She felt like a temptress until the moment his eyes opened and Cullen looked at her. Then, she felt like a goddess of night and shadow and desire. An entity that could bring a man to his knees and leave him wanting and begging for more. Eira had never considered herself a highly sexual being. But now she understood why this insatiable drive left people yearning for more.

"I… I've never…" He trailed off, panic alight in his eyes.

"I haven't either," she whispered. "We don't have to if you're not ready."

"I want to."

"Are you sure?"

"I think so."

Think wasn't enough for her. It wasn't an enthusiastic yes. She had arrived at her own conclusion, in her own time. But she needed him to do the same. It wouldn't mean anything if he wasn't as committed as she was.

"Do you want to tonight? With me?" Eira pressed. Wanting to as a general thing and wanting to here and now were very different.

His throat constricted as he swallowed. Eira watched the panic and worry evaporate from his eyes. "I have never wanted anything more, so much that it scares me." Cullen caressed her cheek. "I'm just worried I won't be good enough for you."

"My dear Cullen…" She tilted her head into his hand. "You are more than I deserve. More than I ever dreamed of. Love was something I had written off a long time ago and then you came into my life."

"And complicated everything." He laughed softly.

"Such a blissful complication you are." Eira leaned forward to kiss him again. She didn't want to think of complications. They just reminded her of the world beyond that wanted to hold them both back at best, or see them dead at worst. "Take me," she whispered. "Now, later, whenever you want me, I'm yours. I will wait eternity for you."

"I hope I never keep you waiting so long." He propped himself up on his elbows and then pressed farther forward. They twisted once more until he was atop her. Her hands roamed down and farther down still. When she hesitated, he grabbed her wrist and guided her hand to him.

With shuddering gasps and strangled moans, they explored each other until there was nothing left between them. With a tent of sheets over his shoulders, cast in shadows, they merged together in the darkness. His heat, his scent, the delightful sensation of tension both relieved and stretched to the breaking point overwhelmed her. When he moved, she moved with him. Eira rasped his name into his ear, over and over again. Cullen bit on her neck, a little harder than he likely should have, forcing her to smother a moan that would otherwise wake up the whole manor.

They treated the night like those fleeting hours were the only ones they would ever have. And when their bodies were exhausted, they fell into each other's arms. Eira's head on his chest, his hand in her hair, they submitted to slumber, sweat-slicked and satisfied.

***

Once more, morning came too soon. Eira woke to Cullen shifting. Ever the gentleman, he tried to place a pillow where his body had once occupied, but she noticed the change instantly. Drowsy and bleary-eyed, she woke to see him dressing. A brief streak of panic raced through her. Would he regret what they had done in the early hours of a gray dawn? Was he trying to sneak out and pretend it all never occurred?

That would be apt. That would be what she'd always expected from such things. Because Eira had never imagined herself for love. She'd never contemplated that a man like Cullen would turn and smile just at the sight of her.

With a knee on the bed, he leaned over and kissed her temple lightly. "I didn't want to wake you."

"It's all right." Eira stretched, stiff in all the right places with an ache she would not want Alyss to relieve.

"I figured I should leave before anyone else wakes."

"For the best." She nodded and sat as he finished dressing. "Do you regret it?"

He paused and turned to look her straight in the eyes. "Mother above, no. I will treasure last night for the rest of my life."

"Me too." Eira smiled, but there was a twinge of sadness in the air that she couldn't pin down. It hovered over his shoulders, weighing them down.

"I love you." Even though he said it, something about those words sounded like goodbye.

No, she was imagining that… These doubts were her fabrication from years of telling herself that this type of love would never be hers—that she didn't *deserve* it. Eira forced the thoughts from her head and smiled.

"I love you, too."

He grabbed her hand. "No matter what, Eira. That will be true. I hope I proved that to you last night—I will always find my way to your bed." Cullen kissed her lips and left before she could say or do anything else.

The rest of the day was a blur.

The seamstress, Estal, appeared in the later hours of the morning following breakfast and popped about each of their rooms, adding last-minute lace and trim or making adjustments. Eira was grateful they were dressing in the manor. She had been dreading the idea of going back to the woman's atelier.

Around lunchtime, Mistress Harrot delivered refreshments in the form of tea and finger sandwiches. Eira watched her movements through the room from the corner of her eye. The woman was definitely lingering beyond what was necessary.

"Excuse me a moment," Estal's assistant said, standing from where she'd been working on Eira's hem. "I need to get a bit of lace."

"Of course," Eira said with a smile.

As soon as the door was closed, Harrot turned. "Do you have everything you need?"

"I do, thank you." Eira kept her magic at the ready. The woman was certainly suspicious, but, oddly enough, Eira continued to feel no threat from her. Even though Eira was certain she was a Pillar and Ferro's mother…Harrot seemed disarmed today.

"The ball is certainly quite the event," she said softly.

"Indeed."

Harrot stepped forward and Eira took a step back, keeping her distance. Pain flashed through the woman's eyes. She lowered them, adjusting the hair that had spilled from her bun and tucking it back in. "Please, there must be another way."

"Pardon?"

"Don't… He's all I have," Harrot begged.

"I don't know what you're talking about." Eira looked out the window.

Taking her eyes off of Harrot was a mistake. The woman closed the gap with a speed Eira didn't expect her to possess and she gripped Eira's hand.

"Unhand me!"

"He's all I have!" she repeated. "There must be another way to rekindle the flame. I kept the dagger safe. I can keep more relics here, hidden. What else can I do? If the flame must be ignited again, then let me do it, not him."

Tonight. The Pillars had the relics they needed. They were going to try to reignite the Flame of Yargen at the ball. Eira had to tell someone.

"Glory to the Champion," Eira muttered.

"Of course…you really are one of them." Harrot slowly released her, the pain in her eyes doubling. It gave Eira the keen sense that, somewhere along the line, she had misjudged the woman.

Harrot was Ferro's mother. But she wasn't a zealot like the rest of the Pillars. She was just someone looking out for, and looking to connect with, her son. She had taken the dagger not for the Champion and reigniting the flame, but because it was Ferro—her son—who asked.

Ugliness poisoned Eira's thoughts. It swam through her, staining every corner of her emotions. This mother was so desperate to do anything for her son that she would ignore everything else she knew was true. That her son was cruel, wicked, abusive, and a power-hungry murderer. Yet, here she was, still looking after him.

Ferro had such a mother.

When Eira had none.

She frowned, feeling her face twist into something that likely more resembled a snarl. Harrot released her and backed away. She looked at Eira as though she had transformed into a wild beast.

"You can't change what's going to happen tonight." Malice kissed her words. A hatred that had been festering for weeks underneath a thin veneer had been ripped to the surface.

"He cares for you. You must—" Fortunately, for her own sake, Harrot didn't get to finish. Otherwise Eira would've spared no explanation as to what Ferro's "care" really looked like.

The apprentice returned. "Apologies. That took longer than expected. One of my companions had the lace in your friend's room."

"No problem." Eira plastered a sweet smile on instantly. She glanced to Harrot. "Did you need anything else?"

"No," Harrot murmured, bowed her head, and left.

Eira stared out the window, confident that even if Harrot wasn't a zealot, Eira's performance had given her no fodder to report back to Ferro with. Eira had played her role as loyal Pillar in hiding. She inhaled sharply as the laces of her corset were tightened. It felt like armor.

Tonight was the night all the pieces on the court's table finally converged.

***

They had carriages to take them to the ball. Alyss let out a monstrous avian-like squawk with excitement at the sight of them. Cullen was distant and quiet as they left the manor. Eira had expected that, but she thought he might have, at the very least, complimented her gown.

Estal did stunning work, that much was certain. Eira stood in a dress of blue and black. Layers of silk transitioned from a frosty cerulean by the swoop neck to an obsidian at the bottom hem. It was fitted to her torso and hung from her hips in scalloped ruching.

Noelle and Alyss were just as stunning in similar styles, but with red and green, respectively, fading into black.

They loaded into their carriage with Levit, sans Cullen. He had been directed into a different carriage to ride with his father and other dignitaries. Eira watched the world drift by as they rocked over the cobblestones of Risen. She twisted one of the layers of her dress in her hands over and over again until Noelle's hand covered hers.

"You might tear the lace if you keep that up," Noelle said softly.

"You're right." Eira stopped.

"It'll be fine."

"It's all right to be nervous for your first ball," Levit encouraged, oblivious. "I certainly was for mine."

It wasn't her first ball, but Eira didn't correct him. Instead, she thought back to that winter's night when she'd first laid eyes on Taavin and Vi. How different those two had appeared then. What was real? The blushing bride and groom to be? The strategic marriage uniting two worlds? Or the deadly couple charging into the Court of Shadows with fierce magic that one of them shouldn't possess?

Finally, the carriage came to a stop and the footman helped them out. Eira recognized the castle from the execution they'd attended. But there were no signs of such grim dealings tonight.

Music drifted through the twilight air. Men and women laughed as they poured into the great hall of the castle. Eira walked with her head high, trying to be seen.

Come and get me, she thought. *I'm here for the taking, Ferro. But it will be the last thing you do.*

THE GREAT HALL of Lumeria's castle glittered with the light of a thousand candles refracting off four massive, crystal chandeliers that were suspended along the length of the room. At the far end was a dais where the queen sat on her throne. At her right hand were Taavin and Vi, appropriately perched in two smaller thrones. At her left was Jahran.

The competitors were held off in the wings of the entry, stealing glimpses as others entered. A crier announced noblemen and women as they passed through the great, fortified doors. Eira watched each of their faces, but didn't recognize any of them as Pillars or shadows. Whatever her orders were, they were waiting until the last second to get them to her.

Movement at her side distracted her from the flow of people. Cullen's jaw was set tight and he kept his eyes forward.

"You finally freed yourself," Eira said under her breath without looking at him. Yemir was only a few people behind them.

Cullen snorted. "I've never been less free," he said bitterly.

"What?" Despite herself, Eira looked at him.

He faced her as well. In shifting, his hand brushed against hers. Their fingers slotted against each other as effortlessly as their bodies had the night before. Yet the movement brought her no comfort. Eira swallowed thickly. She had enough to worry about tonight. She didn't need whatever *this* was.

Cullen's eyes drifted back to his father before he straightened, eyes ahead once more. His hand, obscured by Noelle and Alyss behind them, remained against hers. "I meant it."

"What?"

"Everything." The word was pained. Her chest tightened. "Last night, everything I said, I meant it all."

"I know you did." So why was he pleading with her as though she was about to argue? Why was he doing this *now* of all times?

"All right, we'll announce you next." One of the knights came over. "We'll start with Solaris and go back in groups. Dignitaries will have their own announcements," he said hastily.

Without giving them an opportunity to question, the crier boomed, "Presenting the competitors from Solaris: Eira Landan, Cullen Drowel, Alyss Ivree, and Noelle Gravson."

The four of them strode into the room, Levit and the ambassadors behind, walking down the cleared path to polite applause. Eira was certain most of these people had been watching them in the training grounds for weeks now. But the spectators gaped as if this was the first time they had laid eyes on the four of them.

Before the raised thrones, the whole of the Solaris contingent bowed.

"Good competitors, I welcome you to Meru. May your competition be fair and victories be glorious," Lumeria said formally.

And, with that, it was over. They stepped off to the side and Eira breathed a sigh of relief. The crowd surrounded them and the morphi were up next, following the same script.

A light tapping on her hand drew her attention. Eira half expected to see Ferro, but it was Deneya standing at her side. She felt a folded strip of paper slipped between her fingers.

"Your dance card," Deneya said by way of explanation. "Read it, then have the Firebearer burn it. Once you finish dancing, get somewhere that Ferro will find you. We should have enough eligible men to draw him out. Once you have him, lure him back onto the dance floor. We'll take it from there."

"Deneya—"

"That's all."

Before Eira could even breathe a word on the relics or flame,

Deneya was gone. Eira took the slip of paper and unfolded it. There were five names scribbled on the paper. But Eira only recognized one and the importance of the rest, Eira didn't know. Why these people? Why did they think her spinning around on the floor would do anything?

A wave of nausea passed over her. Deneya and the Specters knew her parading would goad him. Ferro had threatened anyone who merely touched her. How could he resist her dancing the night away with a parade of eligible men? All Eira could hope for was that Deneya's plan worked, and the Pillars didn't have the chance to act first.

Eira folded the paper and passed it to Noelle.

"Yes?" Noelle arched her eyebrows.

"Burn it." Eira appreciated Noelle all the more when her friend didn't question, just took the slip of paper and, with a small flash, immolated it in a second.

All too soon, the introductions were over and with a wave of Lumeria's hand, music filled the hall. Eira gripped her dress, hovering awkwardly. Cullen had disappeared back to his father's side, engaged in some kind of intense discussion.

A tap on her shoulder jolted her back to the present. Eira turned, expecting to see one of the people Deneya had listed, but Alyss held out her hand.

"Would you care to dance, fair maiden?" Alyss said with a dramatic bow.

Eira bleated a laugh and the tension in her shoulders unwound some. "I would love one."

Alyss linked their arms and led them to the dance floor. Her friend assumed the lead role, placing her palm on Eira's hip. Eira took Alyss's other hand and rested her right hand on Alyss's shoulder.

"Do you remember when we first learned to dance?" Alyss said with a small smile.

"I remember bumping into everything in your room as we tried to figure out the basics from that horrible book." Eira laughed softly at the memory. Alyss had read about a ball in one of her romance novels and promptly found an illustrated tome on how to properly dance. It was a night of much trial and error and comedy.

"Aren't you glad we did though? Now you're a proper vision on the dance floor." Alyss extended her arm and Eira twirled with a laugh.

"You are the vision." Eira beamed at her friend as they turned. Alyss stilled.

"What is—"

Someone tapped Eira's shoulder. She looked to see an utterly striking gentleman. He was so handsome that Eira was certain he wasn't a shadow. She would've remembered a man this perfectly chiseled.

"Excuse me, Miss Landan." He bowed. "I'm Sir Crestwall; might I cut in?" He was one of the names on the list Deneya had given her.

"Don't let me get in your way." Alyss released her with a wink.

The strapping gentleman with the long, dark hair and medallions pinned to his chest scooped up Eira without a moment's hesitation. His footwork was dazzling as they spun across the dance floor. He flashed her roguish smiles, accented by the stubble across his jaw.

They'd hardly exchanged any more words than small talk before there was another tap on her shoulder. Another man introduced himself and Eira recognized the name as the next on her card. He was just as handsome as the last with a title that was a mouthful to say.

By the third gentleman, Eira was noticing a pattern. All of the men had impressive pedigrees and even more dazzling smiles. Deneya seemed to have assembled a list of the most eligible bachelors in Risen and, somehow, convinced them to dance with her. She was tempted to ask them what they'd been promised, but knew better. Nothing good would come of the inquiry.

Yet, wondering sat heavy and uncomfortable in the back of

her mind. None of these men *wanted* to touch her. Not really. None of them would be dancing with her were it not for Deneya's and the court's coercion. Eira wished she could say that to the envious stares she was getting from men and women at the edge of the dance floor. She caught the other competitors whispering on a turn.

They don't want me, Eira wanted to scream. Instead she smiled and laughed. She threw the gentlemen coquettish grins and tried to keep up with their far superior footwork as best she could.

Number five was the name she recognized, Olivin.

"May I cut in?" he asked number four smoothly, his Meru accent turning up the words just slightly enough to be effortlessly attractive.

"Of course." Her previous dance partner excused himself with a polite smile and without so much as a second look back.

Olivin assumed his position. The song alternated between fast and slow steps. Movements she was certain she read in one of her books, but couldn't remember with everything else weighing on her mind. Luckily, Olivin had no shortage of grace.

"You dance well."

"You lie." She gave him a tired grin.

Olivin's black hair fell forward, threatening to get into his eyes as he tipped his head forward to meet her gaze. "You've been dancing around Risen's politics and secrets since the first moment you stepped foot on our lands. Not an easy feat."

Shadow or Pillar? He had to be a shadow if Deneya managed to get him to dance with her. Unless Olivin was a just a worthy noble Deneya had picked and secret Pillar.

"I do my best," she said cautiously.

"So I've heard. Ducot told me your best could have spared us all below from that fiery night, if you'd been heeded." *Shadow, then.* He leaned forward, tightening his arms around her as Eira dipped back. Olivin's mouth pressed into a thin line. "Then again, you also threatened our existence and operation."

"Do you admire me, or resent me?"

He swept her out to the side and waited until they came together to answer. "Oh, you have something far worse, Eira, than my admiration or resentment."

"And what is that?" She was suddenly keenly aware of his hand sliding across the small of her back. Of how close they stepped now.

"My curiosity," he said, whisper soft.

The surrealness of the situation finally hit her. Here she was, dancing in Lumeria's castle, in the capital of Meru, with an elfin man who was—by every traditional measure—achingly handsome. She was bait in a deadly game. She would outmaneuver a zealot and murder.

And yet, her mind kept wandering back to…

A tap on her shoulder. Olivin stepped away and Eira braced herself to be face-to-face with Ferro.

But Cullen was there instead, hand hovering, waiting, a face of worry and hope and bittersweet despair. "My lady, might I have the next dance?"

"Of course, my lord." Eira heaved a sigh of relief. It was as though he materialized from her thoughts—from her raw need of him. She rested her hand lightly in Cullen's and a jolt shot through her. Just his touch, the bare skin of his fingers sliding against hers, was enough to make the room spin. Her dress was suddenly too tight. She couldn't get a breath in.

This was what she wanted, what she longed for. Her daydreams were no longer consumed by handsome elfin and Meru…but an Eastern man with intense hazel eyes and plain brown hair.

The music drifted into a slower waltz. Cullen took leisurely, large steps across the floor. Eira struggled to keep up with his wide strides.

"Sorry, I'm a bit lightheaded," she said with a soft laugh. "Must be all the spinning."

"May I do the dancing for you?" He arched his eyebrows, lips quirking.

"Pardon?"

His hand glided across the small of her back, pressing her closer to him. "Don't panic, I have you," he whispered over the shell of her ear.

Despite the warning, Eira let out a soft yelp of surprise as she stepped and her foot didn't meet the ground. Cullen kept his grip on her, holding her steady, keeping her from stumbling. Her other foot landed on air as well and a strange, bubbling sensation filled her as she realized it was his magic underneath her feet, hidden by her skirts.

She danced on air. Effortlessly spinning and gliding across the floor with Cullen, overcome by a grace not made for mortals.

"You're doing it for you too, aren't you?" she asked.

He grinned, dangerously handsome in that moment. So dangerous she could kiss him in front of everyone if she wasn't careful. "How do you think I learned to dance? Practice? No, this is all a show. The gowns, the clothes, take me across the world and nobility is all the same. A performance hammered into me by force." His grip on her tightened slightly. A half turn and they were closer, hips flush. "But you, you're the only thing that's real here. You're the only person that matters."

She soared, and not just because of the air underneath her feet. The air in the room had been replaced with something lighter. His magic glided across her, within her. They moved together, just as they had done the night before, entangled in a very different dance.

"We should stop," she whispered. Surely their connection must be evident to everyone. Surely it was their love that had saturated the air, turning it sweet and heady.

"Just a little longer." His eyes were solely on her. Nothing else existed. There was a dangerous invitation in his gaze to lose herself as well. "We only have a few more moments before it ends."

"What ends?"

"The song." There was so much more left unsaid.

"Cullen," she breathed, searching his face and not liking what she found. "What is it?"

"I—"

The music stopped. Her feet touched the ground once more as his magic gently released her. And, in the void, a new voice appeared.

"My dear, should we dance?"

My dear? Eira found herself face-to-face with a woman whom she'd seen around Noelle on occasion. Her sharp green eyes, her dewy, fawn complexion, her spiral auburn hair carefully pinned looked drastically different than how her practical clothes on the training grounds.

Lavette, Alvstar's daughter. Her father was the man Cullen had been speaking to in hushed tones the other day. Eira's head plummeted out of the clouds as she began to realize that while she had been so focused on Ferro's threat to Cullen, she hadn't considered another game was at play that would take him from her.

Cullen's eyes drifted to Yemir, who was standing next to Alvstar. The two men looked on with large smiles.

"What's going on?" Eira asked—no, *demanded* of Cullen.

"We…" He couldn't seem to make up his mind on who or what he wanted to look at, but it wasn't Eira, that much was certain. "Our fathers, that is…"

"There will be an announcement soon," Lavette said kindly. Though Eira could feel discomfort radiating off her as well. Both of them wanted to dance around whatever this was, not touching on the topic outright. And not because of some kind of announcement. But because there was palpable dread hanging over both their shoulders. The music swelled once more. "Shall we?"

"I suppose." *We must*; that was the other half of the sentence Cullen so clearly wanted to say.

Eira stepped away as they danced, distant, stiff armed, and with forced smiles. She crossed over to where Yemir hovered, wondering if he was about to cause her to make a scene. He gave a nod of his head as she stood next to him at the edge of the dance floor and for half the song they pretended to ignore each other. But Eira could feel him steeping in a horrible smugness.

"Not interested in dancing any longer?"

Eira considered it a victory that she wasn't the one to break the silence. "My head is feeling a bit light."

"You seemed to have quite the array of partners."

"It was a fortunate surprise." She should be searching for Ferro. But all she could look at was Cullen and Lavette.

"Perhaps this will be good for you, Eira. No one here knows of your past transgressions. You could make a smart match and live on Meru as you've always wanted." Yemir could wrap manure in a compliment if he had to. "It does seem to be the time for politically savvy matches." Alvstar chuckled on the other side of him. "First our princess, and now—*ah*, well, best to wait until the announcement."

"What did you do?" Eira whispered, dangerously quiet, eyes still on Cullen and the woman.

"What I had always planned on doing." Yemir looked down at her, speaking just quietly enough that Alvstar wouldn't hear over the music. "I made an advantageous match for my son that will secure our family's political advantage not only in Solaris, but now in a new, key trading partner as well."

She pressed her lips tightly together, not trusting herself to speak.

"You didn't actually think…" He chuckled. "I don't know what my son has told you, but he's always known his position and has accepted it gladly."

No he hasn't, she wanted to scream. But those were words Cullen had to say to his father. They were meaningless if they came from her.

"But I suppose such infatuations can't be helped for a young man as eligible as—"

"When was the engagement arranged?" Eira asked, done sidestepping around what was now so painfully obvious.

"About a week ago."

The wind was knocked from her. Eira placed a hand on her lower stomach just to remind herself that she was still breathing. *A week ago.*

"When did he know?" she breathed.

Yemir didn't have to tell her. But he no doubt delighted in watching the torture that was spreading across her features. He had the audacity to smile. "About a week ago. Why do you ask?"

Cullen knew…he knew and he didn't tell her…he knew last night when he…when they…

Eira spun, unable to stare at the dancing couple. She was ready to charge out the door when Yemir grabbed her wrist. She glared at the man.

"You would do well to take no action that might risk this union. We might be across the sea, but don't think that I couldn't make your life difficult if I wanted to. You're still of Solaris. *I* still have power over you." He chuckled. "You look so offended. I'm merely giving you some helpful advice."

"I find everything about you offensive, Senator," Eira hissed. "Now unhand me."

"With pleasure."

The second she was free, she started for the wall of windows that overlooked the city, relieved to find that they were actually doors that opened to a series of balconies. Eira practically bolted down the line, looking for the balcony that was the most secluded. Looking for a place she could breathe. Her dress was too tight, the music was too loud, the people were too oppressive, the eyes on her were too much—it was all too much.

She inhaled a gasping breath as her hands landed on the balcony railing. Eira exhaled, inhaled in the quiet, and stared up at the stars above. She blinked several times, refusing to allow herself to cry. Cullen loved her. He'd said so knowing the truth. He assured her nothing would change that.

But…what did any of that matter when he was going to marry another? There was no way Yemir would ever allow the engagement to be called off. She pressed her eyes closed and lodged every curse at herself that she knew. How foolish she had been. How—

"He doesn't deserve you. None of them do." A sinister voice slithered on the night air like poison through wine. "Men like that will toy with you." Ferro slid a finger down her spine. Eira couldn't suppress a shiver as his bare skin touched hers, continuing even after he'd crossed over her dress. His breath moved her hair as he whispered into her ear, "I'm the only one who could ever love you, spawn of Adela. I'm the only kin you will ever have."

She bit her lip, staring forward, willing this horrible moment to be a hallucination. She'd rather have been broken by the news of Cullen than have this be her reality. All she'd wanted was a moment to breathe.

"Now, what would you like me to do to really get this party started? Kill them?"

IT WAS HARD to smile, harder still to lean back into his hand and tip her head so she could glance at him from the corner of her eye. Yet Eira managed it all and what she hoped read as a relieved smile.

"Ferro, I was wondering how long until you came for me. I have missed the Pillars and wish to return to their loving embrace." As soon as she said the words, she wondered if she went too far.

He hummed, a little too low and for a little too long. His hand slipped around her waist, yanking her to him. "You didn't look as though you missed your new family out there."

"I danced with whoever asked. I don't want to raise suspicions." She stopped herself before her panic over-justified her actions. *Let him not target Cullen.* Even if Eira hadn't combed through her feelings surrounding the engagement and how he handled all that, she never would if he was dead. She forced laughter. "I even danced with Alyss."

"Very true." His demeanor shifted slightly—from play to work. "Did you bring it?"

"I did." Eira fished the piece of plaster she'd taken from the Archives out of a secret pocket she'd asked to be sewn into her gown. She used it as an opportunity to get some distance between them and angle herself so she could have a better view of the ballroom and other balconies. The nearest balcony was empty, but a couple was leaning against the railing two balconies over. Shadows? Maybe? Hopefully they were watching to make sure the princess's and Deneya's plan went smoothly—whatever it was from here on out. "What are we going to do with it?"

Ferro lifted it from her fingers and turned it over. "To think, something so small will be my father's absolution," he said to himself.

"Long may the Champion reign," Eira intoned with all the blind faith she could muster.

"Indeed." Ferro beamed at her with a wild glint to his eye. "You and I will be the first to march into his brand new world—a world illuminated by Her holy fire."

"What must I do?" Eira tried not to seem too eager to get any information on his plan.

"First, we will absolve him using your power. Then…" Ferro unsheathed a familiar golden dagger from his hip. Eira's eyes widened slightly. It was the dagger she had first discovered in the manor, the one the Pillars had stolen back from the court. "You will come with me into our new world."

He held out the dagger to her. Eira accepted it with both hands. After all the Pillars had done to get the blade, he was just *handing* it to her? New world? She must've looked as confused as she felt, because Ferro chuckled and hooked her chin with his thumb and knuckle.

"Do you want to be worthy of Yargen's love, even though you were born in the shadow of Raspian's tomb?"

"Yes." She'd agree to anything if he started making sense and telling her how everything fit together.

"This is how you will. When the time comes we will use this dagger, a sacred relic of Yargen, to rekindle the flame."

"What *are* the sacred relics?" She counted to three while looking down at the dagger in awe to hopefully display the appropriate reverence.

Ferro placed his hands over hers, one on the dagger's grip, the other on the scabbard, and he unsheathed it. There was a thin line of red down the center of the blade. It looked like a rod of ruby had been set down along the fuller.

"This is the blade my father used to kill the last Voice. Knowing the flame was stolen, and likely extinguished, he preserved some of her blood." Ferro spoke with excitement, as if he wasn't outlining a grim tale. His grip tightened around hers. "He is the Champion of Yargen. And with this and the Ash of Yargen—"

"Ash of Yargen?" Eira pretended she'd never heard the words before. Ferro seemed to buy it.

"Her power had crystallized to seal Raspian away. But when your people set him free of his tomb, it fractured and turned to dust." Ferro cupped her cheek. "We have all we need. Now you will help me ascend as we reignite her flame, together. Then, they will not be able to deny my father and he will rule this land in her light."

"Your father… Ulvarth?" she breathed. "Is it truly him?"

Ferro nodded slowly.

"I heard that Ulvarth was…"

"Dead?" He arched his eyebrows. "Did you hear that from the light traitor Deneya?"

"Among other lies and slander that I don't believe," she said quickly.

"I have no doubt." Ferro chuckled. "They think him dead, because they left him to die. He fell from the great tower of his estate and into the goddess's loving arms. Then, he was reborn."

Just once. Could he not speak in cryptic riddles *just once*? "He fooled them into thinking he was dead?"

Ferro had a knowing glint to his eyes. He'd been involved somehow in Ulvarth's escape, Eira would bet her life on it. "I am his general, his loyal servant, his right hand and blood. I ensured his death would be nothing more than an illusion—but an effective one at that. And now he will return from the dead to the people, to be their Champion." He rested his hands on her shoulders. "Are you ready?"

"Yes."

"Good. We are gaining control of the room. The last true Voice gave me a word of power for this moment. Wait here. You will know when the time is right." Ferro leaned forward and placed a sweet kiss on her forehead. Eira tasted bile in the back of her throat. He left her, dagger in hand.

She should go inside. She should grab his arm and demand he go out on the dance floor with her. *One dance before we usher in the new world*, she could imagine herself saying. The Pillars were on the move. The vacant balconies down the castle meant the shadows were on the move as well.

But Eira was stuck. The golden dagger glinted in the moonlight. The ruby line of blood from the last Voice—if Ferro was to be believed—ran down its center. She could spare a minute. One minute to find out if she was right. If there was more to be heard of that conversation and what it held.

Magic gathered in her palm. A thin sheen of frost coated the dagger. It dripped onto the stones around her feet as her powers smothered it. The darkness grew around her and Eira welcomed it. She had learned how to feel deeper magic in that pit and honed the skill with her friends.

"Tell me everything," Eira breathed. A connection she'd never felt before clicked into place.

I've been waiting for you, Ferro's distant voice said, just as it had the first time.

You know I can't move freely—that was the Champion's voice…Ulvarth. Eira could recognize it now thanks to her time with the Pillars.

I know, that's why I was worried. I thought you might have lost your way out. Way out… This conversation must've occurred when Ulvarth was still in captivity.

They are none the wiser of my movements, or our plans, Ulvarth preened. He had been able to sneak out of his prison without anyone knowing. He had time and means to arrange his "death."

What are my orders?

Always so eager. Let me just look at you a moment; it's not often I get to see my son. You are growing up strong and capable. You will be worthy, when the time comes.

I pray I shall be.

That time draws near.

Ferro snarled softly. *Lumeria's ambition will be her demise. She ignores the evil that threatens to consume us all. We are the only ones who can save this land.*

We alone shall stand against the darkness, Ulvarth agreed.

Ferro gasped. This must have been when he was taking the dagger from Ulvarth. *Father, are you sure?*

Yes. We must implement our plans.

I am ready. Eira gripped the dagger even tighter as Ferro's voice began to waver.

You know what to do with this.

I will bring it to her.

Then you shall go and collect the Ash of Yargen and begin unraveling Lumeria's deal with the heretics, Ulvarth commanded. *Once we possess the four relics, we will reignite the flame that guides this world.*

And when that happens, you will rule.

The real world had disappeared for Eira. There was only the dagger and this sole conversation. She poured all her focus and magic into it. Eira held her breath, not wanting anything to distract her from what came next. This was as far as she'd made it the first time.

And you will ascend, Ulvarth said. *You will take the Ash of Yargen and the blood of the Voice. The blood of the Champion flows through your veins and you—*

Have been born and baptized to be the sacred kindling of a new Flame of Yargen. Ferro's voice trembled with excitement.

Once we ignite the flame, we will use it to guide the wayward flock of Meru back to Her love. We will be undeniable henceforth. Risen will be under the protection of the divine once more.

And under your control, Ferro added.

Yes, and you, my son, will dine at her table in the highest place of honor a mortal could ever attain.

I pray I am worthy.

You will be, Ulvarth said. *Now go. Take the dagger. Hide it under their noses where it can rest until the time is right. I can't risk keeping it here any longer.*

I will not let you down.

The conversation slipped away as her magic slid off the dagger in chunks of ice. She had been right… every careful maneuver and plot, had been to lead them to this moment. The Pillars had worked to collect these relics—ashes, blood of the Voice and Champion, and a person to kindle. Tonight they would reignite the Flame of Yargen. There were enough people here to witness that the Pillars would gain the minds of the general public. They—

The doors to the balcony suddenly snapped open. Eira staggered back. Pillars lined her path in their drab robes. The gathered masses had been parted and they stood frozen in place, making a clear walkway for her to unite with Ferro on what was once the dance floor. He had ended up right where the shadows had wanted him after all…but nothing looked like it was going according to plan.

He beckoned to her, as he held up the plaster in his other hand.

Eira staggered forward, mind and heart racing. What was happening? What had she missed? Had her absence been the cause of this shift in power? The air was heavy with the sort of pregnant silence that promised—one way or another—the night would end with screams.

An invisible force drew her toward Ferro, dagger in hand. She was delivering what he wanted right to him. She should run. She should chuck the dagger over the balcony while she still could.

But she was drawn toward him with the allure of a finality too sweet to ignore. There were hundreds of people gathered, but none of them mattered. It was like that night in the forest, and the later night in the Pillars' hideout. In the end, it came down again and again to just her and him. But this time, she wasn't going to let him go. Too much was at stake. She'd end it here and now. Her heart raced in time with her thoughts; the former threatened to rip out of her chest, the latter threatened to rip open her skull.

As she neared, she noticed that the light now illuminating the room was not just from the chandeliers. A large glyph swirled in the vaulted ceiling, mirroring a smaller one rotating between Ferro's shoulder blades. Was that what was keeping everyone so still? She was walking in a living sculpture garden. *Loft dorh* were words of power that could freeze people in place, but she'd never heard of it being able to be used on an entire room. There must be another word—some kind of magnifier.

"I have here," Ferro said, holding up the plaster, "a fragment from the halls of the Voice of Yargen. And this woman holds the power to uncover the truth. She can listen to the annals of the Goddess in order to seek out that which came before." He pointed to Eira while looking at Vi, who was rigid on her throne. Mouth frozen in initial shock. "The Emperor and Empress of Solaris recognized her power. The Empress Solaris herself said that the words Eira Landan heard were true."

Eira's heart raced. She scanned the room, but the only people in motion were the Pillars. Two stood in the back, creating barriers over the doors, which were bolted shut. They were all trapped.

"I submit new evidence!" Ferro roared. "To the crown, to Meru, to every man and woman gathered, that the last, *true* Sword of Light, Ulvarth Vaspana, was unfairly accused and punished. He did not extinguish the Flame of Yargen. But he will bring it back to all of you if you give him the chance. If you return to light."

Eira glanced between Ferro and the dais where the royals were gathered. Pillars had separated the queen's knights and Swords of Light alike from their charges. Standing behind Ferro was a collection of six other Pillars, morphi and elfin, magic at the ready. But none of them moved. It wasn't necessary; Ferro had the room under his control.

"Tell them what you hear," Ferro commanded, holding out the piece of plaster toward her. "They can see and hear, but they cannot move."

Eira glanced around, searching for Alyss, Noelle, or Cullen. *Let them be safe*, she prayed.

"Speak!"

Eira flinched at Ferro's shouting and focused on the plaster. She made a show of staring at it. Slowly, gripping the dagger as tightly as possible, Eira drew her eyes back to him.

She wasn't going to let them win. She wouldn't absolve Ulvarth. And she wasn't going to let them ignite anything. It no longer mattered what happened to her. As long as he lost. She would die here and now if that's what it took.

"I hear nothing." She watched as he staggered back, shocked and shattered.

His magic wavered. Let him break into a hundred pieces. "You... *You lie.*"

"There is nothing to learn from this rock and Ulvarth is guilty."

"Evil witch," he seethed. He shifted toward her, movements jerky and forced, as though the magic he was maintaining had every muscle rigid and tense. "Liar of the Dark Isle. Spawn of Adela! I will show you all the righteousness of the Pillars. Now give me the dagger, you unworthy child of evil."

Eira took a small step back, getting just enough distance to have momentum, sinking her weight lower and tensing her muscles.

"Take it from her!" Ferro commanded of the other Pillars. He must be using too much magic on his glyph to attack her himself.

"You want it? Fine. Have it." Eira gripped the dagger with all her might. Maybe she was finally living up to their assumptions, because Adela's spawn wouldn't have hesitated and, finally, neither did she. Eira lunged and thrust, and the blade met its mark, burying straight between his ribs. Plunged to the hilt, her shoulder bumped against his as Ferro went heavy. He coughed and she felt blood splatter down her back.

None of this was according to plan. Everything had been broken along the way. Marcus was gone. The Court of Shadows had been decimated. The trust Eira had placed in them had evaporated.

But she had her vengeance and the Voice's blood in the blade was now lost, mingling with Ferro's and spilling onto the floor.

She twisted the dagger and he grunted. The room stared at the scene unfolding in their trapped stasis. Dozens of knights. Over a hundred sorcerers. And they were thwarted by one man and his robed minions. Eira twisted the blade in the opposite direction. He let out a satisfying scream of pain.

None of you could do it, Eira wanted to say to the people and their unblinking eyes. What judgment would they pass on her for this when they could move once more? Did she finally prove to them she was the killer they had been saying she was all along? *It had to be done. And it fell to me.*

"I vowed I would kill you," Eira whispered for him and for Marcus, watching from the Father's realms. "Let it end."

"No, Eira," he rasped. His arm snaked around her, clutching her to him with a force a dying man shouldn't possess. He rasped a horrible, final laugh. "This is only the beginning." Ferro tilted his head back, using her for support as his body was going limp. "Ashes of Yargen!"

The men behind him rushed forward, tossing a fine, shimmering black powder around them. He said he'd collected the ashes on Solaris, from the "tomb." *The Crystal Caverns*. Eira's eyes widened. It was crystal dust. Suddenly every conversation they'd had about the war of the Crystal Caverns returned to her. Had she told him anything that he hadn't used against her?

"Blood of the Champion in my veins. Blood of the Voice, imparted to me from the dagger. Yargen, I am your servant, the vessel to channel your power. My life is yours to use as kindling."

He gripped her hand, Eira was too numbed with confusion to put up a fight as he ripped the blade from his chest. Blood streamed from his mouth and torso as Ferro lifted the dagger high above him. Eira wrenched herself away.

"This blade carried the blood of the last Voice, the last *true* Voice."

Four relics—blood of the Voice, blood of the Champion,

Ashes of Yargen, and kindling. She'd been wrong. *Kindling.* Not someone to kindle the fire. Ferro had meant he was a willing sacrifice. Horror tilted the world in a nauseating way.

"With these four sacred relics combined, I beseech you, Yargen. Reignite the flame. Guide your lost children back into your embrace. Restore your light to this forsaken land for the glory of your Champion and faithful!"

Ferro held his arms up as if reaching for an embrace. He was met with fire.

THIRTY-SEVEN

A COLUMN OF FLAME blazed where Ferro once stood. Eira staggered back, shielding herself from the immense heat, drawing on her power to keep herself from getting burned. The flames flickered white, tinged with blue. Ferro's screams filled the room, cries of ecstasy more than pain—a horrible sound to match the wretched scent of his skin bubbling and meat burning from bone.

The other Pillars raced around him. They swayed and waved their hands to the heavens. They rasped, chanting in tongues. As Ferro immolated himself, the room came alive once more and his glyph disappeared for good. People who were once frozen by magic now were held prisoner by shock and awe.

Eira looked toward the dais, wondering if the flame was from the crown princess. But if she had summoned the blaze, she'd managed to do so under Ferro's magic. *No, it couldn't have been her.* If Vi could've summoned her powers, she would've well before now. Did this mean Ferro really was channeling the power of the goddess?

The flames subsided, leaving nothing but a charred circle with the golden dagger at its center, miraculously unharmed. Tongues of white fire danced on the blade's edge.

"This is the Flame…this is the Flame…" the Pillars chanted, swaying. "By her might. By her blessing. May Yargen guide us once more. May the Champion wield her holiness." Every Pillar knelt before the burning blade, and murmurs rose throughout the room. Even though people had autonomy again, they clearly didn't know what to do with it.

"That is no Flame of Yargen," Taavin's voice rang out, clear and true.

The Pillars ignored him, continuing their chants. "Yargen, guide us with your light."

"It looks like the flame," someone said from the crowd behind Vi.

"Could it be?" another said.

"Impossible."

"Yargen bless, grant us your light once more."

"You heard him. He had relics…"

"Grant us your light…"

Doubt and confusion settled upon those gathered. It rode on an undercurrent of awe and reverence. This was just what Ulvarth wanted, Eira realized. She stood covered in the blood of his son and somehow he had won. Even in death, Ferro had bested her. She'd played right into his plan as they had created what Pillars would claim as the True Flame of Yargen. And even if Taavin cast doubt on it, the display had been enough that it would give them credibility.

Lumeria's control on Meru was chipped away.

"It is impossible to reignite the Flame of Yargen once extinguished," Taavin said. "Those relics were not sacred."

"You lie," one of the Pillars shot back.

"I am the Voice of Yargen; I am the authority."

"You are a puppet for Raspian, fraternizing with his followers, and desecrating the clothing of her holiness." The Pillar reached forward, reverently taking the dagger from the pile of ash. The pale flames continued to dance only along its edges. "This will be wielded by Yargen's Champion, the *true* Champion. When he returns, heed us, Meru, embrace his light or fall into darkness."

More murmuring throughout the room.

"What if it *is* the Flame of Yargen?"

"Did the Pillars actually do it?"

"Is the Champion real?"

"*Who* is the Champion?"

"What do you know about the Pillars?"

Eira staggered, drawn to the flame.

"The Champion will return to you all!" The Pillar shouted.

"He will not because Ulvarth is dead!" Taavin blurted. All eyes swung to the Voice. Eira saw panic light his face.

The Pillars had never said the name Ulvarth. And, according to what the populace knew…Ulvarth was still in his prison. As the whispering grew louder, Eira focused on the flame. The Pillars held it aloft, marching toward the exit. None of the Swords of Light moved to stop them. Lumeria's knights were equally still. After the shock of the evening, no one seemed to know what to do.

Were they just going to let them leave?

The final straw was when she saw men and women bowing their heads, dropping to their knees, clasping their hands in reverent prayer as the Pillars passed.

"Is no one going to stop them?" She projected her voice loud enough that it echoed off the chandeliers.

Inaction was her response.

A current of rage swept through her. Ulvarth, Ferro, all of them were going to get away with this. And no one was going to take action. Be it from fear of more power like what Ferro possessed, or reverence of the flame, or sheer uncertainty, the Pillars were going to walk out triumphant.

"Stop." Eira strode to the center of the room. The brigade of Pillars ignored her. "I said *stop*!"

Ice exploded across the floor. It rippled like a wave of cold hatred. Her spiky magic prickled underneath the feet of people standing at the edge of what was once the dance floor but had now become the first arena of the tournament. The ice raced ahead of the Pillars, sweeping up with a curl of Eira's fingers, pointing sword-like shards toward the men and women.

The one holding the dagger like a torch raised an eyebrow at her. "Let us pass, Dark Isle dweller. You sought to kill our

Champion's right hand out of malice. You do Raspian's work. Yet her light will prevail."

"Is that truly the Flame of Yargen?" Eira asked.

"Do you not feel its radiant power?"

"Can the flame of a goddess be extinguished by mortal magic?" Eira asked.

Taavin was the one to answer. "No. An immortal flame cannot be extinguished by mortal magic."

"Good," Eira said, mostly to herself.

While they had been talking, her magic had seeped into the feet of each of the Pillars, her chill soaking into their flesh. Without them realizing, she'd been lowering their internal body temperatures. The brief discussion and showmanship bought her enough time to catch them off guard so they would not notice how her frosty clutches were wrapping around them.

Slowly balling her hands into fists, Eira condensed her magic on them. She watched as they went as rigid as the first Pillar she'd chased from the Archives. They were held in a cold stasis, unable to move as Eira slowly approached, careful not to move too quickly or else she'd risk their escape. Ferro wasn't the only one who had powers that could turn people into living statues.

For too long she'd been trying to hide her magic—be it from the command of her uncles, or fear of herself. But Eira was done hiding. She had killed her hesitation when she had finally taken Ferro's life. So what if she was Adela's daughter? She held power and she was tired of concealing just how much. She would never doubt again and she would make sure no one else did, either.

Eira pried the blade from the man's icy fingers. She closed her hand around the golden dagger. It bit into her flesh, blood running down the hilt. But there was no heat.

Her guess had been correct. Deneya mentioning how the brazier in the Archives had held a fake flame for years had stuck out to Eira. That fake flame would've been burning when Ulvarth had been in control. Why wouldn't he resort to the same tactics again? Especially since most people hadn't known about his previous lies.

"It's nothing more than an illusion." Eira condensed her magic around the blade, tighter and tighter, until it was a solid block of ice that she threw toward Taavin's feet. "Voice of Yargen, am I wrong?"

Taavin approached the dagger. The fire had gone out as it slid across the floor. "As I suspected, it was not the Flame of Yargen."

Lumeria took a step toward the top of the dais where the thrones were perched. "Enough of this theater. Knights, arrest these men."

As the queen's knights moved to apprehend the Pillars, whispering cut the silence, barely audible over the clank of armor. But the one phrase Eira did hear was, "She extinguished the Flame of Yargen." Eira forced herself to ignore the bitter note in the woman's voice and focused on the Pillars being arrested. Without Ferro and whatever glyph he'd used, the knights made quick work of overpowering the zealots. But the Pillars didn't put up much of a fight. They all stared at her with their haunted eyes and eerie smiles.

"He will come," the man who'd wielded the dagger said. He looked at Eira, but his voice echoed, reverberating into the bones of everyone gathered. "The Champion will return and he will destroy evil's spawn, like you."

"You are nothing more than usurpers," Lumeria said in her powerful, whispering tones. "Get them out of my sight."

The knights escorted the Pillars out the main door, and Eira wondered where they would be taken. There was no hole deep and dark enough for them. There wasn't a cell secure enough. If Ulvarth could escape, then anyone could.

"As for you, Eira Landan."

Her spine went rigid and Eira turned to face the Queen of Meru.

"Knights, please escort her somewhere that we can properly attend her."

A man stepped forward and gave Eira a salute by bringing his fist to the center of his chest. "If you'll follow me."

Eira did as she was told. She was too tired to object. Her head was so full it was hurting. As she left the room, she felt the weight of over a hundred eyes on her. The murmurs of the nobles gathered was the spark for wildfires of gossip that would burn for months to come.

***

The rest of the night was a blur. Eira's focus tunneled on the strangest of things. She remembered the delicate filigree on the spigot of the castle tub she bathed in. She remembered the duvet, as red as Ferro's blood, in what she'd assumed to be the room of a lady-in-waiting, repurposed for her. All these little details, like the lone black thread dangling out of the hem of the plain gown she was given, stuck out to her.

But Eira couldn't recall the names or faces of the people who attended her or the knights who questioned her. She knew that Deneya wasn't among them. Nor were any other shadows she recognized. But, most of the other shadows were dead now, weren't they?

The details of how she got back from the castle to the manor were also hazy. There was a carriage involved, and a brigade of knights. Slipping out a back door… It all vanished in the hours that followed, muted by the memories of Ferro's screams. The final taunt he'd given her.

Only the beginning.

She'd wanted to play the Pillars for fools and, yet, at the end of it all, what had she accomplished? Ferro was dead…but he'd won because she killed him. Was Marcus avenged? Or had she forever lost that chance? She'd proved the Flame of Yargen wasn't real. That was something, wasn't it? It had to be. She needed it to be, desperately.

Eira returned to her body somewhere between entering the

manor and the knight opening the door to the Solaris quarters. She could feel again when Alyss threw her arms around her. Eira's cheek was wet. Was she crying? Oh, no, Alyss was.

"It's all right, Alyss." Eira patted her back.

"You shouldn't be saying that to me, I should be saying that to you." Alyss pulled away, wiping her nose. "You have to stop worrying me like this."

"Sorry."

"Alyss is right." Levit sighed. Though it sounded more relieved than frustrated. "How is it that whenever there's trouble, you're always at the center?"

"Lucky, I guess?" Eira flashed a wild grin. She could feel it unhinge slightly, the expression sliding on her face into a shape she hadn't made before. Alyss blinked twice over. Even Levit seemed startled that she was capable of making such an expression. "I'm going to bed."

"Do you want to talk?" Alyss gripped her hand tightly, as though she wasn't going to accept no for an answer.

"I promise I will in the morning with my dearest of friends." Eira squeezed her fingers and started for her door. Maybe she had learned something throughout it all. She wasn't going to shut her friends out, even when the world was trying to smother her.

Throughout the whole interaction, Cullen hovered, looking incredibly uncomfortable. Eira ignored him, passing by without so much as a glance on her way to her room. Everything was exactly as she'd left it. Everything was familiar. But the world had tilted yet again. She'd taken another step tonight on a path that Eira wasn't sure when she'd started down.

"Where am I going?" Eira whispered. *No*, the better question was, *what am I becoming?*

A flurry of four knocks, a pause, and then two slow knocks interrupted her thoughts. Her blood ran cold. *Marcus*. Eira opened the door to reveal Cullen.

"Forgive me?"

"What am I forgiving you for?" Eira tilted her head slightly. "There's quite the list."

"May I come in?" he asked.

"No."

A wounded expression crossed his features. Yet he was still determined. "Forgive me for using Marcus's knock. But it was the only way I knew to ensure you'd answer."

"Never do it again," Eira said softly. He was beginning to invent ways to hurt her and she hated it.

"Fair. I'm sorry I didn't help you more tonight." He had the audacity to look guilty, to stare at her with those honeyed eyes of his. She went to close the door in his face and he stopped it. Eira glared up at him.

"Are you sorry for sleeping with me when *you knew* you were engaged?"

His lips parted and he stared at her in a stunned silence. "You…" Then his brow twisted with anger. "My father."

"Good thing he told me. Were you going to keep it a secret forever?"

"I will sort it out."

"*Sort it out?* This isn't something that can be 'sorted out.' Arrangements have been made, another person hangs in the balance here," she growled, glancing around to make sure the others had gone to bed. Maybe she had learned more than just to rely on her friends. Maybe she'd killed some of her impulses alongside Ferro tonight. "You can't just act like this is nothing. Lavette matters, too."

"I don't care about her," he protested.

"You don't *love her*, maybe." Eira ached even at the implication that he loved her still. The pain only grew as she tried to defend Lavette. She had to think of others. She had to be more thoughtful and calculating than she had ever been before. "But you should *care* about her, think about her, as a decent person would. And that means you can't continue this—this—" she choked on the word "—affair."

"It's not an affair," he objected.

"You are promised to her!"

"But I will *not* marry her."

"Tell your father that."

"I have." He pushed on the door, opening it just slightly more. "I love you, Eira. Only you. Nothing will change that."

Eira shook her head. The wounds were too fresh, too deep. "Cullen, I can't do this. Please, I am trying to learn from every mistake I've made, which are many. I'm trying to be better."

"You are already enough," he whispered.

"No, I'm not. I'm not looking for your validation, I'm looking for your support. Do I have it?" She looked him dead in the eyes.

"Always."

"Then leave."

He finally didn't protest and Eira shut the door, wondering if that soft click was the last bell tolling on their hopes for happiness together.

THIRTY-EIGHT

S HE'D BEEN SUMMONED to the Archives, though they wouldn't tell her why. Eira had her theories. But she didn't press the Swords who escorted her for information. They likely didn't know.

Down one of the bridgeways and through a narrow hall, the Swords stopped at the foot of a stairway, leaving Eira to ascend alone. At the top was a shut door that Eira listened at for a moment. Hearing nothing, she gave a soft knock.

"Enter," Vi Solaris called from within. Eira stepped inside.

The crown princess stood at a series of windows that overlooked a courtyard. Taavin sat at a table and chairs, flipping through one of the heavy tomes he'd brought from the main tower of the Archives. Their attention was drawn instantly to her.

"Your Highness, Voice of Yargen." Eira bowed. "To what do I owe this honor?"

"Even though you did not abide by our plans—" the princess started, but what Eira feared would devolve into chiding was quickly interrupted by Taavin.

"We wanted to give you our personal thanks for what you did last night, since we didn't manage to find you while you were in the castle." Taavin stood. "Were it not for you, that night might have gone much worse."

Eira frowned. It had gone pretty horribly from where she stood. "They got what they wanted. They summoned the flame."

"But it wasn't real."

"Real enough that it's stoked doubt in the populace of Risen." She'd heard the whispers in the ballroom. She'd seen the way people looked at her in the streets. Even the other competitors were regarding her with wary stares, buzzing as she passed. Enough people had thought the flame was real. And enough of them thought she was the one who had smothered it.

"We're working on that." Vi sighed. "But the Court of Shadows isn't what it once was, and our influence is slower. The best thing you can do, for now, is put up a show that can't be ignored in the tournament. Something that will make the people cheer for you. I presume you can do that much."

Eira had seen the state the court was in with her own eyes. They didn't have the manpower to be defending her honor. And, frankly, Eira didn't want that. There was enough to worry about with the tournament starting in a few mere hours.

"I'll do my best." Eira smiled thinly.

"We intend to show our gratitude by giving you an advantage on the tournament." Vi walked over to the table, retrieving a folio. She held it out. "Here's information on each of the different areas of competition. Lumeria's explanation of the tournament's design at the opening ceremonies tonight should make all our notes clear."

Eira stared at it, chuckling softly. "No, thank you, Your Highness. I'd rather not."

"Excuse me?" Vi blinked. Eira couldn't tell if she merely wasn't accustomed to being refused, or if she really thought she'd been doing Eira a favor.

"The last time I cheated for the Tournament of Five Kingdoms, my brother ended up dead and I ended up entwined with a madman."

Vi slowly slid the folio back on the table. Eira wondered if the princess saw it as another instance where Eira was thwarting her plans. "If not this, then what would you like? I, personally, would like to extend my gratitude for what you've done."

"Bring Ulvarth to justice."

The two exchanged a look. It was Taavin who finally spoke. "We are looking into the Pillars and, as you might know, have already made several more arrests—including Mistress

Harrot at the manor, which I believe Ducot said was at your recommendation."

Harrot was the least threatening of them all. And she hadn't heard "we have Ulvarth." Until those words were said, none of them were safe. "Have you found their main base of operations?"

"We're closing in on a house or two that are prospects," Vi said.

"Their main base of operations is underground."

"You think that only because of an illusioned window." Vi folded her hands and leaned against the table. "We are not ruling out the possibility of there being something underground that the Court of Shadows wasn't aware of…but we also are operating with more information than you ever knew. There are pieces here you don't see. Trust us."

She bit the insides of her cheeks, stopping herself from pointing out that, when she had, two-thirds of the court had ended up dead. "I'm only trying to help."

"We know. And I think I will have use for you in the future. But for now, focus on the tournament."

It wasn't enough. "You *must* go after Ulvarth."

"All of our information has supported that Ferro was the leader of this group," Vi said in what sounded like an attempt to be consoling.

"Your information is wrong," Eira said sharply.

The princess stared down the ridge of her nose at Eira. "Even if it is, I have been dealing with Ulvarth longer than you could possibly fathom. I know what he is and isn't capable of and I am unafraid of him."

"You should be afraid."

Vi Solaris smiled thinly. "You have no idea what powers I wield. I fear very little."

That will be your downfall, Eira resisted saying.

"You must begin trusting us, Eira," Taavin said thoughtfully. "We're not your enemies. Trust that we have your—and everyone else's—best interests in mind. We see the whole picture, or as close to it as we can."

"Very well." Eira sighed. She'd given up on the Court of

Shadows at her last interaction. Honestly, she didn't even know why she was trying.

"But if you have any additional *concrete* evidence, we would hear it," Taavin added.

Eira didn't know if she'd bring something to them ever again. But she nodded anyway. "Thank you for your time."

"There's nothing else you want?" Taavin asked.

Eira thought about it. She still was no closer to finding out the truth of her origins. But they'd kept the knowledge of Adela's location from her on purpose. She was too "risky" for them. So even if they knew if she was really Adela's daughter or not… there was no way they'd tell her.

Still…she could try.

"Adela. Do you know where the Pirate Queen is?"

Vi's eyes shone with what looked like amusement. "Last sighting was to the far west of Meru. She knows better than to traverse waters much closer than that."

"So the Pillars weren't working with her then?"

"Doubtful."

"What of the flash beads and the Empire of Carsovia?"

"We're looking into it," Vi said with a note of finality.

"Very well, thank you." With that, she left.

The knights escorted her back to the manor. The sounds of laughter and music drifted up to her from the common area below. Excitement for the looming tournament was reaching a peak. But Eira didn't think that she was up for celebration at the present moment. Nor would the celebration last very long after she showed up.

Instead, she drifted upstairs to her room, debating how to best spend her last few hours before the tournament began. Adela's books? Sleeping? Plotting her next movements with her friends?

Eira knew someone had been in her room the second she'd opened the door. There was the faint aroma of incense that almost made her gag with how horribly familiar it was. It hung in the air, cloying, scraping under her skin at the darkest parts of her that she pretended didn't exist. That she pretended didn't still wake her up at night in a fit.

Laid neatly on the center of the bed was a golden dagger. Her breath caught as she approached, examining it. Was it the same one as that night? No, this had to be a replica. She'd heard Taavin had collected the dagger from the ball and locked it away in the Archives.

But there was only one way to be certain. Eira held out her hand and gathered her magic around it. A thin layer of frost condensed atop and she closed her eyes, listening.

Eira Landan, Ulvarth's voice echoed in her mind, as horrible as she'd last heard it. *Did you really think you could thwart me? No, foolish girl. The games are only just beginning and I am the one making the rules. I do hope you and your Dark Isle friends are willing to fight like your lives depend on it.*

Eira withdrew her hand, balling it into a fist and drawing it to her chest. She didn't bother to hunt down whoever had placed the dagger here. They were long gone.

"The games are only just beginning," she repeated softly. "All right, Ulvarth, I'm ready to fight for my life. Are you?"

Want more from the world of Air Awakens while waiting for
A TOURNAMENT OF CROWNS?

Read Vhalla's story in AIR AWAKENS.
A library apprentice discovers she has
a rare elemental magic and falls in love
with a sorcerer prince.

Learn more:

https://elisekova.com/air-awakens-book-one/

How did the crown Princess Vi Solaris
discover Meru, Lightspinning, and
the elfin? Read her story of action,
adventure, and love deeper than time
itself in VORTEX VISIONS.

Learn more:

https://elisekova.com/vortex-visions-air-awakens-vortex-chronicles-1/

The Golden Guard is the most elite
fighting force in all of Solaris. Learn
about how they were formed in a series
of three stand alone stories of action and
deep friendship.

Learn more:

https://elisekova.com/the-crowns-dog-golden-guard-1/

About the Author

ELISE KOVA is a USA Today bestselling author. She enjoys telling stories of fantasy worlds filled with magic and deep emotions. She lives in Florida and, when not writing, can be found playing video games, drawing, chatting with readers on social media, or daydreaming about her next story.

She invites readers to get first looks, giveaways, and more by subscribing to her updates at:
http://elisekova.com/subscribe

Visit her on the web at:
http://elisekova.com/
https://www.tiktok.com/@elisekova
https://www.instagram.com/elise.kova/
https://www.facebook.com/AuthorEliseKova/
https://twitter.com/EliseKova

See all of Elise's titles on her Amazon page:
http://author.to/EliseKova

More books by Elise...

THE AIR AWAKENS SERIES

A young adult, high-fantasy filled with romance and elemental magic

A library apprentice, a sorcerer prince, and an unbreakable magic bond. . .

The Solaris Empire is one conquest away from uniting the continent, and the rare elemental magic sleeping in seventeen-year-old library apprentice Vhalla Yarl could shift the tides of war.

Vhalla has always been taught to fear the Tower of Sorcerers, a mysterious magic society, and has been happy in her quiet world of books. But after she unknowingly saves the life of one of the most powerful sorcerers of them all—the Crown Prince Aldrik--she finds herself enticed into his world. Now she must decide her future: Embrace her sorcery and leave the life she's known, or eradicate her magic and remain as she's always been. And with powerful forces lurking in the shadows, Vhalla's indecision could cost her more than she ever imagined.

Learn more at:

http://elisekova.com/air-awakens-book-one/

${\mathcal{A}}$CKNOWLEDGEMENTS

The Man—you have helped make this story come alive. Thank you for all you do for me, my readers, and for my worlds.

Danielle Jensen—I miss your face. I hope our paths cross again soon because we have all the catching up to do in person. But in the meantime I'll settle for our copious amount of texts.

Rebecca Heyman—thank you for always telling it to me straight and making sure I know just what works and what doesn't in my stories.

Melissa Frain—your comments always make me smile. I couldn't get the story to the place it is without your wise editorial eye.

My Tower Guard—to all of my dear guards, you're incredible. Thank you so, so much for all you do for me. I might not be always able to express the true depth of my gratitude, but I assue you that it's always there.

Mom & Dad—love you both. Sorry (but not sorry) for filling up your bookshelves.

Meredith—love you sis. Thanks for always having a charcuterie board out and a bottle of wine open.

Michelle Madow—I'm so grateful for every virtual happy hour we've spent together. Cheers to more books and more years as friends.

Mary—thanks for making sure my wrists and shoulders are always ready for the next writing sprint.

NOFFA—the best place on the internet. Like home without the cleaning. I appreciate you all so very much.

To My Patrons—Bookish Connoisseur, Tarryn G., Cassidy T., Kathleen M., Alexa A., Rhianne R., Cassondra A., Emmie S., Emily R., Tamashi T., Milos M., riyensong, Bri L., Amanda L., Stephanie Y., Caitlyn H., Katie M., Veronica R., Courtney L., Amé, Siera H., Brianna S., Karpov K., Malou7, Kelley, Jule M., Donna W., Chasity Y P., Katrina S., Cassidy, Sam van V., Ashley S., Maria D., Moryah D., Gracie S., Tiffany G., Kate R., Skylar C., Halea K., Alexandria D., Katelynn M., Amelia S., Taylor, Bridget W., Olivia S., Bethanie E., Nancy K., Sarah [faeryreads], Macarena M., Kristen M., Anna B., Kelly M., Audrey C W., Jordan R., Amy M., Nicola T., Kaitlyn, Allison S., Keshia M., Chloe H., Renee S., Ashton Morgan, MelGoethals, Mackenzie S., Kaitlin B., Amanda T., Kayleigh K., Shelbe H., Alisha L., Katie H., Esther R., Liz R., Kaylie, Heather F., Shelly D., Emily G., Alisa T., Hazel F., Angel K. H., Tiera B., Andra P., Melisa K., Serenity87HUN, Liz Aldrich, Nichelle G., Sarah P., Janis H., disnerdallie, Giuliana T., Chelsea S., Carmen D., Alli H., Matthea F., Catarina G., Bri B., Stephanie T., Heather E., Mani R., Elise G., Traci F., Beth Anne C., Jasmin B., Shirin, Samantha C., Lindsay B., Lex, Sassy_Sas, Karin B., Eri, Ashley D., Amy P., Michael P., Stengelberry, Dana A., Michael P., Alexis P., Jennifer B., Kay Z., Lauren V., Sarah Ruth H., Katie L., Sheryl K Bishop, Aemaeth, NaiculS, Lauren S., Justine B., Lindsay W., MotherofMagic, Hannah, Charles B., AzFlyGirl, Kira M., Aanja C., Tiffany L., Kassie P., Fran Rivas Lecturas H., Melissa F., Emily C., Angela G., Elly M., Michelle S., Sarah P., Asami, Amy B., Betsy H., Meagan R., Axel R., Ambermoon86, Delilah H., Jennifer C. Rebekah N., Emily S., Tessa J., Paige E., Madi, Rebecca T., Bec M., Caitlin P., EJ N. — it has been a crazy, wonderful, and exciting year with you all. I cannot thank you enough for all the support you've given me along the way. Here's to another fantastic year together making stories!

And to every other reader who has read and spread the word about my books—THANK YOU. I do this for you and I couldn't do it without you. I hope that I can continue writing stories you enjoy for years to come. Thank you for being on this wild adventure with me.

www.ingramcontent.com/pod-product-compliance
Lightning Source LLC
Chambersburg PA
CBHW030358200726
48286CB00015B/1540